Anita Shreve is the author of the ~~...~~
Close, Strange Fits of Passion, Wh~~...~~
The Weight of Water and the inte~~...~~
bestsellers *The Pilot's Wife, Fortun~~...~~*
They Met and *Sea Glass*. She divides her time between
Massachusetts and New Hampshire.

Praise for *All He Ever Wanted*

'*All He Ever Wanted* is an in-depth exploration of a constricted Victorian society . . . Shreve is prolific, polished,
unputdownable'
Guardian

'Writing a novel is an enterprise fraught with difficulty.
But there are novelists who take a virtuoso delight in
raising the bar even higher than it is generally set, and
Anita Shreve is one of them'
Sunday Telegraph

'Shreve's elegant pace and sureness of character have
given her bestseller status without sacrificing quality, and
this is a thoughtful, intelligent story of desire, love and
betrayal'
Sunday Mirror

'Shreve has given us a highly modern tale of an inner
life where all seems straightforward, but never is'
Scotsman

'Shreve explores love and obsession in a classic that'll
take you to another place . . . Memorable'
Mirror

'Shreve delivers, as always, a carefully worked, harrowing conclusion'
Daily Mail

'This is a classy page-turner of the most well-mannered kind'
Image

Praise for *Sea Glass*

'This is a finely written story of human beings pushed to the edge and Shreve is a powerful but still accessible writer'
Sunday Mirror

'Anita Shreve's prose is deceptively simple and her words are spare and elegant'
Mail

'Shreve does not use her characters frivolously . . . the true power of her novel comes from the appalling social conditions she describes so vividly'
New York Times

Praise for *The Last Time They Met*

'An agonising sadness that is wholly credible, genuinely unsettling . . . Shreve's most lyrical, most self-consciously elegaic book to date'
Independent on Sunday

'One cannot help being drawn in . . . it is impossible to put the book down'
Mail on Sunday

'Beautifully written, this is a fascinating insight on love, loss and forgiveness'
Sunday Mirror

Praise for *Fortune's Rocks*

'A painterly novel, full of lovely Bonnardesque detail'
The Times

'The structure of the book is accomplished and symmetrical, like a planned palace'
Observer

'Shreve's elegant narrative and attention to detail create a memorable impression'
Literary Review

'*Fortune's Rocks* represents commercial fiction straining at the boundaries of its form'
TLS

Praise for *The Pilot's Wife*

'This is a writer who handles mystery with aplomb while brilliantly capturing the sense of a person succumbing to the shock of an emotional tidal wave'
The Times

'Shreve's prose is astonishing; this is a powerful story, beautifully written'
Sunday Times

'An excellent novel about the ultimate unknowability of those closest to us'
Daily Telegraph

Also by Anita Shreve

Eden Close
Strange Fits of Passion
Where or When
Resistance
The Weight of Water
The Pilot's Wife
Fortune's Rocks
The Last Time They Met
Sea Glass

ALL HE EVER WANTED

Anita Shreve

An *Abacus* Book

First published in Great Britain in 2003
by Little, Brown
This edition published in 2003 by Abacus

A CIP catalogue record for this book
is available from the British Library.

ISBN 0 349 11558 3

Typeset in Bembo
by Palimpsest Book Production Limited,
Polmont, Stirlingshire
Printed and bound in Great Britain by
Clays Ltd, St Ives plc

Abacus
An imprint of
Time Warner Books UK
Brettenham House
Lancaster Place
London WC2E 7EN

www.TimeWarnerBooks.co.uk

for Katherine

The fire began in the kitchen and spread to the hotel dining room. Without warning, or perhaps just the one muffled cry of alarm, a ball of fire (yes, actually a ball) rolled through the arched and shuttered doorway from the kitchen, a sphere of moving color so remarkable, it was as though it had life and menace, when, of course, it did not – when, of course, it was simply a fact of science or of nature and not of God. For a moment, I felt paralyzed, and I remember in the greatest detail the way the flame climbed the long vermilion drapes with a squirrel's speed and agility and how the fire actually leapt from valance to valance, disintegrating the fabric and causing it to fall as pieces of ash onto the diners below. It was nearly impossible to witness such an event and not think a cataclysm had been visited upon the diners for their sins, past or future.

If the fact of the fire did not immediately penetrate my consciousness, the heat of the blast did and soon propelled me from my seat. All around me, there was a confusion of upended tables, overturned chairs, bodies pitched toward the door of the dining room, and the sounds of broken glass and crockery. Fortunately, the windows toward the street, large windows through which a body might pass, had been thrown open by an enterprising diner. I remember that I rolled sideways through one of these window frames and fell onto the snow and was immediately aware that I should move aside to allow others to land as I had – and it was in that moment that my altruism was finally triggered. I rose to my feet and began to assist those who had sustained cuts and bruises and broken bones, or who had been mildly crushed in the chaos. The blaze lit up the escaped diners with a light greater than any other that could be produced in the night, so that I was able to see clearly the dazed expressions of those near to me. Many people were coughing, and some were crying, and all looked as though they had been struck by a blow to the head. A few men attempted heroics and tried to go back into the hotel to save those who remained behind, and I think one student did actually rescue an elderly woman who had succumbed to paralysis beside the buffet table; but generally there was no thought of re-entering the burning building once one had escaped. Indeed, so great was the heat that we in the crowd had to move farther and farther across the street until we all stood in the college quadrangle, surrounded by bare oaks and elms and stately sycamores.

Later we would learn that the fire had begun with a few drops of oil spilled onto a kitchen fire, and that the undercook, who stood near to the stove, had felt compelled to extinguish the fire by throwing upon it a pitcher of water and then, in her excitement, fanning the flames with a cloth she was holding. Some twenty persons in the upper stories of the hotel were trapped in their rooms and burned to death – one of these Myles Chapin from the Chemistry faculty, and what he was doing in a hotel room when his wife and child were safely at home on Wheelock Street I should not like to speculate (perhaps it was his compromised circumstances that made the man hesitate just a second when he should not have). Surprisingly only one of the kitchen staff perished, owing to the fact that the back door had been left open, and the fire, moving with the particular drafts between door and windows, sped toward the dining room, allowing most of the staff to escape unharmed, including the hapless undercook who had started it all with her fluster.

The hotel was situated directly across from Thrupp College, where I was then engaged as the Cornish Professor of English Literature and Rhetoric. Thrupp was, and is (even now, as I sèt down my story), a men's school of, shall we say, modest reputation. Its buildings are a motley collection, some of them truly hideous, erected at the beginning of the last century by men who envisioned a seminary but later contented themselves with a small enclave of intellectual inquiry and classical education. There was one impressive Georgian building that housed the administration, but it was surrounded by altogether too many dark brick structures with small windows and oddly placed turrets that were emblematic of perhaps the most dismal period of American architecture, which is to say early Victorian Gothic. Some of these edifices surrounded the quadrangle; the rest spilled along the streets of a town that was all but dominated by the college. Because the school had elected to retain the flavor of a small New England village, however, the colonial clapboard houses that lined Wheelock Street had been left intact and served as residences for the more eminent figures in the various

3

faculties. At the outskirts of town, before the granite hills began, lay the farms: struggling enterprises that had been witness to generations of men trying to eke out a living from the rocky soil, soil that always put me in mind of thin, elderly women.

We ousted, and therefore fortunate, diners stood at the center of this universe, too stunned yet to begin to shiver in earnest from the cold and the snow that soaked our boots. Many people were squinting at the blaze or had thrown their arms over their eyes and were staggering backward from the heat. Somewhat bewildered myself, I moved aimlessly through the throng, not having the wits to walk across the quadrangle to Woram Hall, where I might have attained my bed. And so it was that my eyes were caught, in the midst of this chaos, by the sight of a woman who was standing near a lamppost.

I have always been a man who, when glancing at a woman, looks first at the face, and then at the waist (those shallow curves that so signal youth and vitality), and then thirdly at the hair, assessing in an instant its gloss and length. I know that there are men for whom the reverse is true or men whose eyes fix inevitably upon the bodice of a dress and then hope for a glimpse of calf, but on that night, I was incapable of parsing the woman in question in such a calculated manner simply because I was too riveted by the whole.

I will not say *plain*, for who of us is entirely plain in youth? But neither will I say *beautiful*, for there was about her face and person a strength of color and of feature that rendered her neither delicate nor pliant, attributes I had previously thought necessary for any consideration of true feminine beauty. She had immoderate height as well, which is often off-putting in a woman. But there was about her a quality of stillness that was undeniably arresting. If I close my eyes now, here in this racketing compartment, I can travel back in time more than three decades and see her unmoving form amidst the nearly hysterical crowd. And even the golden brown of her eyes, a color in perfect complement to the topaz of her dress, an inspired choice of fabric.

(As it happened, this was a skill at which Etna had no peer – that of matching her clothing and jewels to her own idiosyncratic charms.)

The woman had almond-shaped eyes and an abundance of dark brown lashes. Her nostrils and her cheekbones were prominent, as if there were a foreign element to her blood. Her acorn-colored hair, I guessed, would unwind to her waist. She was holding a child in her arms, which I took to be her own. My desire for this unknown woman was so immediate and keen and inappropriate that it quite startled me; and I have often wondered if that punishing desire, that sense of fire within the body, that craven need to touch the skin, was not simply the result of the heightened circumstances of the fire itself. Would I have been so ravished had I seen Etna Bliss across the dining room, or turned and noted her standing behind me on a street corner? I answer myself, as I inevitably do, with the knowledge that it would not have mattered in what place or on what date I first saw the woman – my reaction would have been just as swift and as terrifying.

(In a further aside, I should just like to add here that I have observed in my sixty-four years that passion both erodes and enhances character in equal measure, and not slowly but instantly, and in such a manner that what is left is not in balance but is thrown desperately out of kilter in both directions. The erosion the result of the willingness to do whatever is necessary to obtain the object of one's desire, even if it means engaging in lies or deception or debasing what was once treasured. The enhancement a result of the knowledge that one is capable of loving greatly, an understanding that leaves one, paradoxically, with a feeling of gratitude and pride in spite of all the carnage.)

(But, of course, I knew none of this at the time.)

When I had attended with some impatience and distraction to a man who had attached himself to my arm, an elderly gentleman with rheumy eyes looking for his wife, I turned back to the place where the woman and child had stood and saw that they were gone. With a sense of panic I can only describe as wholly uncharacteristic and quite possibly deranged – fortunately such agitation was hardly noticeable in that crowd – I searched the quadrangle as a father will for a lost child. Many people were already dispersing to their homes and to cabs (a fact that did little to ease my anxiety) while others had emerged from the surrounding houses with blankets and coats and water and cocoa and even spirits for the victims of the blaze. Some of those who had been in the dining room were now huddled in garments that were either too big or too small for them; they looked like refugees who had beached themselves upon the quadrangle. By now the fire brigade had arrived and was turning its hoses on the hotel. I am not aware that they saved a single soul that night, though they did drench the charred building with water that turned to icicles before morning.

I wiped at my cheeks and forehead with my handkerchief. Strangely, I do not remember feeling cold. I walked amongst the thinning crowd, my thoughts undisciplined. How was it that this woman had escaped my notice all the time I had been at Thrupp? After all, the village was not so large as to produce general anonymity. And why had she been dining at the hotel? Had she been sitting behind me as I had eaten my poached sole in solitude? Had the child been with her then?

I went on in this manner for some time until I began to slow my pace. It was not that desire had ebbed but rather that fatigue was overwhelming me. I became aware that I had suffered a terrific shock: my knees grew shaky, and my hands began to tremble. I finally noticed the cold as well; it cannot have been more than twenty-five degrees Fahrenheit on that night. I decided to seek refuge and was recrossing the quadrangle for perhaps the fifth time when I heard a child's cry. I turned in the direction of the sound and saw two women standing in the darkness. The taller of the two was half hidden beneath a rug thrown over her shoulders and in which she had wrapped the child. Next to her, and clinging to her arm, was an older woman who seemed in some distress. She was coughing roughly.

When I drew closer to the threesome, I saw that the stillness I had observed in the woman with the golden brown eyes had now been replaced by concern.

'Madam,' I said, approaching swiftly (as swiftly as the fire itself?), 'are you in need of assistance?'

And whether Etna Bliss actually saw me then, or not until the following day, I cannot say, for she was understandably distracted.

'Please, I must get my aunt home,' she said. 'I'd be grateful if you could find us transportation, for she has inhaled a great deal of smoke and cannot walk the necessary distance to her house even under the best of circumstances.'

'Yes, of course,' I said. 'Will you stay put?'

'Yes,' she said simply, thus placing the utmost trust, and perhaps even the well-being of her aunt, in my person.

I discovered that night that a man is never so capable and alert as when in the service of a woman he hopes to please. Almost at once, I was in the street with paper dollars in my hand, which caught the eye of a cabdriver who already had a fare, but who doubtless saw an opportunity to squeeze more bodies onto his frayed upholstered seats. I completed his calculation by leaping onto the carriage and giving immediate instructions.

'Sir, this is irregular,' he said, looking for the extra tip.

But I, and rightly so, dressed him down. 'A disaster has occurred of the most serious proportions, and people all about are in dire need. You should be lending your aid for no pennies at all,' I said.

Astonishingly, for I had in the interim begun to doubt the reality of my encounter with the arresting woman under the tree, the two women with the child were where I had left them. I helped the older woman, who was by now shivering badly, into the carriage first, and then gave my hand to the woman with the child – the hand surprisingly warm in my frozen one. The other passengers could barely suppress their annoyance at being delayed to their hot baths, but they nevertheless moved so that my party could fit.

'Madam, I shall need an address,' I said.

The ride cannot have lasted half an hour, even though the driver took the other fare home first. I sat across from the aunt, who was still coughing, and from the couple, who might have been thinking of their lost possessions in the cloakroom (a dyed fox coat? an alligator case?), but I was aware only of a slight pressure against my elbow, a pressure that increased or decreased as the woman beside me attended to the child or leaned forward to put a hand upon her elderly aunt's arm. And just that slight pressure, of which the woman beside me was doubtless completely unaware, was, I believe, the most intensely physical moment of my life to date – so much so that I can re-create its delicate promise and, yes, its eroticism merely by closing my eyes here in my moving compartment, even with all that came after, all that might reasonably have blotted out such a tender memory.

We traveled the length of Wheelock Street until we came to an antique house of beeswax-colored clapboards. It was an unadorned residence, like so many of the houses of that street. These I much preferred to the frippery that passed for architecture on adjacent Gill Street: large, rambling structures with gables and porches and seemingly no symmetry, although these newer houses did have better accommodations for indoor plumbing, for which one might have been willing to trade aesthetics. The Bliss house had seven bedrooms, not counting attic rooms for servants, and two parlors, a dining room, and a study. It also had, as of a year previous, steam heat, which hissed and bubbled up in silver radiators. I sometimes used to think the appliances might explode and scald us to death as we played backgammon or took tea or dined of an evening in those overly furnished and fussily papered rooms.

'But, Madam, I know this house,' I said. 'It is the home of William Bliss.'

'My uncle.'

I then realized that the woman sitting across from me was not elderly at all, but rather was the middle-aged wife of the Physics Professor, a woman I had met on at least three occasions at the college.

9

'Mrs. Bliss,' I said, addressing her, 'forgive me. I did not realize . . .'

But she, unable to speak, waved my apology away with a flutter of her hand.

I walked the two women to the front door, which was almost immediately opened by William Bliss himself.

'Van Tassel, what is this?' he asked.

'A fire at the hotel,' I explained quickly. 'We are all lucky to have escaped with our lives.'

'Dear God,' he said, embracing his wife and leading her farther into the house. 'We wondered what all the bells and horns were for.'

A housemaid took the child from the woman with the golden brown eyes, who then turned in my direction, simultaneously slipping the blanket from her shoulders and giving it to me to wear.

'Please take this for your journey home,' she said. 'My aunt and I are very much in your debt.'

'Nicholas Van Tassel,' I said.

'Etna Bliss.'

Once again, she put her warm hand in mine. 'How cold you are!' she said, looking down and withdrawing her hand almost immediately. 'Will you come in to warm up?'

And though I dearly wanted to enter that house, with its promise of warmth and its possibility of love (the mind leaps forward with hope in an instant, does it not?), one knew that such was not appropriate under the circumstances.

'Thank you very much, but no,' I said. 'You must go inside now.'

'Thank you, Mr. Van Tassel,' she said. And I think already her mind was on her aunt and the child and the hot bath that would be waiting, for with that, she closed the door.

Perhaps a brief word here about my own circumstances at that time, which was December of 1899, for I believe it is important to pass on to subsequent generations the facts of one's heritage, information that is often neglected in the need to attend to the day-to-day and, as a consequence, drifts off into the ether of time past. My father, Thomas Van Tassel, fought in the War Between the States with the Sixty-fourth Regiment of New York and sacrificed a leg to that conflict at Antietam, a calamity that in no way hindered his manhood, as I was but one of eleven children he subsequently sired off a succession of three wives. My mother, his first wife, perished in childbirth – my own – so that I never knew her, but only the other two. My father, clearly a productive man, was enterprising as well, and built three sizable businesses in his lifetime: a print shop to which I was apprenticed at a young age; a carriage shop; and then, as horses quite thoroughly gave way to motors, an automobile showroom. My memories of my father exist primarily in the print shop, for I hardly knew him otherwise. I often sought refuge in those rooms of paper and ink and type from my overly populated house in Tarrytown, New York, with its second and third wives: one cold, the other melancholy, and in neither case well disposed to me, who had issued from the first wife, the only woman my father had ever loved, a fact he did not shrink from announcing at frequent intervals, despite the impolitic nature of the sentiment and the subsequent sadness and frigidity that resulted. I was not altogether bereft of feminine warmth during my childhood, however, for I was close to one sibling, my sister

Meritable, the very same sister whose funeral I am even now journeying toward.

Perhaps because I was so engaged in the world of ink and broadsides, I developed an early and passionate appetite for learning and was sent off to Dartmouth College at the age of sixteen. I can still remember the exquisite joy of discovering that I should have a room to myself, for I had always had to share a room with at least three of my siblings. The college has an estimable reputation and is widely known, so I shall not linger upon it here, except to say that it was there that I briefly entertained the ministry, later abandoning it for want of piety.

After obtaining my degree, by which time I was twenty, I traveled abroad for two years and then was offered and accepted the post of Associate Professor of English Literature and Rhetoric at Thrupp College, which is located some thirty-five miles southeast of my alma mater. I took this post with the idea that in a smaller and less well known institution I might rise more quickly and perhaps one day secure for myself the post of a Senior Professor or even of Dean of the Faculty, positions that might not have been open to me had I remained at Dartmouth. I had not thought of taking a post outside of New England, though there were oppor-tunities to do so, the reason being that I had adopted the manners and customs of a New Englander so thor-oughly that I no longer considered myself a New Yorker. Indeed, I had occasionally taken great pains to present myself as a New Englander, once even, I am a bit cha-grined to admit, falsifying my history during my early months at Dartmouth, a pretense that was difficult in the extreme to maintain and hence was abandoned before I had completed my first year. (It was at

Dartmouth that I dropped the second 'a' from Nicholaas.)

Because my father was, by the time I had returned from Europe, modestly well off, I could easily have afforded to have my own house in the village of Thrupp. I chose instead, however, to take rooms in Woram Hall, a Greek Revival structure affectionately known as Worms, for the reason that I did not particularly wish to live entirely alone. I had as well a somewhat misguided idea that boarding nearer to the students would allow me to come to know them intimately, and that this would, in turn, make me a better teacher. In fact, I rather think the reverse was true: more often than not, I discovered, close proximity gave birth to a thinly veiled antagonism that sometimes baffled me. My rooms consisted of a library, a bedroom, and a sitting room in which to receive guests and preside over tutorials. In adopting New England ways, born two centuries earlier in Calvinistic discipline, I had furnished these rooms with sturdy yet unadorned pieces – five ladder-back chairs, a four-poster bed, a dresser, a cedar chest, a tall stool and a writing desk in which I kept my papers – eschewing the more ornate and oversized furnishings of the era that were so fashionable and so much in abundance elsewhere. (I think now of Moxon's rooms: one could hardly move for the settees and hassocks and English desks and velvet drapes and ornate marble clocks and fire screens and mahogany side tables.) And as form may dictate content, I fit my daily habits to suit my austere surroundings, rising early, taking exercise, arriving promptly to class, disciplining when necessary with a firm hand and requiring much of my students in the way of intellectual progress. Though I should not like to think I was regarded as severe by my students and colleagues, I am quite certain I was considered stern. I think now, with the forgiveness that comes with reflection in later years, that I often tried too hard to show myself the spiritual if not the physical progeny of my adopted forebears, even though what I imagined to be the license of my New York heritage, as evidenced in my father's excessive procreativity, would occasionally cause me to stray from this narrow and spartan path, albeit seldom in public and never at Thrupp. For my parenthetical pleasure, I traveled down to Springfield, Massachusetts, as did many of my unmarried, and not a few married, colleagues. I remember well those furtive weekends, boarding the train at White River Junction and hoping one would not encounter a colleague in the dining car, either coming or going, but always ready with a fabricated excuse should an encounter present itself. Over time, as a result of such encounters, perhaps five or seven or ten, I had to develop a 'sister' in Springfield whom I had twice monthly to visit, even though said 'sister' actually resided in Virginia, prior to moving to Florida, and wrote to me upon occasion, the envelopes with the return address a source of some anxiety to me. I shall not here set forth in detail my activities while in Springfield, though I can say that even in that city I proved to be, during my visits to its less savory neighborhoods, as much a man of loyalty and habit as within the brick and granite halls of Thrupp.

More dazed than sensible, I took the cab back to the hotel, which was by now beginning to form its fantastical icicles as a result of the sprays of water from the fire hoses. I lingered only briefly, however, due to the combination of penetrating cold and shock, which had begun to make me shiver in earnest. I went back to my rooms at Worms, where I directed the head boy to make a good fire and to draw a hot bath.

Worms did not then, nor does it now, have private bathrooms within its suites, and so I locked the door to the common bath as I customarily did. The steam had made a cloud upon the cheval mirror, and I wiped away a circle of condensation so that I could just make out my bewildered face. There was a bloody scratch on my cheek I had not known about. I was not accustomed to spending any time in front of the glass, for I did not like to think myself vain, even in private, but that night I tried to imagine how I, as a man, might appear to a woman who had just met me. At that time – I was thirty – I had a considerable thicket of light brown hair, undistinguished in its color (this will surprise my son, for he has known me for a decade now as only bald), and what is commonly called a barrel chest. That is, I had strength in my body, a body quite out of keeping with my sedentary and intellectual occupations, a strength I could not refine but instead had learned to live with. I do not know that I had ever been called handsome, my excursions to Springfield notwithstanding, for my lips were thickish in the way of my Dutch forebears, and the bone structure of my face was all but lost within the stolid flesh bequeathed to me by generations of burghers. To dispel that somewhat unpleasant image, and to appear more academic, I had cultivated spectacles I did not actually need.

After my inspection, which taught me nothing I did not already know, except perhaps that one cannot hide one's naked emotions as well as one might wish, I lowered myself into water so hot that my submerged skin immediately turned bright pink, as though I had been scalded. The boy, who I knew was angling for an A in

'Logic and Rhetoric', had set out a cup of hot cocoa, and I indulged in these innocent pleasures, all the while seeing in my mind's eye the form and face of Etna Bliss and feeling anew the exquisite pressure of her arm against my own. Happily, the bath, as a hot soak will often do, produced a drowsiness sufficient to send me off to my bed.

In the morning, I woke in a state of agitation and was forced to complete my toilet in haste and miss breakfast altogether in order not to be late for my first class of the day, 'The Romantic Lyric Poets' (Landon and Moore and Clare and so forth). When I arrived at the classroom, I saw that the fire in the stove had gone out for want of tending and that the students sat with their coats still on, their mufflers wrapped round their necks. Though cold, my classroom was not an unpleasant one. The wainscoting had recently been painted white, an inspired touch that lent an illusion of light and air previously denied by the dark walnut paneling so ubiquitous in those rooms. Above the wainscoting were large windows that looked out over the quadrangle's elms and sycamores. As one could take in this view only while standing, I often laid my arm upon the deep sills and gazed out as the students wrote their exercises and examinations. That day, of course, the view was severely compromised by the black maw of the hotel fire and the soot-dirty snow; in any event, I was too distraught to appreciate a view of any kind – beautiful or not.

It was immediately obvious that the students' attentions were not on their lessons either. The talk was all of the fire, during which I attained some slight celebrity as a result of having actually been present in that ill-fated dining room; and like all good tellers of tales, I perhaps embellished some incidents and details to improve the narrative. I described the ball of fire and the mêlée that followed.

'Many persons were in need of assistance,' I said, adopting an uncharacteristically casual pose by sitting on the edge of my desk. I removed a piece of lint from my trousers.

'And what were the injuries, sir?'

This from Edward Ferald, a slack-jawed boy with narrow eyes, who was always currying favor, but behind my back, I knew, referred to me, as did some of the other students, as 'Scrofulous', which is taken, of course, from the Latin, *sus scrofa*, for pig. Well, not pig exactly, but boar. Wild boar, to be precise. Why, I do not know, since I don't think I resembled a boar, but no matter. Almost all the faculty had unflattering nicknames then: John Runciel was 'Rancid'; Benjamin Little, as I recall, was 'Little Man'; Jonathan Whitley was 'Witless'. (Surely 'Rancid' is worse than 'Scrofulous'?) Ferald's pleasure came not from learning but from provoking an unattractive earnestness in his tutors that he blandly pretended not to understand. Thus a tutorial with Ferald could prove to be a wretched exercise. On the few occasions I had tried to resort to cunning to outwit him, I had failed dismally, verbal agility not being my strong suit.

'Many cuts and bruises and broken bones,' I said. 'And smoke inhalation. Twenty perished.'

'And yourself, sir?' Ferald asked unctuously. 'I hope you yourself were not harmed.'

'No damage to myself, I am happy to report.'

'Happy indeed,' said Ferald, blinking lazily.

'Twenty burned to death, sir?' asked Nathan Foote, a fair-haired young man who wore on his face an expression of genuine horror, though this cannot have been news. The college had been abuzz with the statistic since the night before.

'One hopes . . .' I began. But in that instant, time slowed and came altogether to a stop, and I saw, through the window, a woman with a child, a vision so vivid and visceral that I feared I was hallucinating. I put my hand to my forehead, which was clammy despite the frigid air of the classroom.

'Sir?' asked Foote, alarmed not only by my truncated sentence, but by my appearance.

I forced my eyes to focus on his face.

'One hopes the unfortunate victims perished as a result of smoke inhalation and not of the flames themselves,' I said, struggling to regain my composure.

There was a long moment of silence in the classroom.

'I have suddenly realized,' I said quickly, 'that it is inappropriate to be having class on a day when we should, in fact, be honoring those wretched persons who perished – and, indeed, for whom our college flag is this morning at half-mast. And so I have determined that we shall have no more lessons now. You are dismissed to your rooms and to the chapel for contemplation upon the brevity of life, the capricious hand of fate and the necessity to remain continually in a state of grace.'

Some of the more alert students, Ferald for one, were on their feet at once, sensing the unexpected opportunity for an hour of leisure, while the others sat stunned for a moment before gathering notebooks and texts. How soon the classroom emptied I do not know, for by then I was briskly on my way to Wheelock Street.

(I did sometimes wonder if my Latin nickname wasn't,

after all, a mistranslation, or an attempt at homonymical wit. Had the student who had invented the name meant *bore*? Wild bore?)

The ice ruin of the hotel was now beginning to melt in the bright sun of mid-morning, and as I passed that godforsaken structure, the continuous sound of dripping from a thousand icicles, a rain that glistened and sparkled as it fell, tinkled like fine crystals. I saw two young boys, clearly truant from the local grammar school, poking at the rubble, possibly for valuables that had survived the fire. I barked at them to leave the area at once, as any fool could see that the entire edifice was in danger of toppling (and would, in fact, collapse three weeks later during a particularly wet and heavy snowfall).

The sense of urgency within me to see the woman who had captured my thoughts was such that I had to force myself to walk at a normal gait so as not to attract undue attention. I wanted to reach the beeswax-colored colonial as soon as possible, for I had an apprehension (as it happened, unwarranted) that Etna Bliss had already left the residence to return to wherever she had come from. I didn't think she lived with Professor Bliss. If she did, I reasoned, I surely would have heard of this person in their household, or, more likely, have encountered her at a college function. Thrupp had approximately fifty faculty, most of whom lived as if in glass boxes, subject to the keenest scrutiny on the part of students and fellow faculty alike; so much so that it often seemed as though one knew everything there was to know about another in that college and in that village, when, of course, one did not, secrets being the most zealously guarded of possessions.

My gait slowed somewhat as I approached the Bliss

residence, naked in December without its canopy of elms. Such a spontaneous decision as I had made to visit this house was quite out of keeping with my habits, and I felt, as a result, uncomfortably rattled and incautious. But with a momentum for which I could not easily account, I was propelled to William Bliss's front door. Thus I lifted the door knocker and tipped the hand of fate.

It was some moments before my summons was acknowledged, and when the door was opened, it was by Etna Bliss herself.

Had I had any doubts, in the intervening hours since I had last seen her, about the reality of the thrall in which this woman held me, such uncertainty vanished in her presence. Though she must have moved, to open the door and so forth, there was again such a quality of stillness that one felt recklessly drawn to her as one who traverses a cliff occasionally feels perilously like throwing oneself over the edge. She wore a black-and-bronze striped dress with bronze lace at the collar and cuffs, a dress that was cut in such a way as to present her bosom as upon a sort of shelf, the effect of which was to make my breath tight within my own chest. Her face shone in the snow-reflected sunlight, and one could see that her hair had been freshly washed and refashioned into coiled plaits that one longed (I longed) to unravel. I was unraveling in her presence.

'Miss Bliss,' I said, removing my hat.

'Professor Van Tassel,' she said, gazing at me and failing to add the expected pleasantries.

And I felt then – what?— that already she could see through my fragile carapace? That she understood all there was to know of me? That she knew why I had come and what I would do even before I did?

'Forgive the intrusion,' I said, 'but I was passing, and

I could not help but wonder if your aunt has recovered from her ordeal. I hope I'm not disturbing you, but I was thinking this morning about the shock of the event and how it must have affected her.' I paused. 'And you as well, of course.'

'Thank you for asking,' she said. 'My aunt has had the doctor,' she added, and oddly it was not she who invited me to step inside, as good manners surely required, but rather Bliss himself, who moved into the vestibule, half spectacles perched at the end of his nose, and said, 'I thought I heard a familiar voice. Van Tassel, come in, come in, so that I may properly thank you for so safely conveying my wife and granddaughter and niece out of harm's way last night. What a fright my wife has had. And you, too, of course.'

'No fright at all,' I said, 'though others certainly did and rightfully so.'

I stepped over the threshold.

'You must stay for a hot drink,' Bliss said, removing his glasses and folding the newspaper he held in his hands. 'I should like an account of the event, if you feel up to it.'

'Of course,' I said.

Did Etna Bliss hesitate just the one second before accepting my hat and gloves? Yes, I am sure she did. I remember distinctly the sensation of holding out my things and for a moment having no taker. What did she see in me that made her pause? The vast hunger that had shaken me to the bone? And would she have recognized this hunger for having seen it before on the faces of other men, or was she merely prescient, already intuitive about human want and greed?

(And why, *why*, I have often asked myself, was it that woman and not another? Why the curve of that particular cheek and not another? Why the gold of those eyes and not the blue of others? I have in my lifetime seen a hundred, no a thousand, beautiful women – lifting skirts to step over piles of snow, fanning long necks in restaurants, undressing in the dim electric lights of rented rooms – but none has ever had upon me the effect that Etna Bliss had: a sensation quite beyond that which can be explained by science.)

She took my coat then and hung it on a hat rack in the corner. She turned slightly toward me.

'Etna, I wonder if you would . . .' William Bliss began, not unkindly but perhaps suggesting the nature of Etna's place within the household. There was no further need to elaborate, for already she had turned toward the kitchen to tell the cook that tea was needed.

What relief it was for me to see her retreating form! The respite allowed me some moments to collect my wits and speak to Bliss in the manner to which we were accustomed, the manner of men who do not know each other well but are regarded as colleagues and thus have immediately a common vocabulary that must be respected before any dislike or love can form.

I did not often encounter William Bliss at school, since he was married and therefore did not reside in college rooms; nor did we ever have occasion to work together, coming as we did from separate disciplines. Also, Bliss was older than I by a good twenty years, and thus I regarded him as from a different generation. He directed me to the front parlor.

I cannot exaggerate the feeling of claustrophobia that room produced, the claustrophobia of months spent indoors, of oxygen seemingly sucked from the air by the plethora of ornate pieces and dozens of objets, each demanding the eye's attention, so that one felt not only breathless and oppressed, but also as though a migraine were imminent. It was a room that with its rosewood spool turnings and carved oak trefoils, its gilded mirrors and marble-topped tables, its serpentine tendrils of overgrown plants and cast-iron lanterns, its stenciled stripes and floral motifs, its flocked wallpaper and glass curtains, its oriental rugs and Chinese vases and fringed tablecloths and its iron clock – not to mention the dozens of daguerreotypes in silver and wood and marquetry frames that seemed to cover every available surface – leached the vitality from the body. (A man's body, at least, for one deduced immediately that the room reflected a woman's taste; even Moxon's rooms, at their very worst, might have been considered spare by comparison.) Because of all the plants in the windows, only the dimmest light entered the room, and how Bliss had been able to read a newspaper there, I do not know, though perhaps he had been reading in his study. It was evidence at the very least that William Bliss must have loved his wife very much to put up with so much excess.

'Van Tassel, do sit down.'

'Thank you.'

'There might be good. Oh, let me move that for you.'

'No, I can do it.'

'You know, I cannot thank you enough. My wife says you were a hero.'

'Nonsense, it was no more than any man would have done.'

'You are too modest. Is the college abuzz?'

'I daresay. I have canceled my classes.'

'Have you indeed? What a splendid idea.'

Sometimes it seems to me that all of life is a struggle to contain the natural impulses of the body and spirit and that what we call character represents only the degree to which we are successful in this endeavor. At that time in my life, when I was a younger man, it was often a desperate struggle – to take exercise when one did not want to, to refrain from striking a student who much deserved the blow, to put aside one's naked ambition in the service of others, to conquer rampant desires that if left unchecked might manifest themselves in shocking behaviors – and as with all struggles, I was occasionally not victorious in these battles. Thus, I fear there were disturbing ruptures in my composure, as when I lost my temper and berated a student most harshly, satisfying the anger in myself but leaving the student trembling; or as when I was unable to refrain from speaking badly of a colleague to gain the favor of another; or as when the mask of impeccable deportment dropped for a moment and revealed the depth of want beneath, as must have happened, however briefly, in the silence that followed Etna's entry into the room in which her uncle and I were sitting.

Bliss and I stood politely, and already I was anxious lest the color I could feel rising at the sides of my neck and into my face (another legacy of the Dutch blood of my ancestors) betray me. My mouth trembled, a twitch I sought to hide by pressing a knuckle to my upper lip; and thus I discovered, to my deep chagrin, the blush rising all the while like a flood tide on the night of a full moon, that I had not shaved that morning and that a coarse stubble covered my cheek and jaw.

(I was never well – though often joyous, never well – in Etna's presence.)

She set the tray down and gestured for us to sit.

'Professor Van Tassel. I hope you did not suffer as a

result of your service to our family,' she said.

'Van Tassel tells me that twenty perished in the fire,' Bliss said to his niece.

Etna accepted this news with remarkable equanimity, unlike so many of her sex who might have felt it necessary to exclaim at the announcement of ill fortune.

'I am afraid our fire brigade proved itself most inadequate in the event,' I said. 'I am sure there will be an inquiry.'

'I should like to know who it was who had the foresight to open those windows in the dining room,' Etna said, offering me a cup of tea. 'I should like to thank him personally.'

And already I was jealous of this imagined man – for surely it was a man, though no one had yet stepped forward – for being the recipient of Etna's gratitude. 'One so often does not wish to be singled out for heroics,' I said inanely.

Etna Bliss had a habit, I would later discover, of smiling slightly even though her eyes were expressionless, thus giving the impression of inward thinking while not appearing to be impolite. This she did then; and I will say that when she smiled (lips not parted, only the slightest upward curving of her mouth), her face softened so thoroughly that she seemed altogether the diminutive and pliant woman one hopes for in a lover, and something else – even pretty. Yes, though she was not beautiful, she was pretty in those moments. In later years, it would sometimes be a torment to me to be shut out from the inner thoughts that produced that fleeting smile.

My fingers were slipping badly on the cup handle, causing the china to rattle in its saucer. I was forced to bend to my tea in rather boorish fashion. This disconcerted me so much that I set the cup down and folded my trembling hands in my lap. I crossed my legs and noticed that my foot was jiggling.

'And the little girl?' I asked. 'Has she recovered from her ordeal?'

'I rather think that had it not been for the cold, she would have found the event terribly exciting,' Etna said. 'This morning, she could speak of little else.'

I watched Etna bring her own cup to her lips and noted that there was no trembling in those long fingers.

'Van Tassel teaches English Literature and Rhetoric at the college,' Bliss said.

'An acceptable passion,' I added, smiling in her direction. She did not smile back, but neither did she look away, and I fancy she studied me for a moment then. 'And are you in Thrupp for an extended visit?' I asked, unable to stifle my curiosity any longer.

'Yes, I am,' she said. 'You do not like your tea?'

'I like it very much,' I answered, lifting the saucer and once again attempting to put the cup to my lips.

'My niece is here,' Bliss explained, 'until such time as she can settle herself, though we are enjoying her company so much that I hope that moment shan't be for a long while yet.'

'My mother passed away recently,' she said. 'And unfortunately I was forced to put her house up for sale. I am staying with my aunt and uncle until such time as a settlement of the estate can be made.'

'I am sorry about your mother,' I said, though how could I have been at all sorry if such an event – even death – had brought Etna Bliss to Thrupp? 'I hope it was not sudden.'

'No, she had been ill for some time.'

'And your father?' I asked.

'My father passed away some years ago,' she said.

'Forgive me,' I said.

'Not at all,' she said. 'I also have two sisters, who are married.'

'I see. And where was your house?'

'In Exeter.'

'Etna's arrival is most fortuitous,' Bliss said, 'since my daughter and her husband are in San Francisco, visiting his family for Christmas.'

'I see,' I said again, remembering vaguely a thin, smartly dressed young woman who had sometimes accompanied Bliss to college social occasions.

'Evelyn and I should be quite lonely without Etna and my granddaughter in residence. I hope she shall stay on long after my daughter returns.'

I am certain it was then that I first saw a faint look of alarm pass across the features of the woman who sat opposite to me, and I believe I understood at once that the prospect of confinement within those overfurnished rooms was not one that Etna Bliss relished. Perhaps she, too, felt the oxygen being sucked from her body by the side tables and the spiky vines. At that moment, a door within me opened.

I sat forward, already a petitioner.

'You have a most excellent escort in your uncle, I am sure,' I said, 'but I should be delighted to show you some of the modest treasures Thrupp has to offer, namely the Metcalf Library and the Elliot Collection. Have you been to either?'

'No, I have not,' she said, and I sensed once again that the prospect of leaving that house might not be an entirely unpleasant one to her.

'Etna has been helpful with my granddaughter, Aurelia,' Bliss said by way of explanation. 'But I am afraid we have kept her from enjoying herself with persons her own age.'

I wondered how old Etna Bliss was exactly. Surely twenty-four at the least, but not more than twenty-eight? Just off the cusp of marriageable. I thought I detected in Etna a slightly new scrutiny of me as well, one that had been summoned forth by my bold petition. I wished then I had spent the necessary minutes that morning at my toilet so as to present a more pleasing and prosperous aspect, both to her and to Bliss. He would not think a professor's salary an adequate sum on which to raise a family (and indeed it was not), and I should have to inform him, when the moment was appropriate, that in fact I was in possession of a modest fortune and could afford to keep a wife. I let my thoughts run ahead in this fantastical manner until Etna abruptly stood.

'I fear I have left my aunt too long,' she said. She put out her hand. 'Good-bye, Professor Van Tassel.'

Again, her hand was warm in my own. I could not help from glancing at the presentation of her bosom, a lovely promontory that seemingly begged to be examined, and I wondered then (how quickly thoughts of possession cause jealousy to blossom) if some other man had once put his hand there, if, in fact, this handsome and stately creature before me had had many lovers. Perhaps this thought – and certainly my wayward glance – betrayed me, for she put a hand to the very place I studied, as if to cover herself.

And then she was gone.

I exchanged some further pleasantries with Bliss, so as not to seem rude, but it was all I could do to linger even a moment longer in that fetid greenhouse, craving as I did not only a breath of fresh air but also an opportunity to think upon the person of Etna Bliss and add to my small cache of memories, which I should continue to mine ceaselessly in her absence: a half dozen sentences, the strain of black-and-bronze silk over a bosom, and an entirely naked, if fleeting, glance of fear at the prospect of imprisonment. Armed with these precious, if fragile, possessions, I then went in search of my breakfast.

The view outside my window has deteriorated from the muted blues of the Vermont hills and the navy ribbon of the Connecticut River as we make our way south from White River Junction, where I boarded the train. I have had the good fortune to secure a compartment to myself on this, the first leg of my journey; and as I shall be taking a sleeper from New York City, I have hope of remaining secluded, which is what I wished for when I made the booking. I confess that I am somewhat nervous about the prospect of a visit to southern Florida, since I have heard worrying tales of scorpions and fire ants and malaria-ridden mosquitoes, as well as the terrible heat. Accordingly, I have packed, amongst my books and papers and Etna's tin cake box, two white linen suits, several thin cotton shirts, and a new pair of canvas shoes. My only difficulty will be my mourning clothes, which I cannot avoid, since I shall have to wear them to my sister's funeral, the point of my journey. I had these garments taken out of storage and delivered to my tailor directly for pressing, for I could not bear to have to look at them, the clothes giving off, as they must, the scent not only of death, but also of nearly annihilating guilt – not to mention the heart's ruin.

We are passing now the mill towns of Holyoke and Chicopee in Massachusetts, blights upon the New

England landscape that, however necessary, always put me in mind of the drearier essays of Hazlitt and Carlyle. But I have found, if I narrow my eyes just so, that I can blur this geography somewhat and fix my gaze upon only those attributes of these cities that are bearable: the uneven planes of glass in the windows of the abandoned mill buildings, for example; or a polished black-and-maroon automobile parked intriguingly at the end of a deserted street; or a woman in a short skirt and kerchief fighting her way against the wind toward a church. And perhaps it is this trick of willfully blurred but occasionally keen vision, or the rocking of the moving compartment, or the comforting clacking of the train wheels upon the rails, or, more likely, the idea of a desk (a table, really) on which I have set my pen and notebook, inside a moving vehicle – the sense of one's own library at speed – that invites me now to begin a personal narrative I have long wanted to write, but for which I have always lacked the necessary strength ... (and in that ellipsis, I have just engaged in a lengthy debate with myself as to whether or not to reveal, with complete honesty, the events I wish to record, and I have decided that this document will be as worthless as a floating fragment of ash if I resort to fiction, even fiction by omission. So I will tell the entire truth on these pages, even if this causes me the greatest pain – and it will, it will!) ... (though I must add, in a further parenthesis, that I am only too aware that I can cross out offending sentences later and recopy the text and then edit the narrative should I find the resulting truth too unbearable to read. And is this not so for every story one writes or speaks in one's lifetime? How, for example, will the death of my sister be portrayed to me when I reach my destination? Will the anecdotes of the death watch not change radically depending on the teller of the tale and on the details *which have been left out*, such as particular physical agonies that a daughter or a cousin might deem too unseemly to reveal?)

I have some understanding of the potential benefits of committing one's thoughts – and in this case, one's memories – to paper, for I have published various monographs and essays within my field, most notably my celebrated treatise on Scott's *Marmion*, and my less well-known but no less critically well-received commentary upon the Sir Roger de Coverley Papers in the *Spectator*. Of course, such a venture as upon which I now embark this twentieth day of September 1933 is filled more with terror than with imagined reward, for I know not what feelings such a narrative may evoke; but I am determined to do so for the sake of my son, Nicodemus, who will almost certainly one day ask a question it will take all of his father's courage to answer.

We have had some slight excitement here aboard the train, and I confess I am just now recovering from the shock of the event. Approaching New Haven, there was a great screech and then a jolt of terrific proportions. The car that I was in derailed itself, so that all was upended within my compartment, and I was knocked quite hard against the luggage rack. I have sustained a nasty bruise on my forehead as a result, but I hope that such will have largely disappeared by the time I reach Florida.

I will not write here of the fright the accident gave me, but I did think for a moment that I might die, and in the next instant (how swift the imagination) contemplated my own funeral; but then I began to worry about who should come to such an event, and so I abandoned this avenue of thought. I did ponder, as the trainmen were taking us off the injured vehicle, the prospect of not continuing on my journey and instead returning to New Hampshire. Although it then occurred to me that I should have to do so by train, and, if that were the case, what was the difference between that trip and one to Florida, apart from duration? So I am once again ensconced in my moving library (a different compartment, in fact a sleeper), my books no worse for the accident, but the tin cake box, in which Etna's letters remain, so severely dented at one corner that it lists badly to one side as it sits across from me on the seat. (Accusingly, I rather think.)

I have just had a good meal of roast pork and prunes with a fruity wine, as well as a shimmering apple custard for dessert, so I am more than a little satisfied and can with complete contentment contemplate a pleasant evening of writing (for this part of my narrative contains not a little joy) and then a night of good sleep, which doubtless shall be swiftly induced by the rhythmic rocking of my vehicle.

Inspired by my brief visit to the Bliss residence, I set out with an ambition not equaled in me before or since to win the hand of the woman whose voice and hair and skin seemed to have permeated every membrane of my body and breached every boundary of my soul. Such a state, I have sometimes thought, must be akin to that rapture that defines the life of the religious mystic — a sense of the body filled with the spirit of God. I hope it is not blasphemous to make such a comparison, but I do not think I have ever been so close to a state of grace as I was in the weeks and months of my courtship of Etna Bliss, a state of grace that showed itself in my speech and gestures and a nearly irrepressible smile. I was seen by others to be not only kinder and more compassionate during this period, but also more physically appealing than I had ever been, perhaps explaining why Miss Bliss was not entirely put off by the prospect of accompanying me on various outings.

Students remarked upon my new leniency, and if they took advantage of it, I did not care. Colleagues, unaccustomed to encountering in me anything but a serious mien, seemed at first puzzled by and then responsive to my transformation. I was asked, during this period, to head up a committee that was to look into the notion of revitalizing the English Literature curriculum for the coming academic year. I was also invited to chaperone the Winter Ball (I remember being delighted and thinking immediately that of course I could invite Etna to share this pleasant duty with me). Noah Fitch, the Senior Professor of English Literature and Rhetoric, asked me to spend Christmas with his family (though secretly I was angling for − but did not receive − an invitation to the Bliss household for Christmas dinner), and John Birch Clark, a former tutor of mine at Dartmouth, gave a soiree to which I was invited. Alas, I could not persuade Etna to join me at this event, since it would require an overnight stay in Hanover, which was, of course, bliss for me to con-template. (I will try to refrain from playing endlessly upon Etna's patronym, however tempting; though in those early weeks I exhausted the word in my thoughts, as if I were creating endless variations upon a rhap-sodic phrase of music.) During this time, I cultivated a tailor and ordered three new suits of clothes, my pre-vious garments bearing the somewhat shabby look of the schoolmaster. I scarcely remember my weeks at col-lege then. I have no doubt my students' examinations benefited from my exuberant spirits, for I shed, in those few months, the dull persona of the professor in favor of the more impassioned demeanor of the suitor. If my students learned anything at all that winter term of 1899, it was only that love is capable of transforming even the most self-disciplined and emotionally shuttered of persons.

Four days after the fire, and three days after our brief tea together, I sent a note to Etna Bliss, asking if I might call four days hence to take her for a walk. It seemed a benign request, one she might reasonably grant, as it would allow her to escape the stultifying and airless atmosphere of the Bliss household, while simultaneously permitting her to hover near to home, as a walk necessarily must. Indeed, I had a reply by return mail. (For months afterward, this brief missive, being the first such in Etna's hand and therefore of great significance to me, was attached to the mirror over my dresser in my rooms.)

December 9

Dear Professor Van Tassel,

I should be pleased to accompany you on a short walk on the twelfth of December at three o'clock in the afternoon.

Most sincerely,
Etna Bliss

As chance would have it, we had another snowstorm in the interim and then, on the day of the intended walk, a rather spectacular thaw, so that the streets were awash with that dreadful mix of melting snow and soot and mud we New Englanders call *slush*. I was in a bit of a quandary, having purchased my first new suit of clothing, a frock coat of English worsted, and a new pair of leather shoes from Brockton, both of which would be ruined if I ventured forth in them. I compromised by donning the new suit – thinking to sacrifice the cuffs of my trousers – but wearing my old boots, a concession to the weather. I was dressed near an hour too soon and so remained in my rooms, walking from window to window, sitting upon my bed, glancing at myself in the mirror (how vain we become when infatuated with another), and all the while ignoring the neat sets of copybooks on my desk, examinations which I was required to read and correct — testimonials all, I was already certain, to my somewhat pedantic and desiccated lectures of the fall. The copybooks reproached me in my perambulations, and yet I, in turn, mocked them — for what single sentence amongst those hundreds of sentences could attest to even a fraction of the truth that held me in its grip? I had a fleeting moment of concern lest I never be able to return to my former demeanor and routine, a worry I dismissed in the next instant when I glanced at the clock and saw that the day had reached that longed-for hour of forty minutes past two o'clock, which meant that I could now reasonably set out to fetch Etna Bliss at her uncle's house.

She was alone when I called, which was fortunate, since I was not required to converse with William Bliss, who might have wondered at my intentions and who would almost certainly have regarded me anew were he to have ascertained them. Etna had on a blue-and-gold dress of no coarse material, the gold calling to her eyes as if singing arias to them. Her hair was done up with some care, fashioned in intricate coils that seemed to disappear like roads vanishing on a map. The dress fetched in rather tightly at the waist, and I could not help but be gratified by the sight of the severe taper of her torso flaring generously, both above and below, into modestly veiled bounty. But did I not say it is the face I notice first in a woman? And this, of course, I did on that day, though the expression there, I am bound to report, was somewhat less than generous, even wary, as well it might have been. I was, after all, a stranger.

We exchanged some pleasantries, most having to do with the uncooperative weather, and of course I made inquiries as to the health of her aunt and niece (both wholly recovered). Then I watched for a moment (privileged witness) as Miss Bliss set upon her hair a gold velvet toque that perched just so at the crown of her head, affording me a captivating view of the back of her neck as she adjusted the hat in the hall mirror. Indeed I was so mesmerized by that sight that it was some moments before I realized she was waiting for me ⟨…⟩ cloak for her and help her into it.

⟨…⟩ rm in mine (so many ⟨…⟩ we set out along the ⟨…⟩ ereupon we directed ⟨…⟩ farther out of town. He ⟨…⟩ had even turned the co⟨…⟩ cloak so that her feet mi⟨…⟩ snow, but of course I co⟨…⟩ ning excess of the gestu⟨…⟩ ened away any sane w⟨…⟩ mpracticality of doing so⟨…⟩ strong sunlight, I could se⟨…⟩ I ever had before, and p⟨…⟩ relaxation of her features⟨…⟩ she took her first deep b⟨…⟩

'Professor Van Tassel, it's a lovely day,' she said suddenly and disarmingly.

'More lovely above than below, I fear.'

'No matter,' she said. 'Far better that boots should have to dry of the wet than one's body and spirit dry up for want of fresh air and exercise.'

'Just so,' I said. 'You have been feeling confined?' I asked disingenuously (I who would liberate her only to possess her).

'My aunt and uncle have been exceedingly kind, and I couldn't wish for better company, but as I am new here and have not yet had opportunity to make acquaintances of my own, I have had few occasions to venture out.'

'I'm sorry to hear that,' I, who was not, said in reply.

There were not many persons on the street, and the going was messy and awkward. I felt then the slight embarrassment that attends a foolish decision, as we had sometimes to part and then come together again. Occasionally, the path had been cleared of snow by an industrious Yankee, and we were able to walk normally for a time.

'It's awful,' she said, 'to contemplate the ordeal of the victims of the fire.'

'One cannot imagine,' I replied.

'I was surprised by the fire's speed. It's a wonder more did not die,' she said.

'A wonder.'

'Shock is a strange reaction in the body and in the soul, don't you think?' she asked. 'I was calmer the night of the fire than I was when I woke the next morning. My hands were trembling then, and I had to lie down again in my bed.'

'It is common,' I said, distracted by the thought of Etna Bliss in bed. Was she wearing a silk nightgown? Were her sheets rumpled with sleep? Was her hair in disarray?

She stopped walking. 'Professor Van Tassel,' she said suddenly, pausing in her journey, 'I should like to see the hotel.'

'It is a disastrous ruin,' I said.

'Nevertheless.'

She stood her ground, and I had the distinct impression she would not be moved. I gently turned her in the opposite direction, and we walked on in an uncomfortable silence. While I thudded corporeally over the muddy ruts and snow, Etna seemed to glide just above the surface, a feminine trick of walking that no man can master. Significantly, as we passed the Bliss house, neither of us glanced in its direction.

'What classes do you teach at the college?'

'A bit of everything. English literature from Chaucer forward.'

'Then you must spend your days in the company of Spenser, Milton, and Jonathan Swift,' she said, and from that comment, I deduced that Etna Bliss had some education (an academy? self-schooled?).

'I fear I spend my days in the company of too many dull and restless students,' I said.

'Oh, surely not, Professor Van Tassel. Surely the students of Thrupp are well above average.'

'Perhaps so, Miss Bliss. Perhaps it is only the professors who have grown dull and restless.'

'I'm certain you would never be considered dull,' she said politely; and how my heart leapt at this first compliment to my person, however much manners may have dictated her reply.

'Do you anticipate swift settlement of your mother's estate?' I asked as we walked up Wheelock toward the village center and the college quadrangle, myself scarcely able to think for the pressure of her gloved hand upon my arm, an exquisite sensation even through layers of clothing.

'No, I don't think so. I have two married sisters whose

husbands are – how shall I put this? – perhaps excessively protective of their wives' financial interests in the
matter.' I heard in this forthright reply the suggestion
of herself as the sole unmarried sister.

'Are you close to these sisters?' I asked.

'I was close to my mother,' she said in half reply.

'Couldn't you have remained at your house until the
estate was settled?' I asked.

'The estate is being settled for debts. The largest creditor, my sister's husband, Josip Keep, has taken the house
for himself.'

'I see,' I said, beginning now truly to see. I steered
her out of the way of a passing carriage.

'I envy you your freedom to live alone, in a room
of your own, to study in your chosen field and thus
be of service to your community by teaching,' she said
suddenly.

How did she know I had rooms of my own? I wondered. Had she asked her uncle for details of me? And
might I take this as a sign of some interest on her
part?

'Freedom, Miss Bliss, is entirely relative. Some religious believe, for example, that true freedom lies in perfect obedience.'

'I should like, for once, to be obedient to myself!'
she said quickly in the way of someone who has spoken
a thought before it can be edited. I must admit I was
taken aback by this remarkably forthright statement.

'Then why haven't you?' I asked.

'I have remained too long under the loving protection of my mother and sisters, and now, like many of
my sex, I have forfeited certain necessary skills to go
forward on my own.'

'Where exactly should you go?'

She looked up at me in keen appraisal. 'That is precisely the question, Professor Van Tassel. Where should I go indeed?'

She disengaged her arm from mine and was quiet for a time, and I had, once again, to accustom myself to her silence. But not before I had detected, beneath the blue-and-gold silk of her dress, an underskirt of desperation. Or perhaps I only hoped it so.

'Might I ask you to call me Nicholas?' I asked, emboldened by her frankness.

I was at once furious with myself for reaching forward too greedily, for she stepped away from me and studied the dismal ruin of the hotel. It was a dispiriting sight, the blackened maw now soaked through and rotting. A terrible smell I had not noticed before was in the air, and I shuddered to imagine its origin.

'To think we might have died that night,' she said with some awe.

I withdrew a handkerchief from my pocket, shook it out, and reached across the space that separated me from Etna Bliss. Boldly, I put that square of Belgian linen up against her nose and mouth, covering her, smothering her, so to speak, so that the stench from the fire might not enter her nose and soil her senses. I was actually trembling with the audacity of the gesture.

She was startled but did not flinch. After a moment, her hand replaced my own. And after another moment, she removed the cloth.

'Of course I shall call you Nicholas,' she said, turning toward me. And I could hardly speak for the proffered boon of this hoped-for intimacy.

'Miss Bliss,' I said, 'would you like a cup of cocoa?'

'If I'm to call you Nicholas, it is only fitting that you should call me Etna,' she said easily. 'And yes, I should like something hot to drink. This walk has done me good.'

'Well then,' I said, unable to speak further.

We entered a small tearoom on Kimball Street, assaulted at once by its overheated bustle, the smell of wet boots, and the steam that clouded the etched glass. There was a fire in the stove, and on the muddy boards of the floor were various mufflers and mittens and gloves and knitted hats and even children's cloaks that had been abandoned under tables and chairs and occasionally lost mid-aisle, as if the entire population of the café had shed their outer garments en masse. We were shown to a table by a serving girl in black taffeta and white lace, a matching cap on her head, her hair frizzing in the heat. Etna and I sat down. She ordered tea and apple cake, and I ordered hot cocoa. There were patches of red upon her cheeks that spoke of outdoor exercise and of considerable vivacity. She looked a woman now bursting with health and even a sort of lust for life, as if a restless spirit that had lain dormant all these weeks in Bliss's fetid parlor could now breathe and move.

'Are all of these people from the college?' she asked.

'Most will be,' I said, turning to examine the crowd. There were the usual pockets of students by the window and some ladies who had been shopping in anticipation of the coming holiday, wives or daughters of faculty, I guessed. Then, as I strained to see into the corner, I spotted Moxon, sitting alone with a book. And, bad luck, he glanced up at the very moment my head swiveled in his direction. Our eyes met, and he waved a smart hello, which meant that he was bound to get up and introduce himself to my companion, and, if I could not somehow signal in the negative, accept Etna's almost certain invitation to join us.

Moxon was a lanky man of biscuit hair and pale complexion who, though our tastes were, as I have said, nearly opposite (Moxon being the fellow with the ornate marble clocks and the fire screens), was my closest colleague at the college. We often joined each other in the dining hall and spoke easily together of thorny lines of verse or of the unyielding prose of certain essayists (and occasionally of wayward students one hoped to rein in). Moxon liked the horses and was continually fetching down to his bookmaker to place a bet, and he was a keen follower of college athletics, which I was not, but apart from these dissimilarities, we got on well enough that we had dined together on more occasions than I could number.

'Your name is interesting,' Etna said. 'Is it . . . ?'

'Dutch,' I said stiffly. 'The Van Tassel that is. Nicholas, of course, is old English.'

(And it occurs to me now that there may have been an entirely other meaning to my old nickname. Could the student responsible for its coinage have meant *wild Boer*?)

'How many students are at the college?' she asked.

'Nearly four hundred,' I said.

'And do you like it there?'

'Well enough. I hope one day . . . well, I shouldn't say. And I shouldn't like this repeated, of course.'

'Of course not.'

'Only that I should like one day to improve my position within the college. Noah Fitch, the Hitchcock Professor of English Literature and Rhetoric, may be moving up to an administrative position in a few years, and I have reason to hope for his post. I have many ideas I should like to implement.'

43

'I suppose a few years is not a very long time to wait for something one is not certain of receiving?' she said.

'Don't most things worth waiting for require patience?' I asked. 'You seem to have remarkable patience yourself.'

'Do I?' As she pondered my comment, there was, beside us, an awkward flutter of limbs. I looked up to see Moxon putting on his coat.

'Van Tassel, have you parsed your Newman?'

'Miss Bliss, let me introduce my colleague Gerard Moxon. Gerard, this is Miss Etna Bliss, niece of William Bliss, the Physics Professor.'

Moxon raised his eyebrows. 'I'm happy to make your acquaintance,' Moxon said.

'And I yours,' Etna said.

Moxon had meant, with his question, had I read the volume by John Henry Newman entitled *Essays and Discourses* that had been sitting on the table in my sitting room only the day before?

'I trust I know the Newman well enough to require it of twenty-five students next term,' I said.

'You think "On Saints and Saintliness" worth their time?'

'"The Illiative Sense", surely,' I answered with some impatience, wishing only that the man would leave us.

'Miss Bliss, are you from Thrupp, or are you visiting?'

'I am visiting, Professor Moxon.'

'Well, I hope you are enjoying yourself and that Nicholas here is not too thoroughly a bore.'

Though the comment had been meant to be a joke, Moxon had failed to deliver the line with any humor; thus the moment was merely pained. Etna looked down at her hands, and I beseeched Moxon with my eyes to leave us. Undoubtedly, he read this wish on my face, for he began to put on his gloves.

'I hope we'll meet again,' Moxon said warmly to

Etna, and I do believe he meant it. As I watched him walk away, I reflected that Moxon was not a bad man, really; indeed, I do not think he had ever had a malicious thought. Still, I knew that he would not be able to refrain from mentioning our encounter to any number of our colleagues. I was seldom seen in the company of striking women.

'Might not "The Illiative Sense" be too difficult for your students?' Etna asked when Moxon had gone.

I flinched in surprise, a reflexive insult I sought to hide in the next instant by fussing with my cocoa, which had just arrived.

'So you've read Newman?' I asked, attempting a casual tone.

'Yes, I have.'

'Do you . . . ? Are you fond of Newman?'

'You're shocked, I can see that. It's perfectly understandable. How, indeed, should I come by such a book, and why should a woman of my position, which is to say no position at all, bother her head with such masculine discourse?'

'No, no,' I said, somewhat flustered. 'Not at all.'

She seemed amused.

'I'm promiscuous in my reading, Professor Van Tassel,' she said (and how quickly she seemed to have forgotten her promise to call me by my Christian name). 'I read whatever I can obtain, by any means available to me – lending libraries, secondhand-book shops, books borrowed from relatives . . .'

'Then you are self-schooled.'

She laughed. 'If I am, it is an education riddled with holes, though I hope one that will continue for a lifetime. My father, before he passed away, was a teacher of Mathematics at Phillips Exeter Academy.'

'An academic family.'

'But I myself know nothing of mathematics or of the sciences. I'm sure that my Uncle William thinks me hopelessly dull.'

'Oh, I seriously doubt that,' I said, somewhat recovering my composure and adjusting my portrait of Etna Bliss to include this new information. Such qualities were slightly unnerving in a woman but might prove valuable, I could see, in a wife.

We reached forward together for the silver sugar bowl, and our hands touched. She withdrew hers at once, and there was between us an uncomfortable silence. And that, I was soon to discover, was to be the pattern of our small outings. If we spoke of books or of ideas, Etna was animated, as though she had not had benefit of conversation in some time. But if I tried to speak to her of personal matters, or if I inadvertently touched her, she withdrew so quickly it was as though a cloud had covered the sun, the light going out of her face that swiftly, that absolutely. I had to learn, therefore, to speak so as to draw her out and not allow her to retreat into silence. I was, for the remainder of that first outing, moderately successful in this endeavor, successful enough to put a foot forward when she said, rather abruptly, that it was time for her to return to her uncle's house.

She stood, and I stood with her. 'I hope you will allow me to call upon you again,' I said.

Surely she hesitated too long for good manners, under the pretext of searching for her gloves. She turned to me.

'Yes, thank you,' she said simply. But did Etna Bliss understand that the freedom, both physical and spiritual, that she longed for might come only with a price?

★   ★   ★

My suit began in earnest. If the way to Etna Bliss's heart was through books, then I should become, I determined, an extensive lending library of one. And I believe I saw, even on the first day I went calling with Rider Haggard's *King Solomon's Mines*, that Etna understood the currency of my petition. Though she gave little away, it was difficult not to take her acquiescence as something more than acquiescence. In other words, I had hope.

I established a pattern of calling twice a week, and there cannot have been any doubt in that household as to my intentions. Indeed, I should have been regarded as entirely dishonorable had I occupied so much of Etna's time with no future in mind at all. I could see that Bliss himself was baffled, though less baffled, I am bound to say, when I began to reveal, in odd bits of conversation, the extent of my modest fortune. Perhaps, in the end, he regarded me as a solution to a mildly thorny problem.

As often as was feasible that winter, Etna and I left the Bliss house and went walking, returning at the end of these excursions to take tea with Bliss or with his wife. I would arrive punctually at three o'clock, nearly desperate to see Etna after an absence of three or four days. Following some brief pleasantries, Etna would don her cloak and hat and then take my arm, and I would feel a profound excitement. I craved the sensation as a man will his laudanum, and it seemed proof that Etna Bliss was someone with whom I had been destined to mate, someone whom I was fated to have loved. (I cannot help but wonder, however, if we do not invent our own destiny, design our own fate, to suit our circumstances. How much of love is a trick of the mind, a mere feat of verbal acrobatics, to accommodate persons who just happen to cross our path and who suit our needs at one particular moment in time? I have never known the answer to this conundrum, and indeed I do not think it possible to determine such an answer, since the physical effects of either are equally profound, so much so as to blur any distinction between merely convenient and truly decreed.)

(A train of thought is an out-of-control vehicle, is it not, careering wildly from place to place, more dangerous than my own derailed one?)

Etna would take my arm, and together we would stroll out into the elements; and was there ever a man who wished more for spring to come early, not only so that there might be more fine days for our outings, but also so that there might be fewer layers of clothing between Etna's hand and my arm? Our discourse tended toward the books I had brought the previous visit. She read voraciously and, I must say, rather attentively. Truth to tell, I had read nearly all of the volumes at an earlier point in my life, either for my classes or for my own studies, and some of them, such as the Haggard, bored me utterly. But I feigned interest when necessary, which was not hard to do, since Etna's own enthusiasm was so infectious. I did think at times how marvelous a teacher she might herself have become (quite possibly a better teacher than I, I am compelled to write here), and what a waste it was that this woman had no one upon whom to bestow her considerable gifts. I began to see that she would be an excellent mother, for she had great tenderness, which I had occasion to observe in her relations with her young cousin Aurelia, as well as a true love of learning, which can be no bad thing in a mother, particularly if she is able to impart such a desire to her sons.

(I daresay I sound opportunistic here, but these are thoughts formed more in retrospect than at the time, when I was in a state of such helpless physical thrall that I could not have made sound or even calculated decisions. And though much came later – and though I have found some ease in a life devoid of passion – I cannot say other than that I miss it.

Oh, how I miss it!)

(But was I *fond* of Etna Bliss? Did I actually *like* her? Certainly she had many charming qualities, such as a talent for patience and a helpless laugh, and she had a lovely way of swooping down to a child's level to speak with him or her that was enchanting to witness; but, truth to tell, I was always a little afraid of her, in awe of Etna, in the way of a supplicant before a benefactor. Though I do not think she ever used that power against me, I believe she was always aware of it and understood this great imbalance between us.)

The weeks passed in this manner. I cannot say *pleasantly*, for the word is, I think, too tame. Rather, I remember those days as fraught with a certain kind of peril lest I do or say something that might cause Etna to regard me with alarm. They were as well days of great turbulence of the heart, of unparalleled joy of the spirit, and of a thrill within the blood such as I had never known before. And, if I may say so, there was, upon occasion, a glimmer of joy upon Etna's face as well. I remember vividly, for example, one afternoon in January – the sky so clear it seemed artificial, its blue and the snow's white nearly garish in their audacity and adamantine sparkle – when I had arranged for a long sleigh ride through the nearby countryside that so delighted Etna that she lost her reserve altogether. It had been some time since I had traveled by sleigh myself, and so I had forgotten the speed, the sheer rush of air, that such a conveyance can produce. Etna and I had soapstones in our laps that had been set near to a fire and still retained considerable heat. The rugs that were wrapped over us thus made a kind of cocoon. Only our faces stung with the bitter cold, but we could not mind as the air was exhilarating. As we rode, the sleigh bells keeping time with the rhythmic movement of the horses, the sun began to set, turning the plains of snow and the branches of the trees – even the firs – a deep but vivid rose, so that all the world appeared to be glowing from within as if with a benevolent infusion. As this stirring color reached its zenith, the horses, per- haps sensing this moment of perfection (or, more likely, wishing to return to a warm barn), sped around a corner so fast that the sleigh tipped onto one runner. Etna squealed and grabbed my hand. She and I continued to hold onto each other in a seeming transport of delight that closely mimicked, if not actually was, a kind of pas- sion. Then, to my surprise and bliss (there it is again, that word), she did not release my hand when the sleigh righted itself. Rather, she laced her gloved fingers into my own, a gift so unexpected, I went rigid with hap- piness. The driver, a local farmer down on his luck, muttered an apology on behalf of the reckless horses, when I, of course, wanted only to thank the man. Thus it was that Etna and I reached that marvelous physical milestone – that of holding hands in affection – allowing me to make this a habit on subsequent occasions.

Occasionally, our outings diverted from this familiar pattern. I remember one time in particular when Etna came to me – that is, I went to fetch her, but she came to the college. On Sundays at Thrupp, faculty were per- mitted to invite guests to dine with them after church.

Sometimes these guests would be relatives from out of town, or colleagues one had business with the next day, or a professor's wife and children who for one reason or another had decided not to eat at home. Toward the end of February, I invited Etna to join me for one of those Sunday dinners. I did this partly to repay her hospitality (I had had several meals at her uncle's house), and partly to announce her to my colleagues. Etna always provoked a little flurry of attention in public, about which I sometimes felt ridiculously proprietary, as if I had fashioned her.

It was snowing the day I called for her, an icy snow that stung the skin, and, as I walked, the sleet blew horizontally, straight into my nose and mouth. I had to hold on to my hat and fold my cloak around me. It was, in truth, a filthy day, and had my desire to be with Etna not been so keen, I surely would have canceled our engagement.

When I arrived, she opened the door to me at once, as if she had been watching out for me, and I could not help but be pleased.

'Etna,' I said, shaking the weather from my coat and hat. Wisely, I did not say more at that time, for I did not want to overemphasize the wretchedness of the day. I still had hope that the afternoon would develop as I had planned.

Etna had to turn and back into the door to shut it against the wind. 'I wondered if you would be lost,' she said, and in her voice there was an unmistakable note of relief. Her face was flushed, as if she had the fever. She brought her fingers to her temple in the manner of someone who has a severe headache.

I had a new thought, a dispiriting one. 'Are you ill?' I asked. If I was concerned for her health, I confess I was also worried that I should have to return to the college without her.

'No,' she said, removing her fingers from her face. 'It is just . . . Sometimes I find it hard . . .' She shook herself slightly. 'Is it so very bad outside?'

'It's not impossible,' I said carefully. 'Unpleasant, perhaps, but there will be a good fire in the dining hall, and the meal today is goose.'

She raised her chin. I noticed that her hands were trembling. Though I very dearly wanted to believe that she trembled for me, I knew otherwise. She was gasping for oxygen.

I took a step toward her, but she put a hand out as if to stop me. Had it been at all within the realm of possibility, I would have crossed the distance between us and forced her face to mine. I would have dug my hand into the small of her back so that she was pressed hard against me. I would have lifted her skirts and run my hand along her thigh and tucked my fingers into her stocking. I would have done all those things, and perhaps she saw this, for she drew herself together in an instant, as if she had plunged her wrists into icy water. Of course, I did nothing, but I cannot help wondering what might have happened between us had I been bold enough to touch her then.

I looked at my outstretched hands. To give them occupation, I reached over toward the hat rack and took her cloak from it. I held it to her, and she stepped inside, wrapping herself in the wool. Perhaps I let my arms linger around her a moment longer than was proper. Her hair had been freshly washed and smelled of castile. She pulled away and put her hood over her hair.

'We should go,' she said quickly, 'before my aunt detains us.'

There was no need to say anything more, since I was as eager as she to quit that house.

(What bargains – what bargains – did I force Etna Bliss to make?)

The storm had increased in its ferocity. Etna held her hood low over her face, and I had to lead her in what I hoped was the right direction. It was madness to be outside on such a day, and my thoughts were split between embarrassment for having allowed this foolish outing at all, and a kind of exultation that comes with adventure and risk.

By the time we had arrived at the college and stepped into the hallway of Worms, the fronts of our cloaks were sheeted with ice. My mouth had frozen into a grimace, and it was hard to speak properly for those first few seconds. A college servant helped us off with our outer garments and even encouraged us to remove our wet boots, which Etna would not do. We went immediately into the dining room and stood by the fire, warming ourselves. Etna's cheeks and nose were crimson from the stinging snow – but, my God, how lovely her face was! She could not suppress a smile: we had survived an ordeal. As the warmth rushed back into her face and her limbs, so also did the words pour from her lips. I had hardly ever seen her so animated.

'Once I went ice-skating with my sisters,' she said. 'I was very young, no more than six or seven, I think, and while we were there, a sudden storm came on, very like this one, actually, and I don't remember exactly why now, but whoever had been sent to watch us was not there; perhaps it was thought that my sister Pippa could look after us. The storm came on so suddenly, we could not find our way back, and we were forced to take shelter in a kind of cave, and oh, the thrill of that, of being on our own! I remember that Pippa had brought a jug of cocoa wrapped in flannels in a sack. Miriam was too anxious and couldn't drink much, but I did, all at once, and, my dear, I was so sick later! But it remains, it remains . . . it is a wonderful memory.'

She was rubbing her hands by the fire. She had large hands, nearly as large as mine.

'And how were you found?' I asked.

'There was a search party. It was feared we had slipped through the ice. I don't know how long we were lost, it can't have been more than an hour or two, which can be a lifetime in a child's imagination, no? I suppose also in a mother's. I remember that I was so disappointed to be found.'

She laughed. The hair at the top and the sides of her face was damp and curled against her forehead and cheeks. I glanced around the dining room, which was only partially full. There were no other women. Some men who had been watching Etna turned reluctantly away when I looked at them; others nodded and smiled knowingly.

'Oh, it is so wonderful to be warm,' she said. 'One hardly appreciates these comforts when they are too easily come by.'

'We should sit down,' I said, 'and have our meal. You must be hungry.'

'I am,' she said, looking around for the first time. 'I'm starved, actually.' (That was another thing about Etna; she had a marvelous appetite for a woman.)

We spoke, we spoke of . . . what? I cannot remember now. How I wish I could recall every word of that afternoon, that afternoon of childlike conspiracy and warmth and good food and wine. Perhaps we talked of books, but I don't think so. That day felt different from all of the others.

We lingered long after one might reasonably have left the table. I was light-headed with possibilities. I, who could invent a lifetime in an instant, had visions of Etna having to spend the night in college rooms, of an embrace she would allow me before she entered those rooms, perhaps even a kiss snatched in a dark corridor. I imagined sleeping in the same building as she and fetching her for breakfast, a meal we had never taken together. (Delicious intimacies, erotic in their content, and how strange, for we were to take nearly five thousand breakfasts together, none of which ever produced comparable sensations.)

As the meal drew to a close and the staff was compelled to remove the linens and silver from the other tables and I saw the lovely afternoon slipping away (and perhaps because of my bold fantasies, which I later had to remind myself Etna could not have known and certainly did not share), I reached across the table and seized her hand. She stopped her sentence before she had finished it. I could see that she was holding her breath. I laced my fingers into hers.

'Etna,' I said. 'You are so very beautiful.' It was a joy simply to say the words aloud. I had not done so yet.

'Professor,' she said.

'You have promised to call me Nicholas.'

'There are others in the room.'

'Who envy me,' I said.

Her fingers were frozen in my own. I don't know if she tried to withdraw them; perhaps she saw that for the moment she could not. The stillness I had observed before in her crept over her body and her features like an incoming tide saturating the sand beneath it. She began to breathe slowly, and her face lost its flush. I had the distinct impression (God forgive me) of an animal in a wood standing absolutely still to make itself invisible. She would not look at me.

But on that day, I chose, in my besotted state, to take her demeanor to be only feminine modesty and physical shyness, both of which were, I thought then, endearing and charming qualities in a woman. I wondered as well if this fear in physical matters was testament that she had not had other lovers before me, a question that had vexed me no end since the day I had first visited her uncle's house.

I released her hand, which she immediately tucked into her lap.

'This has been the most wonderful afternoon of my life,' I said truthfully.

She raised her eyes to mine. 'Thank you for the dinner.'

'It will be a dreadful walk back,' I said. 'The storm does not appear to have abated much.'

'No, it doesn't,' she said, looking out the massive windows of the college dining hall.

'You could spend the night here,' I ventured. 'There are rooms for college guests. And then I could take you back in the morning. We could send a messenger to your uncle and aunt so that they won't worry. A boy will have an easier time of it in the snow than we.'

'I would not send a boy out in this blizzard on my account,' she said. 'No, I must go. I don't have my things.'

'Yes, of course,' I said, reluctantly standing with her.

Our cloaks and mufflers had been dried next to the fire by a college servant. I tipped the fellow and inquired about a sleigh, and one was fetched for us. During the journey to her uncle's house, Etna and I held a blanket above our heads, wrapping ourselves in a kind of tent. I could feel warm breath all about my face. At her door, she invited me in, but I had sympathy for the boy and the horses with the sleigh, and could now see what I had not been able to before: there were large drifts in which even a sleigh might be lost.

'I'll call on Tuesday, then,' I said at her door.

She nodded, but she seemed distracted. I could not let her stand in the snow a moment longer.

'Go inside,' I said.

She nodded again, and she stepped into the house. She glanced once at me before she shut the door. I walked back to the sleigh, suddenly painfully aware of the snow that was now considerably higher than my boots.

As it happened, Etna became ill with fever the next day, a development for which I chastised myself unmercifully. Had I warned her sufficiently of the perils of the storm — as any decent man would have done — she would not have taken sick. (Although it did occur to me that the preternatural flush I had seen upon her cheeks in the Bliss vestibule might have been due to incipient fever, but never mind.) I did not discover this until Tuesday when I called at the accustomed hour and was told so by Mrs. Bliss, after which it was necessary to endure an interminable cup of tea and an intolerable conversation in the parlor (in which I must say Mrs. Bliss seemed to thrive like a rare tropical flower, or was she too coming down with the fever?). I could think of little but the fact that Etna might be lying in her bed not ten feet from my head. She was sick for a week, after which she was able to come down into the parlor for brief intervals, the evidence of the contagion in her cough and reddened nose. On my visits, I brought sweets from the baker and hothouse flowers and, on one occasion, a rare orchid from the college greenhouse that the Biology Professor, Everett Tucker, had given me. And, of course, I brought books for Etna to read. Despite these gifts, our conversations in that parlor (Etna settled in a chaise, myself sweating profusely beneath my suit jacket and waistcoat) were always desultory and unconvincing – and whether this was a result of our confinement in that dreadful room or of the unfortunate contrast to the brisk animation we had known together in the college dining room, I could not tell. Needless to say, it was with a feeling of tremendous relief that Etna determined she was well enough to again venture forth.

During our courtship, I was generous with my gifts, most of which I purchased at Johnston & Herrick's in Hanover. I remember a pair of topaz earrings Etna particularly liked. (Have I said how much Etna attended to her dress and accessories? In a modest way, of course, but with an arresting mix of artfulness and taste.) I also gave her a moonstone necklace, and even now I cannot forget the pleasure of fastening the clasp at the back of her neck. Was I wrong to imagine that if I offered these gifts (a jet brooch, a tourmaline comb), and she accepted them, she was accepting me and my attentions, each present given and received an entry to my credit in the ledger of our courtship? And so I had hope, even some confidence, and began to think about a proper occasion on which to ask her to marry me.

It happened on a mild afternoon in March. It was unseasonably warm, indeed, it was the first good day we had had in weeks. The college had paths for walking that prior to that afternoon had been covered with snow and shortly after would be too muddy to negotiate, but on that day, betwixt the winter and the spring, the ground was hard enough for travel.

We left the Bliss household, and I led Etna to the head of the college paths, a walk already longer than any we had taken together. I was in a state of considerable anxiety, as any suitor about to make a petition will be, but I took heart from the fact that Etna did not demur at the entrance to the meadows. Indeed, I think she hardly noted it, so great was her restlessness, as if her limbs were suffused with the very fluid that was rising in the maples all around us. The path we embarked upon kept to the water's edge, the river boisterous that day with early freshets. Not only was the air mild, but so also were the colors – the sky muted to a milky blue, the sharp outlines of the trees blurred by the soft air. Etna held her skirts as she walked, but even so, her hem was soon soaked. She seemed not to mind at all. In fact, she walked at some speed, as though she had a destination. She wore that day a blue and gray and brown plaid skirt that had a short matching cape with a gray rabbit's-fur collar. When she lifted her skirts, I would sometimes catch a glimpse of layers of heavy cream-colored petticoats.

'I don't much care for Upham's stories,' she was saying. 'I thought I would, but I do not. They are fussily written and weighted with the sort of writerly flourishes I find so distasteful.'

'Just so,' I said, for she had expressed this distaste before to me.

'What a lovely scent. What is that, do you know?'

I sniffed. I could smell only the river.

'And what was he thinking, to create a character so fundamentally blind that he does not even understand the true import of his utterances?' she asked.

'It is a device, I believe,' I said.

'To what end?'

'To show us a character who deceives himself.'

'Well, I for one cannot believe in such a device. It makes the reader distrust the narrator. How are we to know what truly happened? And besides, no one can be so self-deceived.'

'You don't think so?' I asked.

'I think the promise of spring has addled your thoughts this afternoon, Nicholas. You're unusually distracted.'

'Perhaps I am,' I said.

Within the half hour, we had come to a sheltered spot, a rocky outcropping that produced a hollow under which we could stand and rest a moment and survey the scene before us – a pleasant vista of rust-colored grasses bowed from the weight of the snow and ice that had so recently left them. Etna had been willing to follow me to the shelter; perhaps she had to catch her breath. Her legs cannot have been used to such exercise. I moved a step closer to her, my hands in the pockets of my coat, my own body soaked with perspiration beneath my waistcoat (I had overdressed). She did not move away, but allowed me this proximity as we gazed for a moment at a flock of starlings that were swooping in a complicated pattern at the edge of the river. She smiled and seemed content.

'My dear Etna,' I began, and there must have been an inadvertently reverential tone to my voice, for she turned to me at once with a look of puzzlement. She tucked her hands beneath her cloak. In the matted leaves, I could hear the rustle of some wood animal – a chipmunk? a squirrel?

'I have a matter of the utmost importance to discuss

with you,' I said, and then paused, for already this was not going as planned; already my words had the ring of a business transaction. 'That is to say, I wish to confess to you . . .' I took a quick breath. '. . . I love you,' I said.

This pronouncement cannot have been entirely unexpected (after all, what had she imagined the topaz earrings and jet brooch signified?), and yet she seemed taken aback, astonished in the moment. I suspect the idea of marriage had been very far from her thoughts just then; certainly her flushed face had been the result of exertion, not of expectation.

But as was so often true for Etna in situations of fright or surprise, she became utterly still. Even her eyelids seemed to blink more slowly as she regarded me steadily.

'I adore you,' I said with a fervor that must have seemed bizarre in contrast to her quiet. 'I cannot sleep at night for thinking of you. I wish you to be my wife.'

(When I recall this event, I cannot help but see a scene from a play in which one of the principles is overacting as a consequence of nerves, while the other appears entirely to have forgotten her lines.)

Perhaps Etna was truly alarmed at this bold declaration, which I immediately sought to soften. 'That is to say,' I continued, 'I should like you for a wife if the prospect pleases you. Indeed, I am asking you to marry me. I know this can be neither sudden nor entirely unexpected, and, of course, you must take your time deciding; but I tell you now that you would make me the happiest man on earth if you would say yes.'

For a long time, Etna remained silent. I cannot ever be certain of her thoughts then, but I believe that though the possibility of marriage had occurred to her, and though she knew that she must in the end say yes if she was to escape the quiet tyranny of a life lived in exile, she had refused actually to *imagine* it. She had warded it off, so to speak, and thus was at a loss for reply.

I withdrew from my pocket a box that contained a ring I had recently purchased at Johnston & Herrick's (at considerable expense, I might inform the reader; I cannot see the harm in mentioning it now). 'I wish to give you this,' I said, 'as a token of . . . to commit myself . . .' But I was unable to go on. The voluble, at times pedantic, Van Tassel was rendered as silent as a stone – as silent as Etna Bliss, for that matter. I held the ring, an emerald and white gold confection, in my palm.

She did not reach for it, but did bring her hands out from under her cloak, perhaps to use them in gesture, and I, nearly desperate lest she refuse me (a possibility that was growing more and more likely with each passing moment), seized one of those gloved hands and wrapped it over my own, so that the ring lay between us. I wrapped my free arm around her long back. I felt her stiffen, her limbs unyielding. But then, when it became clear I would not willingly release her, she relaxed enough to permit the embrace, though I cannot say she responded in any way. She remained motionless, in a state of neither giving nor receiving. Perhaps she was testing herself, watching herself for a reaction. (I believe an entire story, an entire marriage, was written in that embrace, though I could not have foreseen it then. And based on that experience, I would advise young lovers to be as attentive to the first embrace with the beloved as one would be to a soothsayer.)

Yet even Etna's passivity was bliss (I apologize to the reader, but no other word will do): to feel her breath on my neck, to feel the rise and fall of her breast next to my hand. Slowly, so as to give her a chance to pull away (but she did not!), I allowed my face to slide along hers so that I might kiss her on the mouth, a highlight of my hourly imaginings. I had nearly achieved my goal when a great bird came fluttering along the path, that bird being Moxon in his coat – his hair and arms and tails flapping vigorously. Etna and I instinctively twisted apart. Moxon stopped abruptly.

'Van Tassel, what a surprise!' he said.

'Moxon,' I said.

'Miss Bliss. How nice to see you again.'

Etna turned slightly in his direction, but kept her eyes averted.

Moxon seemed oblivious to the scene he had stumbled upon. I was trembling, as much from rage as from the dashing of expectation.

'I am taking exercise,' Moxon said, stating the perfectly obvious, wiping his damp forehead with a handkerchief pulled from his coat. 'My doctor tells me it's the only antidote to college food. To keep the bowels moving and so forth.'

I was speechless, appalled that the man would discuss so boorish a subject in Etna's presence.

(*Wild boor?*)

'Oh, by the way, good luck I ran into you,' Moxon said, replacing the damp handkerchief in his pocket. 'Fitch has been searching for you all afternoon. He seems most exercised and has left messages everywhere for you to appear at his office at your earliest convenience.'

'Fitch,' I said distractedly. 'Looking for me? Today?'

'Most assuredly.'

'Whatever for?'

'I have no idea.'

Etna was as still as a deer that has heard the snap of a twig. I rather loved that quality in her – of not dissembling, of not pretending something was acceptable when clearly it was not.

'I should be off,' Moxon said. 'My doctor tells me I mustn't allow the blood to slow on these outings.'

'By all means,' I said, waving him away.

I still held the emerald ring and was anxious to deliver it to its future owner. But when I turned to Etna, I could see that Moxon had ruined the mood of passivity.

'Etna, I am sorry,' I said.

'Don't be,' she said. 'I'm chilled now, and I think I'd better return home. I don't want to risk another fever.'

'No, of course not,' I said.

'We've come rather a distance.'

'It seemed no distance at all to me,' I said.

In desultory conversation and (for me) dismal silence, we walked back to the Bliss house, my frustration and my fury given vent only in my silent imprecations. When we arrived at Etna's door, she turned and put out her hand in the ordinary way. I was in turmoil, for I was anxious to give her the ring, but I was loath to do so in so public a setting, since I feared that an inopportune moment would almost certainly facilitate a refusal. Thus, I couldn't speak. But she did, somewhat easing my rattling heart.

'Professor Van Tassel,' she said, employing my surname, which I took to be a bad omen, 'I know that an offer of marriage is not easily tendered.' (Oh, but it was, I so wanted to say; and perhaps she sensed this, for she held up her hand to stay my speech.) 'But neither can such an offer, if it is sincere, be easily accepted,' she continued. 'And so you must allow me time to think about this so that I can make an honest and clear decision.'

'I'll call in two days,' I said, eager to mark the boundaries of this decision-making.

'No, let it be a week before we see each other again. I need time to contemplate my future.'

'You wish leisure to think,' I said.

'Not leisure, Professor Van Tassel. But time for meditation. I cannot make such a momentous decision in a hurry.'

'Shall I speak to your uncle?'

'Not at this time.'

'Please,' I said, unable to keep the desperation from my voice, 'don't take too much time. I doubt I'll have a restful night until I hear from you.'

And I think that naked confession moved her somewhat, for she nodded – not in amusement or with pity, but with true sympathy, an emotion to which, I would shortly discover, Etna Bliss had ready and ample access.

The office of Noah Fitch was located at the end of a long stone corridor, so that to reach it, one had to walk that corridor's distance, each boot step echoing between the polished mahogany panels of the walls and announcing the visitor well in advance of arrival. The journey's reward was but a lone white bust of Franklin Pierce on a plinth before a massive window that overlooked the college quadrangle. Familiar with Fitch's office (and somewhat out of breath from both exertion and anxiety), I knocked confidently to dispel an aura of timidity. Hearing a tentative knock upon one's door, I knew only too well from having often been on the other side, put one in an unnecessarily superior frame of mind; and though Fitch was, as Hitchcock Professor, my natural superior, I did not like him to think me cowed by the summons.

Fitch was an impressive man, with tin-colored hair in the muttonchops mode and, improbably, a mouth of perfect teeth – an attribute of heredity or diet, I cannot say. He was a renowned vegetarian and had not taken meat in twenty years. He dressed formally on all occasions and held himself erect – even at fifty-five – and

I often suspected it was his imposing and appealing physical presence as much as his scholarship that had garnered for him his post.

'Yes. Van Tassel. Come in.'

He led me into his office, and perhaps it was the drawn drapes at the windows that lent that office such a somber air, even in the daylight. Needless to say, the walls were lined with books, though here and there a cherished objet interrupted the monotony: a birdcage, a lead rooster, an orange studded with cloves. There was also a rather good portrait of his wife, which was later to find its way into the Elliot Collection.

We sat across from each other, a large expanse of cherry wood between us. There was a folder in front of him.

'You wanted to see me, sir?' I asked.

'Yes, Van Tassel, I did.'

He glanced away for a moment, as if gathering his thoughts. The urgency of which Moxon had spoken earlier was nowhere in evidence. I had then, as I had had sometimes in the past, the faint impression that Fitch did not actually like me very much – a feeling, I must say, he took great pains to hide – and I had long ago decided that the cause of this mild dislike was that I was not born and bred to my adopted New England heritage and thus lacked a certain authenticity.

'This is a delicate matter,' Fitch began.

The heat came instantly into my face. What might such a 'delicate' matter be? Had a student complained about excessively harsh treatment? Had I, in my current state of distraction, been missing tutorials? Had I been unfair in my grading?

He pushed himself away from his desk. I became aware that I was leaning forward in my own chair in the attitude of a supplicant and so made an attempt to readjust my posture.

'As you know,' he began, 'we share an interest in the writings of Sir Walter Scott.'

'Just so,' I said.

'And we are, as we should be, acquainted with the scholarship regarding this author.'

I nodded, resisting the urge to sniff, as I fancied myself better read in this field than Fitch, whose interests were necessarily broader, allowing him less opportunity for depth in any one area.

'And so it is that I have come across your monograph on the early novels of Sir Walter Scott.'

(Was there then the briefest jolt of alarm within my breast? I think not. Not yet.)

'Sir,' I said.

'And, just by the merest happenstance, I have also had occasion to come upon a monograph written by Alan Dudley Severence of Amherst College, which is – how shall I put this? – remarkably similar to yours.'

I was silent.

'And, well, to be frank, Van Tassel, there is, I am afraid, a question of plagiarism.'

The word singed my ears and made my mouth go dry. 'Sir, you cannot suggest . . .' I said.

'But I'm afraid I do,' he said.

'It cannot have happened,' I said.

Fitch fiddled with the gold chain of his pocket watch. 'Certain phrases do seem, shall we say, remarkably co-incidental.'

'But coincidence, sir, is not a crime.'

'Not if it is unintentional.'

'It is, sir. It is. I cannot think. I have had an impeccable—'

'Yes, yes, so you have.'

Fitch regarded me for some time. The fire in the grate popped suddenly, startling both of us. He rolled himself closer to the desk and set his elbows upon it.

'I confess I was most surprised,' he said. 'You are, after all, a man of extraordinary discipline.'

'I am, sir.'

'You possess a scholarship that rises well above the average.'

'Thank you, sir.'

'There should have been no need.'

'There was no need.'

'Yes, well.'

Fitch studied me at great length, and I forced myself to return his scrutiny.

'Perhaps you would like to take this monograph of Severence's with you to your rooms to review the co-incidences for yourself,' he said. 'Certain phrases are, as you shall see . . . here, I have marked them: "*a fey man, living in a remote world of pain*". And this one: "*swift, competent and careless narrative*". And this here: "*marching fatality unbroken by the awkwardness of invention*". Need I go on?'

It was some seconds before I found my voice. 'But, sir, are not certain phrases, such as *if we admit* and *we make no sufficient allowance* and *at first sight*, built into common discourse?'

'Yes, certainly, but I am afraid those are not these.'

'But the principle is the same, is it not?'

Fitch swiveled in his chair, nearly putting his back to me, and gazed for some time into the fire. I guessed that he was pondering his dilemma and making judgments. I groped wildly for a subject that I might introduce to distract him from the matter at hand, but my thoughts were too confused. I longed for an open window, a hint of light in that gloomy room. The silence was so profound that one could hear each tick of the clock over the mantel. After a time (after an agony of time, it seemed to me), Fitch turned around.

'Well, Van Tassel.'

'Sir.'

My nerves had pitched my voice embarrassingly high. I cleared my throat.

Fitch sighed once. A decision had been made.

'I should not like to lose you after all this time,' he said. 'But I shall be forced to if there is a second offense.'

'There was no first offense.'

'You seem firm in your denial.'

'I must. There was no crime.'

'I shall have to pay great attention to your work.'

'I hope you have been doing so all along,' I said.

'We shall say no more about this now,' he said, making a small notation on a piece of paper in the folder. I strained to see what he had written but could not in the darkened room.

'No, sir.' I sought to hide my considerable relief (not to mention my trembling hands) by crossing my arms and once again clearing my throat.

Fitch folded his fingers under his nose and regarded me for some time. Beyond the door, I could hear the echo of boot steps making their way along the corridor.

'I hear you have been walking out with a young woman,' he said.

'She is not a young woman,' I said inanely, rattled by the abrupt change in subject. 'She is twenty-five.'

'Van Tassel, sometimes you strike me as excessively . . . accurate.'

'I should hope so, sir.'

'Well, I know the person in question. I have dined with Etna Bliss. You're a lucky man.'

'Dined with her?'

'Yes. It must have been, let me think, three weeks ago. Bliss had a few of us to dinner.'

Us to dinner? Who exactly were the *us*? I wondered. And why had I been excluded? The thought rankled.

'A handsome woman, Van Tassel,' he said.

'Thank you,' I said.

Fitch stood. The interview was over. Across the desk, he handed me Severence's monograph, which I had no choice but to accept. 'I believe we have said all there is to say on the subject of coincidence,' he said.

'Thank you, sir.'

'And unless I were absolutely convinced of a delib- erate, as opposed to a careless, wrong, I should see no point in discussing the matter with any other person.'

Fitch, I knew, was a man of his word. And perhaps I did then betray some relief, for he fixed me with his gaze, as if in final assessment.

There was a knock upon the door, my own sum- mons to depart. With quickening step, I brushed grate- fully past a worried-looking student.

When the door had closed, I leaned against the wall in the corridor. It was the worst infraction I had ever been accused of. I thought of Moxon's importunate appearance, of my missed chance with Etna on the col- lege path, and of Fitch's intolerable suspicions; and I imagined the day could not possibly get any worse, until I happened to glance at my pocket watch and saw that I was late for my tutorial with Edward Ferald.

Ferald was waiting for me in my sitting room – leaning

with a languid pose against a stool near the window, one foot on the floor, the other on a rung, his hands insouciantly folded upon his thigh. He was looking out at the view and pretended not to notice me when I entered the room.

'Yes, Ferald,' I said. 'Sorry for the delay.'

My breath was short and tight, and I was perspiring mightily, which put me at a distinct disadvantage with the preternaturally cool Ferald; but there was little I could do about it beyond sitting down in one of the wing chairs by the fire and unwrapping my muffler.

He turned slowly in my direction.

He was, as always, impeccably dressed in an expertly tailored suit coat with a long pearl silk scarf. His shirt-front was so white and so crisp, I decided it must be new. Ferald had impressive manners as well, though I knew those to be a mask that hid a canny nature.

'No trouble at all, sir.'

The 'sir' that I had employed just minutes earlier with what I hoped was true deference to Noah Fitch sounded faintly mocking from Ferald's lips.

'Have you been here long?' I asked.

'Since five.'

It was now twenty-five minutes after the hour.

'Then I shall simply go over time,' I said, opening my case.

'Sir, I am afraid I cannot. I have promised myself to Merrit.'

I tried to think. Merrit was a third-year student rumored to be a bookmaker.

'For what purpose?' I inquired.

Ferald hesitated. 'I do not wish to seem rude, sir, but is that relevant? The fact of the promise would seem to be the point.'

'Have you read *The Bride of Lammermoor*?' I asked, abruptly changing the subject.

'Yes, sir, but I am having difficulty with your seventh question – that of the historical novel versus the "turbid mixture of contemporaneousness", as you put it. I cannot see how a work not from one's own time permits the isolation of essentials from accidentals. It seems to me a false endeavor, since the author cannot know or ever write authentically about the past. We are, of course, referring to *Waverly*, which is just outside Scott's period. And which rather begs the question, don't you think?'

'Perhaps you have not read your text carefully enough,' I said.

'I have done the work,' he said in an aggrieved tone. 'I simply have it all in a muddle and shall need your help in sorting it all out. Indeed, I am looking forward to your commentary.' He took no pains to hide his slight smile. 'As ever.'

The gall, I thought.

'Very well,' I said. 'Take out the text.'

Ferald's feigned pedagogical and literary interest irritated me no end, particularly as he had so little need of an education, and I doubted he should ever use it. He would, I knew, shortly come into considerable property nearby and would retire, at a young age, to the life of a gentleman farmer.

I told Ferald to take the seat opposite mine. He did so with a languor that, were he not my student and were I not impatient to be done with him, I should have admired. I reflected then that there would always be a Ferald. Sometimes his name would be Wiles or Mutterson or simply Box, but there would always be one boy who clearly mocked his teachers, though never openly, and by his behavior played at a labyrinthine game of wits, one that would necessarily amuse him greatly, and one that he almost certainly would win.

But in the game of teachers and students, the teacher will always have the last word; and I must confess that as I sat there and watched Ferald take out his Venetian glass pen and his Italian leather notebook (doubtless souvenirs of tours abroad), I began to consider seriously the notion of being unable to find sufficient merit in his final examination and so having perforce to fail the boy.

When Ferald left, I paced in my rooms in an emotionally exhausted state. The monograph Fitch had given me lay on my desk, but I ignored it, having no desire to read it or to compare it to mine, for I knew only too well what I should find. It was a clerical misstep only, I told myself, a consequence of being preoccupied and overtired and thus somewhat careless. And the sentences were not *precisely* the same, were they? If there seemed a marked similarity in ideas, were ideas the sole property of one mind, one voice? Might not a brilliant critic arrive at the same conclusion in the same year as another as a result of normal evolution in a field of study? Besides, were not the questionable passages Fitch had referred to but a tiny part of the whole? Nevertheless, I reminded myself, I should have to guard against haste and distraction in the future and return at once to my disciplined ways.

The week did not improve. Etna sent a brief note saying she deeply regretted that she would not be able to see me on Wednesday, as we had planned, since she was otherwise engaged with an unexpected visit from her sister and brother-in-law, but she would be happy to see me the following week. This meant I should have to wait more than a week for an answer to my question, a wait that seemed agonizing. I suffered through an interminable weekend, trying to catch up on all of my course work, which I had much neglected, only to receive a nasty shock at an all-college faculty luncheon on Monday, when William Bliss surprised me at my table in the dining hall.

'Van Tassel,' he said as he passed my table. 'I am surprised to see you with such a hearty appetite, considering our sad news.'

I did not understand the man. I noted that he did not seem sad, however.

'What sad news?'

'Did Etna not write you? No, perhaps not. It was very sudden. Her sister and brother-in-law came abruptly to fetch her back to the family house in Exeter. I gather Keep, the brother-in-law, thought it unseemly to have Etna board elsewhere, even though he seems to have snatched the family homestead right out from under her. Quite frankly, I rather think the man has it in mind to make a governess of her for his children.'

'Etna gone?' I asked, stupefied.

'I'm afraid so.'

I stood. 'This is not possible,' I said in a voice loud enough that several of our colleagues glanced up at us from their meals.

Bliss put an avuncular hand on my shoulder. 'I am afraid that it is so. Forgive me for having informed you in so public a place. I thought you knew.'

Bliss had gone pale. He was a gentle scientist, unused to displays of emotion. 'Shall we step outside a minute?' he asked.

I went, as a steer will be nudged toward the abattoir.

'Of course, we were much dismayed ourselves,' Bliss added when we were safely outside the building. 'But Keep is formidably persuasive. And my niece apparently made little protest, or if she did, I do not know about it. Doubtless she was glad to see her sister again, and perhaps to return to her home, even if the circumstances are a bit . . .' (he hesitated) '. . . compromised.'

I could not absorb the blow. 'What is the address?' I demanded. 'I must go to see her.'

'Now, now,' said Bliss, again employing the restraining hand on my shoulder. 'I shouldn't want you to get too exercised about this. I am sure she will write you in good time.'

'But I love her!' I blurted. 'I wish to have her for a wife! It is all I wish for!'

'Oh, my dear man,' Bliss said, dropping his hand. 'Van Tassel, you surprise me.' But I could see that he was surprised only by the occasion and the vehemence of my declaration, not by the fact of it, which he had doubtless anticipated. 'Has Etna returned this . . . this love?' he asked gently.

'Not in so many words,' I said. 'But I believe she is not averse to my affection.'

'Have you spoken to her of this?'

'Just five days ago,' I answered.

I spun away from him, my hands in my hair. I could scarcely think. Etna gone? Etna *gone*?

'You must get a hold of yourself,' Bliss said. 'I am sure she is carefully considering your proposal. Allow my niece to write you and explain her abrupt departure for herself. Perhaps in that letter you will have the answer to your question.'

I shook my head, too bewildered to reply.

'Now let us go in to our dinners, which have grown

cold in our absence,' he said. 'I shall call for some brandy to restore your color.'

But I could not reenter that dining hall, nor converse further with any person, and so I bolted across the lawn, leaving a doubtless much relieved Bliss to return to his Indian pudding. I made it to my rooms without encountering anyone with whom I should have felt compelled to converse. I staggered up the stairs, wanting only privacy. On the hall table just outside my rooms, there was a letter waiting for me.

March 25, 1900

Dear Nicholas,

Please forgive this sudden and abrupt correspondence, but I write to tell you that I have left Thrupp and the household of my kind aunt and uncle to return to my former home in Exeter, now that of my brother-in-law Mr. Josip Keep. The departure was sudden, as Mr. Keep had urgent business at home and could spare only the weekend to come and fetch me. I tell you truthfully that though I had no inkling of his mission prior to his arrival, the choice to leave was mine alone.

I fear I have overstayed my welcome at my uncle's house, though I assure you they gave me no hint of this at any time. And since I do wish to be useful in my life, and not merely dependent upon the kindness of others, I thought it best to take up residence with my sister so that I may help to educate her children. My sister, alas, has no love of learning.

But do not imagine that I have made this decision lightly. I have appreciated your company and have valued your friendship greatly. It was always stimulating for me, and I doubt I should have borne my exile with as much good cheer had I not had the anticipation of your visits and the distraction of the lovely books you lent me. (The Hardy, by the way, is with my uncle. He said that he would have it delivered to your rooms.)

As to your offer of marriage, I cannot consider your proposal at this time, as I am sure you must know. I release you from all commitment whatsoever and shall understand perfectly if you should choose to take my departure for a refusal. I cannot say to what decision I should have come had I remained at Thrupp; I had no time to ponder your grave request and the equally grave responsibility of answering it.

I know that this will not be easy for you, but you must not think it was easy for me either. I shall miss your companionship. I hope you will find solace in your work and that the Lord will keep you safe in all your endeavors.

I remain, most sincerely yours,
Etna Bliss

It was fortunate that I had thought to bring the letter into my rooms before opening it, for I then behaved in an unseemly manner that might have made another cringe to behold. How long I was in this state I cannot say, but gradually I calmed myself, and though I was subject to intermittent and brief seizures of both anger and grief, I was finally able to regain my composure. I had not come so far to go down so easily in defeat.

Perhaps there is some truth to the notion that stars collide or are out of balance in the universe and thus, in disarray, exert an influence upon individuals here on earth. I say this for want of any other explanation for the confluence of unpleasant events that day and the next.

There was at the college a battle brewing between two opposing factions, and I had somewhat unexpectedly found myself the informal leader of one of them. Perhaps this was a consequence of my newfound confidence and popularity during the winter months; more likely, it was because of the passion of my convictions. I could not then (and still cannot) countenance the idea of a department of physical culture at any college of classical learning, nor, moreover, the conferring of degrees in this nondiscipline upon matriculating students.

To give a degree to students whose chief occupation for four years has been employing wood-and-iron dumbbells in rhythmic motions or running circles in a gymnasium, all the while yelling like Rebels, is nothing short of absurd. Perhaps there is a place for physical exercise in the life of an individual – in the *private* life of the individual, that is, and to be carried out *in private*, as are other bodily functions – but to make of it an academic discipline with all the same rights and privileges as, say, Mathematics or Biblical History and Interpretation is an idea that would have been laughable had it not been proposed so seriously.

The Tuesday following the Monday of my hideous news, I was scheduled to speak at a meeting of college faculty and administration. I was to debate (and then vote upon) a proposal which would allow Professor Arthur Hallock (who did have, I am bound to say, a degree in medicine from the Medical School of Maine at Bowdoin College and who taught Anatomy and Physiology at Thrupp) to create a department of physical culture, which would elevate its study (what *study*? I ask) to the status of Literature and History. Worse, all college students would be compelled to take courses in this field and to keep to a regular regimen of physical exercise on pain of forfeiting their degrees. Even now – in this moving compartment and so far removed from the fray – I can work myself up into quite a froth on this subject.

The faculty had divided itself on this issue; two-thirds were in favor of instituting the new discipline, and one-third were against. Mine was, unfortunately, the minority view, and thus it was all the more necessary to exhibit the courage of my convictions in a stirring speech before the assembled staff of the college. To say that I was not in a fit condition to do this is an almost ludicrous bit of understatement. I was barely able to stand and was completely unable to take food of any kind, since I was still in shock over the distressing news of Etna's sudden departure. Worse, I could not gather my thoughts properly. I had left the drafting of my argument until the last minute, an uncharacteristically procrastinic gesture on my part, though, as I have said, during that time I had let a certain laxity undermine my normally excellent discipline. Thus was I faced with the horror of having to compose a speech within hours of having read Etna's letter. That I was able to do so at all is testimony to my considerable willpower, for I remember having the utmost difficulty concentrating. In addition, I kept succumbing to intense fits of despair. Only by remaining awake most of the hours of the night was I able to fashion something that at least resembled an argument.

The next morning, the faculty assembled in the Anatomy amphitheater. Hallock and I and the President of the college, Isaac Phillips, sat on the stage. By common though unspoken agreement, the faculty had seated themselves more or less according to their convictions – two-thirds on one side of the theater, the remaining third on the other side, which made the room look a bit like a state legislature. As mentioned, I had not slept much the night before, and I knew I presented a poor argument for the continued absence of physical culture at the college. I looked pale, even haggard, and though I took great pains to position my features and my limbs so as to convey a brighter aspect, the center of my being felt aged to the core.

Hallock, by contrast, radiated good health and seemed to anticipate the debate with genuine relish. One could not fail to notice his impossibly erect spine or the way his muscled limbs nearly burst from his frock coat. He was reported to have had an excellent arm in his time and, consequently, he coached, in the springtime, the fledgling and seldom victorious Thrupp Throwing Team.

After an introduction by President Phillips, Hallock took the podium. He began by assembling an impressive number of facts about the deteriorating health of Thrupp students. Though I had to feign politeness at the beginning of the assembly, I grew more and more agitated as Hallock's argument evolved. He insisted upon a natural link between poor health and intellectual inferiority. He had the audacity to call upon the Greek ideal of the palaestra in his comparison with the physical characteristics of the typical Thrupp student: that is, misshapen limbs, slumped posture, pale visages, and difficulty with breathing brought on by indifference to matters of the body. He called attention to cases of disease and feebleness and, in some instances, premature death among the students. (I thought this was going a bit too far.) If every student were required to participate in physical exercise daily, he insisted, the general health of the student population would improve. Worse, he had the audacity to suggest that faculty ought to be required to exercise regularly on the theory that their teaching and their relationships with the students would improve as well. To house such activity, Hallock proposed, the college should erect a gymnasium.

I was on my feet at once, though it was some moments before I could speak over the cheers from the gallery. The proposed site of this 'gymnasium', I informed my audience, was none other than the college's beloved Strout Park, a particularly serene bit of landscape nestled among the severe granite hills. Was such a precious natural resource to be squandered in the pursuit of an enterprise that ought best to be performed in private and certainly not under the auspices of the college? To then endow, I asserted, this endeavor with all the hallowed privileges of, say, the faculty of Literature and Rhetoric was obscene. There was a faint titter of laughter, which I tried to ignore, despite the fact that I feared that my cause was lost (the simple geometry of the audience could tell me that).

Nevertheless, I persevered. Was it truly the charge of the college, I asked, to take over the physical education of a man? Was this not more properly a task suited to the military, which depended on a man's fitness, or to the physician, whose job it was to preserve the health of any individual? Did the college really think it could dictate health and then, piling absurdity upon absurdity, grant a degree for it? Were the precious financial resources of the college to be spent on a facility in which young men might run around with balls, or were they not better apportioned to the improvement of the library, which sorely needed more books, or to the erection of an observatory, so that our understanding of the heavens might increase?

'Surely men are entitled to the pursuit of physical health,' I argued, softening my tone a bit, as is necessary in any rhetorical argument. 'Surely anyone who actually *enjoys* throwing a ball around a field can find like-minded fellows with whom to do this in his spare time. This is the essence of *recreation*, by definition an adjunct to education, not its point.'

'Hear, hear,' someone from my side called out.

'Nonsense,' shouted someone from the other side.

President Phillips had to ask for order. William Bliss was seated to my right (in the pro-gymnasium two-thirds), and I dared not look at him lest I be derailed completely.

'But to make such an activity *compulsory*,' I said, 'is beyond reason. One cannot dictate physical health any more than one can dictate good teeth or good breeding. The college is in danger of straying into an arena in which it has no place and, further, of risking becoming a laughingstock. Do we really imagine that sober parents will send us their children? Will they not want more for their one hundred and fifty-five dollars a year than this misplaced commitment to harden their sons' bodies?'

The shouts and calls had reached a level uncomfortable enough that I was forced to raise my voice above the fray.

'Of what possible use will a degree in physical culture be?' I asked, nearly shouting now. 'Are we not in danger of releasing into the world students with no skills beyond what might be useful in the miliary? The business of a university . . .' I said, and then stopped.

'The business of a university . . .' I tried.

I could not finish my sentence. An odd and unpleasant sensation had taken hold of my eyes so that the audience before me had broken into a hundred – no, a thousand – brightly moving dots.

'The business of a university . . .' I began again, but I could not think how I had intended for the sentence to end. My mouth opened and closed, and I am sure I must have winced, for I was certainly wincing inwardly from extraordinary pain. I felt light-headed and gripped the podium. It was then that I found myself most grievously indisposed in a manner I should not like to set forth in any detail here. After a time, I felt a hand on my arm and looked up into the face of Arthur Hallock, who, as a physician, undoubtedly felt it necessary (and politically expedient) to see to my distress. I shook him off, humiliated by his attentions. 'Go away,' I think I actually said as I fainted to the floor.

I awoke moments later on the stage of the amphitheater. I could hear Hallock telling Phillips that he thought I had had a seizure, and though I wanted to protest this misdiagnosis, I found that I could not; that, for the moment, I had no speech. In a state of confusion and deep chagrin, I was brought to a sitting position and then to my feet. When it was determined I could stand on my own – even though, mysteriously, I still could not talk – I was led like a child to my rooms.

Though I regained my speech before the night was out, I was too exhausted to move or to eat – my collapse, I am convinced now, more emotional than physical. I tried diligently to convince my would-be physician of this, but I could tell that he was no more persuaded by my argument than he had been by my impassioned rhetoric in the amphitheater.

I remained in my rooms for several days. The vote to institute a department of physical culture was delayed a week. The outcome might have been predicted. And although by then I hardly cared about the matter, I have often wondered whether I should have been more persuasive and perhaps even victorious had Etna not abandoned me and had my voice contained a natural and convincing enthusiasm for my cause, or had I not presented such a haggard appearance on the stage. Thus there might not be, even today, a department of physical culture at Thrupp College. Which makes me ponder the nature of fate and coincidence: A man is propelled one minute sooner to his automobile because he decides not to stop to kiss his wife good-bye. As a consequence of this omission, he then crosses a bridge one minute before it collapses, taking all its traffic and doomed souls into the swirling and angry depths below. Oblivious, and safely out of harm's way, our man continues on his journey.

I waited the week out in a feverish grimace. On Saturday, I hired a coach to take me to Exeter. I gave no advance warning of my visit, for fear either Etna or her apparently formidable brother-in-law might forbid it.

The journey from Thrupp to Exeter could be made in one very long day and was then a rough journey, since there were no direct highways to that part of the state. One had to resort to the twisting lanes and village roads of a countryside not best known for its easy landscape. Thus I was in somewhat disheveled condition when I arrived in Exeter. Though my need to see Etna was keen, for once prudence held sway; I asked the weary driver of the coach to take me to a boardinghouse instead.

I doubt Exeter has changed much since I was there. It is a handsome academy town with many fine residences along its High and Water Streets. As the driver brought me into the village, I tried to imagine in which house Etna was prisoner. For that is how I saw her then – a servant, even a slave, in her brother-in-law's possession. If I had before been determined to liberate her from the kindly though stifling household of her uncle, I was doubly resolved then to free her from the employ of the man who had contrived to steal from Etna her entire capital.

I spent a restless night in the home of a widow who had been forced to open her own considerable abode to the public. In my distraction and haste, I had neglected to pack a suitable kit and was forced to borrow from my landlady a razor and clean shirt and so on, which I promised to return as soon as my mission was accomplished. After an odd dinner of chutney and potatoes and brussels sprouts, I retired to my room and sat in a chair and thought about my plight and my mission. It was clear to me, as indeed it had been clear all along, that Etna did not care for me in the same way that I cared for her. (Would I have left Etna behind in Thrupp? Never.) At that time I attributed this imbalance to the physical and temperamental differences between men and women. Certainly men were capable of greater passion than women, were they not? And so, perforce, must always be the predators? And was there not a certain sport in the chase? Was I not expected to pursue Etna, no matter where she had gone? By then, of course, I had persuaded myself that she had left Thrupp against her will, whatever she had written in her letter. Though I had never met Josip Keep, I imagined him to be an intimidating presence, a man accustomed to having his wishes obeyed. And would Etna not have felt duty-bound to help her sister with her children? Yes, surely she would. I had seen the way she was with her young cousin and had already admired the humor and patience she had displayed. But all of this was merely idle speculation on my part. I could no more have given Etna up than I could have taken my life. Indeed, she was my life now. I could not envision a future that did not include her.

And there was something else that I must admit to here: I could not cease from my pursuit until I had known Etna Bliss. I mean this in the sense it will be understood. It was not a desire I would freely have confessed to at that time, but there was in me the keenest need to touch and to experience Etna Bliss, a need I had recognized from the first time I saw her the night of the fire, a need that had grown only sharper as the days and weeks had progressed. Do all men feel this way when they meet their beloved? I do not know, for it is not a discussion I have ever had with any man or woman. I know only that the alternative was for me intolerable. If I did not pursue Etna, I was convinced, I would be tormented all my life by longing – a longing that no other woman would be able to slake. (And I must say that even today I am not certain that I was not correct in this assumption.)

That night, as I slept in the boardinghouse, I was haunted in my dreams by images of Etna: her skirts tangled in tree branches as she sought to fly, sheltering under a shelf of rock that quite suddenly fell upon her, and then soaring up and out from Noah Fitch's office like a gull caught on an updraft. The next morning, I inquired as to the whereabouts of Keep's home, and it gratified me to be told by my widow-landlady that the house was still known as the Bliss house and would be for years to come, the townsfolk preferring to pay homage to the ancestral owners and not its usurpers. I walked the not-very-great distance of a mile to the house I sought, the day clear and cold; and it was not the glory of the morning that increased my pace. No, it was the thought of seeing Etna again that gave me vigor: the knowledge that if I failed today I was likely to fail for a lifetime.

One could see at once that the Keep residence (the *Bliss* residence) had been newly painted and the windows freshly glazed. I passed through a gate and approached a large paneled door. A manservant opened it. I stated my business. He asked me to wait in a parlor.

Despite my nerves, I could not help but notice that the parlor was in considerable disarray. All about the room were ladders and drop cloths and putty knives and paintbrushes laid out upon newspaper; and the smell of turpentine was much in evidence. It seemed obvious that Josip Keep, having taken up residence as the largest creditor of the Bliss estate, was now making repairs that the late Mrs. Bliss had been unable to afford in her declining years.

I heard footsteps on the stairs and turned.

'Professor Van Tassel, you surprise me very much,' Etna said.

She had on an extraordinary dress of navy and cream that set off the color of her hair in a marvelous way and seemed to give it hues I had not noticed before. Her eyes, above her pronounced cheekbones, appeared wary. I had interrupted her in the act of fashioning her hair, for I saw that loops and curls were suspended from a knot at the back of her head, the sight of which stirred me greatly, for I had never seen her with her hair down.

'I could not stay away,' I said at once. 'I must speak to you.'

She did not seem precisely alarmed to see me, but neither did she appear pleased. It was difficult for me to determine exactly how my arrival was being received.

'We are shortly to leave for church,' she said.

'I don't have much time,' I said. 'I must be back at Thrupp for my classes tomorrow afternoon.'

'You are well?' she asked.

'As well as can be expected.'

'Why have you come?'

'You must know why I have come.'

From the hallway, behind Etna, I could hear rustling on the stairs. I saw her stiffen at the certain interruption.

A diminutive woman entered the room, and Etna turned politely.

'Etna, you have a guest,' the woman said with some surprise. And then added, 'Your hair is not done.'

'Miriam,' said Etna, 'this is Professor Nicholas Van Tassel. He has come from Thrupp. Professor Van Tassel, this is my sister, Miriam Keep.'

It seemed scarcely possible that the two women before me could be related. Where one was dark, the other was fair; while one was tall, the other was petite and delicate in her look; while one had arresting features, the other was truly beautiful in a more conventional manner: that is to say, she possessed the nearly perfect beauty of wide green eyes, naturally pink lips, and skin so luminous it seemed to have the sheen of marble. She held herself with the bearing of a woman who had used her beauty to advantage, and I surmised immediately that it had been her comeliness that had secured for her a rich husband. It would be interesting, I thought, to see if the man was worth so dear a sum.

'So you have come a distance,' Miriam said, taking a step farther into the room.

'Yes,' I answered.

'To pay a call on Etna, or are you engaged in business here?'

'My business is with Etna,' I said.

'Your timing is unfortunate. We are just on our way to services.'

'Yes, forgive me. I did not think,' said I (who had done nothing but think).

'Etna,' said Miriam, surveying Etnas's coiffure. 'Josip will not want to be kept waiting, not for church, which, as you know, begins promptly at ten o'clock.' I winced to hear Etna spoken to in this manner.

'Miriam,' said Etna, 'would you be kind enough to entertain my guest while I go upstairs for a moment. I shall be right back.' I understood this as my cue to leave, but I could not. Etna left us — whether gratefully or in a state of confusion I did not know.

'So, Professor Van Tassel,' Miriam said, seating herself on the only uncovered chair in the room, 'what brings you to our house so early on a Sunday morning?'

I heard in the question another mild rebuke for having disturbed a family on their day of religious worship.

'I have something of importance I must discuss with Etna,' I said plainly.

'Is that so?' she said, bestowing upon me a cool glance. I had the distinct sense of being in the presence of a diamond even as I preferred the golden glow of the lesser jewel, the topaz.

'I'll not pry,' she said, though I could see that she dearly wanted to. 'Unfortunately, I fear the Reverend Young will not wait upon our arrival at services. As for myself, I confess I could easily forgo the man's dusty sermons, but my husband has a keen sense of piety and religious obligation. And though he has many excellent qualities, he is often impatient with tardiness.'

'I myself appreciate punctuality,' I said. 'And do forgive me for intruding upon your family. If I could have waited until tomorrow, I would have done so, but unfortunately I must be back at Thrupp for my classes.'

'You teach at the college.'

'Yes.'

'Your business must be urgent,' she said in another attempt to ascertain the reason for my call.

I was silent.

'I am sure the college is quite wonderful, but Thrupp is a dreary little town,' she said.

'I think a town may be dreary or not depending upon its inhabitants, Mrs. Keep,' I said. Miriam Keep bristled, and I hastened to amend my reply. 'But Thrupp is in no way equal to the charm of this village,' I added.

'No,' she said, and smiled thinly. 'I hope that my sister shall rediscover this charm for herself shortly,' she added.

'And I have hope that she will not remain long enough in Exeter to test its charm,' I countered boldly.

'Really, Professor Van Tassel,' she said, surprised but also intrigued, 'you reveal yourself at last.'

'It is a joyous revelation, I assure you.'

'You have strong affection for my sister?' she asked.

'The strongest.'

'And does she know of this?'

'She does.'

'I am surprised, then, that she did not mention this to me. You are aware, are you not, that Etna did not put up any impediment to leaving her uncle's household?'

The slight had been meant to wound, and it did. 'Perhaps she felt it her duty to return with you, however briefly,' I said. 'Or perhaps she thought the change of venue might bring a swift and happy conclusion to her deliberations.' Then I hastily added, so as to defuse the mild tension between us, 'And, of course, I am certain that she has missed her sister a great deal.'

Miriam Keep did not yield at the compliment. 'My sister is deliberating a proposal?' she asked. 'A proposal of marriage?'

'Yes, she is.'

'How extraordinary,' she said, examining me so thoroughly this time that she actually narrowed her eyes. Perhaps she was shortsighted. 'I had no idea. And how doubly extraordinary that she has remained silent. Well, I cannot say whether or not I wish you to succeed, Professor Van Tassel, since I do not know you at all.'

'No.'

'But I can assure you that I have the greatest desire for my sister's happiness,' she said.

'And why should your sister not have happiness?' said a voice from the hall.

Josip Keep's sudden and massive presence in the doorway matched the rich baritone with which he spoke. The man was nearing forty, I surmised. He had a head of silky black hair that had been richly oiled and waved back from a slightly receding hairline. It was a handsome face, one used to entitlement.

'Dearest,' Miriam said, rising at once, which seemed an odd reversal of manners. 'This is Professor Van Tassel, who has come to see Etna.'

'At this hour? On a Sunday?'

'Forgive me,' I said.

'We are off to worship,' he said (somewhat rudely, I thought; he had not even introduced himself). He drew on his gloves. 'Are you a man of faith?' he asked.

'Of some faith,' I answered carefully.

'And where do you worship?'

In fact, I was not fond of worship at all and did not do so as often as I ought to have. Consequently, I had attached myself to a Presbyterian parish some five miles from the college on the theory that few men of the faculty would be drawn to such an inconvenient venue. (Though one day I was surprised to see Moxon in a pew opposite; but since he was as irregular as I in attendance and as loath to expose his laxity further, we did not greet each other after the service, nor speak of this coincidence, much in the way that men who have frequented the same brothel will fail to recognize each other at a place of business some days hence.)

'I am a Presbyterian, sir,' I said.

'I see. We are Unitarians.' Somewhat dismissively, Keep turned away from me. Presbyterian had failed to impress him. 'Miriam, where is your sister? We shall be late.'

'She will be here shortly, dear.'

'I hope this is not indicative of her habits,' he said.

'I'm sure not,' Miriam, who seemed somewhat cowed by her husband, said.

'And the children?'

'Etna will bring them.'

'It will be crowded in the pew,' Keep said. 'Perhaps Etna might sit with the children?'

'If you think it absolutely necessary,' Miriam said, with a quick glance in my direction.

I could see then how Etna's situation might be intolerable – an unwanted guest in her sister's home (once her own home), at best a governess to her sister's children. Thus was I doubly determined to press my suit.

Etna entered the room, the lovely loops and coils of her hair now dutifully harnessed. Miriam invited me to dine with them upon their return from services, and I accepted, though Keep cast a sullen glance in my direction.

But Etna surprised us all. 'Miriam, forgive me,' she said, 'but I will not be attending services with you today. Professor Van Tassel has come so far, and I must speak with him now.'

Miriam looked rebuffed but had no reply. She could not reasonably insist that her sister accompany her to church. I was pleased for Etna's sake that she had stood up to her sister, but I could also see that for Etna life in Exeter might have to be a constant series of negotiations.

There was a flurry of leave-taking then, during which Etna and I waited awkwardly, not wishing to seem rude in our haste to speak with each other. I occupied myself during this time by composing sentences I might use in my petition. Impatient to begin, I started to speak before the Keeps' carriage had even pulled away.

'Hear me out,' I said, raising my hand to forestall any protest. 'I offer you a life as mistress of your own household, as mother to your own children, as wife to a man who adores you. Though your situation may seem pleasant now, your life here will grow unbearable. Even I can see this in the short time I have been here. You say that you wish to make yourself a governess to your sister's children, but who knows what position you will occupy when these children are grown? And would you not prefer to be a governess to your own children? I offer you everything a man has to give a woman, including his mind and heart and modest fortune. Would you turn away from such an offer?'

The more I spoke, the more heated I grew. Did she not know her own worth? I asked. Was she so willing to settle for such a life? Surely this could not be her idea of happiness. Had she given up all hope of marriage, of her own home, of her own children at her feet? My anger was honest indignation, even if it did neatly dovetail with my own hoped-for future.

I clenched my hands to my sides. The silence that followed seemed overly long and agonizing.

Finally, Etna spoke. 'I could not lightly turn aside so generous an offer, Professor Van Tassel. Nicholas. What woman could, when it is so sincerely meant? And I do have admiration for you, I do. And some fondness. And . . .' She smiled slightly. 'You are often amusing in spite of your earnestness.'

I did not quite know how to take this, but if the thought had produced even a slight smile on Etna's lips, then the teasing surely was worth it.

'But,' she said and stopped. To her credit, she did not avert her eyes. 'This must be said: I do not love you.'

There was a great silence in the room. My heart paused in its workings. I could not move or speak. It was not that I couldn't have anticipated such a response (indeed, I'd often feared it in my imaginings); it was that hearing it aloud and spoken in such a plain way had the effect of a blow taken to the center of my body. I had so wished for this not to be true. I had thought somehow that my own love for her might have been infectious. At the very least, I had hoped that if such a sentiment were true, she might not actually voice it, and in time would develop true fondness for me.

'You understand my meaning in this,' she said somewhat tentatively.

Perhaps I nodded. I do not know. I remember only that I couldn't speak.

'I don't think that I could . . . love you . . . in the

way a wife must love a husband,' she said with great difficulty.

I stood immobile for some moments while she watched me. And then, to my utter shame and horror, tears came unbidden to my eyes. I blinked furiously to send them back.

She reached out her hand and touched my arm.

'Nicholas,' she said quietly, 'you move me.'

I had no voice. I shook my head.

'Am I really so dear to you?' she asked.

I removed my handkerchief from my pocket. I did not answer her, for no answer was necessary.

'My poor man,' she said in a surprised but gentle voice.

We stood in that attitude for some time. In the corner, the ticking of a clock could be heard. Beyond the gracious windows of the room, a carriage passed, the driver calling to a passer-by. In an upstairs room, there were footsteps. Any minute now, I thought, we would be interrupted by a servant asking us if we wanted tea.

Etna turned away and gazed out the window. I can only imagine what was in her mind. After a few minutes, she turned back to me.

'I shall accept your proposal,' she said in such a low voice that I was not at all certain I had heard her correctly. But I didn't dare ask her to repeat her words. I held myself rigidly, terrified lest I had heard wrong and that I should soon discover that that was not what she had meant at all; and I knew that I would not be able to bear a second disappointment.

(Of course, an honorable man – an *honorable* man – would not have let a woman sacrifice herself in such a manner.)

Etna leaned forward and kissed me on the cheek. 'We

shall speak no more of love,' she said, 'either of its presence or its absence.'

I found my voice then, though it was cracked with an emotion that was beyond all that I had ever known. 'I promise to make you content, if not actually happy,' I said. 'And my own happiness shall be so great as to be more than enough for both of us.' (Were ever more foolish words uttered than those by a man who assumes he has love enough for two people?) I fumbled in my vest pocket for the ring I had nearly bestowed upon her eleven days earlier. I slipped it on her finger. And once that ring was in place — signifying what? a deposit of my love? a token of possession? — I dared to breathe again and allowed myself to feel some of the joy to which I was now entitled. The ring sparkled on her finger, and I took her hand in mine. But as I was in danger of again embarrassing myself with tears, I dared not embrace her. Nor did I want to dispel with further words the lovely magic that now lay all about that room with its drop cloths and ladders and paint buckets.

'I shall not ask my brother-in-law for permission,' Etna said, 'for I am of sufficient age to make such a decision for myself.' She looked away. Did she already regret her momentous decision? Was she trembling inside from the audaciousness of her pronouncement?

'You will not be sorry,' I said boldly. (But how could a man promise such a thing? He could not, he could not.) 'I will always love you,' I said.

She glanced down at our commingled hands and then up at me.

'I know,' was all she answered.

Keep was shocked, I could see, and he blathered on a bit, a harmless tirade to which I was blissfully (have I not earned the right to use the word here?) immune. Miriam pretended happiness but did not, I think, feel it, doubtless thinking, as did her husband, of the inconvenience of Etna's departure. I hardly remember the rest of that afternoon now. I had come on a desperate mission and had been successful, a fact I could scarcely comprehend. I held Etna's hand at intervals, and when she walked me to the vestibule later that afternoon to say good-bye, I kissed her on the mouth, my desire now knife-edged and whetted by good fortune. I must reveal here, however, that she did not respond passionately. Indeed, she hardly responded at all. But my imminent departure emboldened me, and it was some moments before I let her go. Then the door was opened, and I was standing on the front steps: battered, wrung out and radiant with happiness.

Did I have, either that day or the next, misgivings? Did I sense that my greed to possess had overwhelmed my judgment? Might not another man, in better control of his faculties than I, have been deterred at the declaration that his love could not be returned? No, I do not think I did. Not then. For such a thought is one that comes of experience and in retrospect, and not in the moments of greatest joy. I told myself I would teach Etna Bliss to love me, a tutorial I anticipated with the greatest pleasure.

The porter has just come by to turn down my bed and refill my water pitcher, and so I think I shall retire now. Sometimes when I am writing, I feel as though I were not reliving the events I describe here, but rather *living* them. That there is no distance, either in time or in space, no distance at all, and that I do not know how my story will end. It is an extraordinary sensation, since, of course, I know only too well how it will all end.

My compartment (have I written this already?) contains the most intriguing devices for the traveler. The table on which I scribble can, with a turn of a lever, drop down to the level of the upholstered seats. A cushion hidden behind a backrest fits like a puzzle piece between the two benches and makes up into a rather good-sized bed, one that can certainly accommodate a man as large as myself. Above the washstand is a mirror that snaps down to cover the sink, transforming it into a nightstand, complete with water pitcher, glass, and a small lamp by which to read. Behind the opposite back-rest is a clothes locker in which one can hang a suit jacket and pack away one's socks and underthings. It is all rather ingenious. Apart from the toilet, which is just down the corridor, I do not want for anything. I have brought with me a copy of Emerson's *American Scholar*, which I am looking forward to reading before the rhythmic clacking of the train wheels along the rails sends me off to sleep.

I cannot help but think of newlyweds and of how they would enjoy this self-contained universe.

This is now the second day of my journey south (the better part of a day lost to the aforementioned derailing), and I am feeling dispirited by some of the sights that I have witnessed through the window of my compartment. One has heard, of course, of breadlines and of homeless tramps, but to see for oneself the extent of the degradation and poverty in our nation's capital is alarming. Men dressed in rags are lined up for blocks, presumably hoping for a bowl of soup; women with small children sit on sidewalks and hold out tin cups; cardboard shanties line the tracks for miles, and vagabonds hover over fires. It is, at times, too much to take in. I should not like to boast about my own New Hampshire, but it can hardly escape notice that breadlines are few and far between in that state of self-reliance and industry. Of course, we do have our share of people fallen on hard times – the smaller enrollment at the college is but one example; the seizure of Gerard Moxon's property is another; and, now that I think of it, one might have to attribute to the dismal economy the suicides of Arthur Hallock and of Horace Ward Archer – but we in New Hampshire like to think we help our own. I cannot count the number of times that my cook, Mrs. O'Hara, has fed itinerant beggars from the back door of our kitchen; indeed, I think she bakes more than she normally would simply to be able to do this. I cannot mind, since my own living is ample and reasonably comfortable, and there is only myself to feed in that cavernous and drafty house.

But enough of dismal news! I shall turn my eyes away from the window and peer instead at my notebook, for I should not like to taint my tale with bulletins from the future. Indeed, at the time of my story, which was 1900, the mood of the country, perched as it was on the precipice of the twentieth century, was one of unbounded optimism. Never had we as a nation known such prosperity, nor had we experienced such a period of peace. The rupture of the civil conflict was long behind us, and the nearly constant appearance of new conveniences and inventions such as the automobile and the telephone promised a life of greater comfort and interest than any of us had ever known. It was a bright age with myself positioned squarely in its center (or, rather, in its northeast corner), and it seemed a particularly propitious time to enter into a marriage.

Etna and I were wed on the 28th of May in a small ceremony at Thrupp College Chapel. Etna wore a dress of beige silk and carried a bouquet of lilacs, which had just come into bloom in profusion all over the campus and lent the day, and even the wedding itself, such a lovely scent that even now when I happen upon a lilac bush and am gifted with its perfume, I am transported back to that May morning. There had been a rain shower the night before, and when we woke, the grass and buds and flowers were washed clean as though they had been laundered for the occasion. New Hampshire produces precious few fine days in the spring (spring being the worst of the seasons in the northern New England states – unusually late to arrive and more sodden than anyone would like), but that day was a rare gift and seemed, I am bound to say, an omen. Or at least I wished it so.

William Bliss, who appeared to be relieved to have the turmoil of the late winter put to rest, brought Etna from a side door of the chapel to the altar. One of the college's many preachers married us with a minimum of ceremony, and owing to the considerable affection in which the Bliss family was held (and due perhaps to my own small portion of notoriety), we had quite a few guests in the chapel to wish us well and send us on our way. Etna's mouth trembled at our first kiss as man and wife, a pale fluttering that might have seized the heart of any bridegroom and, indeed, seized my own, as if she had taken it in her fist.

As it happened, I had hardly seen Etna since the day in Exeter when I had made a proposal of marriage to her. While I had returned to Thrupp, she had stayed on with her sister. Though I minded her absence, I was so busy during those weeks that the pain of separation was somewhat mitigated by occupation. Chief among my tasks was the securing of a house in which we might live following the wedding trip. I wanted it to be grand, suitable for my lovely bride, and one that would, of course, eventually contain a brood of children. There were not many estates to be had that spring in the center of Thrupp, and so I was forced to travel to the outskirts of the town more than a few times to view properties. In April, I found a candidate that excited me for its potential, though its owner had mismanaged the place and the house was in a state of some decay. The land was the finest I had encountered, with magnificent sloping lawns that ran down to a good-sized lake and with unparalleled views of modest granite mountains in the distance. The house was stately, a Federal structure of warm redbrick with white trim, three stories high with a shingled barn and a carriage house in the back. The public rooms had high ceilings, which I knew would be difficult to heat, but which lent the house a grandeur absent in so many of the colonials on Wheelock Street (Bliss's house, for example). There was a formal dining room that ran the length of the house on one side, and I immediately began to imagine that room as the locus of festive suppers or even, upon occasion, gala balls. When I was shown the bedrooms on the second floor, I pictured Etna and myself asleep within the four posts of a massive bed, our five or six children not far from us, tucked beneath their own comforters. That vision alone was enough to seal the bargain.

I paid cash on the spot on the condition that the owner and his family vacate the premises at once so that carpenters and painters and so forth could enter the house to begin the work of restoring it to its former glory. (Hard not to think of Josip Keep here, with his ladders and drop cloths.) The fellow I hired to manage the restoration was charged with working overtime to complete the task by the third week in June, when Etna and I would return from our wedding trip to take up residence. It was a daunting assignment, but the man came through admirably, and though we were sometimes plagued with painters and even plumbers (the indoor plumbing being unaccountably difficult to install), I could hardly complain at the transformation he eventually wrought.

It was remarkable as well to note the transformation

in myself – and though I do not think it would be quite true to say that we grow or shrink in character and spirit so as to inhabit our surroundings, I did feel that I began to take on the role of the property owner and to shed the somewhat dismal image of a schoolmaster consigned to college rooms. My humiliating collapse on stage was behind me (indeed, I was able to congratulate Arthur Hallock heartily, if not sincerely, on the day of the physical culture vote), and though I was never again to regain my former brief popularity (one could not erase altogether the image of that unmanful collapse in the Anatomy amphitheater), my colleagues seemed, for the most part, genuinely pleased about my forthcoming marriage.

But what can I say of Etna during this time? I hardly knew her true thoughts, and I felt somewhat disinclined to ferret them out, since, I confess, I was fearful lest she change her mind about the wedding. I allowed our correspondence to remain on a pleasant, even-tempered plane, and if it was a trial not to run on at length in my letters about my love for her, I comforted myself with the thought that I would soon be able to say whatever I wanted. I longed to possess Etna, a desire I sincerely hoped would be reciprocated. Whether I was hopelessly naive or simply ignorant of a young woman's fears regarding her forthcoming physical responsibilities, I cannot say. Of course we had never spoken of such matters (although we did once discuss in great detail the notion of passion within a framework of restraint in Hawthorne's novel *The Scarlet Letter*, a thrilling conversation, if I may say so, not only for its intellectual rigor, but also for its thinly veiled erotic content), but I guessed she had some knowledge of them. At the very least, I assumed she would query her sister about certain necessary aspects of the wedding night.

(However often in these pages I might appear to be opportunistic, my love for Etna Bliss was genuine. I had never before known such a feeling, nor have I since. Though I could not help my imaginings – can any man? – I had but the purest of motives in anticipation of my marriage. I wanted first and foremost to make Etna happy, whatever sacrifices that might entail on my part. I think that any man who does not feel similarly about his bride-to-be should not entertain the idea of wed-lock. Marriage entered into with even the best of intentions can sometimes be both baffling and trying. To do so with baser motives beggars the imagination.)

(Not that I was immune to the pleasurable anticipation of physical love, however. No, no, to the contrary, I rather think I enjoyed the sexual act more than most, for it allowed me that rare opportunity to escape myself – to shed constricting inhibitions and enter, if for moments only, another universe entirely, one in which I ceased to be a man named Nicholas Van Tassel.)

Etna and I walked arm in arm (man and wife) back to the home of William Bliss, who had generously offered to host a wedding breakfast. I was tongue-tied during this brief journey, and Etna was as well, and had it not been for my loquacious sister Meritable, it might have been an awkward walk indeed. But Meritable, who had journeyed up from Virginia for the occasion, loved to chatter and had any number of questions and pronouncements for both of us. As she was a product of my father's second wife, we were only half brother and sister, but the resemblance between us was unmistakable. Unfortunately, the physical characteristics of my Dutch forebears do not normally contribute to delicacy of limb or fineness of facial feature in women, and in this Meritable was very Dutch indeed. She was a stolid woman with a broad face and thickish lips similar to my own. She was prone to heaviness, so that she had to walk briskly on stout legs to keep up with Etna and me, lending her queries a breathless air. Where would we be staying the first night of our wedding trip? Had we hired a coach or would we drive ourselves? Had I looked into the matter of purchasing the oak Roycroft dining set she had seen for sale in the newspaper? Did I think that the President of the college would come to the breakfast, since she so very much wanted to meet him? My sister punctuated these queries with bits of news about her brood of seven children (prolific daughter of prolific father): Peter was turning into quite the young scholar and Quincy, unhappily, had broken his leg. Meritable closed her eyes and uttered a short prayer when she said this, as she was likely to do whenever she mentioned any ill fortune in regard to her children (she was terrified lest she lose a son or daughter to accident or illness); and I cannot help but think these small missives sent heavenward successful, since the seven children of 1900 subsequently became eleven, all of whom are alive and well today – an unlikely, though happy, statistic.

'I like her very much,' Meritable said when we had reached the Bliss house and found ourselves alone in a hallway. Etna had gone upstairs to make herself presentable for the breakfast, though I thought her more than presentable already. I minded her leaving my side and longed for her return. Meritable put her hand on my arm. 'She does not dissemble, which I admire,' my half sister said. 'Though silence in a woman can sometimes be a trial.'

'I think Etna feels shy today,' I said.

'Of course she does,' Meritable said, smoothing the voluminous skirts of her dress and kicking a clod of caked mud from her boot. (Boots nearly as large as my own, I noted.) And then she added, as if explanation enough, 'It is her wedding day.'

'I count myself lucky,' I said.

'She is tall.'

'Stately, I think.'

'Yes. And not too young, I am happy to see. But in the matter of children, you will want to begin straight away. There is no time to lose.'

I was silent.

'You'll begin tonight, no doubt,' she said wickedly, and there might even have been a wink. 'I hope you're not journeying far.'

'Not too far.'

'A child conceived on the wedding night will be clever and charitable,' Meritable said with the assurance of a countrywoman.

'I promise you I shall do my best,' I said, and she laughed — a throaty laugh that threatened to sink beyond the realm of good taste.

'Nicholas, you are sometimes very pompous.'

Perhaps it was the talk of sexual matters, or simply that I felt bereft without my new bride on my arm, but I excused myself and climbed the stairs, hoping to surprise Etna and kiss her quickly out of sight of her family and the other guests. I found my wife in her aunt's bedroom.

She was standing at the mirror in an attitude of perfect immobility. Another woman's hands might have fluttered all about herself, correcting imagined flaws, enhancing precious charms – pinching her cheeks or refastening her hair, for example – but Etna was completely still. So intent was her commune with her image that at first she did not notice my presence. But it was not vanity that made her oblivious to her spy; no, it was something else, something far more dispiriting.

The golden eyes to which I had attributed so much beauty had taken on a look of despair. The luster had gone out of her skin, and her lips, that lovely mouth I wanted nothing more than to kiss, seemed almost bloodless. It was as if I were seeing Etna as she might be forty or fifty years hence: as an old woman who had learned to live without joy.

Do I sound excessively melodramatic? I wish I did. I had to bite my own lips to keep from calling out, and perhaps some sound escaped me, for Etna started and swiveled in my direction. For one second, before she could compose herself, I experienced the full force of that despair: bottomless, black, and irreparable. And though she managed a smile and put (for my benefit) some warmth into those golden eyes, and, further, seemed at great pains to demonstrate a modicum of fondness for me, my own joy teetered and momentarily collapsed, and it was some moments before it could pick itself up again.

Etna crossed the room.

'Husband,' she said. Whether this word had emerged deliberately or not, I do not know, but I later thought it a remarkably brilliant choice; what other greeting was so guaranteed to please?

'Wife,' I said in kind, though something inside me was still off-balance and wavering like a dislodged ladder.

Etna put her hand upon my arm. Instinctively, my fingers closed over hers.

'The guests are arriving,' I said.

'I will go down with you.'

'The Reverend Mr. Wilford did a creditable job.'

'It was a lovely ceremony.'

'Your uncle seems pleased.'

'I like your sister. She has no pretensions.'

'We shall stay for an hour and then go,' I said.

'Yes,' she said, linking her arm in mine.

'Etna,' I said hoarsely – joy tentatively on its feet now and daring to stretch its limbs.

(I should explain here the abrupt change in ink. Immediately upon finishing that last sentence, I began to feel wretched. I sat back in my compartment, resting just a moment – perhaps I was experiencing some motion sickness, I thought – but then, as the distinct nausea I was experiencing grew worse, I remembered the crab croquettes we diners had had just hours before on the train. They had had a peculiar smell, and I had thought of bypassing them altogether, but, unfortunately, hunger had defeated common sense. I quickly succumbed to a violent fit of nausea; in fact, I was so ill the train was forced to make an unscheduled stop in Richmond while a doctor was brought on board to attend to me. Fearing food poisoning, though vociferously denying it, the train personnel have been solicitous of my well-being. They have given me another berth, a more luxurious one with leather upholstery and a mahogany table and even gold-plated fixtures in the hidden bathtub, which the conductor tells me was once used by Woodrow Wilson during his campaign for the presidency. Unfortunately, at some point during my illness, or perhaps during the move to my rolling parlor, my pen was lost – or stolen – and I am now using one given to me by the conductor. I am saddened to have lost that cherished writing instrument, one that Etna gave me when I turned forty. I am also, oddly enough, missing my previous compartment, which suited my temperament and seemed conducive to solitude and memory. Will luxury alter my narrative? I sincerely hope it will not.)

I had hired a carriage to take Etna and me north and east to an inn in the White Mountains. As will happen in the spring in New Hampshire, the day turned abruptly cooler. Etna and I rode side by side but had few words between us. Shortly after we left, she fell into what appeared to be a deep slumber from which even the jolts of the muddy ruts couldn't rouse her. Her head listed onto my shoulder, and I was quite happy to be, for the duration of the journey, her bulwark. I slipped my arm around my bride, and though she was not conscious, I imagined her at least content. We stopped only once, for nourishment. Our driver, familiar with the route and mindful of the fact that we were hours wed, took us to a small inn. As I recall, Etna ate little, while I, nearly ravenous, devoured lamb chops. There were several other diners in the restaurant, and their boisterous spirits provided a welcome buffer, allowing Etna and me to eat in relative silence. Though I was rendered nearly mute with anticipation of the night to come, I considered blurting to the assembled crowd the fact of our marriage just hours before. Each time I glanced at Etna – at her thoughtful face with those seemingly foreign cheekbones (surely there must be some Indian in her, I thought) – I felt buoyant, nearly giddy, not unlike a man who has unexpectedly come into a large sum of money as a result of a game of chance.

As we left the inn, I noted a trinket shop across the street. I helped Etna into the carriage and asked her to wait for me. I wanted something – some tangible gift – to give to my new wife, to mark the day. I was dismayed, however, to find that the shop contained only second-hand items. I fingered a veil of lace and discovered a moth-eaten hole; I looked at a silver-backed brush that might have done but for a small stain in the bone of the handle; I had high hopes for a Florentine writing case until I lifted the lid and saw it was connected by only one hinge. I was ready to abandon my idea altogether when I moved a worn velvet hat from a display case and saw, beneath the glass, a matching set of items such as a woman might carry in a purse: a small mirror, a pillbox, a case for calling cards. Each was made of gold with an intricate mother-of-pearl cover. The shapes were pleasing – the round mirror, the oval pillbox, the rectangular card case – and seemed like treasures a child would find tucked away in a grandmother's jewelry box. The set had some age, and I exaggerated what flaws I could find (the silver backing of the mirror was beginning to flake) to get the price down, though in the end I needn't have bothered. The shopkeeper seemed not to know their value. I paid for the set, had it wrapped, and brought it to the carriage.

'But I have nothing for you,' Etna said when I put the package in her lap.

'Of course not,' I answered. 'This was merely a whim. Well, more than a whim. I wanted you to have something to mark this wonderful day.'

I held my breath as she untied the package. It was

the purest gift I had ever given. I felt, as she let the silk ribbon slip through her fingers, that the best of me was now available to her. I had never wanted so to please another human being as I did then. All of hope, I believe, was contained within those folds of tissue.

She opened each small case in turn and then ran the tips of her fingers over the mother-of-pearl inlay. 'Thank you, Nicholas,' she said. 'They are very beautiful.'

'Love me,' was all that I could manage.

I cannot now recall why I chose the Mountain Inn for our honeymoon. I suspect it had something to do with my finances, nearly exhausted as they were by the renovations to the house. Surely one might otherwise have gone to Paris? Or even to Italy? Yet I had selected a lonely inn perched upon a granite summit in the heart of the White Mountains, which, at that time of year, was still host to inhospitable winter. (I can't think how I'd have known about the hotel. I must have booked it on the recommendation of a colleague. Was Moxon to blame?) Even now, just the visual image of that monstrous inn causes something inside of me to empty out with despair.

It was immediately clear that we were not expected, that the person to whom I had written and from whom I had received a reply was nowhere in evidence. Nevertheless, said the young fellow who finally answered the door, a room could be made up. He would not turn us away, he said, his phrasing having the unfortunate effect of making us feel like unwanted refugees. I was more annoyed than I wished to be; I could barely restrain myself from upbraiding the man. Etna was embarrassed, I think, and tried to soothe my ruffled temper. 'It doesn't matter,' she kept saying. 'It doesn't matter.'

'But it *does*,' I said, too sharply to her, for she turned her head and did not comment again.

We were shown to a room on the second floor. The view was, most assuredly, impressive, as had been promised, but it was a feature I was too distraught and cold to notice just then. A gust of wind had blown the ashes from a previous fire in the hearth across the floorboards, and one could see from the doorway the sag of the bedsprings. The chamber was frigid and smelled of mildew.

'This is all you have?' I asked.

'It's not really the season, sir, is it?'

'Can you make a fire?' I asked the boy.

'I will,' the boy said.

'And what about a meal?'

'You'll be wanting a meal then?'

'Of course we'll be wanting a meal. Many of them, in fact.'

'Many of them, sir?'

'Damn you, this is our wedding trip!'

Etna put a restraining hand on my arm. The boy smiled, which I took for insolence.

'Never you mind,' I said sharply. 'You see to that fire.'

A marriage, I now think, should never begin with a wedding trip, for the excursion places upon the couple, who may be nearly strangers to each other, too great a burden of expectation. Except for those persons for whom physical pleasure is paramount and who are content never to venture from the bed (and who do not care whether or not this is ever noticed by the innkeeper or other guests), the enforced togetherness – the endless hours of togetherness – sets up the assumption of continuous happiness, in reality an impossibility. Better that newly betrothed couples should plunge into the responsibilities of the quotidian, coming together at odd moments during the day (and of course during the night) than have to maintain the pretense of wedded rapture.

Etna and I sat in silence in the room while the boy made the fire. As it was growing dark already, a walk outdoors was out of the question (nearly out of the question during the day as well, owing to the precipitous drop from the cliff edge). Since the hotel remained unheated but for the dining room and one or two other of the public rooms, wandering the hallways of that cold building was also unappealing. As we sat there, a sense of claustrophobia threatened to sink my spirits altogether, and, oddly, it was Etna who broke the stillness when the boy had finished the fire and had left the room (I could not help but notice the knowing smirk on his face as he shut the door).

'Nicholas, I should like to lie down,' she said.

'Yes, of course,' I said, standing.

'Just for a few moments. A rest.'

'I shall go for a walk.'

She was silent.

'I'll just go down and have a cup of tea.'

'That would be nice.'

'Shall I send some up to you?'

She shook her head. 'No, no. A short rest is all I need.'

With some relief, I left the room then and went down to the lobby. Stepping out onto the porch, I noted the remarkable view in the twilight and could see how the inn might come to life in the warmer months. Aware of a sudden thirst (and needing some courage), I searched for the insolent boy and found instead a woman cooking in the kitchen who agreed to send some tea and sherry to a sitting room. I made my way toward said sitting room, where I smoked a stale cigarette that was on offer in a silver box on the table. The boy brought the tea and a decanter of sherry and set them down on the table beside the wing chair in which I was sitting. I gave him some pennies for his trouble. The sherry warmed me almost at once. The room grew dark but for the fire in the grate, which snapped and hissed pleasantly.

As I smoked, I began to think about Etna upstairs asleep on the bed. I wondered if she had undressed. Of course she had, I mused; a woman would not sleep in her wedding dress, would she? I must confess that at that point in my life, I had had little experience with women who were not skilled in sexual matters. Indeed, I think it is safe to say that I had seldom ever been with a woman who was not, in some sense, a professional. My sexual life with Etna would be very different, I knew; it would be I who was the more skilled, the greater teacher. Not for me the slim volume entitled *What the Young Husband Ought to Know* that was supposed to be of use to the bridegroom on his wedding night. (The servants who cleaned the dormitories at the end of term would routinely find a dozen or so copies of the college-banned book when the undergraduates moved out for the summer.) I understood that Etna would be a virgin, and I was, I admit, a bit concerned about my ability to cross that most sacred of all barriers. I hoped that I would not hurt her, and I hoped something else as well: that the raw physicality of the act would not frighten her and forever stunt the pleasure that might someday come her way.

(I have always been amazed by the secret world of sex in the same way I have always regarded the common occurrence of birth as a miracle. Nearly everyone who grows to adulthood experiences the sexual act, and yet, removed from the event itself, it seems astonishing that human beings should behave in the way that they do. Sometimes, during a worship service or when I am having a cup of coffee in a crowded tearoom, it will occur to me that most of the well-composed persons there have had sexual relations, perhaps even that very day. I will look at a middle-aged woman, for example, who sits primly with her purse on her lap, barely concealing her impatience with the waitress, and I will think: What secret pleasures has this woman known? Is she prim in public places but wanton in the night? Does she squander herself in various transports of connubial delight? Does she favor, in private, practices that she might feel compelled to condemn in public? The woman, laced and buttoned as she sits at a corner table, her packages beneath her seat, seems incapable of such animal-like activities. And yet one guesses – one *knows*, unless the woman in question is that rare species, a spinster with no experience of love whatsoever – that she has once or twice or often, or even daily, comported herself in a manner that we, in polite society, might label shocking. In my youth, when I was a man of great passion, which I tried to contain with varying degrees of success, such idle thoughts and fantasies plagued me hourly; it was a favorite game of mine, I must confess, to spot in a room the person who appeared to be the most priggish and invent for him or her a sporting sexual life. I am, I am happy to say, less troubled by such thoughts in my old age.)

I entered the bedroom lit only by firelight. Etna lay beneath a dimpled quilt. She stirred when I moved closer to her, and she opened her eyes. I removed my boots and then my frock coat, and when I opened the wardrobe, I saw that the beige silk wedding dress was hanging inside. The sight of that dress and the knowledge that Etna lay beneath the covers in her underclothes or a nightgown was enough to ignite my senses, and I no longer had any fear of being able to perform the act. I quickly undressed, crossed to the other side of the room, and slipped between sheets that Etna had already warmed. Because I sensed that to hesitate even a moment might make any further action impossible, I embraced her at once. Her body was warm and loose inside her shift; she had, I was thrilled to discover, already removed her corset, that tantalizing yet annoying garment.

'Wife,' I said to her and pressed her hard against me.

I draw the curtain now as I must, and it is not a coy gesture that I make. I do so to spare the reader of this narrative the full harrowing nature of that encounter. I will reveal only these details. Etna trembled beneath the weight of my body and yielded to me only as far as her wifely duties dictated. That I could have borne. That I might cheerfully have borne, content in the knowledge that with careful tutoring, her fears would vanish and that it would not be long before my pupil would be greatly pleasured and pleasuring in return. No, it was the other thing that so chilled my heart, that disturbed me so greatly I was nearly unable to complete the act. Though one can never be absolutely certain about such a thing, human anatomy being as variable as it is, I was sure that entry into my new wife's body had been made easier by another before me. Even as I was experiencing those moments of the greatest physical pleasure a man can know, I was composing questions that would haunt me for years. *Who?* I cried silently. And *when?* I shuddered in the way that all men will do and then rolled onto my back. Beside me, Etna was silent. I thought of the good Meritable's pronouncement, that a child conceived on the wedding night would be clever and charitable. There would be no life conceived on this night. The act would, instead, give birth to jealousy – intense and fruitless and all-consuming. Love, which just moments before I had thought too domestic and tame a word for my nearly transcendent feelings for Etna, was replaced by something for which I have never been able to find a suitable name: the helplessness that descends when a cherished object has been stolen; the anger that one feels when one has been deceived.

I have often wondered if I had spoken at that moment, if I had expressed to Etna all the emotions I have just described, we might not have had an unpleasant hour or two (a hideous hour or two, I imagine) that we would always be saddened to remember, but that might have cleared the air and allowed us to go forward with some intimacy.

But I could not do that. No, no, Nicholas Van Tassel could not ask his new bride why there had been no barrier to her body. He could not demean himself in that way. Instead he lay on the bed, in the dark of his imaginings, his new wife breathing quietly beside him.

We have had a brief stop, during which I debarked from the train to stretch my legs. I stood on the platform and watched the sun and steam create a kind of luminous fog under the vaulted ceiling. A large clock, whimsically fashioned in the shape of a pocket watch, glistened in this mist I write of. Men and women alike (I remember in particular a dark-haired woman in a short cloth coat who stared straight ahead and smoked a cigarette) were blurred in the eerie light. This unlikely cloud produced both an ethereal and a prosaic sight: the platform dirty with litter and oil stains, the shimmer so beautiful I wished I owned a camera. Unwilling to leave my momentary oasis (which was strangely quiet apart from the hissing of the steam engine), I had to run to catch my train when it began to move, doubtless a comical sight to those who had already attained their seats.

I take up my narrative on a morning fourteen years after my wedding day. Etna and I sit in a breakfast room papered with crimson roses and trimmed with dark mahogany. The year is 1914, and somewhere in the house are two children – happy children, one would have to say – not abed, both already up and noisy, and in the case of Clara, our elder at thirteen, already dressing for her classes at the Thrupp Girls' Academy. There are sounds throughout the house that indicate activity: a drawer closing, a shoe dropped, the scrape against the stove of a cast-iron pan. In the sunlight of the transom windows, dust motes sparkle against the dark wood-work. The pungent smell of coffee stirs the senses.

All this I remember as clearly as if I had just walked through the door. Yet when I look at the years pre-ceding this memory, it is as though time passed the way the leaves of a book caught in a breeze will do: the pages fluttering by so quickly that it is sometimes not possible to glimpse but an expression or a phrase. 'What words were said?' I ask myself as I hover now over my journal. 'What looks exchanged?'

I can recall a sense of how my marriage was – truths more felt than spoken – but not its precise content. Occasionally, scenes or facts present themselves out of context, floating in the ether of time lost. I have an image of the baby Nicodemus at Etna's breast, his eyes as wrinkled as an old man's, his hair stiff with birth matter. I recall a wonderful dress of Clara's, a sort of red velvet and crinoline confection that sounded like paper as she moved. I remember the first day Nicky walked by himself: he strode wildly, pitched forward, and fell into my arms. And, of course, the larger facts about our life together are clear enough (I do not mean to suggest a doddering fool); it is just that from the per-spective of a sixty-four-year-old man, many details bleach into a life composed equally of daily content-ment and nightly anguish.

The daily contentment is easy enough to explain.

After my wife and I returned from our wedding trip, Etna settled in to prepare for motherhood, an event that was not long in coming, though I was not to prove as prolific as my father. We had only the two children, seven years apart; Etna had miscarried twice to her great sorrow. As anticipated, she proved to be an excellent mother, and we were able to share a considerable joy in our boy and girl. Etna was a superb teacher and had an aptitude for play that not all mothers are able to summon (certainly neither of mine ever did). Thus I might find her in the nursery sitting on the floor, her skirts beneath her, manipulating with considerable skill a pair of puppets to Nicky's delight. Or I would sometimes see her with Clara in the garden, a slender pair in their spring dresses, chasing each other all around in the manner of schoolboys. Etna had a strong constitution as well as an unusual affection for the out-of-doors, both of which made her a splendid playmate. I was glad of this (and not one bit disturbed by her lack of femininity in this regard), since I, as the reader will not be surprised to hear, felt disinclined to sport. Etna was insistent that both Nicky and Clara learn to play tennis and croquet, and to that end, we had had various lawns and nets installed on the premises. My wife always looked charming in her tennis dresses and was a disciplined yet encouraging teacher. Over time, I came to understand that in these games with Clara and Nicodemus, my wife found appropriate release for an inherent restlessness – one that I had seen fleetingly on her face when she was living in the home of her uncle; indeed, one that I could be said to have taken advantage of.

Occasionally, this restlessness became something more: Etna needed to be away. As a consequence, she was a great one for wanting to go on holidays. In the summers, she and I took Clara and Nicodemus to a small seashore community on the coast of New Hampshire. We rented a cottage there for a month or so, or took rooms at a hotel called the Highland. In my memories of those holidays, we always have sand in our boots and the children are slightly sunburnt. Etna is in her linen duster, the black ribbon of her straw hat snapping behind her in the east wind. She stands looking out to sea, or she is simply walking along the shoreline. Or she is wading in the water in her mohair bathing suit, her hair captured in her turban, her long legs and arms deliciously white and bare.

As often as I could, I joined her on the beach or went walking with her, for I, too, was equally happy to be 'away'. Thrupp, I had long since learned, could be only too confining. I had continued on at the college and had risen to the post of Hitchcock Professor of English Literature when Noah Fitch had moved on to the position of Dean of Faculty four years earlier. (The word *Rhetoric*, much to my sorrow and before my time as the senior professor, had been dropped. Students didn't like it, it was thought. I, of course, found such pandering thoroughly detestable, but Fitch had argued, and successfully, that one could certainly continue to teach the subject, albeit in a surreptitious manner, and that there wouldn't be much teaching of anything if enrollment didn't go up. Every discipline had been told to 'improve' its curriculum so as to be more appealing. Slippery standards all around, I said.) It was a post that suited me well, as I was an able administrator and had implemented some few ideas in the department, such as stricter requirements for a degree in English Literature and the awarding of the Kellogg Prizes for superior essays.

When we returned from the shore each September, Etna would again take up the overseeing of the education of our children, at first tutoring them herself in rudimentary mathematics and in the principles of reading in preparation for entering grammar school. More recently, however, Etna had also taken on charity work at a settlement house in an adjacent town. The Baker House on Norfolk Street in Worthington was an establishment that took in the poor and the sick. We had Mary, our cook, and Abigail, the maid, and because the house had long been seen to (Etna unleashing in me a decorating streak I had not known I possessed) Etna was able to volunteer her services at the charity house several hours a week. Indeed, she had, just the year previous, learned to drive a motorcar in order to accomplish this. I had purchased for her a Cadillac Landaulet coupe, one of the first cars to have an electric starter, thus enabling a woman to manage it. It was quite a lovely little thing, a green boxy affair with a gold stripe. Etna was one of only four women in Thrupp who could drive an automobile, and I must say she made a most spirited picture in her lovely driving hat as she sat behind the wheel. I would sometimes catch sight of her speeding by the quadrangle as I crossed it for my classes. The tails of her scarf would be fluttering, a dust cloud would have risen up behind her, and I would think, with considerable satisfaction, *That is my wife. That is Nicholas Van Tassel's wife.*

So these are the facts of daily married life. But beneath this pleasant narrative there is another story – that of a nightly struggle I could not win.

I try now to understand. Was there something I might have done differently? Was I being punished for having grasped for more than I was due? I cannot say. Never have I experienced such a fraught and complex entanglement as is a marriage. The most vexing student or the most abstruse essay are as nothing compared to the challenge of negotiating the delicate marital truces we forge and live by.

To wit: though Etna proved to be an excellent mother and we were happy in our children, our relations, cordial enough by day, grew strained as evening approached, so that silence replaced conversation, glances became more guarded, distractions were sought and welcomed. As was our custom, we passed our evenings together in the parlor, a sentence neither one of us was willing, or able, to commute. Thus I would read in preparation for a lecture and Etna would bend over her needlework, and it would be so still, so quiet, that I could actually hear my wife swallowing across an expanse of Persian carpet. If she felt imprisoned, then so did I – doubly so – not only by my desire for her, which seemed never to abate, but also by the tension that thrummed between us as I read Dreiser and Etna embroidered dresser scarves.

It will come as no surprise to the reader that the cause of this considerable unease between Etna and me was the existence of the marriage bed, a mahogany monstrosity we had purchased in near silence on our wedding trip. Though Etna seldom refused me outright, she took no pleasure in the event. Night after night, I would slip between the sheets and embrace a woman whom I had seen only that morning lift our son from his carriage or plait our daughter's hair, the woman who only hours before had handed me a shirt she had just mended or who had looked up from her book, pleasantly distracted, to answer a question from our cook, to discover that I was, in essence, as barred from her body as I was from her soul. Though she was dutiful in that bed of trefoils and flower medallions, Etna could not love me. Time, which I had imagined to be my ally (would not a woman come to discover the joys of physical love with patience? might not the alchemy of time transform respect into love, duty into passion?), proved only to pass too slowly during those agonizing hours before we met in our bedroom. As a consequence, I had learned to hold myself back, and an unnecessary coldness had set in, made chillier still by the fact that each night I was reminded of the first, of my hideous certainty that Etna was not a maid when she married me. Thus was jealousy refreshed, renewed, doomed to repeat itself. It was my constant companion in the night, more trustworthy than love, more faithful than my vows.

I cursed myself for having kept silent on our wedding night. Later, the right moment for such a confrontation having passed, I could not find a suitable context in which to broach the delicate subject. Then, as the weeks slipped by us, as we entered into the daily routines of our married life, the notion of raising such an appalling topic grew more and more difficult, until it became impossible even to imagine querying her on this point. (A moment lost is a moment lost forever, is it not?)

One evening several months after we had returned from our wedding trip, I stood impulsively and crossed the room and knelt before my wife. Etna had been poking at a knot for some minutes with her needle in an effort to release the threads, and perhaps it caused me to think about the tightening knot of our marriage, for I seized her hand and cried out that I loved her dearly and wished only for her happiness. She looked at me with an astonished, perhaps even alarmed, expression on her face. 'Nicholas,' she said. (For years, my wife retained a slight reluctance to use my Christian name. It was as though she had been about to utter *Professor Van Tassel*, but had stopped herself in time.) She still held her sewing needle with one hand; the embroidery hoop had fallen into her lap. Her eyes, normally so lovely, were pink tinged from eyestrain (I would have to find her a better lamp, I thought to myself), and before I could stop the words, I exclaimed, 'How cold you are!' Her hand was unexpectedly chilly in my own, and I could not help but recall the evening after the hotel fire when I had conveyed Etna to William Bliss's house, and she had put her hand in mine and had exclaimed, with like astonishment, *How cold you are!* It was as though, in the months since our wedding, I had leached the warmth from my wife's body.

Only one other time did I speak of love to Etna. One late afternoon, we stood at a second-story window looking down together at our children playing in a side yard. It was a moment such as only parents can share – pride commingled with the purest sort of joy – and it seemed that day that Etna smiled not only upon Clara and Nicodemus, but upon me as well; indeed, so encouraged was I by that entirely spontaneous smile that I blurted out, startling her, 'Love me, Etna. Please love me.' It was, I know now, the purest sort of howl in the desert, and I could see at once that I had frightened her. She turned slowly and left the window, not unkindly or harshly, but almost reluctantly, as though, if it had been in her power to do so, she would willingly have summoned love.

(And what to say of our physical relations? I was knowledgeable, if not necessarily accomplished, in the more exotic practices of the sexual arts, an interest that has proven to be lifelong. Though I would not for all the world have introduced these arcane acts to the marriage bed, nor would I have sullied Etna with my considerable knowledge, I did, unlike so many new husbands, know something about the female body and how it may receive pleasure. Etna did not rebuff me, but neither did she respond; and though failure to pleasure a woman will not extinguish the sexual flame in a man – endlessly reignited – it curbed extraordinary effort, so that our relations became more habitual than inventive.

But enough of this. Dear God, enough.)

So it was that Etna and I sat among the twinkling dust motes that October morning in the breakfast room, a habit I would not ever have willingly forgone. Though we were strangers in the night, we were, in the light of morning, once again husband and wife, involved amiably in the quotidian. As we ate our breakfast of toast and eggs and meat and so forth, we would – without tension of any sort – parse the hours to come. She kept beside her plate a pen and ink pot and notebook, and as we chatted she would fill its pages with notations, tasks to be completed or food to be purchased. I loved to watch her at this activity, since she had grown only lovelier with age and was, at forty, more beautiful than when I had met her at twenty-five. Each woman has, I am convinced, a specific age at which her beauty peaks. For most, this occurs at fifteen or sixteen years of age when they are still girls. But though these perfect creatures are lovely and have great promise (yet how many later disappoint!), one cannot touch, as it were, these treasures, and thus their beauty cannot be fully appreciated. Of course, I cannot ever know what Etna looked like at fifteen years of age (sadly, no photographs of her then exist), but I feel confident in saying that Etna was, at forty, at her best.

'Will you join me at the reception tonight?' I asked my wife as she buttered her toast.

I referred to a gathering that would be held that evening to introduce to the faculty the men who had survived thus far what was proving to be a rigorous search for a candidate to replace Noah Fitch. Fitch had ascended to and held for four years until his death several months earlier the position of Dean of Faculty. I had made no secret of my ambitions and still remained as one of the final candidates. (Against all likelihood, the hapless Moxon had nearly made it too; he was well liked and had had considerable success with his popular biography of Lord Byron.) My two remaining rivals were Arthur Hallock, the man who had brought physical culture to Thrupp, and Fisher Talcott Ames, an historian from Bates College. All fall, the Board of Corporators of the college had brought in other candidates – Atwater Hall, from Princeton, William Merriam Hatch, from Dartmouth, are two that I recall – and though it had been disconcerting to see what can only have been rivals walking the halls of Thrupp, I was fairly confident of a happy outcome.

The reception would be at the home of Edward Ferald, who had swiftly ascended to the Board of Corporators by dint of his considerable fortune. Thrupp was only too glad to have him: an 'old boy' as well as a patron was well nigh an unbeatable combination (Ferald was rumored to have in excess of two million). Though Ferald had a vote in the upcoming election (a vote I did not expect to garner; the memory of that failing grade in his Scott tutorial doubtless lingered in his mind), his would be but one of seven, and I felt fairly certain of at least three of their number.

'I look forward to it,' Etna said, rolling back the cuff of her serviceable white blouse. I could always tell, by what my wife wore at breakfast, what she would be doing that day; and as she had on a gabardine skirt and a pair of boots not her best, I deduced that she would be spending a portion of her day at the settlement house. She functioned there as an administrator and was much appreciated for her secretarial skills. The settlement house took in indigent women and girls and children only, which was reassuring to me, as I should not have liked my wife exposed to the sort of men who would have been forced to resort to such charity. It was bad enough that Etna had to know of the horrors that befell girls of poor moral character, but I comforted myself by imagining the great pains my wife would take to insure that our daughter, Clara, fell to no such harm. 'Is it for dinner?' she asked.

The telephone rang in the kitchen, and I hoped it was not for me. I did not like my early morning interludes with Etna interrupted for any reason. 'I believe so,' I said.

'Then I should dismiss Mary after she has prepared the children's dinners. We won't be dining at home this evening, and neither of us will be home for lunch.'

'No, you're quite right,' I said, distracted by the day's headline: WILSON APPEALS TO NATION TO PRAY FOR PEACE.

'Although she could do the marketing,' Etna said more to herself than to me.

'The reception is to introduce to the faculty the remaining candidates for the post of Dean,' I said.

My wife looked up from her list. 'It is a post you should have,' she said.

'I think I am a strong candidate,' I said. 'If it weren't for these by-laws that so shackle the board, I might have the post already.' I spoke with equanimity, but beneath my calm exterior, I was annoyed by the necessity of the college to consider candidates from outside the school.

'When is the vote?'

'December fourth.'

'Why so long a wait?'

'The date is stipulated in the by-laws. It must be precisely four months after the search has begun.'

'Perhaps this would be a good day to have the painter in, to finish the hallway,' Etna said, putting the top of her pen to her chin. 'He could work undisturbed through the late afternoon and evening.'

'Yes,' I said, 'that might be wise.'

And then she said, in a quieter voice, 'I shall be needing some more money, Nicholas.'

I looked up at her. 'For . . . ?'

'Fuel for the motorcar,' she said. 'And there are other expenses I have. Of a more personal nature.'

'Yes, of course,' I said, not wishing to inquire further what these expenses of a 'more personal' nature might be.

'And Clara has a cough,' she added.

'Clara does not have a cough,' I said, glancing at the letters Mary had just put by my plate.

'You heard her this morning,' Etna said.

'It is my opinion,' I said, opening the first envelope on the stack, 'that our daughter is a remarkably gifted actress when it suits her.'

'Our daughter does not lie.'

'I love her dearly, Etna, but I happen to know that

132

Clara has a particularly odious examination on plane geometry this afternoon and that she would resort to any ruse to get out of it. Tell me you didn't say she could stay home from school.'

'I'm afraid I might have,' my wife said.

'You are altogether too soft,' I said, not unkindly. I stood and walked to the hallway and called up the stairs. 'Clara, come down here, please,' I said, reading what was not a letter after all but rather an invoice. 'This can't possibly be right,' I said.

'What is it?' Etna asked.

'It's a bill for a chandelier,' I said, turning to her. 'White iron, six sconces. From March's in Hanover. Did we order a chandelier?'

'Let me see that,' Etna said. After a moment, she added, in what I took to be an annoyed tone, 'I sent it back. I don't understand why we should have received a bill.'

'Then we *did* order a chandelier.'

'I did,' she said. 'I thought it might look pretty in the side entrance. But it was far too big. I sent it back.'

'I'll just telephone the man and remind him.'

'Let me,' Etna said. 'You have enough to do. This is a household item. I will see to it.'

I cannot say whether or not we discussed the matter further, for Clara, whose presence was always vivid (even when she was feigning illness), came down the stairs and into the room. She had been born a year and two days after our wedding and was growing into a comely girl. For some time, I had thought that she would be a frail and slender child, since she could hardly keep any weight on her bones, but lately she had become sturdier. Clara had inherited Etna's height and the blond, blue-eyed coloring of my Dutch ancestors (though I myself had brown hair), and she had exquisitely textured skin. I had to suppress a smile when she entered the room, for she had misbuttoned the sweater she wore over her uniform.

'Clara, are you ill?' I asked. 'I warn you that you must tell me the truth.'

Our daughter opened her mouth to reply, but something in my voice, or perhaps in my face, gave her pause. She had entered the room with a wan demeanor imperfectly masking the bloom of good health. Now she seemed more confused than sickening from a cough.

'My dear,' I said, softening my tone, 'do you think that you might try extra hard to make it to school today because of the importance of the geometry examination?'

She pondered this request and glanced at her mother.

'Clara, I agree with your father,' Etna said. 'Perhaps you are feeling better now.'

Clara coughed once feebly, but even she could see that the game was lost. And it being lost, there was now no reason to pretend to no appetite. She gazed longingly at the spread on the buffet. 'Is there jam today with bread?' she asked.

I set off for the college on foot, as I did every weekday morning that the weather was hospitable, though even in inclemency I tried to make the journey. The walk was my only form of exercise. As I may have mentioned, I did not, as did so many of my colleagues, exercise for sport. I did not ride, for example, or bowl or play baseball. But my step was brisk, nevertheless, abetted by the nearly translucent color of the autumn leaves – golden ochre and tulip red, interspersed with grass green. The New England soil and air and water produced this rampant color, and no matter how much one anticipated it, it was always a surprise (and that surprise a further surprise, since I had been a New Englander for well over twenty years). The mind forgot, through the white winter and the humid summer, just how brilliant nature could be. Indeed, one could scarcely credit the color, nor the blue above it, and I thought how seldom it was that nature was accurately described in literature. (Wordsworth, possibly, though then again it was more the *idea* of nature than nature itself that had so engaged that poet.) It was enough to put one in mind of one's maker (autumn in New England being one of God's better creations), despite my tepid acquaintance with God – though I thanked him often enough for the miracle of my children and the more unlikely miracle of my fourteen years of marriage to Etna Bliss.

My journey that morning took me past two dairy farms, neither picturesque, and then along the outskirts of the village where the modest houses were not pleasing to the eye (the houses of college staff and village shopkeepers and so forth), and then finally to the foot of Wheelock, ablaze with a canopy overhead that produced a fiery tunnel through which one yearned to walk. I recalled then my autumn walks with Clara not so many years previous and the manner in which she would clap her hands, and her mouth would form an astonished 'O'. She would sprint ahead, gathering up the loveliest blots of color – scarlet and tangerine and butter yellow – so that when we returned home, our pockets would crinkle with dried leaves. (How I adored those walks and adore the memory of them now!)

I strode up Wheelock Street with somewhat more decorum than Clara would have done. Though the world had changed considerably since 1899, the houses on that street had not. I paused in front of the home of William Bliss, who until recently had been a frequent visitor to our house; our children called him 'Papa', as one would a beloved grandfather. But now, sadly, the man had been diagnosed with the cancer and was, I knew, resting in an upstairs bedroom. Etna and William had grown closer over the years, and she visited him several times a week. I believe she looked upon him as a father, a role he was only too happy to play. I often visited myself, and thought of doing so that day, but after a few seconds' consideration, decided to move on, reluctant, on such a sparkling morning, to enter the darkened rooms of death. And as with nearly all such selfish decisions, I found, as I made my way to the college, that I could think of little else but the thing I had hoped to avoid, which was death, Bliss's and my own one day. That line of thought led almost immediately to a seizure of thought such as might produce a sudden intake of breath: Were I to die before the end of the semester (which was Bliss's sentence), what would be my legacy? Where would Nicholas Van Tassel have left his mark?

I stood in an attitude of contemplation and thought about the ambitious Van Tassel who had arrived at Thrupp so many years ago. Other men of the college had written better than I, had published more, had garnered more awards and prizes. The trajectories of their careers had been swifter, the ascent steeper. Mine had not been an altogether insignificant career – I had taught hundreds of students and perhaps even inspired one or two; and I had proved myself an able administrator (indeed, it was the successful supervision of what was now a full-fledged English Department that spoke most eloquently in favor of my ascending to the post of Dean of Faculty) – but still, these small successes did not add

up to greatness. No, I thought as I stood in the quadrangle, if I had come close to greatness in my life, it
was in loving the woman who was my wife. I knew
that few men of my acquaintance would have said that
greatness could be had simply in loving another: it was
too easy, too common, too *uxorious*, they would doubtless have argued. Indeed, I had seldom heard a man
speak of love; it was understood to be a discourse
reserved exclusively for women and poets. Yet I knew,
as I stood there, that I had, in loving Etna, touched
something extraordinary in myself. It was the one occupation that had engaged all of me: my senses, my intellect, and my emotions.

I took a step forward and walked on for a bit and
then stopped abruptly, assaulted by a new and troubling
thought. Would it not be necessary to have that extraordinary love returned in order to have achieved true
greatness? Etna had never spoken the words of love to
me, and I had been disinclined, after those two previous
(and distressing) encounters, to press her on this point.
She was more fond of me than she had been at the
beginning of our marriage – of this I was quite certain
– but did she love me? It is with some heartache – even
now, after all these years, even after all that was to follow
– that I must write here that she did not. Not as I loved
her. This was the bargain we had made, was it not? She
had agreed to be my wife in exchange for the freedom
to be a mother and mistress of her own home, and,
more recently, to come and go in an automobile to a
place where she was able to find some satisfaction in
her charitable work. For a long moment, as I watched
the students bisect the quadrangle's green – that brisk
autumnal geometry – I felt sad, quite out of keeping
with the glorious day. But then I reminded myself that

I did, in fact, actually *have* Etna Bliss for a wife. Were not such questions irrelevant in the face of so great a truth? I shook off my fleeting melancholy and set off for my classroom.

I heard the voices even before I had turned the corner. There was no mistaking Ferald's self-satisfied drawl or Moxon's high-pitched queries (the very voice of sincerity), though there was a third voice I could not identify, a voice with an English accent that had perhaps blurred over the years. I thought of slipping unseen into a classroom, since I did not welcome an encounter with Edward Ferald under any circumstances, but it was already too late. Indeed, had I not pressed myself against the wall, there might have been a collision.

'Van Tassel,' Ferald said, and even in that greeting an entire universe was hinted at: a pecking order, mild amusement, and, of course, dismissal. 'I'd like you to meet Phillip Asher, lately of Yale.'

Asher stood a head taller than I and had a leaner frame. He wore a suit of gray worsted that matched his eyes (though perhaps it was the other way around, and the eyes had taken on the coloration of the cloth). He smiled slightly, but unlike Ferald's grin, Asher's contained nothing of malice or of mischief. He wore his pale hair longish and brushed straight back from a young man's forehead. He had a pleasing aspect – one might even have said handsome – and radiated, in addition to general decency, a keen intelligence. I could well believe the man from Yale.

'What brings you to Thrupp?' I asked.

'Professor Asher will deliver the Kitchner Lectures,' Ferald answered for him.

'Congratulations,' I said.

The Kitchner Lectures were a series of talks structured around the eternal conflict between the common good and private gain. Senior students in the departments of Philosophy, History, and English Literature were required to attend, though all students and faculty were invited. Typically, the talks were given by a distinguished man of letters, and they lent the college a bit of prestige. As might have been expected, they often provoked intense, collegewide debate as well.

'Asher is a man of many talents,' Ferald said. 'In addition to being a Professor of Philosophy, he is a scholar of Milton, an economist, and a poet.'

'Truly,' I said.

'I believe I know your work,' Asher said. 'Your field is Scott?'

I could not help but be pleased that my work had come to Phillip Asher's attention. I could not, however – to my chagrin – put Asher's name to any critical work I could think of. It was Moxon who came to my rescue. 'Asher's particular field is Nietzsche,' he said.

I thought a moment.

'*I am afraid we are not rid of God,*' I quoted, the pedant in me rising to the fore, '*because we still have faith in grammar.*'

Ferald actually laughed. 'Van Tassel, you impress us with your scholarship.'

Ferald had grown only more insufferable over the years, if such a thing be possible. What had been incipient in Ferald at nineteen was, at thirty-four, fully fledged. He had developed an elegance matched only by his arrogance. His clothes, imported from England, were of the finest that could be made at the time. He had cultivated an ironic drawl, one that I thought had quite twisted the shape of his mouth; in repose, he appeared to be sneering. I detested the man – his ostentatious wealth in the face of so much genteel academic poverty, his unearned authority (though he was clever, he had been a poor student – indeed, he rather prided himself on this fact), his nattering interference in college matters (he favored the addition of a medical school, a proposal I violently opposed, as it would all but exhaust the fragile resources of the college). Mostly, however, I loathed his half-lidded gaze, a look he fixed upon me as we stood in that hallway.

'Will you travel back and forth from Yale?' I asked Asher.

'I'm on sabbatical,' he said. 'Actually, I'm staying at the Hotel Thrupp.'

Beside us, Moxon was a choreography of nervous tics – ruffling his hair, putting his hands in and out of his pockets, removing bits of lint from his lapel. Even Ferald seemed anxious to move on. Only Asher had poise.

'Professor Asher,' Ferald said, nudging his guest forward. 'We mustn't delay Professor Van Tassel any longer.'

Asher put out his hand. 'Very happy to have met you, Professor.'

'And I you,' I said in kind.

I must stop now, for my eyes are aching from the strain of trying to write in a moving vehicle. It has grown quite warm in my compartment, but there is always mechanically cooled drinking water available in bubblers, not to mention a pitcher of iced tea upon request, and so I am keeping as comfortable as possible in this North Carolina heat. (I had no idea September could be so *humid*.) To find some relief this morning, I went through to the observation/library car, which is the car farthest to the rear, where I sat on the back deck with several fellow travelers and took in the countryside. The land whooshed away from me as we traveled along at sixty miles an hour, and I couldn't help but think this sensation not unlike the writing of a memoir: one attempts to write forward in time, keeping to a reasonable chronology, all the while trying to seize the past as it speeds by and recedes into the distance — finally disappearing at the vanishing point.

I met Etna at the foot of the staircase and was again reminded of how handsome she had grown over the years. She no longer looked as tall as she had when I met her. (Can that really have been possible? No, of course not. It was simply that she did not seem as formidable as she once had.) She wore that night a high-necked satin gown of a burnished copper color that had a daringly raised hemline (only three inches above her evening slippers, however, so not as audaciously raised as hemlines are today; shamelessly, I often think, though I have never been immune to female charms). She had matched the hue of her silk stockings to her dress, and I had no doubt that every man at the party would admire those strong, copper-colored ankles. She was also wearing her outrageous driving hat, a black-and-brown concoction with a wide brim and veil and two sashes with which to tie it underneath the chin. I adored the hat and had often said so; it was, by now, a familiar feature in our household.

I helped her with her coat. 'Shall I drive?' I asked.

'Heavens, no,' she said. 'You're far too nervous a driver, Nicholas. So I will, if you don't mind.'

She was entirely right. I was a dreadful driver, hunching over the steering wheel, gripping its rim with such force that my fingers were stiff for some minutes after I had arrived at my destination. I couldn't get the hang of it and was never relaxed. 'I don't mind at all,' I said.

I followed Etna out the side entrance and along a garden path that led to the carriage house. There had been, a half hour earlier, a ferocious thunderstorm, but now the sun was setting within a clear ribbon beneath a blanket of cloud. Most of the light was gone, but one could still see the garden, or rather the autumnal remains of same. There were some phlox in bloom (how I loved their scent; I have thought from time to time of reviving the garden simply to have it again, but as it would be only myself who would enjoy it, and as I would be certain to feel a sort of melancholy there, I do not think it wise). The garden was of Etna's design, and it was her pleasure to work in it of a morning. She would don a gardener's apron and straw hat and a pair of boots, and would look both comical and endearing. She had a deft touch with the roses, which still lingered and would do so until a killing frost. Indeed, we normally had masses of the things on the hall table right up until the middle of October.

'Should I become Dean,' I said to Etna's splendid back, 'I shall have two parties a year: one in the fall for the faculty only – a men's-club sort of thing with cigars and brandy and so forth – and then in the spring a family party in the garden. In May, I think. I should like to see the garden full of children.'

'That sounds lovely,' Etna said.

As it will sometimes do with its dying gasp, the sun just then lit up the rose canes and the stalks of phlox and the picket fence Etna had insisted upon and the lawns and the fruit trees and even my beloved wife in her mad hat with such a glow that I was struck with awe (and am even now, remembering it). The world became, for that instant, salmon colored and shimmering. Above it, against the retreating dark cloud, a sunset rainbow, a rare enough sight, rose straight up from the field adjacent to ours.

'Look, Etna,' I blurted.

My wife stopped, and we watched the phenomenon together, and I could not help but think that my life and my possessions were receiving a pagan blessing. I was a fortunate man, was I not? Apart from my nightly disquietude, which in that rosy light I was more than willing to ignore, Etna and I had a good marriage, rather better than most. We never quarreled, nor were we ever dismissive of each other, a quality I have witnessed far too often in other couples. *How lucky I am!* I thought as I stood transfixed on the garden path. Happiness, which had eluded me all my life, seemed so much within my grasp that I labeled it as such. 'I am so happy,' I said.

'My dear,' Etna said.

'I shall very much enjoy tonight,' I added.

'Of course you will,' Etna said.

Ferald's house was ostentatiously grand and quite out of keeping with the general modesty of the Yankee countryside. It was built in the Georgian manner of English limestone that had been imported for the purpose. (I cannot conceive of the cost – and with New Hampshire granite all about!) It had a massive portico with columns that rose two stories high. The unadorned windows were large as well, and I suppose, if one forgave the excess, the house might have been regarded as stately, a comment that was, in fact, often put forth that evening by men eager to curry Ferald's favor. (Said house, I am pleased to report, is now a school for the blind.)

'My goodness,' Etna said when we had driven up the circular drive.

'Mutton out of lamb, if you ask me.'

'Still, though, it's quite extraordinary.'

'There are no limits to which some men are willing to go to demonstrate their wealth, better left undemonstrated, in my view.'

'You don't like him much, do you?' she said.

'I'm required to be civil to the man,' I said.

'Do you think it wise to be merely civil? Under the circumstances?'

'His is but one vote out of seven. No more, no less. And I am certain of at least three of the others. Fortunately for me, the board is a democratic one.'

As we entered Ferald's house, he greeted us with a faint smile. 'Professor Van Tassel, may I present my wife, Millicent.'

As I had never before been invited to dine with the Feralds, I had not met his wife of less than a year, a luxurious froth of a woman in her lace jacket and bejeweled tiara. She was slender and delicate of feature, her hair nearly as pale as her skin. She had, however, a somewhat bewildered look about her, as one who is continually startled. It suggested that Ferald's wife might be no match for her wily husband, and, instantly, one felt a sort of pity for her.

'How do you do?' I said, taking her hand. 'This is my wife, Etna.'

(How we men enjoy our possessive adjectives.)

Etna smiled at the younger woman. Quite young,

actually; Millicent Ferald cannot have been more than twenty. 'Your house is lovely,' Etna said.

'Oh, do you think so?'

'Yes, it's quite grand.'

'You don't think it too big?'

'No, not at all. You must do a lot of entertaining.'

'That's what makes me so nervous,' Millicent Ferald said. 'All this entertaining!'

Ferald, barely able to conceal his impatience with this revealing exchange, leaned pointedly around Etna to shake the hand of the man standing behind her. It was an insult I sought to hide from my wife by moving her away from the entry. Fortunately, we were almost immediately accosted by Moxon, who seemed all arms and legs in his ill-fitting suit, the trousers too short for his considerable height. I wondered how he could ever have been put forth for the post of Dean, despite his success with his popular biography. He rambled and could not command an audience and dressed, despite a decent income, like a tradesman. That night he sported a red-striped vest that on anyone else would have been vulgar, but on Moxon was merely curious.

'Hello, hello,' he said in his too-loud voice, his pleasure at seeing a friend (insofar as either Moxon or I had friends) apparent in his tone and in the wide smile on his face. 'And Etna. You look magnificent.'

Moxon, ever hapless, had been engaged to the daughter of a local Methodist minister and had all but been left at the altar when the girl had come to her senses and gone off to Simmons College in Boston. Having read Moxon's biography of Lord Byron and convinced herself that Moxon and Byron were one and the same, the woman had been, for a time, romantically persuaded. I knew for a fact that Moxon had been crushed by the rejection, though he put on a brave face. The evening would be trying for him, as nearly all of the senior faculty were married – all except for the monkish Erling Morse, a prematurely wizened man who taught several dry courses in Ancient History.

'Thank you,' Etna said, accepting his kiss. 'What an interesting vest.'

'Horrid,' Moxon said with genial self-deprecation. 'I must get a tailor. I keep saying that. Nicholas here has a very good tailor. Don't you, Nicholas? Quite a spread, isn't it?'

Etna gazed up at the coffered ceiling, bordered by an ornate gilt molding.

'Who dreams up such flourishes?' I wondered aloud, glancing at the silk walls.

'The house has a swimming pool,' Moxon said.

'I can't imagine Ferald taking exercise,' I said.

'A swimming pool,' Etna said. 'What fun.'

I was so distracted by the image of Etna in bathing costume slipping into the water of an indoor pool (a toga and grapes somehow came to mind) that it was some moments before I realized we had moved into the sitting room in which most of the guests were sipping champagne (an unnecessary extravagance, I thought, typical of Ferald; we were, after all, in the business of providing education, not entertainment). Nevertheless, I noted, the drink was producing a giddiness in the gathering, the effervescence of the beverage transferring itself to musical voices. There was a great deal of laughter, which was not altogether unwelcome. Indeed, some would later recall Ferald's party as having been one of the more spirited evenings in recent college history.

Canapés were produced. More champagne was drunk.

Moxon was lost in the crowd. I put my hand to Etna's back, but as a rowboat will sometimes drift away from its mooring, she became separated from me by various jostlings and greetings. I had a short talk with Arthur Hallock about the state of William Bliss's health (not good) and, while doing so, I noticed that Eliphalet Stone, a corporator, was standing not far from me. Viewing his presence as a welcome opportunity to further promote my candidacy, if only by engaging the man in conversation, I moved in his direction.

'We're to have lobster,' I said when I had reached him.

Stone, eighty if a day, was scarcely five feet tall, and I had to bend to him to make myself heard above the animated din.

'What was that?' he asked, cupping his ear.

'Lobster!' I said, nearly shouting.

'Lobster,' he said with evident distaste. 'Don't eat bottom-feeders.'

'Oh,' I said. 'Really. Well, perhaps not.'

'Had a chat with the fellow from Bates,' Stone said, getting right to the point. 'The one looking for your job.'

'You mean Fisher Talcott Ames.'

'Bit on the dull side,' Stone said, which I thought an interesting comment coming from a man not known for either his conversation or his wit. 'You're my man, you know,' Stone added, as if delivering an unhappy pronouncement. 'Hate change.'

'Yes,' I said agreeably. 'One does.'

'Where's your handsome wife?' Stone asked.

I turned to introduce my handsome wife and realized then that I had lost her.

'Excuse me,' I said to Stone, thinking that Etna was

always an asset and that I should not miss an opportunity to have her speak with Stone. 'I'll just see if I can find her.'

But where *was* my wife? I wondered. Not in the parlor and not in the dining room. I grew distinctly worried. Had she taken ill?

I slipped away from the party and moved along a hallway that held some rather good art (a few of the Dutch masters, I was pleased to see). The general noise of the gathering receded as I walked. The floor was tiled and led, I shortly discovered, to the natatorium. I entered the blue-tiled and humid room. The pool was not as impressive as one had been led to believe; there seemed to be barely room for one exuberant swimmer.

'What do you suppose it's for?' Etna asked, startling me. She'd been standing just to the right of the door when I had entered, and I hadn't, for the moment, seen her.

'Etna,' I said with some surprise. 'I was worried about you.'

'I wanted to see the pool.'

'You should have said something to me.'

'You were talking with Mr. Stone. I didn't want to interrupt.'

'We're trespassing,' I said.

She smiled – a delightfully mischievous smile. 'And shall we be punished, do you think? Sent home without our supper?'

Had the house been anyone else's but Ferald's, I should have insisted that we return to the party at once. But as I had already had two glasses of champagne, I found the idea of violating Ferald's privacy somewhat appealing.

'I imagine Ferald and his wife swim here,' I said.

I had then a brief and unpleasant vision of Ferald sitting in one of the chaise longues by the pool's edge, watching his wife, Millicent, cavort in the nude for his own especial pleasure – an image I sought at once to banish, not only for its lewdness, but also because it had replaced the more felicitous image of Etna with the toga and the grapes. Ferald did have a look of the venal about him – louche and morally corrupt, one might have said – and I find, as I try to recall that evening and put my memories down on paper, that the image of that face keeps intruding upon my narrative.

Etna bent to touch the water, which sparkled from the electric lights overhead. She trilled her fingers along its surface, lost for some moments in a reverie of her own. Perhaps she was remembering a pleasant excursion of ours to the seashore. Contentedly, I watched her.

'You are having a happy memory,' I said after a time.

She glanced up at me.

'You,' I said. 'Just now. You seemed to be remembering something pleasant.'

'I have many happy memories, Nicholas,' she said.

'I hope some of them are with me,' I said.

She stood and shook the water from her fingers. 'I have happy family memories, certainly,' she said carefully.

She moved around the tiled edge of the pool and sat in a wicker chair near its edge. The act of sitting caused her skirt to rise. Drawn by the sight of her copper ankles, I joined her in an adjacent chair. Along the opposite wall, there were many plants which seemed to thrive in the room's humidity. Etna's hair had begun to curl at her temples. I reached over and took her hand in mine.

'Is it so very important to you?' she asked.

'Your happiness?'

'No, I meant the post. Of Dean.'

'Yes, I think it is,' I answered. 'I am ambitious.'

'Not overly so.'

'It is something I have wanted for some years now.'

'Your workload will increase.'

'I regard it as a challenge.'

'Yes, of course,' she said, smiling at me.

'What is so amusing?' I asked.

'I was remembering that first time we had tea in town on Kimball Street. You said you were willing to wait years to gain Noah Fitch's position. I was struck by your patience.'

'That seems so long ago,' I said, thinking of that pleasant outing. 'I remember you spoke of Newman.'

'You were surprised I had ever heard of the man,' Etna said.

'Well, yes, I was. I know I shouldn't have been, I can see that now. You spoke of freedom.'

'Did I?'

She withdrew her hand. 'Perhaps we should go back. We shall be missed.'

'Linger a bit,' I said, unwilling just yet to relinquish her to the party.

There was something I wanted to say to my wife. Now, after all these years. The ripples on the water combined with an element of risk were making me bold. And though I was aware of a sterner, more sensible, voice screaming *no* within my head, I was sorely tempted toward adventure.

'I wish . . .' I said.

Etna turned to face me. She waited. 'What do you wish for, Nicholas?' she asked after a time.

I tried to form the question I so very much wanted my wife to answer. I opened my mouth and then closed it. How should I put this, exactly? What would be the most delicate way of phrasing it? Should I begin with an apology? Should I start by saying that I knew such a question might be offensive, but that I had waited so long for an answer? I had shown patience, had I not? Was this not an answer to which a man, a husband, was entitled?

I opened my mouth again. I may have leaned forward. Etna may have leaned forward as well. It seemed there was a long silence between us.

'I wish I could erase the memory of our wedding trip!' I blurted in frustration.

Etna recoiled slightly – stunned, I think, by the ferocity of my statement. She sat in an attitude of stillness, as I had so often seen her do in moments of fear or confusion. This was the closest we had ever come to discussing the events of our wedding night, and I was now quite horrified that I had lost control of my tongue.

'It is just that . . .' I said, seeking to soften and explain. 'It seems to have . . .' I realized that of course I could not utter aloud my anxieties about that night. I could not ask her if she had had other lovers before me. Sense had won out over boldness. 'I really cannot say,' I said helplessly.

Etna shook her head. 'Whatever is the matter, Nicholas?' she asked. 'You are behaving very strangely tonight.'

'There is nothing the matter,' I said. 'It is just that . . .' But I was unable to continue. She understood, I am sure of it. For she laid her hand over mine with a tender gesture and a kindness that nearly takes my breath away when I recall it now.

'Nicholas, sometimes you make me laugh. You are so earnest and you try so hard,' she said.

'We all try hard in our own small ways,' I replied.

'I'm told there is a conservatory,' she said, standing.

'A conservatory,' I said, rising with her. 'Another English affectation. If Ferald is so enamored of England, perhaps he should simply move there.'

'And would that make you happy?' Etna asked.

I shrugged down my vest, which had risen over my considerable stomach. 'I already *am* happy,' I insisted.

We left the natatorium. Moving from room to room, I could hear the murmur of voices from the public rooms of the house. In time, we found the glass conservatory, through which one could view the stars. We also discovered a remarkably modern kitchen, fitted out with all the latest conveniences: a toaster, a refrigerator, an electric hot plate. Etna and I made a breathless run through a butler's pantry that seemed nearly as long as the southern border of our own decently sized house. We returned to the gathering like children who imagine they have gotten away with something grand.

A waiter produced a tray of champagne in flutes. Etna and I each took one and clinked glasses. The sharp rap of a silver knife upon a wineglass cut short our sense of conspiracy. Heads turned in search of the source of the summons.

Edward Ferald, when he had everyone's attention, put aside the glass and the knife. 'Welcome, colleagues and lovely wives,' he began, the compliment causing a polite titter to ripple through the crowd. One could not help but note, however, that Ferald himself was not standing with his own lovely wife, but rather with Phillip Asher, lately of Yale.

'Thank you for coming to my home on this beautiful October evening,' Ferald continued. 'I will let you get to your suppers in just a moment, but I wanted to introduce to those of you who have not met him my very special guest, Phillip Asher, Professor of Philosophy at Yale. Professor Asher has graciously agreed to deliver the Kitchner Lectures at our college.'

There were some murmurs, even a bit of applause here.

'Professor Asher, who has a degree from Harvard College, was born in London, immigrated to this country when he was six, and was raised in our own New Hampshire. In addition to being an ethicist and a poet, Professor Asher is something of an explorer, having recently returned from an expedition to New Guinea,' Ferald went on. 'He is currently on sabbatical for the term. Unless of course . . .' (and here Ferald winked, a particularly smarmy sight, and snaked his arm possessively around Asher's shoulder) '. . . we can persuade the man to stay on a bit longer.'

Asher, looking for a place to cast his embarrassed gaze, caught my eye, and it was in that moment that the obvious occurred to me.

Asher was a candidate. It was only too clear.

Appalled by this new and certain knowledge, I studied the man. He was everything I was not. An authentic New Englander next to my stolid Dutch-American. (No, *better* than that, an authentic Englishman-turned-New Englander.) An apparently brilliant scholar next to my dull schoolmaster. A poet to my pedant. I thought of the college corporators who might find Asher appealing – the Reverend Frederic Stimson, currently the college pastor (a man who would almost certainly be intrigued by the thought of an ethicist as Dean);

Howard Yates, a banker from an old New England family; Clark Price, a confessed Anglophile; not to mention the ever-present Ferald, who I knew despised me. Could dutiful administration and dogged scholarship compete with a wide-ranging intellect and an artistic temperament from Yale?

Asher's eyes did not leave mine, and I knew only too well what he was seeing: a man grown stouter through the years, formed by his sedentary profession; a hairline receding with the same velocity as the stomach advanced. Would he know I was a candidate as well? Had Ferald apprised him of this fact, or could he sense ambition in another?

In the moment I had first seen Etna Bliss on the night of the fire, I had felt the keenest desire. It was a moment that had altered my life forever. Indeed, I had long grown accustomed to dividing my life into halves: *before* Etna and *after* Etna. So it was as I watched Ferald take Asher under his wing. Jealousy uncoiled itself and stretched its serpentine length, and I realized I had not yet known the depths of its passion, not even in my imaginings as I lay beside Etna in our marriage bed. That had been, in comparison, a cerebral sort of envy that dissipated easily enough in the sunlight of the breakfast room. But this . . . this was something else: the underbelly of admiration; the darker side of love.

(It occurs to me now, some twenty years after the events I describe, that great passion or jealousy may be reduced to an understanding of chemicals in the brain, chemicals that are triggered and retriggered each time the memory of the initial event is retrieved. If so, what a riot of chemicals must be in my brain as I have been writing this memoir – a kind of chemical soup!)

(Are there chemicals in the brain? I shall have to query the Chemistry Professor on this matter when I return to Thrupp.)

That night, I slept fitfully, scarcely at all, and from time to time I sensed in Etna next to me an alertness of which I was normally not aware. I ascribed her restlessness to having caused a bit of unwanted attention at the party. Etna had been apologetic to her host, attributing a dropped champagne glass – which, unfortunately, had fallen during the momentary lull after Ferald's introduction of Asher and was thus all the more noticeable in that crowded room of academics and their spouses – to wet fingers due to the condensation on the flute. As for my own agitation, each time I opened my eyes, I could see only too clearly the patrician features of Phillip Asher, lately of Yale. Thus Etna and I, we two small boats, bobbed along the tempestuous waves of insomnia, one visible and then lost, the other rising from a trough and then sinking again, until such time as we were roused from our bed by our maid, Abigail. My wife, as if she had been anticipating the summons for hours, rose from the sheets so quickly that I did not have a moment to speak to her.

We met, as always after our respective toilets, in the breakfast room. I noted that the relief I normally felt, the relief from the nightly marital tension between us, was not present that morning. We greeted each other not as warm friends will do (no kiss that morning, as I recall), but rather as exhausted or preoccupied colleagues, each engaged in silent dialogues with other persons. Since I cannot know Etna's thoughts (at the time I imagined she was composing a further apology to Millicent Ferald), I can only record mine, which were both exceedingly anxious and highly political.

I sifted through all that had been said the day before – in the hallway of Chandler as well as at Ferald's reception – and, as most of us will do after the fact, I composed replies that were sensible or sharp or even witty, replies that taunted me with their cleverness as they could never be uttered in reality. How I wished I could retrieve time so that I might appear the confident and generous professor who, instead of collapsing at the thought of a serious challenge to his candidacy, rather welcomed, even encouraged, the rival, as men of sport will do. But as I have never been a sporting man, and as I had been blindsided by Ferald's remarks, I felt my mind to be a jumble of confused thoughts, none of which I should have liked to utter in Etna's presence.

Appetite, as well as peace of mind, seemed to have been stolen from me, and I poked the viscous and vile-looking yolk of my egg much as a child will do. I should have to seek Asher out, I determined. I should have to speak to him to ascertain just how much of a threat the man really was. I knew that Eliphalet Stone (the man who detested bottom-feeders) would not be well disposed to an outsider for the post. He believed, and rightly so, that only a man drawn from within the ranks of the college could understand the particular provincial needs of Thrupp. More to the point, he was not in favor of expansion. If Latin and Rhetoric and Biblical Interpretation had been adequate for their own educations, their argument went, such a curriculum was good enough for successive generations as well. I was not as conservative as they, though I favored the direction of funds to the library rather than to further schools of science – with apologies to the ailing William Bliss, who was, in fact, no more interested in this debate than was Mary, who cleared away my nearly untouched plate with a disapproving look.

From the corner of my eye, I saw Etna reaching for the sugar bowl. I was reminded of my boorishness and sought immediately to make amends.

'That was a pleasant reception last night,' I said, puncturing the silence that lay between us.

'It was,' she said.

'You are perhaps too worried this morning about the broken champagne glass,' I said.

'I'm sorry?'

'The one you dropped.'

'Yes,' she said, taking two spoonfuls of sugar (she normally took only the one).

'You were suitably apologetic,' I said. 'I think you should not give it another thought.'

I glanced at her face, which was decidedly pale, causing me to inquire after her health. 'Are you unwell?' I asked. 'I noticed that you took two sugars.'

'Did I?'

She made an effort then to eat a bite of toast, which must have been what was needed, for she smiled at me.

'I'll be at Baker House this afternoon and may not be back until five,' she said.

'Is that so?' I asked. 'You're not dressed for it.'

Indeed, Etna had on a pink silk blouse, not at all suited, I thought, to physical encounters with the poor.

'I hadn't planned to go today, but I feel I need to this morning,' she said, which made me further curious. It was the expression of need, as well as the speed with which she had uttered it, that piqued my interest. It was not often that I saw desire of any sort in my wife, and I began to reflect that charity, though generous, was not entirely selfless, serving as it did the donor as well as the indigent.

'You will be here for dinner?' I asked.

'Yes, surely,' she said, making a notation on the pad of paper beside her cutlery.

I studied my wife in profile as she bent to her task. (She was, in my estimation, nearsighted, though she would not admit to it – a gentle vanity I could well understand and tolerate in a woman; odd circumstance, though, since I had long cultivated spectacles, though I did not, even at forty-five, need them.) The light from a transom window defined the planes of her face – those prominent cheekbones, her straight dark brown eyelashes framing her almond-shaped eyes, the sloping hairline at the temple, the long throat, only faintly lined. She wrote with a formidable and upright hand, and I strained to see her list, but apart from the words *lamb* and *carbolic*, I could make out nothing.

My attention was drawn away at that moment by the happy arrival of our children. Clara, her examination in plane geometry having been successfully negotiated, was in considerably better spirits than she'd been the day before, and, as a result, she tucked straight into her porridge (I so appreciated her good appetite), while Nicodemus, ever a finicky eater, looked at his bowl with suspicion.

'It is only porridge, Nicky,' Etna said.

'I must have brown sugar and raisins,' he said, and Etna, who often indulged him, nodded to Mary, who was standing by the door. We had only the three servants – Mary; our housemaid, Abigail; and Warren, the gardener. Not so many for that era, I think. Nothing, for example, as compared to Ferald's thirteen or to Moxon's seven. (What did they do all day? I often wondered. Moxon was not even married. Have I mentioned that Moxon had had an unexpected success with his life of Byron, a popular volume that had made him a small fortune? Yes, perhaps I have. Did I envy Moxon his success? Well, perhaps I did.)

'You look well today,' I said to Clara. I had been noticing for the past few months that the previously scrawny Clara was filling out admirably, growing taller and developing something of a womanly body. I was glad to see that she was discarding some of her more tomboyish mannerisms (her knees askew when she sat, a propensity to run when she ought to have walked, an entirely unnecessary fidgeting when she was required to be still, such as in church) and was demonstrably more graceful and fluid of limb. Nonetheless, she was still a child, and never more so than in the presence of her brother, who brought out the worst in her.

'Nicky wrote his name on the back of his bedroom door,' Clara announced with unconcealed satisfaction, much to the horror of Nicodemus.

'I did not!' he said, though incipient tears told us otherwise. At six, Nicky was incapable of a successful untruth (and still is today, I am happy to report).

'You did so,' Clara insisted. 'N-I-C-O-D-E-M-A-S. He didn't even spell it right.'

'Is this so?' Etna asked Nicky.

The tears that had threatened to spill fell in earnest down Nicky's cheeks, making him all the more upset with himself.

'With what did you write your name?' Etna asked gently.

'He wrote it with charcoal from my drawing set,' Clara said at once. 'And he ruined the crayon!'

By now one had sympathy for the young Nicodemus, who, after all, had committed no crime greater than the claiming of his door (I had no doubt the charcoal would easily wash off), whereas Clara had committed the graver sin of *informing*. Thus are the joys of parenthood presented daily: sorting out the innocent from the not entirely innocent of misdemeanors.

'Nicky,' Etna said quietly, 'after you have eaten your breakfast, you will wash your name off the back of your door, and you must pay Clara for the charcoal pencil.'

'But how shall I pay her?' Nicodemus asked.

'With money from your glass jar,' his mother said.

'But what is a charcoal crayon worth?'

'Ten cents,' Clara said at once.

I could see that this debate, if left to Clara and Nicky, would have no satisfactory conclusion, and so I said, quite arbitrarily, that Nicodemus would pay Clara one penny, an outcome that vexed Clara, who thought the charcoal crayon more dear than that, but one that pleased Nicky simply because it ended the discussion.

The children returned their attention to their meals, and, in the brief silence that followed, my preoccupation with Asher reasserted itself. I neither heard the rest of the breakfast conversation, if there was any, nor absorbed a word of my newspaper. I could see only the cool and confident visage of the man from Yale. Would not Asher's excellent credentials as well as Ferald's scheming ways sway the board in Asher's favor? For a moment I began to contemplate the notion that I might not, after all, be elected to the post. I must do something, I thought, but what?

'My dear,' I said, standing and bending to kiss the top of Etna's head, 'I must leave you. I am late.'

'Are you?' she asked, looking up.

'A meeting,' I said. 'I'd nearly forgotten.'

'Shall I give you a ride?'

'No, no, it's not necessary. I'll walk. I must have the exercise.'

I did not want Etna to drive me to the college, because I was not, in fact, going to the college, but rather to the Hotel Thrupp. I didn't know precisely what I should do when I arrived; I simply felt that I could not be elsewhere.

The hotel had been rebuilt following the fire of 1899 and had been furnished in the manner of a New England colonial inn, which pleased me; as I may have mentioned, I did not care much for nineteenth-century decoration. Wood floors with good Persian rugs, pale wallpaper with white wainscoting, and simple mahogany and cherry pieces made up the lobby of the hotel, where I hovered, hoping that Asher would pass through. I could then pretend to have run into him and start up a conversation. For I was now intensely interested in speaking with the man away from the prying eyes of Ferald and his cronies. More to the point, I did not want to be seen visiting Asher at the college. An encounter in town, however, a word or two: nothing amiss in that.

I sat in a chair in the corner and read the *Thrupp Gazette* and for the second time that day failed to absorb the news therein. I waited for as long as it might take a man to peruse a local journal and was about to leave the hotel and go to my college office (the office of Noah Fitch was now mine; I had, the reader will be happy to learn, installed electric lights) when I had the idea that Asher might be breakfasting in the hotel. I made my way to the dining room, and there, in the corner, was my prey.

A waiter inquired as to whether I should be dining in the hotel that morning, and I, seizing an opportunity I had not anticipated, answered in the affirmative. As I was led toward a table, I passed by that of Phillip Asher.

'Professor Asher,' I said, sounding (I hoped) suitably surprised. 'Good morning.'

'Van Tassel,' Asher said, holding a white linen napkin to his lap as he stood. He seemed momentarily flustered to be caught so off guard.

'I trust you are enjoying your stay in Thrupp,' I said.

'Very much so.'

'That was quite a pleasant gathering last night.'

'Yes, it was,' he said, using the napkin to wipe a stray bit of egg from his mustache.

'Please, don't let me disturb you,' I said, gesturing to his plate.

Asher was silent a moment, as if considering various replies, and I was happy to see that the man was perhaps not as quick on his feet as I had at first imagined.

'Are you breakfasting here as well?' he asked finally.

'I often do – one or two times a week,' I said, inventing a schedule for myself as I spoke. I leaned in conspiratorially. 'Our cook, upon occasion, makes an appalling porridge, which I only pretend to eat.' I glanced at the second chair at the table, a glance that cannot have been misinterpreted.

'Will you join me?' Asher asked.

And before Phillip Asher could inform me that he had nearly finished his own meal, I accepted his not entirely sincere offer (how could it have been? I had forced myself upon him).

'Excellent,' I said, dismissing the man who had been waiting to lead me to my table. 'I should welcome an opportunity to discuss your lecture series, which I am looking forward to. They begin on Thursday?'

I settled myself at the table. As I seldom ate at the hotel, I did not know the breakfast menu well. I ordered eggs, meat, toast, and orange marmalade when the waiter reappeared.

'They do,' Asher said. He seemed to have lost his appetite, or perhaps he was simply sated, for he sat forward in his chair, wrists poised upon the table, and looked from me to the window and then back at me before he spoke. His face, already pale by nature, seemed excessively fair that morning. 'I hope they will not be too much of a bore.'

'Nonsense,' I said. 'Though you must miss New Haven.'

'I am content to see the New England autumn in New Hampshire. The colors are so much richer the farther north one goes.'

'To a point,' I said. 'They are weak in Canada, I am told.'

'Well, yes,' Asher said. 'I meant New England.'

'But Thrupp can have little appeal to one used to the scholarship of Yale,' I said. 'I envy you.'

'Do you?'

'I envy anyone who has an opportunity to converse in a spirited manner with like-minded men on the work of Bertrand Russell or Hilaire Belloc or Ben Jonson, for that matter.'

'I'm afraid I'm at a loss when it comes to Jonson,' Asher said. 'Quite out of my field.' He paused for a moment, as if he could not remember his field, and I noted that he was studying my face intently — a face surely not worth such a perusal.

'A minor poet,' I said, engaging in a little scrutiny of my own. Asher's was a strong visage, the cheekbones prominent, the eyes truly gray. The man was undeniably handsome, which was a disconcerting realization, since I knew only too well that beauty in a man could well dispose others to favor him. I also knew the reverse of this truism: lack of beauty in myself had occasionally been a hindrance to advancement. (Though, in a slight disturbance of chronology, I will just say here that Asher and I met quite by chance more than a decade later on Newbury Street in Boston, and I was shocked by how unkind the years had been to him. He had quite simply *faded* in the interim. His hair was white, and his eyebrows were so pale as to be nearly invisible. 'It wasn't true,' I said to him as we stood on that charming Boston street. Asher nodded, speechless in the moment.)

'I am afraid you will find Thrupp a very dull place,' I said in the dining room.

'I have not so far.'

'But one that you will soon tire of, I can assure you. I will admit there are some fine minds in the various disciplines, but there is simply so little to *do* in Thrupp,' I said. 'No theater or music of any consequence.'

'Really not?' he asked. 'I was led to believe that the Cushing concerts were worth attending.'

'But they are in the spring,' I said.

'Yes,' he said.

'And you will be back in New Haven by then,' I said.

'I am on sabbatical for the year,' he said.

'So you are, so you are,' I said. 'Do you have family?' I asked.

'I am not married, if that's what you mean.'

'You studied at Harvard.'

'I did.'

'And did you not like Cambridge?' I asked.

'It was not that I disliked Cambridge,' Asher said carefully. 'It was simply that New Haven seemed the best place for me at the time.'

'You have gone from London to Cambridge to New Haven to Thrupp, Professor Asher. You are a nomad. Wandering in the wrong direction, I might add.'

'Or the right direction, depending upon one's point of view,' he said quietly.

'Quite,' I said, and busied myself with my breakfast. 'Forgive my asking, but how old are you?'

'Thirty-four.'

'So young!'

Asher said nothing.

'But time to think of a family, nevertheless,' I said.

'Perhaps.'

'Though one would not want to limit oneself to the eligible young women of Thrupp.'

'No?' he asked.

'There simply aren't any!' I exclaimed.

'I find that hard to believe,' Asher said.

'Well, there is Sarah Griggs, who has an unfortunately high-pitched voice that one cannot abide for more than a few minutes at a time. She is the daughter of the Provost. And there is Julia Phipps, daughter of the Sanskrit Professor. She must be nearing thirty, I should think. She seems to have been eligible for years. And then, of course, one might try the stately Frederica Hesse, whose German blood is as evident in her posture as it is in her chilly mien, not to mention her overbite.'

Asher glanced out the window. (I wince now to recall this patently transparent conversation.)

'I trust they have given you an office in which to prepare your lectures,' I said. 'Or have they consigned you to the library?'

'The corporators have been generous. I do have an office.'

'Very good,' I said. 'Once again, forgive me for intruding into your private life, but if I am not mistaken, you are being considered for the post of Dean of Faculty?'

Asher leaned back in his chair. 'As are you, I am told,' he said.

And so, at last, our cards were on the breakfast table.

'You applied to the post?' I asked.

'I was invited to apply.'

How had that been accomplished? I wondered. Had Edward Ferald himself written to Asher? Yet how would Ferald have learned of such an intellect? Or were others responsible for the arrival of the Yale professor at Thrupp?

'We are such a backwater institution,' I said. 'The train journey to Boston alone takes most of a day.'

Asher made a show of looking at his watch. 'I'm afraid I must go,' he said, rising. 'An appointment.'

I rose as well, as good manners required. 'Well, I cannot say that I wish you luck,' I said.

'No,' he said, extending his hand. 'But I hope we shall remain amiable colleagues.'

'The most amiable,' I said. Asher had a strong, entirely masculine grip, which took me by surprise, as there was something distinctly refined about his features.

'Professor Asher,' I said.

'Please call me Phillip,' he said.

'Well, yes, Phillip then. I wonder if you would care

to come to dinner at my home. My wife, Etna, and I should love to have you. Hotel and college food cannot be much to your liking.'

For just a moment, Asher's eyes widened in alarm, or what I took to be alarm – perhaps it was only surprise: would one rival have another to his home? (Yes, I might have answered him, I would do so, if only to better assess the competition.) I didn't think Etna would mind, though she might decide it was strange I had invited a colleague home at all, since I so seldom did this. Yet, she, too, had been at Ferald's reception and could not have failed to grasp the import of Ferald's public embrace of Asher.

'Thank you, Van Tassel,' Asher said.

'Nicholas.'

'Nicholas.'

'Friday evening?'

He appeared to think a moment. 'I'm afraid I . . .'

'Sunday dinner then.'

Asher nodded slowly.

'There,' I said, once again seizing the moment. 'That's settled. Let me just write down the address. Shall we say one o'clock? To give you time to get home from church and so forth?'

Asher said nothing.

'Do you have need of transportation?'

'No, I have an automobile.'

'Do you?' I asked. 'What kind?'

'A Ford.'

'You drove up from New Haven?'

'I did.' He looked around and seemed anxious to be gone.

'And were the roads tolerable?' I asked.

'There's a direct route,' he said distractedly.

'I keep you too long,' I said. 'These are matters we may discuss on Sunday at my home.'

And before I could detain him a minute longer, he moved away from the table. 'I look forward to it,' he said.

I sat to my cold breakfast and watched his retreating figure. I felt better than I had after our two previous encounters. I had seen a momentary weakness in Phillip Asher, a sign that the man might fear my own candidacy. Perhaps all was not lost after all.

As it happened, Asher did not come to dinner that Sunday, or on the Sunday after that, owing to the fact that William Bliss died the Friday following our breakfast at the Hotel Thrupp, and Etna and I had perforce to enter a period of mourning. Etna was understandably distraught, and I was required to remain close to home for the better part of a week to comfort her. She found some solace in her sister Miriam, who came up from Exeter to attend the service. (Pippa, Etna's other sister, was visiting her husband's family in Chicago and did not attend.) Keep, Miriam's husband, came with his wife, and, of course, the couple stayed with us. I did not care for Josip Keep, but, in such a situation, one is more generous of spirit than one might be otherwise. Besides, I was not at all unhappy to dispel the image of my boorish and unconfident intrusion into their household on that long-ago Sunday morning. Though Miriam had visited yearly for a weeklong stay each time, Josip Keep had not accompanied her to Thrupp; and while I had no illusions regarding his impression of the village ('Dreadful,' he pronounced it upon arriving), I thought he might at least be more impressed with our house. (In fact, he was not: 'I wonder, Van Tassel, that you did not situate the house so that it avoided the dismal prospect of those granite mountains,' he said.

'It was already situated,' I answered, seething.)

The funeral was impressive, with the Reverend Mr. Frederick Stimson delivering a personal and moving homily on the benevolent brilliance of our Physics Professor. Etna wept copiously (her sister Miriam did not; indeed, she appeared hardly to have known the man), and I, too, felt the masculine lump in the throat that will lodge when tears are not seemly. I was moved by Etna's obvious grief, by my affection for William Bliss (quite genuine; it had, after all, been in his house that I had come to know Etna), and by the memory of our wedding, fourteen years earlier, in that very same chapel, a memory further enhanced by the recollection of that first fluttering kiss with my wife. The chapel was filled to overflowing with mourners. I had not known that Bliss had been held in such affection, though I might have guessed; he was a gentle man with a keen mind in a difficult field. Following the ceremony, there was a buffet luncheon at the home of Evelyn Bliss, who appeared visibly exhausted from the effort of tending to her husband during his illness and then having to watch him die.

Etna and I stood in the hallway of the Bliss residence, greeting the mourners who had come to have a meal (a bizarre custom, I often think: who wants to partake of food following a death, which inevitably leads to an unhappy contemplation of one's own?). Occasionally, Etna would leave my side when freshets of grief threatened to embarrass her, and it was after an exceptionally long absence that I went to find her. I searched through the crowd, and when I couldn't locate her, I climbed the stairs. I could hear a sound in one of the rooms. Approaching it, I hesitated just the one second outside the doorway as the memory of coming upon Etna on our wedding day pushed itself forward through fourteen years of marriage. I refer to the sight of my wife as she stood gazing into the mirror but an hour after our wedding, and the hollow and ravaged reflection from said mirror, a look such as I had hardly ever seen on another human's face. I shook the vision from my thoughts and allowed forward momentum to propel me across the threshold, where I beheld no more harrowing a sight than that of my wife sitting on the bed, her eyes red-rimmed and swollen. She took a breath of air and raised her head.

'My dear,' I said, 'I have been worried about you.'

'I should have come to visit Uncle William more often,' she said.

'You came whenever you could.'

'Not enough. The man suffered. I have been so selfish.'

'Nonsense, Etna. No one could have been more dutiful.'

'I have thought only of myself!'

If I was surprised by my wife's outburst, I was tolerant nevertheless; she was, in essence, losing a father for the second time. 'Etna, I do not understand you,' I said. 'You think of everyone *but* yourself. You take excellent care of the children and me.'

'I deceive you, Nicholas. You think me virtuous when really I care so little about virtue. You think me selfless when really I save everything for myself.' She studied me a moment. 'I have not taken care of you, Nicholas. Not at all. I have been cold in wifely matters, and I am sorry. I am so very, very sorry.'

I touched her shoulder. 'You have not been cold,' I said.

'But I have not loved you!' she said.

My fingers froze upon her dress. I felt a paralysis such as that which may attend one in moments of extreme shock (I think of the woman who succumbed to paralysis by the buffet table during the hotel fire and had to be carried bodily from the room). I had known – of course, I had known – that my wife did not love me. But to hear it said. To hear it said!

'Nicholas,' she said, 'forgive me. That is not what I meant.'

'Yes, it is.'

'I have hurt you.'

'It is no matter.'

'Look at me, Nicholas,' she commanded.

I did so.

'Please sit down.'

Again, I did as she asked.

'You have loved me with all your heart,' she said.

'Yes, I have.'

'It is a treasure. To be able to love someone in that way. So thoroughly. So freely. Do you understand? Do you know how much that is worth?'

I must have looked startled. I shook my head *no*.

'Yes, yes, Nicholas. I envy you!' my wife repeated.

I was stunned by the ferocity of her statement. This was so unlike Etna. For a long moment, neither of us moved.

And what am I to say of what came after? That out of death comes life? That in the darkest hours, grief gives the body license? I have known such grief and the gradual emergence of desire that follows, a desire that may swiftly develop into a keen appetite for life (a hedge, I often think, against annihilation). Thus it was, that day on the bed, when Etna turned to me and took my face in her hands and searched my features for . . . for what was she so desperately looking? I do not know, but I do remember clearly the kiss that followed, a kiss that both moved and aroused me. It was the first taste of true passion I had ever had from my wife, and, as such, it produced a joy made all the sweeter for the wait.

I hesitate to trample here upon the most private of memories, but as it is part of my narrative, and part of my attempt to understand Etna, I set it down in writing. Etna kissed my eyes and cheeks. She found her way again to my mouth. She touched me gently on my neck. She tucked her fingers behind the knot of my tie and unfastened it with a surprisingly deft movement. With both hands slipped beneath the lapel of my jacket, she slid it over my shoulders and along my arms. I began to help her, scarcely able to believe my luck.

Etna touched me in a way she had not ever done before (*me*, Nicholas Van Tassel), and I experienced in that half hour such bliss (I do not think that William would mind having his name used in such a manner; he always struck me as a man who had known happiness in sexual matters) that it now seems like a dream. I kicked the door shut and let my wife undress me. For the first time in our marriage, Etna made love to me.

I needed no skill to please her. Indeed, it was effortless, sublime. And I recall thinking, as we lay in a state of considerable disarray afterward, that this was how it was meant to be: husband and wife, intertwined and sated, no barrier between them.

If only such a state could have continued indefinitely.

I heard voices just outside the door and nudged Etna, who had drifted off to sleep. She flinched and sat up and, to my dismay, immediately began to rearrange her clothes and hair. I wanted to tell her to *stop*, but I knew that she would be shamed were she to be caught in such disarray by one of the mourners. As for me, a great lassitude had overtaken my body, so that I was barely able to fasten the buttons of my shirtfront, buttons that had, but a half hour earlier, been so deliciously undone by my wife.

'Forgive me, Nicholas,' Etna said with her back to me. She was pinning up the strands of hair that had fallen to her shoulders. I adjusted my position on the bed so that I could see her face.

'There is nothing to forgive,' I said. 'Far from it. Etna, I am celebrating.'

'I am not myself.'

'You are delightfully yourself.'

'Nicholas.'

'It is how a man and his wife should be,' I said, protesting. 'Indeed, you as much as said so yourself.'

Etna pressed her fingers to her temples and then drew them back through her hair. She folded her arms over her head as if to hide herself.

'Etna,' I said.

She let her arms fall. She assessed herself in the mirror and saw that she had mussed the patient pinning of her hair and would have to begin again.

'My dear,' I said. 'I hope you are not feeling ashamed.'

'Ashamed?'

'Then what is it?' I asked, hating the distance she was already putting between us. I could feel my wife retreating. Or perhaps the retreat was already complete, for she turned to me and gave me the half smile I had seen so often – the one directed to me in kindness or to the children always, or even to Mary when praising her. A smile that was half of nothing. Nothing! I would rather have seen despair in that moment or even deep chagrin than this indecently rapid return to the wife I had known for more than a decade. I felt shut out, and I hope I do not blaspheme here, but it was akin to that experience described by religious mystics of being shut away from the light of heaven. I did not want my former wife back; I desired the one who had just revealed herself to me in all her sensual glory.

Etna turned, touched me on my ankle (I had not even removed my shoes), and then she was gone.

That abruptly. That fast.

I lay as a man will when he is spent, desiring only sleep (desiring it all the more when it is not possible). Gradually, I found the wherewithal to finish buttoning my shirtfront and fastening my trousers. If circumstances had brought forth such passion in Etna, I reasoned, perhaps they would again, the path having been forged, the way easier. I might have to draw her out, or I might have to be alert to moments of vulnerability, but what had happened once could happen again, could it not?

In such a manner, I reached a kind of equilibrium, one that was entirely necessary in order to return to the other mourners downstairs.

I do not recall much of the luncheon that followed the funeral, with the exception of a strange encounter with Josip Keep, whom I had been trying to avoid. Toward the end of the affair, however, when I was watching Etna say farewell to Arthur Hallock across the room, Keep surprised me at my elbow. Perhaps my brother-in-law was still feeling outmaneuvered by that long-ago Sunday morning at his house in Exeter. Whatever his motive, he chose that moment to ask a question that startled me.

'Did she sell the painting?' Keep asked in a baritone that had grown only deeper through the years.

'What painting?' I asked, turning to him. Keep's silky black hairline had receded to a vanishing point. His massive frame had softened some, and his handsome face – that face so used to entitlement – had blurred a bit with age.

'Oh, I am mistaken, then,' Keep said. 'I was under the impression that Etna had sold a painting she had inherited.'

'A painting of what?' I asked.

Keep sipped from a glass of sherry. 'My dear man, if you don't know, how should I?'

'Etna has sold no such painting,' I said. 'If she had, I surely would have known about it.'

'Of course,' Keep said.

'I can't imagine what made you think she had inherited a painting,' I said. 'We own many paintings, but none that she inherited.'

'Quite so,' Keep said, taking another sip from his glass of sherry (an amontillado I myself had purchased for the occasion).

'Do you know the artist?' I asked.

'There can hardly have been an artist if there was no painting,' Keep said with evident impatience.

'There is none.'

'I believe you said as much.'

I sniffed. 'Really, Keep, whatever gave you that strange idea?'

'Perhaps a Claude Legny?'

'A Legny, indeed,' I said with mild amusement.

I might have pursued my denial further in this somewhat deranged manner had not the word *Legny* suddenly triggered a memory: a memory of a conversation with William Bliss I had had late in the summer, when he had first become ill and was resorting to morphine for the pain. (He was later to abandon the drug, as it addled his mind, he said.) He had just taken the tonic, and perhaps he had misjudged the dose, for he was rambling on a bit. He was asking questions and making pronouncements, none of which made any sense at all. Occasionally I would say *yes, yes* or *there, there*, but in truth I was paying very little attention to his disjointed statements. But I suddenly remembered, there in William Bliss's dining room, on the day of his funeral, as Josip Keep stood at my elbow, that Bliss had said the word *Legny* in the same breath as the word *Etna*. It was a conjunction of names such as normally nestles innocently in the mind and might remain there until it decomposes in the grave, unless summoned by a similar confluence of words at a later date.

Legny. Etna.

'There was never a painting,' I said.

'No, of course not,' Keep said. 'I can't think of where I should have gotten the idea.'

'I must go to my wife,' I said.

'By all means,' Keep said.

The man beside me in the dining car is poking at his baked ham with his fork, even as he is debating the matter of the new German chancellor with the gentleman seated across from him. I gather they are strangers. Farther along in the dining car, an elderly fellow is reading his newspaper, an awkward task at the best of times, nearly impossible on a moving train with one's lunch spread before one. PROMOTER WHO ATE

OWN SALVE DEAD AT 96, the headline says. (I believe the article refers to the inventor of Vaseline.) And even farther along, I see a man whose face is familiar to me. I cannot place it exactly; it is a face I associate with sport. To judge from his imperfect table manners, I may be right in this. (He emptied the contents of his nose into his white dinner napkin, a boorish gesture I cannot abide in a man.) With him is a man of the cloth, reading a volume of Thoreau. I am lingering at my table as I write this, hoping once again to encounter a Mrs. Hazzard, a widow from Holyoke, Massachusetts, who appears to have inherited a half dozen sizable mills from her husband, one of which is in South Carolina, the point of her journey. We were seated together at breakfast this morning. Two very large families – each with at least seven children – took up most of the other seats and made an immoderate amount of noise, so that the widow and I had to huddle over our omelettes (with guava jelly) to hear each other, a circumstance that produced, in me at least, the beginnings of something like affection, enough so that I am desirous of seeing her again. I have not been entirely bereft of female companionship these many years, but I have seldom *liked* the women I have been with, and so it pleases me to converse with such a spirited and clever female. She is determined, she told me, not to be a mere figurehead for her husband's businesses but rather to learn everything she must know in order to take them over. Indeed, she seemed reasonably knowledgeable about looms and balance sheets and commercial loans, none of which I know a thing about myself. I did not hold it against her that she had never heard of Thrupp. She has a lovely laugh and, though I guessed her to be in her late forties, an estimable figure as well. But even as one who can see the future in an instant, and is capable of imagining a lifetime in a face, I did not entertain thoughts of marrying.

I will never marry again. It is a penance to which I shall ever be faithful.

Mrs. Hazzard and I had dinner together this evening, and I was glad of her company. Over our braised beef tips, we chatted amiably of her husband, and I learned, among other things, that he was not only a devotee of moving pictures but also a collector of automobiles. There was some suggestion that he was a philanderer as well, though the widow Hazzard did not seem particularly bitter about this fact. After a moment's pause, during which it might have been polite to offer some commentary about my own life, Mrs. Hazzard (*Betty*, she insists I call her) did ask a question about how long I had been a widower. I answered politely but then steered the conversation to the safer topic of my son, for I could not bear to discuss Etna Bliss Van Tassel with a stranger, even one as delightful as Betty Hazzard. And, as will sometimes happen, Mrs. Hazzard spoke at some length (though not tediously) about her own children, for whom she clearly has great fondness. Thus the tricky precipice of truth was avoided.

Mrs. Hazzard chided me gently about my pomposity (which I fear has grown only more pronounced as the years have passed), once stopping me when I used the word 'heretofore'. 'Heretofore, Mr. Van Tassel?' she asked. And while *heretofore* may not be a particularly defensible word, I did argue that as a professor of English Literature, one had to decry the more simple (and, to my ear, bereft) speech of today's discourse, since it constricted one's vocabulary and did not allow one to parse the moment – dissect the moment, as it were – with clause upon clause upon clause (boxes within boxes within boxes, I so often think). She mulled this over a bit and then said she enjoyed speaking with me nevertheless, and that she found me *charmingly amusing*. Since it has been some time since any woman has called me either charming or amusing, I daresay I blushed (the blood of my Dutch ancestors no less likely to betray me in advanced age than it was in my youth), which seemed to please her even more, for she tilted her head and smiled, a smile I wish I could retain and take out when I am dispirited. We lingered over coffee, and I found I was anxious about her imminent departure, for I knew that she would be detraining at Charleston. She invited me to call upon her should I have occasion to visit that city on my return. I know that one extends such invitations as a matter of courtesy, not really expecting the invited ever to appear, but for some time after we had left the dining car and returned to our separate compartments, I allowed myself to envision a visit to that southern town, a pleasant stay with Mrs. Hazzard, and possibly even a friendship of some duration.

The days immediately following the Bliss funeral were distressing ones for Etna, who kept to her room, ignoring not only her social work but her family as well. Nicky and Clara and I tried to draw her out, but it quickly became apparent that Etna had retreated to a private place from which she could not be summoned. This went on for some weeks, into early November, and I was on the point of calling for the doctor, since Etna's grief was beginning to feel out of proportion to the event. Perhaps she understood that I was becoming frightened, for I found her one morning at the breakfast table, looking almost normal, the pink having left her eyes. She attempted a smile, and I had the sense that this effort was distinctly Herculean (Minervian?) on her part.

'Etna,' I said. 'I am so happy to see you up and about.'

'I am up, but not entirely about,' she said.

'Still, though,' I said.

'It has not been good for the children.'

'No,' I said.

'I have had a difficult . . .' She took a quick breath, but not before I saw a slight quivering of her lower lip. '. . . time,' she said.

It was clear to me that I should have to tread lightly and try to keep the conversation on an even keel, away from subjects of death or sadness.

'You look very pretty this morning,' I said, which was true. She had on a high-necked indigo silk blouse and a long string of jet beads that matched both the decorative buttons of the blouse and her delicate pendant earrings.

'Thank you,' she said.

'May I get you a cup of coffee?'

'No, I've had mine already. I've been down here for some time.'

'You are making your list,' I said, unfolding my napkin in my lap. I studied my breakfast. There appeared to be meat of some sort. Kidneys, possibly. Or liver. It looked dark and overcooked.

'Yes,' she said. 'I plan to do the marketing today in town. Is there something you need?'

'I need a new shaving brush,' I said to Etna. 'And shoe polish. And ink for my desk. But I can buy these things when I am myself in town.'

'Let me,' she said. 'It's better if I am busy.'

'Well, in that case, I should love some of that blackberry jam we had last month. I should love it right now, as a matter of fact. What is this meat?'

Etna glanced in the direction of my plate. She wrinkled her nose. 'I'll have a word with Mary,' she said just under her breath, for it was clear that in the absence of her mistress's attention, our cook had relaxed her standards considerably.

Etna made a notation on the tablet of paper that lay beside a stack of correspondence – most of it, I guessed, sympathy letters. 'I'm not sure that the jam will be available this time of year,' she said.

And I, who was pleased to hear my wife speak of trivial matters, could only smile. I put my hand over hers. 'I am so happy to have you back,' I said.

Time passed in the way that it will. Throughout those weeks of mid-November, I rose, I breakfasted, I danced lightly around any topic that might cause Etna distress. I went to my classes, I taught my students, I read endless copybooks of dull treatises. But I was in a state of anxiety nearly all the time: cautious around Etna, worried about the impending vote, and sleepless with thoughts of Phillip Asher, whose lectures were as brilliant as advertised. I began to disparage Asher to my colleagues. 'The man does not know his Jonson,' I said, and sometimes I saw an expression of wariness or pity on my colleagues' faces. Was I so transparent? They had picked up the scent of rivalry, and perhaps there was some sport in it, for they also seemed amused.

One afternoon I had occasion to be in Chandler Hall, as I had a book I needed to return to Moxon. I made my way along the corridor, passing by the closed door of Phillip Asher's office. I knew the man was in the Recitation Hall at that hour, delivering a lecture on the nature of good and evil in *Paradise Lost* (hardly a challenging topic). I meandered past the closed door, then pretended to have forgotten something. I turned and walked past it again, this time unable to resist the urge to slip inside. I had no clear idea what I was looking for; it was simply that I felt I needed to be nearer to the man's *things* – as if in so doing, I might learn more about my rival. I entered the room and shut the door.

Asher kept an untidy desk and an open file cabinet (why, indeed, should any man lock up his brilliance?), and one's first impression was of disarray – of books, of academic journals, and of a plethora of personal items on the desk, which I took to be souvenirs of his tours: pressed butterflies within a glass case, a small sculpture made out of soapstone, an intricate Indian mosaic, a copper printer's block with a cow engraving, an odd monocle that allowed one to see to the side rather than straight ahead. Near the typewriter, I discovered a silver frame with a picture of a young woman inside it. She was fair haired and Scandinavian in her looks, actually quite pretty. I immediately began to imagine a fiancée in a distant city – Oslo, possibly. Encouraged by this discovery, I dared to take a closer look at the various papers Asher had scattered about the office. I recall a treatise submitted to the Academy of Arts and Letters about the role of photography in the recording of history. There was also some correspondence with a professor at the University of Virginia about a pre-biblical story of the Flood, and a letter to the Royal Geographic Society asking to be allowed to accompany an expedition to the Arctic in search of the lost explorer Vilhjalmur Stefansson. I found a detailed scientific paper delivered to the Medical School of Maine at Bowdoin the previous spring about Dr. Gaston Odin's discovery of the cancer microbe and how that might promise a vaccine, as well as an essay in the *Atlantic Monthly* magazine in defense of pacificism. I sat back in Asher's oak roll-away chair and contemplated a series of woodcuts, framed in wide white mats, along one of the walls. How had so young a man published so much? The range of the man's talents and interests was astonishing!

Perhaps it was time to come to terms with the very real possibility that I would not be elected to the post, I thought as I swiveled in Asher's chair. Would that be so terrible? Well, yes, it would. Nevertheless, one had to be realistic. One had to prepare.

I sighed and stood and was about to leave the office when I caught sight of a brown accordion folder with a cloth string tied around it on the floor just beyond the reach of the desk. I bent and picked it up and, as delicately as I could, I undid the string. Inside were letters from a professor at Jesus College, Oxford, inviting Asher to come to that college as a visiting lecturer. I read, from copies of Asher's own letters, that he had at least considered such a move. I held the illicitly viewed correspondence and began to think in earnest: if I had been disheartened to discover that Phillip Asher, lately of Yale, was indeed that rare thing, a man of greatness, could I not take courage from the fact that such a man might not agree to a post at Thrupp if he had a better offer elsewhere? I contemplated a new line of attack in my politicking. I could suggest to my colleagues that Asher was too *good* for Thrupp, that such a man would almost certainly grow tired of a provincial college and might therefore allow himself to be hired away by a better-known institution after the board had gone to all the trouble to elect him. Whereas, I, Nicholas Van Tassel, was in it for the long haul. I was a man of loyalty. I had dedicated my life to Thrupp, had I not?

Yes, yes, I thought as I left that darkened office with my purloined intelligence, careful to maintain the state of disarray in which I had found the room, this was an excellent line of reasoning and should be communicated, however subtly, to the board as soon as possible. The vote, as of that sunny November afternoon, was only fourteen days away.

Shortly before Thanksgiving, Etna resumed her charity work. Baker House needed her, she said one morning when I remarked that she was dressed as if to go to the settlement house. She had on a pin-striped suit with a high turned collar. She was, she said; it was time. I concurred heartily, for I was eager to see my wife make a full recovery. Life, after all, must go on. Children could not be inhibited indefinitely, nor would the poor and indigent stop being poor and indigent.

'Very good,' I said.

As I had no classes that day, I decided to spend the morning in my library with my books all about. I had much to do (those endless copybooks), but, as the morning wore on, I found I could not attend to them. I stood in front of a window, looking out at the back garden – all stalks and dried flowers now – and then I meandered into the kitchen to beg of Mary a cup of tea. I made my way back to the library again and hovered over my walnut desk, seeing not the desk at all, but the face of Phillip Asher as he stood behind a podium to deliver his first address to the college faculty as Thrupp's Dean. I wandered from desk to bookshelves to desk and back to bookshelves again, from time to time shaking off my preoccupation only to have it reassert itself shortly thereafter. As a result of all this *thinking*, I was feeling quite exhausted.

I determined that I needed a walk. I should go into town and have lunch there. Yes, yes, good idea, I thought. Perhaps Moxon was around? I needed manly company of an easy sort, someone to take me out of myself. Possibly I was growing ill. One heard of various hysterias in women, of course, but one did not like to think such a state could infect a man; indeed, by definition, an hysteria could not infect a man, being an entirely female condition. But still, one worried that one was becoming a little too lost in one's daydreams. I telephoned over to Moxon and suggested he meet me at the hotel dining room. He was only too eager to accept. (Poor Moxon. I believe he was always lonely.)

The dining room was crowded that noon hour, and Moxon was seated already when I arrived. He hailed me with a flapping gesture of his arms such as one might make upon being found after several nights lost on a mountaintop. He had on a striped wool suit that had a foreign look to it (not Savile Row foreign, more Bulgaria foreign), and where he had got the thing I have no idea. Moxon often looked as though he had dressed in the dark.

'Nicholas,' he said when I was seated. 'How is Etna?'

'Better,' I said. 'She is resuming her charity work.' I

glanced at the handwritten menu. The day's special was veal shanks. As it happened, I rather liked veal shanks.

'She looked pale when I called last week,' Moxon said.

'She has had a difficult time of it,' I said, taking a sip of water.

'The waiter said the pot pie was the thing to have.'

'I've settled on the veal shanks,' I said, putting the menu aside.

'No classes today?' Moxon asked.

'No. How is your sabbatical?'

'Miss the students,' Moxon said.

'Truly?' I asked, much surprised. A sabbatical away from the students was usually considered to be a prize.

'You are looking as pale as Etna,' Moxon said.

'I haven't been sleeping well,' I said.

'You are taking the vote too hard, I think,' Moxon said. Beneath his bumbling exterior, Moxon was a man of great sympathies.

'It is my future,' I said.

'I've heard it put about that Asher has a fiancée,' Moxon said helpfully.

'A fiancée?' I asked innocently. 'Wherever from?'

'Abroad somewhere. Scandinavia, maybe? Keeps his cards close to the vest, no?'

'He does. Secretive man,' I said. 'Not such a good quality in a dean, I should think.'

'I'm taking up snow skiing,' Moxon announced abruptly, much in the same way he was given to gesture.

'This is news,' I said.

'I'm off to Quebec City this afternoon.'

'What fun for you,' I said, and for a few minutes, I contemplated the image of Moxon on snow skis on a mountainside. Despite this highly amusing picture and the blur of conversation that followed, I could scarcely eat the veal shanks I had ordered. I scanned the crowded room with its waiters deftly carrying trays from kitchen to table and back to kitchen, for Phillip Asher, who might, after all, be dining in the hotel as well. When I was not thus occupied, or trying to attend to Moxon's benign if endless chatter, I was thinking of Etna and her first venture back to work since her uncle's death. 'Moxon,' I said, putting down my fork. 'I have a rather large favor to ask of you.'

'Anything,' he said, his mouth unhappily full.

'Could I borrow your motorcar?'

'Of course,' he said. 'Yours is being repaired?'

'No, Etna has it. She's taken it to Baker House. But I'm worried about her. This is her first day out, and she's still very shaky. I thought I might just call by the settlement house and see if she is all right.'

'By all means, take my touring car. Take it.' He flapped his hands excitedly. 'We can walk together now to the garage. I never use the thing. I never have anywhere to go.'

It was impossible not to like Moxon, both for his honesty and for his lack of pretension. Another man in Moxon's position – which is to say hardly any position at all – might have found it necessary to invent a life simply to save his public face.

It was a breathtaking day (I mean this literally, the air so cold it hurt the lungs as it was going in) as we walked together to Moxon's house. I had some trouble getting used to Moxon's motorcar, a yellow Stevens-Duryea that required some fuss with a primer cup and a choke before one could start the engine. Moxon took the wheel for the first several turns around his frozen side yard until I felt fit enough to move over to the right-hand seat to take the wheel myself and venture onto the street. He lent me his skunk-fur coat for the journey, since it was nearly as frigid inside the motorcar as it was outside.

Over the years, I had been to the settlement house on a number of occasions, five or six, perhaps, for teas and receptions, and so I knew the way. The dirt road was corrugated, however, and I had to get used to the slipping and skidding of the wheels. I was glad that there were few people about, as my driving was erratic and I should not have liked to hit another motorcar along the way. Driving the Stevens-Duryea felt a bit like riding a skittish and undisciplined horse.

The house was located at 18 Norfolk Street in Worthington. In 1880, the two sisters Baker had opened their home to the poor and sick in the neighborhood. Since there were few such facilities in that part of New Hampshire at that time, the home had been enlarged to encompass the indigent from a number of towns in the county, including Thrupp. The exterior of the abode belied its usage. It was, in fact, a charming yellow-clapboarded house, of colonial design, with dark green shutters. There were two front doors (I was never sure why), and several stately elms situated along the narrow yard. There was a rather beautiful wrought-iron fence along the street and a wide porch, which on good days usually held a half dozen women and children taking in the sun. It was only in the dress and demeanor of these unfortunates that one could see that this handsome dwelling was a poorhouse and not the abode of an upstanding Worthington family.

I parked across the street from the home. In the driveway, there were three motorcars, one of which was our Cadillac coupe. I crossed the street, holding my hat against the November breeze, unlatched the iron gate, and was on the flagstones when Etna opened one of the doors.

She did not at first see me, since she was still speaking to someone inside the building as she exited. She had on her wool coat with the fox collar and her driving hat, and in her hand she carried a small carpetbag in which I knew she often ferried items from our house to Baker House (hand-me-downs from the children or foodstuffs we had not eaten).

'Etna,' I said.

She gave a small start and turned in the same moment. I cannot exaggerate her surprise; it was the *frisson* of a sudden shock. Her mouth opened and her eyes widened (why does the body do this, I wonder? to take in *more* of the thing which alarms?), and there was the tiniest jolt through her shoulders. I watched as her mouth quivered a moment, and then she set her lips together. She attempted a smile.

All of this took place in an instant.

'Nicholas,' was all that she could say.

'My dear,' I said, 'I have startled you.'

'Well, yes, you have,' she said. 'What are you doing here?'

'I was worried for you. I'm sorry. I just wanted to make sure that you were all right. You seemed shaky this morning.'

She drew herself up then to her full height. The shock had passed, and she seemed composed. 'I'm just on my way home,' she said.

'You're leaving early today,' I said.

'As you said, I am not myself.'

'Of course not. It's a wonder you came at all.'

'It was good for me,' she said, pulling the fur collar of her coat under her chin.

'Well,' I said, 'now we have two motorcars.'

'Whose did you come in?'

'Gerard Moxon's.'

She studied the Stevens-Duryea across the street. 'You hate to drive,' she said.

'It was actually rather fun,' I said.

'Was it?'

Etna had a habit of lowering the brim of her hat to hide her eyes – a not uncommon feminine gesture. Whereas a man must look another in the eye or risk being thought an untrustworthy character, a woman is always permitted a modest glance to the side or at her feet.

'Shall you follow me home?' I asked. 'Or I you?'

'What a nuisance,' she said suddenly, stepping down off the porch.

'Yes, it is. But a small one, no?'

She touched me on the arm. 'It was very sweet of you to come to find me,' she said.

'Thank you,' I said. 'And Etna?' I asked as I followed her.

'Yes?'

'I was thinking of inviting Phillip Asher to the house for dinner.'

My wife stopped and turned. 'Our house?' she asked.

'Well . . . yes.'

She shook her head. 'I don't . . .'

'It is too soon,' I said quickly.

'Yes,' she said with evident relief.

'Then I could have him over for drinks – a cigar-and-brandy sort of thing.'

Etna, carpetbag in hand, was silent.

'You wouldn't have to entertain him,' I went on. 'You wouldn't even have to come downstairs for that matter.'

She looked away from me toward the Cadillac coupe. 'If you feel you must,' she said. She turned back to me. 'Whatever have you got on?'

I looked down at the skunk coat, not a thing of beauty, however warm it was. 'Moxon's as well,' I said.

Etna smiled.

'I should get to know the man,' I said.

'Moxon?' she asked.

I took the carpetbag from her and walked around the car. I set the satchel on the cocoa mat on the floor. I shut the door and looked at my wife over the hood of the car. The sashes of her hat, as yet untied, were blowing in the breeze.

'Asher,' I said.

The following morning, I sent a note around to Asher's hotel inviting him to drinks that evening at the house. I had Mary set up a tray in the library. The room was small, but there were two comfortable chairs there, giving it a masculine feel. At the appointed hour, I was waiting in that library, pretending to work. I was not sure that Asher would come, as I had not had any reply to my invitation, but just before half past five o'clock, I heard a ring at the door. Though I knew that Abigail was in the house, I thought it would be a friendlier gesture if I went and greeted Asher myself.

Asher stood on the front stoop. Though he was a younger man, one could not help but notice a nest of wrinkles at the corners of each eye, the legacy, I thought, of his weather-beaten expeditions to New Guinea or wherever it was he had gone. Under his overcoat, he wore a formal collar and a dotted red silk tie. His mouth was fixed and serious.

'Come in, come in,' I said, making way for the man, who stepped into the hallway, bringing with him a shiver of cold air. I shut the door quickly. The clock struck half past the hour, and I remarked on his punctuality. Abigail arrived then and took his hat and coat.

Asher patted down his hair. 'This is very kind of you,' he said as we stood somewhat awkwardly in the hallway.

'Not at all,' I said.

'I should like to convey my sympathies to your family on the death of William Bliss,' he said.

'Thank you,' I said. 'My wife has taken it particularly hard. She regarded William Bliss as something of a father.'

'Then I should like to convey to her my special sympathy,' Asher said.

'Thank you, Professor Asher,' Etna said from the top of the stairway.

I believe I was even more surprised than Asher to see my wife descending the steps. She moved at a slow and stately pace, the skirt of her dress making a rippling brook behind her. She wore an ivory dress with a lace capelet on her shoulders. She had plum-colored beads threaded through the curls of her hair and knotted at the nape of her neck. Her pendant earrings quivered as she walked.

'Etna,' I said. 'May I present Phillip Asher. If you recall, he was introduced at Edward Ferald's party.'

'Yes,' she said, reaching the bottom step. 'Good evening, Professor Asher.'

Asher hesitated just a moment before advancing to take her hand. In that moment, I now believe, he was making a critical decision. 'You knew my brother,' he said to Etna. 'Samuel.'

Etna nodded. 'Yes, I did,' she said, and I could see that this was not news. 'And how is Mr. Asher?' Etna asked.

I watched as Phillip Asher let Etna's hand go. Though her manner was cool, her fingers trembled. I noted that Asher saw this as well.

'He lives in Canada,' Phillip Asher said. 'But now he is in London. With the British Admiralty.'

Etna blinked and nodded again.

'Because of the war,' Asher added.

'So you two know each other,' I said, a bit bewildered by this exchange.

'Not well,' Etna said. 'I knew Professor Asher's brother when I lived in Exeter. He was a friend to the family.'

'I see,' I said. 'It is not someone you have ever mentioned before.'

This was a boorish statement on my part, slightly insulting to Phillip Asher and his brother.

'I am just on my way to fetch the children,' Etna said. 'They are visiting with their aunt.'

'Just so,' I said, still somewhat confused.

'Good-bye, Professor Asher,' Etna said. 'I hope I shall have more time to visit with you when next you come around to our house.'

'I look forward to that,' Asher said.

'Drinks are waiting,' I said with bluff heartiness to Asher as Etna was putting on her hat, and it seemed the man left the hallway only reluctantly.

I led Asher into my study. I had arranged my books and papers on the desk to look as if I had been writing an essay. He glanced at the disarray and then took one of the leather club chairs. 'What can I get for you?' I asked. 'Brandy?'

'Yes, please,' he said.

'Soda?' I asked, holding the seltzer bottle.

'No, thank you.'

'Very good,' I said, making a drink for myself as well. I sat opposite the man. I reached for a silver box on my desk. 'Cigarette?' I asked. 'Or are you a pipe man?'

'Neither, actually.'

We each took sips of our drinks. Asher had his legs crossed at the knee, exaggerating the length of his limbs. But though his posture suggested an easy elegance, I noted that he seemed to have lost a bit of his poise somewhere between the hallway and my study. From time to time, he jiggled his foot.

'Your lectures have been remarkable,' I said. 'The entire college has been abuzz with them.'

'Do you think so?' he asked.

'Small debates, like brush fires, have been starting up in the least likely of places as a result of your comments. The lecture series is intended to do this, so I think we can say you have succeeded admirably.'

'I still have one left to give,' he said.

'And then you will be returning to New Haven?'

'I'm not sure,' he said, uncrossing his legs. 'There is the vote.'

'You're still a candidate, then?'

'I believe so,' he said, taking another sip of his brandy. I had kept the lights in the study low. A bit of kindling snapped in the grate.

'I wonder,' I said as I swirled the oily liquid in my glass, 'that you have not considered a post at a more exalted institution. Oxford, for example.'

Asher looked sharply up at me, and I could only guess at his thoughts. Was he wondering if I knew that he had had an offer from Jesus College? Or would he assume I had simply made a lucky guess?

'It is not a particularly propitious time to go abroad,' Asher said carefully.

'No, I suppose not,' I said. (There was, after all, a war on.)

Asher looked down at his drink.

'I came across an article in the *Atlantic Monthly* magazine you wrote in regard to pacificism,' I said.

'Did you?' he asked, much surprised.

'Would you not go if asked by your country?'

'I am already too old,' he said.

'So it is a theoretical argument you make. Not one to affect you directly.'

'No,' he said, shifting in his seat. 'But no less heartfelt, I assure you. I hold to it firmly.'

'Are you an atheist, Professor Asher?'

'No,' he said, 'I'm not.'

'Remarkable,' I said.

'Remarkable?'

'Well, the Nietzsche.'

'It is a field of study only.'

'Just so. Are you a Quaker, then?' I asked.

'No, I am not.'

'Well, what are you, if you don't mind my asking?'

It was a rude question, certainly, and even today I am not sure why I pressed him. And did Asher hesitate? I am sure that he did. Not in fear, but in preparation for the reaction his answer would provoke. He looked away a moment and then back again.

'I am a Jew,' he said.

I sat perfectly still, drink in hand, stopped in its progress to my mouth. I doubt anything Asher could have told me would have surprised me more. *I am Chinese. I am a shaman. I am a Gypsy.*

'Really,' I said, finally taking a sip.

Was *Asher*, which had sounded so plausibly English, actually a Jewish name? Did the Board of Corporators know that they were considering a Jew for the post of Dean of Faculty of Thrupp College, a school that had never, to my knowledge, hired a man of the Jewish faith? The unexplained descent from London to Cambridge to New Haven to Thrupp was beginning finally to make more sense to me.

(I cringe now to recall and to reveal these opportunistic thoughts. My only defense, insofar as a defense is even conceivable, is that at that time, Jewish academics were rare outside of Europe and virtually unheard of at a school such as Thrupp. Now, of course, it is entirely otherwise. At our college alone, I can count at least three Jewish academics who have been considered for posts: Isaiah Gordon and Robert Newman and Jerome Sills. Though none of them, I should point out, was hired.)

'There are many of us pacificists about,' Asher said.

'Not in Thrupp, I can assure you,' I said when I had recovered my equilibrium. 'The sentiment is quite the other way in this village.'

Asher gazed around at the shelves of books, at a small Sargent sketch I had on the wall. He reached over and touched the foot of a bronze of Winged Mercury on the desk.

I was near trembling with my news and could scarcely think.

'What a remarkable coincidence,' I said, 'that your brother should have known my wife.'

'Yes, it is,' he said.

'How is it that they met?'

'I believe my brother knew Mrs. Van Tassel's father,' he said. 'They were both schoolmasters at Phillips Academy in Exeter.'

'A tolerant school,' I said delightedly.

Asher glanced up at me but said nothing.

'Your brother is of my wife's father's generation?' I asked.

'In between, I should think,' Asher said. 'My brother is ten years older than I am.'

'My age then.'

'Well, yes, I imagine he would be.'

'And you say he has emigrated to Canada?'

'Toronto. Yes. He had rather settled in, in fact, when he was asked to go to London.'

'Good, good,' I said.

Asher looked at me oddly.

'Though you must miss him,' I said quickly.

'We were not close,' Asher said. 'There was the age difference. By the time I was ten, my brother had left the house.'

'I see. So you personally had never met my wife before.'

'Well, I had, actually. Once or twice in passing.'

'May I refresh that drink?' I asked, now in an intolerably expansive mood.

'Yes, thank you.' Asher shifted in the chair, the creaking leather betraying his unease. A truly poised man, I reflected, could sit for an hour without appearing to move a limb.

'I am guessing that my wife will dine at her aunt's house,' I said. 'We might even take in a meal together later, you and I. In town perhaps?'

'I should like that,' Phillip Asher said. 'But I am promised to Eliphalet Stone.'

'To Stone, you say?'

'Yes,' Asher said.

He did not elaborate. But then again, he didn't need

to. There was only one reason Eliphalet Stone would invite Phillip Asher to his house. Did Stone know that Asher was a Jew? Surely not, I thought.

'Well, another time, perhaps,' I said.

'Yes, another time,' Asher said, glancing at the clock over the fireplace. 'Is it nearly six already?'

'The clock is fast,' I said.

Asher's evident desire to be away teetered on the impolite.

'Britain has had heavy casualties,' I said.

'Not without inflicting considerable damage.'

'They will see an air war soon,' I said.

'Yes,' he agreed. 'It is inevitable.'

'That was dreadful news about the *Hawke*,' I said, referring to the British cruiser that had been torpedoed off the coast of Scotland.

'Terrible.'

We talked further about the war in Europe. While I had another brandy, Asher nursed his first.

'May I ask you a question, Professor Asher?' (This may have struck Asher as odd, since I had been doing nothing else all evening; indeed, our little masculine chat bordered on an inquisition.)

'Yes, of course.'

'Why Thrupp?'

Asher cleared his throat. 'I see an opportunity to bring a provincial college to the status of a university,' he said.

'Then you would institute schools of graduate study?'

'That would be my goal, yes.'

'And with what would you do this? Financially speaking, that is?'

'I should have to become a fund-raiser,' he said.

'I see. Is this not a job more suited to a president

than a dean, whose job is, more often than not, that of a disciplinarian?'

'I must disagree,' Asher said, setting down his drink. 'The job of a dean surely encompasses more than discipline. There is the proper management of the faculty, the planning of a curriculum . . .'

'You would broaden the scope of that position, then,' I said, my voice rising to a near giggle.

'Explore them to the full. Certainly.'

'I fear our small and unprepossessing college will strain and break under your ambition,' I said, trying to bring my voice under control.

Asher regarded me with a quick flicker of something like amusement. 'Are we not all ambitious?' he asked.

'I suppose we are,' I said.

He glanced at his pocket watch. 'I really must go,' he said, standing. 'You have been very kind. Thank you for the drink.'

'Where will you go for the Thanksgiving break?' I asked, standing with him.

'Mr. Ferald has been kind enough . . .'

'I see,' I said, seeing only too well. (But would Ferald knowingly have a Jew to his house, I wondered? I could scarcely imagine such a thing.) 'Pity your brother cannot join you.'

'We will pray for his safe return.'

I walked Asher to the hallway. Abigail was summoned and retrieved Asher's coat and hat. 'May I give you a ride into town?' I asked. 'I have an extra motorcar for the week.'

'I appreciate the offer, but no, thank you,' Asher said. 'I have my own vehicle.'

'So you have, so you have,' I said.

'I hope you'll join me one day soon at the hotel,

where I can return your hospitality,' he said graciously.

'I should be happy to,' I said, opening the door.

Asher stepped out into the starry night. I watched as he drew on his gloves.

'You should not toy with the corporators,' I said.

He looked up at me, his face illuminated by lantern light. 'Excuse me?' he said.

'I cannot imagine that you would remain at Thrupp for very long,' I said. 'You are too ambitious and too accomplished. Thrupp is a backwater college, of little interest to you in the long run. But the corporation takes this election quite seriously. It is meant to be a post for life. I doubt you should hold it for life.'

Asher paused, as if weighing his words carefully. 'That is my business,' he said.

'It is my business as well,' I said.

'Good night,' Asher said. He turned and began to walk to his motorcar.

'*Had not thy pride/And wand'ring vanity, when least was safe,/Rejected my forewarning*,' I quoted to his back, knowing full well that Asher, of all men, would recognize the Milton.

I shut the door. I smiled. I did not believe I would be having the man from Yale to my house again.

I scarcely slept at all that night, agitated and buoyed by my delicious bit of news. I considered various scenarios. Could I casually mention the fact of Asher's religious persuasion to Ferald in conversation? How best could this be accomplished? I must contrive to run into the man, I thought. Yes, I would do that. Was there a matter about which I could plausibly call him?

The Thanksgiving holiday was spent largely at church, with a meal in the afternoon at the widow Bliss's house, during which our spoken thoughts were with the absent William. Nicky and Clara leavened the gathering with a pantomime they had prepared. Nicodemus played an Indian, nearly giddy at being allowed a tomahawk and scalping knife. Clara was a Quakeress, the sole survivor of a family massacre. She thrived in the role, particularly during the part when she was able to demonstrate her Christian benevolence by converting the miserable Nicky, who had to exchange his lovely leather tunic for trousers.

During a brief intermission, I thought about the matter of the painting Keep had mentioned and of William's drug-addled state, and so I leaned over to ask Etna about a painting. Had she ever owned a Legny? I asked.

'A what?' she asked.

'A New England artist, of national repute. He paints impressionist landscapes. Some portraits. Surely you know who Claude Legny is, Etna.'

'Yes,' she said distractedly.

'So have you ever owned one?'

'Owned a painting of my own?'

'Yes. A Legny. Of your own.'

'What an amazing question!' she said.

'And I was just wondering,' I added quickly, since Nicky and Clara were about to resume their little playlet, 'how it is that you did not mention to me that you knew Phillip Asher – particularly when you knew he was coming to the house?'

'I wasn't at all sure if it was the same family,' Etna said with only mild attention. She was all eyes for her children upon the makeshift stage. 'And Phillip Asher is nearly unrecognizable now from the boy he was when my father knew the family,' she added.

And that was all we were able to say of the matter, for Nicky and Clara had again commanded our attention.

That night, Etna had a brief relapse and took to her bed for the remainder of the weekend. By the following Monday, however, Mary was able to report at breakfast that my wife had left especially early that day for the settlement house. I was pleased at this news, for it meant that Etna was once again herself. But just before lunch, as I was passing through the side hallway, I saw that Etna was perhaps not herself after all. She had left her carpetbag at the foot of the stairs. I opened it and noted that it was full of food – cheese and bread and meat pastries, doubtless leftovers from the Thanksgiving weekend. Had the contents of the satchel been clothing merely, I should have let it go. But because it was filled with food, I decided then that I would take Moxon's motorcar, which still remained in our driveway, and deliver it myself. I had rather enjoyed the motoring during my previous visit there, and heaven knew I could use the practice.

The day was a miserable and rainy one, but I was able to congratulate myself on being able to sit back in my seat most of the way and not having to clutch the steering wheel as if it were a life ring. I was on Norfolk Street before one o'clock and was approaching the settlement house when I saw, from a distance, Etna emerging from one of the front doors. Really, I thought, my timing was impeccable!

I watched as Etna held up her umbrella and let it unfurl. She spread her arms out a bit and skipped down the steps to the coupe in the driveway. I stopped my own vehicle and got out of the car and called to her, but with the rain beating down and the sound of her own engine, she did not hear me. With the economic gestures of one used to such a machine, Etna reversed out of the driveway and made a turn.

She did not turn in my direction, however, but rather the opposite way. She hadn't even noticed the presence of Moxon's touring car.

Did Etna have an errand? I mused. Was she taking a shortcut home?

After an initial moment of surprise, I climbed back into the Stevens-Duryea and attempted to follow my wife. The road was wet and slippery, and the rain made a blur of shapes on the windshield. I pressed a bit harder on the pedal in hopes of catching up to Etna, but as I was a less skilled driver than she, I couldn't seem to gather enough speed without skidding. I didn't even know whether I was following Etna's car or someone else's, for a carriage had overtaken me soon after I had set out, and I had to hope that it had passed Etna as well. At some point, I was vaguely aware of having driven into another town, Drury, perhaps. I stepped even more firmly on the gas pedal, frightening myself with the sound of the straining motor (I was traveling at thirty miles per hour, which seemed rattling in those days). After fifteen minutes of this insanity, I was rewarded with a glint of green through the rain. I would pass Etna, I thought, and wave to her, and then she would stop her car.

But as I was formulating this plan, Etna veered left off the road into a driveway. She made the turn too quickly for me to do so as well, and so I bypassed that turning and stopped the car at a clearing farther on. I was shaken at having traveled so fast, though relieved not to have perished doing so. I sat for some minutes until the beating of my heart slowed. I got out of

Moxon's motorcar and walked back to the place where Etna had turned. I thought that I might have to lecture my wife about her driving. Really, I thought, she could have killed herself at such a speed and in such a downpour!

I stopped at the entrance to what clearly looked to be a large estate. Just beyond the main house – a white manse of several stories with massive pillars reaching to the roof – was a small carriage house. It was in front of that smaller building that Etna had parked the Cadillac.

Perhaps my wife was collecting a parcel from another benefactor, I thought. Not many women drove motorcars in those days, and Etna may have offered her services to an acquaintance. As I drew nearer to the main house, however, I saw that it was closed, as a summer cottage will be in winter. The shutters on the first floor were locked, and the curtains at the upper stories were drawn. If no one was in residence, I wondered, then what was Etna doing there?

Hiking my collar over my neck, I walked past the main house and directed myself toward the coupe. The estate had lovely grounds, undulating and benign, even in November. The property, as far as I could make out, was bordered with a handsome stone wall. There were fruit orchards and dormant rose beds and a grape arbor in the back. What I had thought was a carriage house, however, was in fact a simple, unadorned dwelling with a front door that would admit no automobile or carriage. The structure reminded me of a schoolhouse, and for a moment I had the idea that Etna had taken on the job of tutor to a family and I had simply failed to attend to this bit of information. The house was white clapboarded with shutterless windows, and it had a pitched roof with a cupola at its crown. The grounds immediately surrounding the cottage had the look of having been cultivated and then tidied for the winter. There was no sign of activity and there were no other motorcars or carriages nearby. I walked to a window and peered inside.

I looked into a single chamber, neither sitting room nor dining room nor kitchen, but rather one that combined all three in the same way that the most impoverished shacks will do. The walls were painted white, the plaster chipped in places. At the windows, pale linen curtains were knotted just below the sills, and on the wall directly over a davenport hung the frame of a Gothic window, like that from a small chapel. Faded French floral studies were stuck onto the walls with hat pins, and in one corner of the room was a tall apothecary cabinet the color of cream. Atop the cabinet was a tin cake box with a green design embossed in its latched front door. There was a white pitcher of dried flowers on the single table. The light in the room was diffuse, as if it had been sifted.

In the center of the room, a white chandelier hung from the ceiling. The conceit of the chandelier, which was oversized for the room, was of a bouquet of white iron flowers, the rust poking through in patches lending the blossoms a tinge of ruin. Through this thicket of flowers — some daisies, some roses with sharp-edged petals — the six sconces of the fixture spread out with open arms. All about the chandelier, hanging from the stems and leaves and vines of the sconces, were dozens of crystals.

Near a window and with her back to me, Etna sat in an upright wooden chair. She was bent over what looked to be needlework.

I turned away from the window and pressed myself against the clapboards, the rain striking my face. I cannot say why I reacted in such a way, why I did not simply rap at the window to catch my wife's attention, why I did not, more properly, knock at the door. It was, I believe, the shock of seeing my wife bent so serenely over her work in the bleached quiet of the foreign room that confused me.

I was besieged with questions. What was Etna doing there? To whom did the cottage belong? Was this a dressmaker's cottage? Had Etna taken on a bit of sewing to make extra money?

I turned back to the window, aware now of a certain stealth on my part. I watched her at her sewing. I saw her put a pin between her lips. She lifted up the material she was working on, rearranged it, and laid it back down in her lap. Her driving hat and her fox-trimmed coat were on the Davenport, as if tossed in a rush. The furled umbrella was making a puddle in a corner.

I studied my wife in this manner for perhaps half an hour, occasionally glancing at the road lest someone passing by wonder why a man was peering into the window of a cottage. As I stood there, I took in more of the details of the room – a tiny porcelain sink, a cookstove, a hassock on which rested a plate of golden pears – but my eyes were constantly drawn back to the white chandelier, its image melting and re-forming in the rain-washed window panes. I remembered the bill for a white chandelier that I had inadvertently opened and which Etna had explained away by insisting that she had sent the fixture back. *White iron with six sconces.* Etna stood and turned in my direction, as if she had caught me. But she only shook out a piece of silk from an untied parcel on a shelf. She sat back down in her chair.

With each passing moment, the idea of knocking on a window or at the door became more and more difficult to imagine. And if I am to be truthful here, there was some excitement in watching my wife through a glass pane. It was as though I were a disinterested spectator viewing a play, the meaning of which was crucial to my existence. My wife seemed not my wife, but rather a thing apart from me. I could not reach her or touch her or call out to her. She existed in a separate universe from the one which I inhabited.

Etna knelt on the wooden floor and spread the cloth out in front of her, the edges of the silk running in the windowpane. She pinned a paper pattern to the silk and began to cut around the edges. She stood then and took the garment she had already been sewing to the davenport and smoothed it out. She gazed at it for a few moments (I think it was a nightgown), her fingers folded beneath her chin. She tilted her head and frowned a bit and then put her hands on her hips and looked around her. She collected the bits of silk from the floor and put them in a sewing basket.

I watched as she walked to the stove, put a kettle on, and took a teapot, cup, and saucer from a cabinet. She stood for a time, staring out a small window over the sink (fortunately not in my direction), until even I could hear the kettle's whistle. She spooned tea into a pot and walked to another cupboard. She removed a writing case and set it on a table. She waited for the tea to steep. When it had, she poured herself a cup and put it on the table next to the writing case. I had the distinct impression that the table had a wobble. She removed a pen and bottle of ink and a sheet of paper from the case. She began to write, occasionally taking a sip of tea as she did this.

These were perfectly ordinary actions that I should have paid no attention to had I seen Etna performing them in our home. But watching her through the window was altogether different. There was a sort of fascination in it as well as the insistent hammering of the central riddle: What was my wife doing in that cottage?

How long I stood at that window with the rain running down my neck and soaking the backs of my trousers I cannot now recall. I did not move or make a sound. After a time, Etna laid down her pen and put the writing case away. She washed her cup and saucer and teapot in the sink. She shook the water off the cup and then dried it with a cloth and set it back in the cupboard. She shook her hands as well and then wiped them off with the damp cloth. She surveyed the room and walked to the davenport. When she began to slip her arms into her coat, I moved around the corner to the wooded side of the house so that she would not see me. I heard her leave the cottage by the front door, pulling it shut twice, as if it had not properly closed the first time. A few minutes later, I heard the start of a motor.

I slid down the clapboards to the ground, having for the moment lost the strength of my legs. I was as perplexed as I had ever been. Why would my wife, Etna Bliss Van Tassel, drive to Drury, New Hampshire, to sit in a foreign cottage to sew, when she could sew perfectly well – and had done so nearly every night of our married life – at home?

I drove erratically and made several wrong turnings.

Worse, I ran out of fuel and to wait for a passing motorist to lend me a cupful to get home. When I arrived at the house, I saw that Etna's coupe was parked in our driveway. Disheveled and soaked through to the skin, I went inside the house and walked directly upstairs to Etna's dressing room, where she stood in her corset covering, holding a dress she planned to put on for dinner.

'Nicholas,' she said, clutching the dress to her breast.

'Where were you?'

'What do you mean?'

'Where were you?' I shouted. I had not even taken off my wet coat and hat, which were creating a sort of rain on the rug. I knew that I was frightening my wife, but I didn't care.

'I was at the settlement house,' she said. 'I have just got home.'

'I went to the settlement house,' I said. 'You were not there.'

'I must already have left,' she said. 'Nicholas, what is this all about?' She pretended to be both surprised and annoyed by my queries, but her manner was not quite as self-assured and innocent as she might have wished.

'I was there at half past one o'clock,' I said.

'Were you?' She pretended to think. 'Well, I don't know what time I left, but I had some errands to do.'

'Where? What errands?'

'I had fabric I had to buy in Drury,' she said. 'Really, Nicholas, stop shouting at me. This inquisition is offensive. I must ask you to leave my dressing room.'

I stood, poised on the brink of accusation, one that would have been reflected four times in the mirrors that lined the dressing room. Perhaps I opened my mouth. For a long moment, we were husband and wife, across a gulf of silence. Was she about to confess her visit to the cottage? Was I about to tell her I had watched her for nearly an hour through a window but had not announced my presence? Was I afraid to introduce a topic that once mentioned could never be retrieved? I do not know. I know only that the silence between us was so profound that neither of us at first understood the meaning of Mary's shouts from below.

'Mary is shouting,' Etna said.

'What?'

'Mary is shouting.'

I went to the head of the stairs. 'What is it, Mary?' I called, annoyed.

'The machine, sir, the machine!' Mary cried, flapping her hands about her face. 'It is reversing itself down the driveway!'

I moved to the window, through which I could see that, indeed, the Stevens-Duryea was gathering speed as it rolled down the pebbled drive. Worse, I now saw the reason for Mary's hysteria: Clara sat in the driver's seat, clutching the wooden steering wheel in a kind of paralysis.

I ran down the stairs and out of the house, shouting my daughter's name. In my haste to confront Etna, I realized, I had left the motor running. My wet clothes hampered my speed, and though I am, as the reader will doubtless have realized, among the least athletic of persons, I think it is true to say that when his child is in danger, a father may perform miracles of physical prowess. I pursued the errant motorcar the length of the driveway, screaming at Clara to press the brake pedal – Clara, who did not know a brake pedal from a gearshift. When I reached the vehicle, I leapt onto the running board. I clutched the door frame, my sudden momentum causing the motorcar to lurch. I now feared the wheels would catch in the trench at the side of the drive and turn the motorcar over. I shouted at Clara to move to one side. In her fear, she lay down on the floor. With a contortionist's skill, I opened the driver's-side door and threw myself inside. After several stabbings at the floor with my foot, I finally stopped the Stevens-Duryea just inches from a stone wall that bordered the property opposite us.

Heaving for air, I glanced up to see that Nicky and Abigail and Mary had come out of the house to see the chase. Etna, her hands to her mouth, was watching from an upstairs window. I picked up the trembling Clara from the floor and held her to my breast.

I trust we comforted each other.

That night neither Etna nor Clara came down to dinner. Clara I could well understand, but not my wife. Abigail reported that Etna had gone to bed without a meal in the guest room, since she did not want to bother me.

Bother me? I thought but didn't say since I shared the table with Nicky, who was still trembling from the earlier incident. Bother me about *what*? I wanted to know. (Quite possibly Nicky was trembling from excitement; for a six-year-old boy, the wild descent of the motorcar would have been thrilling.) I thought my wife a coward and determined to wake her up after the meal and tell her so; and I might have done but for a phone call I received during the tomato bisque.

Ferald's tone was businesslike. He wanted to speak with me at his home first thing in the morning. Could I come at nine o'clock? Yes, I said, I would be only too happy to do so.

I hung up the telephone and half fell into the hallway chair. What did Ferald want? His tone had been chilly, but, then again, Edward Ferald was not known for his warmth. Was he calling to tell me I was being dismissed from consideration for the post? No, no, I did not think so, for why would he bother, when the vote was only a few days away? It was then I had another, more pleasant thought. Was it possible that word of Asher's Jewishness had reached Ferald via some other route? And, if so, could it be that Ferald, speaking on behalf of the board, was about to offer Nicholas Van Tassel the post of Dean of Faculty of Thrupp College?

I did not sleep well that night. How could any man have done so? When I wasn't wondering why my wife had lied to me about being in a foreign cottage (had she lied to me, though? I tried to recall the precise series of questions and answers), I was thinking about the dialogue that would shortly take place between Edward Ferald and myself. I imagined the conversation, my grateful modesty (modest gratitude), and the solemnity with which I would accept the post. It seemed likely, based on past experience, that Ferald would not be able to refrain from conveying to me that I was not his first choice. But would he not, after all this time, bury the hatchet and congratulate me in the manner of a patron to an academic? No matter. Even if he could not rise to a moment of graciousness, the outcome would still be the same. I would leave his home in time for my ten o'clock class as the new Dean of Faculty of Thrupp College.

I dressed with care, donning my best worsted suit and striped silk tie. I wore a diamond tiepin, a gift from Etna, an ornament I wore only on the most important of occasions. I tried as best I could to groom myself. As I may have mentioned, my hair was beginning to thin, leaving a bald semi-circle at the top of my head, as if someone had taken a bite. I shaved carefully and sprinkled cold water on my face repeatedly in an attempt to reduce the puffiness around my eyes, a result of my excitable condition.

I was glad of the Stevens-Duryea, for I thought I should make a better impression arriving in Moxon's touring car than on foot. I tried to drive steadily and keep my thoughts even, warding off images of Etna in the cottage. I did not want to be preoccupied or distracted on this most important of occasions. I pulled up to the front door of Ferald's house, my opinions about his manse softening as I did so. Perhaps the English limestone and the Greek columns were not as pretentious as I had thought. Why shouldn't a man design a house to suit his fanciful whims?

I stepped smartly from the automobile, and I trust I appeared confident and composed as I knocked on Ferald's door. A butler answered (yes, a full-fledged butler in Thrupp, New Hampshire, but never mind), took my coat and hat and gloves, and said that Mr. Ferald was expecting me.

I followed the man a fair distance to a set of massive double doors that I had not remembered from my previous visit to that house; the porcelain handles were near chin height. The butler ushered me into a large, well-lit room, in the center of which was a highly polished oval table. He suggested I take a seat near the center of the table, which I did.

I folded my hands and was told that Mr. Ferald would be with me shortly. All around the table were shelves of books reaching to an upper gallery that held even more volumes (but the man did not even read! I protested silently). The windows' deep sills and the thick carpet rendered the room so silent that I could hear my watch ticking in my pocket. I waited for what seemed an age, glancing at said watch at intervals. Ten past nine o'clock. Twenty past nine o'clock. If Ferald didn't come soon, I thought, I would be late for my class. No matter, I told myself; by then I would be Dean, and it would not be long before I was excused from teaching any classes at all – a delightful prospect, to say the least.

The latch of the massive doors clicked precisely at nine thirty. Edward Ferald, in moss green jacket, his beard shaved to a point, entered the room. Under his arm, he carried an old and worn folder of the sort that we had once used at the college years ago. I stood, but he waved me down. He sat opposite me at the table.

'I have summoned you here today,' Ferald began (no greeting at all; the man's manners were deplorable), '. . . because there is a small matter which has come to my attention.'

'What small matter?' I asked, uttering my first words of our encounter.

Ferald consulted his folder. 'Noah Fitch kept files on all of the men directly under him when he was Hitchcock Professor,' Ferald said. 'I thought it prudent to go into the college archives and find yours, as we are considering you for the post of Dean of Thrupp College. You were at that time an associate professor.'

'Was that necessary?' I asked, suddenly aware of a ribbon of perspiration on my upper lip. Why did Ferald keep the room so warm? I needed my handkerchief, but I would be damned if I would take it out in Ferald's presence.

'And upon reading your file,' Ferald began, 'I find that

there is . . . how shall I put this . . . a disturbing notation.'

'Yes?' I asked.

'It seems,' he said, 'that there was once a question of *plagiarism*.'

Ferald said the word with evident distaste. 'A monograph on the early novels of Sir Walter Scott?' he asked.
'Does that sound familiar to you?'

The perspiration which had begun on my upper lip
now seemed to have blossomed from every pore of my
body, even from my bald pate. 'Scarcely,' I said.

I had no choice now but to take out my handkerchief and wipe my head and face and neck. Ferald smiled
patiently, waiting until I had put the sodden linen away
before he resumed speaking.

'You did have a chat with Noah Fitch regarding your
paper, did you not?'

'We may well have done,' I said. 'I should hardly be
expected to remember a chat that took place . . . when
did you say?'

'In March of 1900.'

'Fourteen years ago.'

'Nevertheless.' Ferald paused. 'This is a charge of
plagiarism, a most serious crime.'

'I believe Noah Fitch apologized to me for bringing
the matter to my attention,' I said. 'Yes, I am certain
that he did.'

'Then you do recall the conversation,' Ferald said.

'I may,' I said, waving my hand as if to shoo the matter
away.

Edward Ferald took a long sip of water from a carafe
on the table. He had thin lips and a pointed tongue
that curled into the glass. 'Water?' he asked.

'No, thank you,' I said.

'Apparently,' Ferald continued, his thirst satisfied, 'Fitch did not think this a minor matter at all. Not if we are to believe his notes.'

'I'm sorry?'

'To be precise,' Ferald began, 'the notation here, in Fitch's handwriting – and I am afraid there can be no question as to its authenticity – reads, in part . . .' Ferald cleared his throat. '*VT denies the accusation of plagiarism regarding his monograph on Scott and its uncanny resemblance to that of Alan Dudley Severance of Amherst College. I've let this go with a severe warning, as VT is a valuable, if uninspired, teacher of rhetoric, and I doubt we should find another on such short notice for the remainder of the term. Nevertheless, VT's scholarship will be examined with utmost care in future. Perhaps a formal review is warranted?*'

'I . . . There was no such review,' I said, the word *uninspired* having pricked my ears.

'No. Quite,' Ferald said, taking another sip of water. 'To this document is appended a series of phrases, also in Fitch's hand, which seem remarkably similar to phrases contained within Severance's monograph, which was published a good number of years before your own paper, and which, by the way, I have read.' Ferald looked up at me and smiled. 'Would you like to see these addenda?'

'No,' I said, 'I would not. I denied the accusation vigorously at the time,' I added, 'and do so now.'

'Yes, yes. No doubt.'

'It is a very old matter,' I said. 'Of no significance.'

Ferald leaned back in his chair. He folded his hands and tucked them under his chin. 'Ah, but there, you see, Van Tassel, I must disagree with you.' I noted that his shirtfront, as ever, was so white as to appear new. Did he have shirts made by the dozens and wear them only once? 'It is, in fact, why I have summoned you here today. You see, any man we elect to the post of Dean must be above reproach,' Ferald added. 'No blots on the record.'

'There are no blots.'

'There is, shall we say, a faint stain.'

'I . . .'

'And if I may say so, Van Tassel, it seems to me that Fitch let the matter go for pragmatic reasons, and not because he didn't think it was true.'

'Pragmatic reasons?' I asked. 'That is an outrageous misinterpretation of the incident.'

'I think I am rather good at interpreting,' Ferald said.

'You were not in your tutorials!' I said before I could stop my mouth.

Ferald smiled. 'No, I was not,' he said. 'A weakness for which I was severely rebuked, as I recall. With a failing grade. An *F*. Which caused me to have to repeat the second term of my third year.'

'A student must accept the consequences of his short-comings,' I said.

'As must a professor,' Ferald said, shutting the folder. 'If you don't withdraw your candidacy, Van Tassel,' (no *Professor* now), 'I shall reveal this indiscretion to the corporators.'

'You cannot . . .'

'But if you withdraw, no one shall hear of this, and you may stay on at the college.'

I blinked. *Stay on at the college?* 'What do you mean?' I asked.

'Keep your job is what I mean,' he said. He worried a vertical line on his forehead. 'This isn't to say that we might not want to review, at a later late, your suitability for the chairmanship of your department.'

I shook my head. I needed time to think. I unbuttoned my suit coat. 'This is monstrous,' I said.

Ferald shrugged, as if to say, *This is scarcely of any importance.*

'And all this because I once failed you in a Scott tutorial?' I asked.

Ferald stood. 'I'll announce your withdrawal at the December fourth meeting,' he said, tucking the aged folder under his arm. He studied me for some time.

I would have stood with him, but for the moment, I could not. My arms were quivering with shock, and my mouth was dry.

'Did you enjoy your tour?' he asked.

'Tour?' I asked, unable to think. 'What tour?'

'Of my house.'

I wanted to undo my collar. 'I have no idea what you mean,' I said.

'The night of my party, Van Tassel. I'm told reliably by a servant that you had a tour of my house.'

'I . . .'

'The pool?' he suggested.

I retrieved my handkerchief from my pocket and wiped my brow.

'The conservatory?' Ferald asked. 'The night of the reception?'

'I . . . I had lost my wife,' I stammered.

Ferald smiled. 'Had you indeed,' he said.

I forced myself to a standing position, though I had to put my hands on the table for balance. I cleared my throat.

'I assume you are aware that Phillip Asher is a Jew,' I said, a man playing his trump card long after all the other players have left the room.

For a moment, Ferald was silent.

'A Jew,' I repeated.

Ferald regarded me curiously. 'Good day, Van Tassel,' he said.

I hardly remember my drive to the college. I parked the motorcar on the lawn and made my way into Chandler Hall to my classroom. I entered the populated chamber (I was late) and sat with weakened legs at my desk. After a time, I glanced up at the young, expectant faces before me.

I did not recognize a soul, not a single one of the astonished visages.

I sat in an attitude of perplexity for some time, the baffled students waiting for a pronouncement. I could think of no words with which to address them. Had I had a stroke, I wondered? Had an occlusion of a blood vessel caused this hideous memory lapse, this quaking in my limbs?

A figure stood in the doorway, and I turned my head. It was Owen Ellington, a junior faculty member. He carried a cup of tea and he, too, looked somewhat perplexed, though kindly so.

'Professor Van Tassel,' he said. 'What a pleasure. What can I do for you?'

I may have offered a greeting. I stood and collected my briefcase. Ellington moved aside, and I stepped out into the hallway. For an uncertain moment, I did not know in which direction to head.

With deliberately careful strides, I went in search of my own classroom. I could think of little but the humiliating scene I had just endured at Ferald's house. What recourse did I have? Could I not tender an appeal? Yes, I thought, I could do that. I would do that at once. Surely I had more respect than Ferald did among the faculty. And yet . . . and yet . . . to bring such an accusation to the notice of the college might end in catastrophe for me. I leaned against a wall. I knew only too well what such a revelation might do to my career.

I found my classroom and entered it. I walked to the desk and sat in the chair. I looked up at my restless and impatient students, who doubtless wondered how it was that Professor Van Tassel had aged so much since just the week before.

As I drove to the settlement house, I felt strangely calm. Familiar with both the Stevens-Duryea and the road, I felt as if I reached Norfolk Street in no time at all. It was not my intention to go inside Baker House, however, or even to make myself known. What I sought that day was invisibility.

I parked in a clearing behind a stand of oaks that had not yet lost their leaves. I did not believe I could be seen from the house, since I could barely make out the building itself; nor did I think I could be detected from the road. I did not want Etna to know that I was there.

A boy on his bicycle and a man in a rough tweed coat and cloth cap walked past without seeing me. Apart from these two souls, I noted no other person during the hour or more I waited in the clearing. Exhausted from the events of the morning as well as my sleepless night, I believe I may have dozed off for a time. I started when I heard a faint sound: a voice, two voices, one of which I recognized. Sitting up, I saw that Etna had emerged from one of the front doors. I watched her call good-bye to a person who remained behind and then walk to her coupe.

I had not thought beyond this point, nor did I know how I should behave. Was I now to follow my own wife like a common detective? And how was this to be accomplished without her knowing I was behind her? The absurdity of this venture pressed itself upon me, and I nearly got out of the car to call to her as I saw her reversing out the driveway. It did not matter now about the strange cottage, I thought. I simply needed to speak with my wife. She would know what I should do in the matter of Edward Ferald and the post. At the very least, she would comfort me.

Almost immediately, however, I lost sight of Etna. I was confident I could again find the cottage, but in this I was mistaken. In trailing her in the rain the day before, I had apparently taken two turns I had not remembered very well. Thus I discovered myself on an unknown road in a heavily wooded area. I stopped the car and got out to look around, thinking there might be a clue in the clear afternoon. There was nothing, and I had no choice but to travel on, hoping to encounter a farmer who could tell me where I was. I did this for another twenty minutes, until I happened upon a small house set a bit back from the road. I knocked at the front door and was told by a slightly startled woman that I was in Vermont. *Vermont!* When had I crossed over the Connecticut River? The woman wasn't entirely sure how to direct me onto the main highway, but she was able to give me directions to a general store at which I received further directions. My nerves frayed to the point of disintegration, I crossed back over the river and made my way to Drury, the town in which I had seen Etna at the cottage.

It took me nearly half an hour more to find the actual estate. I should have to buy a road map, I determined. I parked as I had done the day previous and approached the house, walking not as boldly as I had done before,

223

but rather keeping to the edge of the woods. I slipped silently toward the cottage, in plain view should Etna have happened to glance out the window. But she did not.

She was once again sitting at the small, wobbly table, this time reading a book that she had flattened against the table's surface. She had on a black silk dress with a rose collar, and pink glass beads at her throat. She was bent over the volume, her hands clasped in her lap. As I watched, she leaned her elbow on the table and put her fingers to her forehead, much as I had seen Clara do when studying for her exams. Etna turned a page and put her chin in the palm of her hand. She shifted slightly on the ladder-back chair on which she sat (it cannot have been very comfortable) and crossed her leg over her knee, a gesture she would never have made in public, or even with me in the parlor. Once again, I had the sensation that I was watching a thing set apart, someone who had nothing to do with me. She stretched her arms over her head.

I walked to the front door and entered the room.

She stood and knocked against the table, toppling a saucer to the floor. 'Nicholas,' she said.

'What are you doing here?' I asked, spreading my arms.

She moved so that the ladder-back chair was between us. 'It is my own,' she said.

'What do you mean it is your own?' I asked, taking another step.

She put her hands on the top rung of the chair. A deep flush, in competition with her pink collar, rose to her cheeks. 'It is mine.'

'Etna,' I said, 'I do not understand you.'

'I own this cottage,' she said.

She owned this cottage? That simply wasn't possible. I took a step toward her. She gripped the chair rung but held her ground. 'What are you talking about?' I asked.

'I bought it,' she said.

I listened as if to a foreign language I had neglected to study.

'With what?'

A sudden, if faint, sheen of perspiration popped to her forehead. 'I inherited a painting,' she said.

'Then there *was* a painting,' I said.

'Yes.'

'You lied to me.'

'How did you find me?' she asked.

'I followed you,' I said. 'Yesterday.' I threw off my hat, heedless of where it landed. 'I never saw a Claude Legny.'

'It was in the attic of my sister's house,' Etna said. 'She brought it to me, at my request, last year.'

'Last year? How long have you owned this?'

'Since January.'

I tried to think. That was eleven months ago! 'You have been coming here all this time?'

She didn't answer, but she didn't need to. The answer was plain enough in the domesticity of the scene, the tidied garden at the side of the cottage. She had come to this place in the winter, when snow was all around, and in the spring, when someone had planted phlox by the side of the house. She had come here all during the summer and the early fall, when I had walked beneath the fiery canopy of Wheelock Street. Did the children know about this? Had they ever been here?

I stepped farther into a room that was perhaps twenty feet long and thirty feet wide. As I did so, I noted objects I hadn't seen the day before: a dress form in the corner, books in shelves under the window, a Chinese grass chair. Under the chandelier, there was a small Persian rug. An area near the kitchen was covered with linoleum. On the shelf over the kitchen sink, there was a glass jar of sugar. I looked up at the ceiling.

'The chandelier,' I said. 'You lied about that as well. The day the bill came.'

Etna's grip tightened on the chair.

'You are my wife,' I said.

'I have been a good wife,' she said.

'A good wife with a secret.'

She bent to pick up the pieces of the saucer. 'It did you no harm,' she said.

'No harm?' I asked incredulously. 'No *harm*?'

She stood, the china shards in her hand.

'What do you do here?' I asked, gesturing to include the entire room.

'I do . . .' She looked all around her. 'I read. I sew. I write.'

'Does anyone else know of this?'

'No,' she said.

'Does anyone come here? A lover?'

'No,' she said again, seemingly shocked at the suggestion. 'Of course not.'

I put my hand to my forehead, as if in doing so, I might be better able to think. 'How can I believe anything you say?'

But, in truth, I did believe her. I believed – and still do – that on that day she told me the entire truth; that, in fact, the experience was akin to a sudden torrent of tears – liberating for her and full of relief.

'You have had me all these years,' Etna said quietly. 'You have had the children. I have given you a home. I have been faithful. I have been dutiful.'

226

'Dutiful,' I said. 'You have been cold.'

'Yes, I have. And I have said I am sorry for that. But that has nothing to do with this.'

I walked over to the apothecary cabinet and touched the white tin cake box. Etna took a quick breath.

'When you would ask me for money, at the breakfast table, it was for this?' I asked.

'I had money from the painting.' She put the pieces of the broken saucer on the drainboard beside the sink. 'It was worth more than I thought it would be.'

'This is madness,' I said.

'It is my price,' she said quietly.

'Your what?' I asked, certain I had not heard her correctly.

She raised her chin. 'My price,' she said.

'Your price for what? I know of no other wife who exacts a price.'

'Perhaps they do not,' she said.

I shook my head. 'Has it been so painful to be married to Nicholas Van Tassel that you must exact a price?' I asked. 'Has it been so distressing that you have needed a place to hide?'

'I do not hide,' she said simply.

'Then why have you not told your husband about this?'

'Because it would not then be my own,' she said.

'I do not understand your logic, Etna.'

And, truly, I did not. Had it been a man who maintained a separate dwelling, I might have understood. A dwelling for his mistress, perhaps. One might not condone the action, but one could at least grasp the idea. But for a woman to have such a thing! It was unthinkable.

'This is not meant to be logical, Nicholas.'

'You had a lover before me!' I said explosively, no

longer able to keep this accusation to myself.

In the silence between us, I could hear geese honking overhead. A motorcar along the road. Etna's eyes slid away from mine. She took a long breath that may have contained a faint shudder.

'Who?' I asked, even as I braced myself for the answer.

She leaned against the porcelain lip of the sink. 'It is not important,' she said.

'I demand to know,' I said, summoning all of the putative power of the husband.

She turned and looked out the small window over the tap. 'And I shall not tell you,' she said.

My eyes took in the room once again, alighting on now-familiar objects: the tin cake box, the Gothic window frame, the chandelier. I spread my arms wide. 'Why?' I asked.

She turned back to me. 'This is a thing apart, Nicholas. It is separate. It has nothing to do with you.'

'There can be nothing separate in a union,' I protested.

'If you were wise,' she said, 'you would stop these questions.'

'We had a bargain,' I said.

'Yes. And I have kept my end of it.'

I sat heavily on the ladder-back chair. Etna moved away from the sink. 'Do you have a lover now?' I asked.

'No, I do not.'

'Why else would a woman need a cottage that her husband knows nothing about?' I asked. 'This is what everyone will think.'

'No one will think anything if they do not know.'

I leaned my arms on the wobbly table. 'You would have me become part of your deception?'

She appeared to think a moment. 'No, I would not,' she said finally.

I gestured in the direction of the larger house. 'Who lives there?' I asked, pointing.

'The woman who sold me the cottage.'

'This isn't her property?'

'The driveway divides the two properties.'

I stood and walked to the window, and from there I could see what in the rain the day before hadn't been apparent: the cottage was bordered by a low fence. 'How did you discover this?'

'I saw a notice in the newspaper.'

I walked to an oak wardrobe to one side of the entry and opened it. Inside were two dresses, a smock, and a garden hat. The sight of the dresses and the hat unhinged me, I who was a door waiting to fall from its frame. I swung my arm across the wardrobe and swept the clothing from its hangers. I flailed, a wild boar after all. I moved away from the wardrobe and tore a linen drape from its window.

'Nicholas,' Etna said.

I kicked over the enameled bucket, sending dried hydrangeas skidding across the floor. I ripped a small picture from its hook. Etna slid away from me, inches from my grasp.

'Nicholas, stop!' she cried.

Would I have hit my wife? No, I do not believe I would. I wished only to violate that room. I opened a cabinet and took out a plate and flung it against a wall. Etna made a sound, and I turned. There was an expression of such alarm on her face that it brought me to my senses. I stumbled forward and collapsed on the davenport, amazed that it held my violent weight.

I put my head in my hands.

I had been cuckolded by a house.

'I will not get the post,' I said.

'Nonsense,' Etna said.

'I have been told.'

'When?'

'This morning. By Edward Ferald.'

'Nicholas,' she said, moving toward me.

'Don't,' I said, putting up a hand. I didn't want her sympathy. Her coldness I could just about bear. But her pity? Never again, I told myself. Never again.

Etna stopped and crossed her arms over her chest. 'I am so very sorry.'

'Tell me your lover was not Phillip Asher.'

'It was not.'

'But you knew him.'

'Hardly at all. I've told you this.'

I sat forward on the davenport. 'It was his brother, then. Samuel. He was your lover.'

Etna briefly closed her eyes. When she opened them, I saw that she was crying.

'Did you know that Phillip Asher was coming to Thrupp?' I asked.

She shook her head. 'I knew nothing until I heard his name at the reception.'

'Ferald's reception.'

'Yes.'

'It's why you dropped the champagne glass.'

'Yes,' she said.

'It's why you shut yourself away all those weeks. You haven't been grieving for William; it is grief for some other.'

'That is a monstrous accusation,' she said.

'You married me under false pretenses,' I said.

Etna pulled a pin from her hair. She sometimes did this in moments of private anguish. 'I did not,' she said. 'You never asked about my former life.'

'It is understood that such a thing is to be confessed before marriage,' I said, somewhat distracted by the sight of the cascade of acorn-colored hair falling from the undone knot.

'And did you not have lovers before me?' she asked, shaking her hair along her shoulders.

'Don't be absurd, Etna. That is hardly the point.'

'It's very much the point,' she said. 'You have had your freedom.'

'I don't *want* my freedom,' I shouted quite truthfully. 'Since the day I met you, I have wanted no freedom.'

'But I have wanted mine!'

I stood in a panic of irresolution. 'Where do they go?' I asked, pointing to a narrow flight of stairs.

'To another room. An attic room,' she said, as I pushed past her. 'But there is nothing up there.'

The stairs were so steep, I had to use my hands. When I got to the top, I looked around and saw an attic room with gabled sides that allowed me to stand only in its center spine. It was sparsly furnished, though there were curtains on the two windows at either end. There was a white iron bedstead with a mattress and a sewing machine cabinet. At the foot of the iron bed was a cedar chest. I opened it and saw a folded quilt. I recognized the quilt as one that had once been on our marriage bed.

I sank to my knees and put my head in my hands.

After a time, I walked back down the stairs. Etna was still standing near the sink.

'I assume you know that Phillip Asher is a Jew,' I said.

She blinked. 'Yes, of course,' she said after a moment.

'You took a Jew as a lover?'

Her mouth opened and then closed. 'This is beneath you, Nicholas,' she said.

'I'm amazed, Etna. I didn't think you capable of such a thing.'

She was angry now. 'How can you think my heart and mind not capable of accepting a Jewish man?' she asked, her voice rising. 'Of loving him?'

'The heart may love, but the mind does not,' I said fatuously. 'The heart has no mind, and the mind has no heart. They are two separate organs, often at war with each other.'

'You are deluded,' she said. 'Your own mind, certainly, is wanting.'

'My *heart* is wanting and I mean that in another way entirely. You knew that Phillip Asher was a Jew, and yet you said nothing, even though it may have aided my candidacy to do so?' I asked.

'Stop this!' she cried. 'You are a fool, Nicholas.'

'This is grounds for divorce,' I said.

The room went deathly quiet, as if awed by the pronouncement.

'You would not divorce me,' Etna said.

'I would,' I said.

(But why had I said such a thing? I wondered. I did not want a divorce. No, no, it was the *last* thing I wanted.)

'You are too rash,' Etna said, and I noticed that her hands were shaking.

'It is *you* who have been rash.'

She backed up a step and sat on the Chinese grass chair. The strength in her legs had at last deserted her.

'You have been coming here secretly for eleven months,' I said. '*That* was rash. You have lied to your husband. *That* was rash.'

Etna shook her head.

'A divorce is a most unhappy act,' I said, bending to pick up my hat from the floor.

Etna made a sound, and if it was a plea, I do not know, for I had opened the door, walked out into the cold, and started down the driveway. I found the motorcar as a blind man will make his way to a house he does not want to enter. I opened the door and sat down. I gripped the steering wheel and would have shaken it loose from its mooring if I had had the strength. I flung myself back against the tufted leather seat, and as I did so, a quotation from *Paradise Lost* rose up through the earth and the floorboards of the motorcar and mocked me with its precision.

. . . Yet well, if here would end
The misery, I deserv'd it, and would bear
My own deservings.

(Book X, ll. 725–727; Adam speaking; in despair over the lost glorious world; knowing his descendants will curse him; wanting only death. Some of Milton's better lines, I think.)

The Hotel Thrupp
October 19, 1914

Dear Mrs. Van Tassel,

This is a difficult matter I write about, and forgive me if I assume unhappiness where none exists, but after having seen your face in Mr. Ferald's hallway tonight, as we were all waiting for our carriages and motorcars to be brought around, I cannot think other than that you were shocked to find me in that house. I had met Professor Van Tassel earlier in the day, but I did not know that he was your husband. Indeed, I did not know that you had married. I write to say that however pleasant it was to see you again, it was never my intention to cause either you or your husband any distress by my appearance in Thrupp. Had I known that you resided here, I assure you I would not have accepted the kind offer of the college to deliver the Kitchner Lectures.

Having committed to this series, however, I find myself in Thrupp for the duration of the term. Worse, it would appear that both your husband and I have been invited to apply to the post of Dean of the Faculty of Thrupp College. After seeing you this evening, I am determined

237

to excuse myself from consideration of the post and to
return to New Haven as soon as the lectures are over.
 With warmest expressions of good will,
 Phillip Asher

Holyoke Street
October 20, 1914

Dear Professor Asher,

Thank you for your kind letter of October 19.
It is generous of you to offer to excuse yourself
from consideration for the post of Dean of the
Faculty of Thrupp College, but please understand
that if it were in my power to do so, under no
circumstances would I ever permit this. Indeed, I
should take it as an insult were you to leave
Thrupp on my account. Though I believe my husband to be the best candidate for the post, his
petition, and ultimate success, would be tarnished
were his competitor to have left because of a distant encounter with his wife. Please assure me at
your earliest opportunity that you will do no such
thing.
 Very respectfully yours,
 Etna Van Tassel

The Hotel Thrupp
October 21, 1914

Dear Mrs. Van Tassel,
 Thank you for your prompt reply to my letter of
October 19. I will honor your request, though I am not
at all confident that this is the right course of action. (It
would appear that the deliverer of the Kitchner Lectures
on the nature of private gain vs. public good is no more
able to answer a simple question of common decency than

is a student.) Since that evening at Mr. Ferald's reception, I have wished that I had never heard of the Kitchner Lectures. My family has caused you enough distress, and I do not want to add to it in any way.

I had occasion on the morning following Mr. Ferald's reception to meet your husband in the Hotel Thrupp. We had a pleasant chat, and as I had no indication from him that he knew anything of past difficulties between you and my family, I said nothing to him at that time. It was an awkward moment, however, one that may cause a breach of trust in the near future. It would appear that I am to dine with you at your house on Sunday. Since it is entirely your decision how I should proceed in this matter, I await your reply.

Your most devoted,
Phillip Asher

Holyoke Street
October 22, 1914

Dear Professor Asher,

To answer your letter of October 21, I should just like to say that it was not your family who caused me distress. Nor was it your brother. What distress I suffered was entirely my own, and I alone am responsible for it. I was of sufficient age to understand the consequences of my actions and to accept them. Indeed, I have reason to be grateful to your brother and to the circumstances of leaving him. A marriage to Mr. Bass of Brockton would have been disastrous for any number of reasons. My relationship to your brother, Samuel, put a necessary, if difficult, end to that betrothal, for which I will always be glad.

As to the matter of my husband and future trust, I see no reason to discuss with him an incident of so long ago. I hope that you will come to our house on Sunday and that my husband and I will come to know you as the Phillip Asher who has so recently arrived in Thrupp.

With much respect,
Etna Van Tassel

The Hotel Thrupp
October 30, 1914

Dear Mrs. Van Tassel,

I wish to express my deepest sympathies upon the death of your uncle, William Bliss. Although, sadly, I did not know the man, the high esteem in which he was held by the entire Thrupp College community is only too evident. If I may be of service to you in any way during this difficult time, please do not hesitate to let me know.

Your obedient servant,
Phillip Asher

Holyoke Street
November 14, 1914

Dear Professor Asher,

Forgive me for having taken so long to acknowledge your kind letter of sympathy. My Uncle William was a loving husband, devoted father, and an esteemed professor. He will be much missed. I am sorry, too, that you were not able to meet him. I am sure the two of you would have enjoyed each other's company.

Your humble friend,
Etna Van Tassel

The Hotel Thrupp
November 16, 1914

Dear Mrs. Van Tassel,

I should not like to intrude upon your period of mourning except to say that I am sorry I did not attend the funeral service of William Bliss. I thought, under the circumstances, it would be best to stay away.

With perfect consideration for your loss,
Phillip Asher

Holyoke Street
November 18, 1914

Dear Mr. Asher,

I assure you that you gave us no offense by not attending my uncle's funeral service. There were many there to mourn him, including, we were most gratified to see, a good number of his former students. This was, I think, a great testament to his success as a teacher of physics.

I do not know when next my husband and I shall be able to invite you to our house for dinner. I find that I have been hit unexpectedly hard by the loss of my uncle. Why, I do not know, since I had ample warning of his death. It seems to have opened a vein of feeling that I thought I had successfully closed. My father died shortly after the unhappy incident with your brother, and I think those two events and this one are linked in my heart.

I hope your brother is well. I should be grateful for any news of him.

Affectionately yours,
Etna Bliss Van Tassel

November 20, 1914

Dear Mrs. Van Tassel,

My brother is in London, having been seconded to the Admiralty for the duration of the war in Europe. All that he is able to tell us about his work is that it has to do with astronomy and navigation, which, as you may recall, was his field when he was teaching at Exeter. My brother emigrated to Toronto shortly after his relationship with you ended. He has been a professor of Astronomy and Navigation in Toronto since 1897. Samuel's wife, Ardith, and their four children will remain in that city until such time as it is safe to travel to London. We all pray for a swift and just end to the conflict in Europe.

I must tell you that the memory of your arrival at my parents' home on that snowy January morning is among the most meaningful of my early adulthood. It was on that day that I first glimpsed the ferocity of love that lies behind the veil of polite comportment. It was a terrible moment for all concerned, but one which I have carried with me for years. I cannot condone or entirely forgive my brother's behavior that day, nor have I ever understood it. Indeed, it was years before we were able to have an honest conversation or correspondence.

Believe me affectionately yours,
Phillip Asher

Holyoke Street
November 23, 1914

Dear Mr. Asher,

I am deeply sorry to learn that I was, however peripherally, the cause of a rift between you and your brother. I hope such a rift is well and truly healed. Samuel and I had a difficult, not to say impossible, situation, and he did what he felt was entirely necessary. Over time, I have come to understand that decision and make peace with it. Samuel had many wonderful qualities, and I loved him deeply. Whatever you saw on my face that day was genuine.

I do not remember seeing you in that house on that snowy morning. I daresay that my mission and my subsequent unhappiness blinded me to the presence of everyone but your brother. I do remember a tennis game at the school courts, however. As I recall, you hit the ball well over the fence and out onto the street.

I hope you will have a pleasant Thanksgiving in Thrupp, though I am sure you will miss your family in Exeter.

Your humble friend,
Etna Van Tassel

The Hotel Thrupp
November 24, 1914

Dear Mrs. Van Tassel,

I am pleasantly embarrassed to think you recall that dreadful shot into the street. I confess I have never been an accomplished tennis player.

Your husband has sent round a note just now asking me to your house for a drink at half past five o'clock tonight. I feel I cannot decline, but I wish I could speak with you on the matter before I go. I look forward to seeing you should you be there this evening.

In the matter to which we have been referring in our previous correspondence, let me just say that the sight of your face on that morning so many years ago has remained for me a standard by which I judge my own affection for any woman with whom I am close, and the affection of any woman for me. I count you among the most fortunate of persons to have felt so strongly for another human being, however unhappy the outcome. Is this not the point of our existence?

Your devoted,

Phillip Asher

The Hotel Thrupp
November 25, 1914

Dear Mrs. Van Tassel,

I scarcely know what to write to you this morning. Though your husband was in no way inhospitable, it was clear to me last evening that he very much minds my presence in Thrupp. Indeed, he delivered what can only be taken as an ultimatum. It has made me realize how inappropriate it is for me to continue to write to you. It causes me great sadness to have to say this, but I do not think we can continue this correspondence, innocent though it has been.

It was a pleasure to see you — however briefly — last night at your home. Permit me to say that you have grown only more lovely with the years.

Yours in affection,

Phillip Asher

Holyoke Street
November 27, 1914

Dear Mr. Asher,

I am very sorry if there was any unpleasantness between you and my husband, Nicholas. I cannot enter into that debate, nor do I wish to know any more about it. While you might be right about my husband's distress were he to discover this

244

correspondence, I trust I am capable of determining on my own whether or not it should continue.

Sincerely,
Etna Van Tassel

The Hotel Thrupp
November 29, 1914

Dear Mrs. Van Tassel,

I did not mean to insult your independence or judgment. Forgive me if I have. But it cannot have escaped your notice that we are in possession of facts about which your husband has no knowledge. While this correspondence has been, as I say, innocent enough, the fact of it, in light of his feelings toward me, so recently revealed, cannot be entirely blameless. Nevertheless, I shall follow your lead in this matter, since I cannot presume to know your husband or your marriage as you do. Indeed, I do not know either him or it at all.

I spent most of the Thanksgiving holiday reading and taking walks. Mr. Ferald and his wife were kind enough to invite me to dine with them at their house for the Thanksgiving meal itself. Though it was only Edward and Millicent and myself, we sat at an elaborate table and partook of a feast such as I have scarcely ever seen. I should not want to sound ungrateful for their hospitality, but I did miss, at times, the noisy bustle of a meal in Exeter at our overcrowded table, and I wished I had taken the trouble to travel there and back for the duration of the holiday.

No matter. The term resumes tomorrow, and I am to deliver the fifth and final of the Kitchner Lectures on Wednesday. I shall attend now to my notes.

With perfect consideration,
Phillip Asher

Dear Mrs. Van Tassel,

I do not know if this will reach you. I had occasion to speak with Gerard Moxon this morning, and he said that you had returned to Exeter. My dear Mrs. Van Tassel, what has happened? Your husband has said publicly that your sister is gravely ill and that you and the children have gone there to tend to her. If this is so, then I cannot say how sorry I am. But I must tell you that Mr. Moxon, in confidence, suggested otherwise. (It is a confidence I promise you I shall share with no one, though I cannot vouch for Mr. Moxon; he is quite innocently incapable of keeping a secret, I think.) Mrs. Van Tassel, I am unhappy for you if what Mr. Moxon says is true. Please write to me to tell me if he and I have got it wrong. I do not wish to pry in any way, and I am sure you have excellent reasons for leaving Thrupp, but if there has been a marital breach, I urge you to repair it by any means. It cannot be good for either you or the children to have been forced to leave your family home.

My distress on your account is exacerbated by the fact that your husband withdrew his candidacy for the position of Dean of Thrupp College, and I was two days ago elected to the post. I have until the eleventh of December to tender my decision. I feel I must have some word from you before I do. I pray that I have not been, in any way, responsible for either a rift between you and Professor Van Tassel or the cause of his change of heart. Please reassure me on this point, and, further, please say if you do not wish me to accept the post, tarnished as it is with the unhappy fact of your husband's withdrawal. I should not like to take advantage of another man's difficult situation.

Professor Van Tassel has sent round a note to all con-

cerned saying that he relinquished any thought of the post of Dean in order to better attend to his duties as department chair. I find this difficult to credit, not only because that was a position your husband seemed to handle with ease, but also because I know how keenly he wanted the post of Dean.

Your devoted and concerned friend,
Phillip Asher

The Thrupp Hotel
December 11, 1914

Dear Mrs. Van Tassel,

I write to tell you that in the absence of any word from you, I have accepted the post of Dean of Thrupp College. I officially take up my duties at the start of the new term. I will shortly move out of the hotel into a rented house at 14 Gill Street, but if you should write to me between now and January 10, you may send it to the hotel, and they will forward any mail to me. I hope that you and your children are well.

Very respectfully yours,
Phillip Asher

14 Gill Street
January 6, 1915

Dear Mrs. Van Tassel,

I write to tell you that I have shifted residences from the Thrupp Hotel to 14 Gill Street, and should you wish to answer this or any of my previous letters, you may do so there. I am renting a small house in anticipation of beginning my new job at Thrupp.

I hope you and your children were able to pass a happy Christmas with your sister and her family.

Yours,
Phillip Asher

Exeter

January 15, 1915

Dear Mr. Asher,

    Forgive my silence.

    Etna Van Tassel

14 Gill Street

January 18, 1915

Dear Mrs. Van Tassel,

    You do not need my forgiveness for your silence. It is perfectly understandable. I wish you a swift and happy conclusion to your difficult circumstances.

    Phillip Asher

Exeter

January 22, 1915

Dear Mr. Asher,

    I put these questions to you as an ethicist. Is a woman, married and with children, entitled to reserve a portion of her life for her own and exclusive use? May such a woman, if she decides that in doing so no harm will come to either her children or her husband, be permitted to retire to an inviolable place, a place to which only she has access, in which only she resides, for the benign and innocent purposes of gentle education and recreation, which might encompass activities such as reading and sewing and possibly the writing of letters or of poetry? Is not a man of a certain education accorded, without difficulty from any party, an inviolable retreat of his own, one in which neither wife nor child is welcome, one in which he may read or smoke or write or engage in contemplation, or even entertain certain friends and colleagues, a room that is commonly called a study or an office or a library? And if so, why then is a woman − married and with children − not entitled to a similar retreat? And if this woman should discover that no retreat may be had within her own home, owing to the traffic of children and servants and even her own husband, who sees no violation in entering such a retreat, and because of the lack of respect for such a place of solitude, is she not then allowed to seek retreat elsewhere, such as at a resident hotel or boardinghouse or at a cottage in a rural area, outside of town, some miles away from the family abode, the whereabouts of which is unknown to any family relative?

I await your reply to these questions, as they are ones I am struggling with moment to moment and which are at the very heart of what you have accurately heard is considerable marital discord.

With respect for your judgment,
Etna Bliss Van Tassel

14 Gill Street
January 27, 1915

Dear Mrs. Van Tassel,

You do me a great honor by confiding in me the details of your marital discord and by assuming that I might be able to help you answer these difficult questions. But I must tell you that I am an academic only and not a superior judge of either human or marital behavior. I am not married, nor have I ever been. Marriage is a special province, the residents of which have access to a knowledge and a language all their own, one that cannot be had by any other means than to be married. (It is for this reason that I have always thought unmarried clergy and magistrates particularly poor counselors for those who seek redress for marital grievances.) But as I am a scholar, I will, if you will permit me, put to you questions that in answering may give you increased insight into your own difficulties.

Is not the personal retreat of this putative husband you speak of — the inviolable retreat within the house that we commonly call the study or the library — agreed upon, in essence, by both parties of a marriage when they take up residence at that specific abode and a room is so designated for that purpose? Or, put another way, can a retreat not agreed upon by both parties of a marriage, or not even known about by one party of a marriage, be accorded the same respect? Might not a wife have reason to distrust a husband were she to discover that he had rented a room in secret, even if the husband planned only to read and write and think in such a place? Might not the discovery of such a room put too great a burden on the fragile thread of marital trust between a man and his wife?

Mrs. Van Tassel, I can only guess at your circumstances, having no knowledge of them. More important, I have no knowledge of your health or well-being. These are serious questions that you ask me, disturbing in their nature, more disturbing since I am in a position to see your husband daily; and I must tell you, as a reporter only, that he is hardly in a fit state to teach a class of young men. I have twice given him leave so that he may travel back and forth to Exeter, and have suggested a sabbatical, as he is certainly deserving of it. Your husband would seem to be a proud man, however, as he has refused this offer. By all accounts, he is in a seriously overstressed state, one that concerns many of his colleagues and friends.

I do not know how your unhappy story shall end, but I implore you to consider returning to Thrupp with your children and repairing, with time and sacrifice, the marriage to which you have committed yourself.

Your humble friend,
Phillip Asher

Exeter
February 3, 1915

Dear Mr. Asher,

You write to me as a man and not as a friend. I do not need to be told to return to Thrupp to repair a broken marriage. That judgment I am more than capable of placing on myself. I was hoping that you might, <u>as a friend only</u>, give me guidance as to the ethical issues involved.

Sincerely,
Etna Bliss Van Tassel

14 Gill Street
February 7, 1915

Dear Mrs. Van Tassel,

I think there is a strong argument to be made that all marriages might be improved if both husband and wife had a private place to which to retreat for the contemplation — in solitude — of issues that the daily noise of life does not permit. But questions of right or wrong can exist only within a framework of convention, the circumstances agreed to by any society. In our society, at this moment, neither a man nor a woman who is married may rent or own a private and separate abode about which the spouse knows nothing. I do not speak about the legal ramifications of such an action (I suspect it is not illegal to own or rent such a room), but rather of the moral. Without trust, there can be no marriage, and a secret as large as a rented house or room puts too great a burden on that trust.

Mrs. Van Tassel, I am in a difficult position. I wish to be your friend and to give you what guidance I have in my power to bestow. But I know so little of your particular situation beyond the observable effects upon your husband. It is my understanding that your son has returned to Thrupp, but that your daughter and you have not. The presence of your son seems to have had a beneficial and salutary effect on Professor Van Tassel. He appears, at least for the moment, to have largely recovered his equanimity.

Yours,
Phillip Asher

Exeter
February 11, 1915

Dear Mr. Asher,

I am grateful to you for conveying to me the improved condition of my husband. It has been achieved, however, at great cost to me. I find myself now embroiled in a battle for the protection and custody of my son, Nicodemus, who is hardly of an age to understand why he has been separated from his mother. Theoretical issues of privacy and solitude within a marriage have vanished in the face of the very real issue of child custody, to which I am now employing all of my wits and about which I pray constantly.

Forgive me for not having apprised you of the details of our marital discord, and forgive me further for not having the necessary strength to do so now. I am grateful for your understanding, and am sorry you are in the difficult position of being privy to the thoughts of the wife even as you are the supervisor of the husband. It is an awkward position I have placed you in, and one from which I now release you. I have realized that it is inappropriate in the extreme to be writing to you in the manner in which I have, and so I shall, with immense gratitude for your patience and solicitude, stop.

With perfect consideration,
Etna Bliss Van Tassel

14 Gill Street
February 15, 1915

Dear Mrs. Van Tassel,

My constitution and wits are, I trust, sufficiently strong to be able to read your letters and to 'supervise' your husband, who, in any event, needs no supervision of any sort that I can offer him. I should be distressed to think I had given you any indication that our correspondence should cease because of a burden upon me. If I can offer any assistance, if only to be a sounding board of sorts, then please allow me to be. Though you do not wish me to mention that earlier matter regarding my family, I cannot forget it, and it assuages my familial conscience, if you will, to be of help to you.

Believe me always your friend,
Phillip Asher

Exeter
February 20, 1915

Dear Mr. Asher,

Thank you for your letter of February 15th. I have realized that in all these weeks we have written only of me and that I have not asked a single question about your new life. Forgive me. I have been, I am afraid, too self-involved to think of others, and reluctant to ask how you are settling into a position I still believe my husband should have had. Though his recent behavior toward me has been most objectionable, and I have been the recipient of his explicit and unreserved anger, I have great sympathy for his lost possibilities. Please do tell me of yourself. Are you settling in on Gill Street?

Since the veil of polite comportment was dropped so many years ago, don't you think it would be more appropriate to address me as Etna? It is, after all, as Etna that you knew me when we played tennis with your brother and your father.

Most sincerely,
Etna

14 Gill Street
March 3, 1915

Dear Etna,

There you go again, reminding me of that horrid tennis date.

I am pleased to be invited to call you Etna and shall do so. Thank you as well for inquiring about my life, which though academically satisfying is largely uneventful on a personal level. This is just as well, I think, since I find I must devote nearly all of my energies to my new post. In that regard, Gill Street is a good address. It is comfortably furnished and well run and the cook is remarkably competent for a college town (my cook in New Haven was appalling), so I have no complaints.

It is, however, difficult to write of my new life when yours is in so much turmoil. The dinners to which I go

*and the meager social life Thrupp has on offer (your hus-
band did warn me about this) pale into insignificance
when compared with the struggle in which you are
involved.*

*I did, on the advice of Gerard Moxon, take up snow
skiing this winter, which was, at best, a highly comical
endeavor.*

Fondly,
Phillip

Exeter
March 9, 1915

Dear Phillip,

I cannot express to you how distressed and troubled I am at the removal of my son from my protection. It is not just the personal sadness that
sweeps over me so many times during the day – a
kind of emptying out of any joy in the moment
and then a filling up, as of a well, with sorrow –
it is the knowledge that my Nicodemus is in the
custody of his father, who has shown himself to
be so violent in his temper and so disturbed by
our marital circumstances that I fear he will be, at
best, a preoccupied parent, and at worst a frightening one. Is this retribution for my wanting the
solace of occasional solitude? Swift and devastating
retribution, if it is, and, I cannot help but think,
so much greater than the crime.

So it is with some trepidation, born out of
parental love and necessity, that I shall be returning
to Thrupp so that I may be nearer to my son. It
is my hope that I shall be allowed to see him on
a frequent, not to say regular, basis until such time
as I am able to regain custody of him. I cannot tell

you my future address at this moment, but as I shall be leaving Exeter before the week is out, I do not think it wise to write to me again until you hear from me.

With respect,
Etna

My dearest Phillip,

Would you be kind enough to meet me at the Payne Street Market in Worthington at ten o'clock next Thursday morning? There is something I should like to show you.

E. VT.

A marriage is always two intersecting stories. I can tell only mine. As for her story (as for *their* story), I was not privy to it apart from the letters I was to find in Etna's tin cake box, letters I append here with a clip, somewhat reluctantly, not only because of their revealing (and, to me, dismaying) content, but also because I rather liked the slim, neat package my leather journal made, as if a life could be contained within its elaborately tooled covers.

Etna was by nature a reticent individual, not given to verbal displays of emotion, and therefore hardly likely to have apprised me of her relationship with Phillip Asher. Had it not been for my accidental discovery of Etna's and Asher's correspondence (my hand nervously strumming the front of the tin cake box, thus tripping the latch of the door), I might never have been aware of it, for it almost certainly would have been destroyed in the fire. I cannot say that the enigma that was my wife is entirely revealed to me here, but some questions are answered.

I learn in Etna's letter of October 22 that she had once been engaged to a Mr. Bass from Brockton, but that the betrothal had been broken off. It is a wonder such a fact was kept from me, that William Bliss, in all innocence, did not reveal it, or that Keep, not so innocently, did not seek to wound (or rather nick) me with this bit of information. A betrothal in those days was a serious matter and nearly as difficult to undo as a marriage. I can conclude only that William Bliss, after having seen me disintegrate so completely upon the news that Etna had left for Exeter to become a governess for Keep's children, thought it best not to trouble me with facts that were, after all, not his to tell. Indeed, both Bliss and Keep might well have imagined that Etna had already discussed the matter with me. Most women would have done so, but, as we have seen, Etna was not like most women. Etna was a woman of secrets.

Indeed, what was I to think of what is clearly revealed in the correspondence to have been a passionate love affair between Etna and Samuel Asher? Truth to tell, this revelation was not as agonizing as I might have expected – I who have shown myself to be quite capable of agony on any number of occasions. In fact, this knowledge was almost a relief, for somehow *I had always known*. I remember speculating even on the first day I met Etna as to whether she had had one or many lovers before me. A woman who has known love has about her an aura of having been – how shall I put this, I do not wish to be indelicate here – *plundered* is the only word I can think of, and I do not think it an inaccurate one in this circumstance. Etna had been plundered, soul and body, however willingly, by Samuel Asher. I will not now dwell upon the images that this avenue of thought produces; suffice it to say that the senses have an intellect that may be denied the conscious mind, and that my senses accurately detected, on my unpleasant wedding night, more than just a previous deflowering of my bride. Etna had been well and truly loved.

I cannot ever know the nature and duration of that love affair. It is not a question I can ask anyone – not Phillip Asher, who, in any event, might not have known a great deal about it (he was only a boy of seventeen at the time); and certainly not Samuel Asher, who may or may not even be alive at this writing. All I have are phrases from the correspondence, more revealing on Phillip Asher's part than on Etna's.

Though Etna asserts that her love was genuine, it is Asher who speaks of passion. 'The ferocity of love that lies behind the veil of polite comportment,' he writes. And this: 'The sight of your face on that morning so many years ago has remained for me a standard by which I judge my own affection for any woman with whom I am close, and the affection of any woman for me. I count you among the most fortunate of persons to have felt so strongly for another human being, however unhappy the outcome. *Is this not the point of our existence?*' (Italics mine.)

We can only imagine what happened 'that snowy morning' in Exeter. Had Etna gone to the house to confront Samuel? To tell him that she had broken off her engagement to the man from Brockton? And why was it necessary to seek Samuel out at his house? Had he already withdrawn from the relationship? Was he about to leave for Canada? Was he engaged to another? And what precisely was the nature of the 'unhappy incident' in the 'overcrowded' house in Exeter? Were there declarations of love? Were there tears? And why, years later, does Phillip Asher find it necessary to apologize for the behavior of his family? Or does he mean by *family* only his brother?

I have pictured the event in detail. (Are not imagined events sometimes more real than events at which one is present?) It is the summer of 1896. Etna, just twenty-three, is engaged to a Mr. Bass of Brockton, Massachusetts, a Mr. *Josiah* Bass, shall we say, an older man, perhaps thirty-six or thirty-eight. He is a man whom Etna does not love, but whose shoe-manufacturing fortune promises her some independence, which, as we now know, is of paramount importance to Etna Bliss, even if she herself does not understand this yet. In the meantime, a Mr. Samuel Asher, tall like his brother, twenty-seven, an academic with – I am just guessing here – a high forehead (perhaps a slightly receding hairline?), a blond beard, and sloping shoulders, has recently had occasion to visit Etna's father, William's brother, Thomas Bliss, an educated and tolerant man who would not shrink from inviting a Jew to his house – particularly an English Jew. (Or does Bliss simply not know about Samuel Asher, who for years may well have been passing for an Episcopalian?) Was this a jointly taught course on the mathematics of navigation? A research project? A steering committee of two? We cannot know. Etna and Samuel have two or three times found themselves alone in the Bliss sitting room while Thomas has been attending to other matters, and they have discovered in each other like-minded souls. They have, at least once, played tennis with Samuel's father and his younger brother Phillip. (Do they discuss astronomy? No, probably not.) Samuel and Etna look forward to their encounters and contrive to make them happen. Samuel Asher, attracted beyond reason to this striking daughter of Thomas Bliss, even as he is engaged to Ardith Silver of Toronto, Ontario, a woman he met when her family lived in Exeter prior to moving to that Canadian city, manages to come round to the Bliss house even when he knows (though he pretends to forget) that Thomas Bliss is engaged elsewhere. (We will not imagine for Samuel the baser motive of needing female company while his intended is elsewhere.) A summer acquaintance turns to autumnal friendship and then swiftly molts into something very like passion before Christmas.

Indeed, Samuel Asher calls upon the Bliss family on Christmas Eve to bid them a happy holiday. Thomas, who does not yet have any inkling about his betrothed friend's secret affection for his betrothed daughter, welcomes Samuel into the house. Etna is in the parlor with her mother and Miriam (Pippa already being married and living in Massachusetts), making last-minute adjustments to an impressive Christmas tree that will be lit within the hour. On the sideboard is a cut-crystal bowl of punch, liberally laced with rum. Etna is wearing a plum velvet dress with perhaps a slightly revealing neckline, and she looks almost beautiful on this occasion. Samuel, cheeks reddened by the weather and his anticipation, greets Etna's mother, then Miriam, and finally, when all other formalities have been observed, Etna, whose cheeks are as red as his. (Might not Thomas, were he alert to romantic oscillations, have detected something amiss in the greeting of Miriam before Etna? Perhaps not.) Thomas mentions how much Samuel must miss his fiancée on the holiday. Samuel agrees politely even as he notes the tiny flinch in Etna's lovely white shoulders.

(And where is Josiah Bass, Etna's intended? Away. He is simply away.)

How will Samuel negotiate this tricky evening? For he has a gift he wishes to bestow upon Etna. He cannot give it to her in front of the mother and the sister, because he has not brought them gifts as well. Nor can he give it under Thomas's scrutiny, for Thomas, though a scientist, would surely detect an unnatural favoritism in the singling out of Etna. A walk is therefore contrived – casually, politely. Samuel invites Mrs. Bliss first, praying that she won't accept. She does not; it is too cold for her. Etna accepts readily, speaking of the pleasure of seeing smoke emanating from other houses, of encountering carolers along the way. Miriam is tired, she says, and miraculously she declines.

Scarcely able to conceal his relief, Samuel moves with Etna to the vestibule, where they dress for the cold, each carefully avoiding the gaze of the other. Each is aware of a sense of conspiracy at this point, though neither gives anything away.

The pair walk in silence for some time – not toward the houses with the warm fires, as it happens, but away from them. They reach one of the many playing fields of the men's preparatory school. Together they look at its snowy expanse, lit by a Christmas moon.

'Etna,' Samuel says.

He gives Etna the package, which she holds in her gloved hand a moment before opening it. (It hurts me to have to imagine that she has considerably more enthusiasm for this unopened gift than she did for my own on the college path, but there it is.) There is fumbling with stiffened fingers as Etna undoes the ribbon. The silver gleams in the moonlight. Samuel takes Etna's hand, removes her glove, and slides the bracelet onto her wrist, nearly as white as the moon. Pointedly, he does not release her wrist.

'I had to give you something,' he says.

'I cannot accept it,' she says.

'You must accept it. You can wear it privately.'

'I am engaged to be married,' Etna says, stating the perfectly obvious.

'As am I,' Samuel says.

Samuel kisses Etna then in a way I think we can safely say Etna has never been kissed before, certainly not by Josiah Bass, for whom we shall invent imperfect teeth and slightly metallic breath. Asher's kiss unleashes a previously unknown physical response from Etna, and for a few moments she is lost to the world, heedless and uncaring: all that exists is Samuel, to whom she is unreasonably and powerfully attracted. She doesn't entirely understand what is happening to her (not as Samuel does, for example), and so she labels the fluttering in her abdomen and the erratic beating of her heart *love* and assigns to it a deathless quality. Already she is imagining an elopement, a sacrificing of her honor.

He loves her, Samuel declares. He says so in the moonlight. He begs her to meet him again – in secret this time – the day after Christmas. He has a suite of rooms at the school, he says, nearly empty now because of the holiday. Etna, quite calm, agrees.

The holiday passes. Etna and Samuel meet in his rooms at one o'clock on the 26th as planned. Etna removes her coat. Samuel slides back the cuff of her dress, revealing the bracelet. He kisses the underside of her wrist. Etna closes her eyes. There is a moment, we shall imagine, when neither of them moves. Then caution is abandoned.

(The reader must imagine the details of Etna's subsequent deflowering for himself. I haven't the heart to describe them.)

Later, lying on a rug in Asher's study, Etna tells Asher that she will leave the unfortunate Mr. Bass. Asher tells

Etna she must not do that. In the aftermath of passion, he has the clearer head of the two of them; a fickle sense of honor is reasserting itself. He tells her he cannot allow her to disgrace herself in such a way. There is no future, he insists. There is only the moment they now have together.

Etna, somewhat bewildered, acquiesces to her new lover.

Etna and Asher meet three times that week in Samuel's rooms, discovering in each other a sexual compatibility so intense as to be almost frightening. On the fourth meeting, just before the term is to resume, Etna once again says she will break her engagement. Samuel is alternately angry and distraught. His own wedding is only a month away. He has a job and a fiancée waiting for him in Toronto. He then tells Etna he is a Jew.

Etna, either so besotted that she doesn't care about the import of the revelation, or else the true daughter or her tolerant father, tells Samuel this information is of no consequence. Indeed, she loves him all the more.

They make love again (wildly? passionately? wistfully?), this time interrupted by a sound from a nearby room. A student has returned early, Samuel realizes. Etna dresses, and there is some anxiety (perhaps a comic episode here?) as Asher spirits Etna from the dormitory. Parting hastily, they each reaffirm their love.

Now we come to the Sunday morning in January (the Sunday before the term resumes), wild with a snowstorm sent from Canada (from Ardith herself?). The Ashers – there must be many of them to produce a happy, overcrowded household – are at home. Phillip, just seventeen, is reading in the sitting room and overhears Samuel being summoned to the door. Phillip, wondering who can have come to the house in such filthy weather, shifts his position on the sofa so that he can better see into the hallway.

An unusually tall and arresting woman in a wet cloak and boots stands before Samuel. Phillip recognizes her as the woman with whom he once played tennis. Bits of urgent conversation make their way into the sitting room. Phillip, intrigued, stands and walks to a library table. At that moment, Etna lifts her face, and Phillip sees there . . . what? *The ferocity of love*, he will later write. Etna is imploring Samuel. She is weeping. Perhaps she puts her reddened hands on Samuel's arms. Samuel tries to calm her, but she will not be calmed. She has broken her engagement, she announces. She cannot marry another man. She loves only Samuel, Samuel who must not marry Ardith. Who must not go away to Toronto. Who must not leave her.

What is a man to do? Samuel tries to take Etna into another, more private room to speak with her, but Etna, nearly wild now, will not go. Samuel offers to fetch a carriage for her to take her home. Etna shakes her head. Samuel tells her finally that he cannot break his engagement, that his honor does not permit this. (Can he really have said that? I suppose so. Honor was then a sturdier concept than it is today.) Perhaps he tells her another truth – that his family would never permit him to break his engagement. Ardith is, after all, from a good Jewish academic family like his. Phillip moves to the doorway, and perhaps Etna looks up, catching the young man's eye. Phillip's father, having heard the disturbance, has made his way into the hallway. What is this commotion? he asks his son.

Samuel tries to give a respectful answer that will send his father back to his study. Etna, her emotions having spiraled out of control, is clearly too distraught to answer for herself. The Asher patriarch fetches his wife, who is at first taken aback by this melodramatic display. She immediately intuits the reason for the visit and the tears, and announces, in a chilly voice, that she will deal with the young woman (the chilliness uncalled for, since she herself has been weeping in her bedroom at the thought of the departure of her favorite son). Etna, suddenly realizing the horror of her position, her perfect humiliation, turns and opens the door. Samuel, temporarily cowed (thus earning him the lifelong scorn of his younger brother), says nothing and allows Etna to go. Phillip, at first stunned and then moved to aid the striking, if not entirely beautiful, woman, runs to the door and out onto the street. By the time he has reached the end of the walkway, Etna Bliss has vanished.

As I say, this is only my imagination.

But how annoying these letters ultimately are! Though one initially admires Phillip Asher (some eighteen years later) for offering to withdraw from consideration for the post at Thrupp on Etna's account – such *chivalry* – he then easily acquiesces to Etna's dismissal of the matter (though she was quite right in refusing to allow him to do so). Already in the letter of October 21, we see the seeds of deception sown: Asher reveals that he has met me in the hotel, but has withheld from me the knowledge that he once knew my wife. On October 22, in the same letter that we learn Etna was betrothed, Etna allows this deception to continue: 'I see no reason to discuss with him [meaning me, N. VT.] an incident of so long ago.' One cannot help but wonder what license this must have given the man from Yale, how this may have made him think in terms of a future for himself with a woman who has, after all, intrigued him for years. How amazing that the mysterious woman he chased to no avail in Exeter should suddenly have appeared at Edward Ferald's party. (Not such a remarkable coincidence, you might say. Both were, after all, from academic families, and Thrupp was an academic town.)

The exchange of sympathy letters that follows is perfectly acceptable, quite within the bounds of common etiquette, although one additionally wonders why it was necessary for Phillip to apologize for not going to the funeral. It seems a patently obvious excuse to continue the correspondence. And note how, in her letter of November 18, Etna likewise requires a response of Asher. 'I should be grateful for any news of [your brother].' She signs this letter Etna *Bliss* Van Tassel. Why? To remind Asher of the young woman she once was?

And why, on November 24, does Asher think it important to have some reply from Etna before he accepts my invitation to have a drink? To decide how to continue the deception? (I take great offense at the word *ultimatum*. I hate exaggeration in any man. I think my quote from Milton was simply a warning at most.)

No one reading this correspondence can deny that something more than common friendship was developing between my wife and Phillip Asher. It is not long before one begins to sense the ooze of decorous flirtation between the lines of Asher's correspondence: '*You have grown only more lovely with the years.*' Why was this compliment necessary? And this in the same letter in which he declares how inappropriate it is to continue to write to her! Clearly the man does not wish for the correspondence to end at all; he is merely waiting for Etna to assume responsibility for it. One does have sympathy, however, for Etna's desire in her letter of November 27 not to be dictated to by her former lover's younger brother; though Asher is correct in his letter of November 29 in suggesting that, with their correspondence, they are crossing a marital, if not moral, line. One can only imagine the poor man's intolerable dinner at Ferald's house on Thanksgiving day. Ferald had position, but never any conversation worth listening to. As for his wife, Millicent – well, one shudders to imagine.

In his December 6th letter, Asher pursues Etna (in an epistolary manner) to Exeter with news of his election. He then places the acceptance of the post of Dean *in her hands*. Is not this token of his affection as tangible as a jet brooch? And when he receives no reply? He accepts the post, as he was certain to have done all along.

I do not wish to speak for any other reader of this correspondence, but I cannot help but point out the manner in which both step outside the bounds of common friendship with the slightly frantic exchange of January 15 and 18: '*Forgive my silence.*' '*You do not need my forgiveness.*' Note that there are no polite salutations in these letters, lending the exchange the breathless quality of that between lovers. Both Phillip and Etna continue to speak of the inappropriateness of the correspondence, but neither seems willing to end it. Indeed, Etna deepens the bond between them with her 'ethical questions' letter. The questions are absurd, and one cannot help but have a little sympathy for Asher, whose discomfort is all too apparent in his reply. (*Of course* it is not ethical to rent a room which is kept secret from the spouse; what was Asher supposed to say?) Etna's syntax is garbled in her letter, as if her thoughts had addled her grammar. The questions are nearly impossible to follow, and, really, one aches to edit this missive. There is, as well, a certain stiff quality to her prose, and – how shall I put it? – a less than rigorous intellect on display here.

Though Asher's response and return questions are perfectly reasonable under the circumstances, I find appalling his presumptuous reporting of my conduct during the early months of 1915. It goes without saying that I find it disingenuous in the extreme when he states, on February 15, that he wishes to assuage his familial conscience. This is mere posturing, I think, and worse – a way to excuse his already inexcusable behavior.

I was, of course, distressed to see that on February 20, Etna invites Asher to call her by her Christian name – a bit coquettishly, I might add. And I cannot pretend to have been anything other than grievously wounded by the final letter of April 20. *My dearest Phillip*, Etna writes (weeks of intimacy leapt o'er in a single endearment!). What happened between the frantic letter of March 9, when the reality of her situation was sinking in, and the short missive of April 20 inviting Asher to meet her? I assume it is the cottage she means to show him. Were there more letters that were not saved? Had they seen each other in the interim?

Though I was hurt to discover this correspondence, and particularly hurt to find that last affectionate letter, I was already, at the time of the discovery, an animal with many wounds. Nicholas Van Tassel was stumbling maniacally, arrows poking out in all directions, spilling blood upon the plains.

A man makes a rash pronouncement and then spends the rest of his life regretting it. In the cottage, I spoke of divorce. I wished to punish, to assert my authority. I would take away the marriage with a word. I would humiliate my wife. A foolish declaration by a foolish man. Did I take any enjoyment in shocking Etna with my decree? Did I take pleasure in seeing her pale face, the way the strength in her legs gave out? For a moment, perhaps, I had had some satisfaction. But to what end had I done this? To deprive myself of the woman with whom I had been obsessed for fifteen years? The only woman I had ever loved?

I don't know how I managed to drive the Stevens-Duryea or even where I drove it, for it was already dark by the time I crossed into Thrupp. I had long since turned on the headlamps of the car, which illuminated the surface of the road but not anything beyond the circumference of the electric light, and so it was as if I drove blind through a landscape deeply foreign to me. As a weary horse will seek the barn, however, the Stevens-Duryea finally made its way to Moxon's house. I parked it in the drive.

A manservant answered my frenzied knock.

'Professor Van Tassel,' Jackson (first or second name, I never knew) said, 'Professor Moxon is not here. He will not be back until Thursday.'

'I'll wait for him,' I said.

I walked into a sitting room and laid myself on the sofa. Jackson was kind to me that night, for which I will always be grateful. He let me sleep and brought me soup and let me sleep again and had the wisdom not to ask me any questions. When I stood up finally, late the next morning, he led me to a bathroom where I bathed and shaved. I ate a breakfast of eggs and toast and sat for some time at the table. I did not think as I sat there; no coherent thoughts were formed in Moxon's house. After a time, I stood up again and went out to the motorcar and drove away.

I don't know what became of my students that day, for I didn't drive to the college but rather to my home, which was empty of everyone I loved. Mrs. Van Tassel was gone, a flustered Abigail reported. To Exeter. She had taken the children with her. I nodded, surprised by nothing now. In the last twenty-four hours, I had been forced to resign my candidacy for a post I had dearly wanted, I had discovered that my wife owned a separate residence to which she had been retreating in secret for nearly a year, and I had declared that I would be divorced – none of which I would have said was remotely within the realm of possibility just the week before.

'There is a letter on the breakfast table,' Abigail announced.

I opened the letter as if it were a bill I had no intention of paying. *Dear Nicholas*, it read.

I have taken the children to Exeter. Please do not follow me. Let us think about the things we have said to each other.

Your loving Etna.

My loving Etna.

I left the dining room, dropping the letter on the hallway floor. I went up to my bed. I don't believe I had yet had a coherent thought. Nor did I the next day or the next. I recall a telephone call from the college asking if I was unwell. Yes, I said, and I would be away from my classes for a week. I remember Moxon coming to visit me and a bizarre conversation in the sitting room, desultory on my part, frantic on his. Etna had left me, I said to Moxon's horror. He was all arms and legs, flapping in companionate misery. Keep the car, he said, keep the car, as if an automobile might help to mitigate the heartache of a foolhardy declaration.

In the days that followed, I grew whiskers and had

to be told by the housemaid to shave them. I ate cheese and eggs repeatedly, as if I had returned to the nursery. On Friday, Phillip Asher was elected to the post of Dean.

On Saturday, I drove to Exeter, remembering that earlier trip of fifteen years previous, when all my life had been contained within a single petition. On the way, I practiced the words of my second plea to Etna Bliss Van Tassel.

Do not think about a divorce, I would say. It was the utterance of an angry man and was to be accorded no more respect than the ravings of a lunatic. Listen instead to the husband of fifteen years who desires to have his wife and children at home. Their absence from the house is unnecessary. Foolish words are often said in the heat of the moment, are they not? Surely a marriage is elastic enough to accommodate them without destroying the union? As to the other matter, as to the separate abode, we would discuss it upon her return to Thrupp. I might leave the college, I would say. I might write a book.

But Etna had another idea, which she communicated to me immediately upon my arrival.

'I agree to a divorce,' she said in that parlor in which she had once announced that she would marry me. She had entered the room as if she had long been expecting me, as if she had already armed herself, had built around her both a moat and a fortress.

We stood across a Persian carpet. I was vaguely aware of damask and crystal and rosewood and silk, the end result of all those ladders and drop cloths of so long ago. Etna's face was drawn, and I saw that she was thinner; perhaps it was that severe aspect to her expression and posture that gave her the glamour of a regent.

'No, no,' I said, shaking my head, certain that sister

Miriam was listening from behind the paneled door. 'I didn't mean it. I was too rash. I was angry. Etna, listen to me.'

She stood her ground and went as still as the ancestral Keep in the oil portrait behind her. Her gaze was steady and unyielding. I studied her and thought again, as I had so often before, that there must have been a foreign element in her blood, perhaps that of a superior race, one that had produced the almond eyes and the high cheekbones, the utter poise that seemed to require no breath. Then I had an astonishing thought, one so remarkable that I was, for some moments, unable to continue the conversation. Why had Phillip Asher blurted out to me – of all people – the fact of his Jewishness? Had he simply assumed I would know this because Etna had once known the family? Or, more to the point, was my wife herself Jewish?

I examined her anew.

'Are you Jewish?' I asked.

Etna was startled by the question. She shook her head. 'I don't know,' she said.

'What do you mean?'

'My mother didn't know her father.'

'I don't understand.'

'My mother's mother was a servant girl who was impregnated by a man she later would not, or could not, identify.'

This was news to me. I had simply assumed for my wife an Anglo-Saxon ancestry on her mother's side. 'Then why do you think you are Jewish?' I asked.

'I could be anything,' she said.

'My son may be Jewish?' I asked, incredulous.

'Does that *matter*?' she asked.

'I don't know,' I said truthfully.

'I can no longer be your wife,' Etna said so quietly that I was not certain I had heard correctly. Or perhaps it was only that I didn't want to have heard correctly. Outside, there was a commotion, as if there had been an accident with motorcars. It cannot have been any more serious, I was thinking, than the collision in the parlor.

'That is no grounds,' I said, adding pomposity to foolishness, as if I knew the law. Spending a precious sentence when simple words of love would have been better currency.

'It will have to be enough,' she said with the tentative authority of the recently coronated.

Etna quit the room, left her husband sputtering, the husband who was prevented from following her up the stairs. I shook Miriam's surprisingly tenacious hand off my arm, but men were brought to the hallway. I was forced to go away, Josip Keep smugly clucking that marriage was a trial.

I drove to Salisbury, a seaside town of poor repute. I found a brothel, my first lapse of a sexual nature in fifteen years of wedlock. After an encounter I do not now remember, I went on to a bar near the ocean and drank a bottle of bourbon. I was left to mutter in a leather booth. In the morning, I returned to Thrupp.

I appeared for some classes and ignored others. My wife had been called away, I said to anyone who seemed poised on the brink of inquiry. Her sister was gravely ill, I added, happily giving Miriam a fatal disease. My colleagues nodded, and if they doubted me, I didn't care. I removed myself before expressions of pity or distaste could form. I was a man of little conversation and even less patience. It was understood that I was reeling.

In January, I was summoned by Phillip Asher, who

had moved into the office of the Dean. (Everyone, it would appear, including Asher himself, had been willing to look the other way regarding his Jewishness.) I went reluctantly and left without a word before the offer of a sabbatical had been completely tendered. It was a sop to a defeated rival, I thought with disgust, unaware at the time of his correspondence with my wife. I knew only that he had once known of Etna years ago. Still, I thought, Asher would have heard the rumors of a dissolving marriage. In his eyes, I would be a twice-defeated man, an academic and marital emeritus.

A week later, I returned to Exeter, nearly losing myself and my newly purchased black Ford in a dun-colored storm. Etna, paler still, was summoned to the parlor. The room was bathed in the flat dull light of mid-season snow. She wore a pale blue daytime dress that showed the new angles of her body, and already I was imagining how I would care for her, how I would instruct Mary to fatten her up with a rich diet. My wife was disappearing in Exeter.

I strove to be composed. I did not beg or wheedle, but I presented my case.

I had made a rash pronouncement, I said. It was a wife's duty to forgive the ranting of a temporarily deranged husband. Any man might have said the same, I said. As to the matter of the cottage, I was prepared to consider the issue in a calmer manner, and I was sure that some arrangement could be made.

'What arrangement?' she asked, settling herself in a yellow-silk-covered chair. She moved as if her bones had become fragile, and I was suddenly worried for my children. Was Keep not feeding my family in exile?

'An arrangement,' I said, though in truth I had not thought much about any such arrangement. Indeed, I could not think about the cottage at all. The very sight of it in my mind's eye – or the sight of it in reality (for I had several times gone there to look at it, the door locked, the thief unwilling to break a window, since he still believed a reconciliation imminent) – caused a tide to flood my brain, like the assault of a rising blush.

Etna folded her hands in her lap. 'You would decree when I could go there,' she said.

'Not necessarily,' I said, treading carefully.

'But you would want to know when and for how long and precisely what I would be doing there,' she said. 'Who I might see there.'

Confinement didn't suit her, I was thinking. It never had. 'How are the children?' I asked.

'They are well,' she said.

'I wish some news of them. I wish to see them.'

'They are away,' she said.

'Away where?'

'Away with Miriam. Visiting Pippa in Massachusetts.'

'You cannot keep my children from me,' I insisted.

'Nicholas,' she said with a flicker of marital concern, 'you are not in a fit state to be with children, your own or anyone else's.'

'And are you?' I countered.

'I have a good deal of help,' she said.

'*Why*, Etna?' I asked, sitting forward. '*Why* are you doing this?'

'I have given you fifteen years,' she said.

'I would have given you my whole life!' I said.

'You say that,' she said calmly, 'but you will not give me one hour of true freedom.'

At last, I begged. 'Etna. Please. Come back for the sake of the children, who desire only that we be together.'

I watched as she struggled with that old emotion – pity. And I am ashamed to write here that for a moment I gladly would have accepted it.

'I will have a divorce,' she said.

'On what grounds?' I said, angry now.

'I have never loved you,' she said, as if that were enough.

And it may have been. It was certainly enough to silence me. With difficulty, I stood, my legs those of a wizened man. 'We will correspond through lawyers,' I said hoarsely from the hollowed-out place to which my wife had sent me.

'Yes,' was all she said.

I found the strength to walk to the door. I let myself out. My wife made no move to stop me.

The divorce proceeded at the pleasure of the court, which is to say it scarcely proceeded at all. I was awash in legal sentence structure and grievous grammar:

It may be averred that the relator's marriage was a sacrifice, the result of an unwillingness, on her part, to recede from an ill-conceived engagement, into which she had improvidently allowed herself to be drawn, and with which she afterwards complied, under the influence of a mistaken sense of duty. That she would not thus have complied or been married to the respondent at all if she had not been assured that her wishes would not be opposed, upon points which she deemed vital to her happiness and welfare, and upon which he did not then consider her wishes as unreasonable.

I sent a lawyer to retrieve Nicodemus. His name was Tucker, and he had strict instructions.

'He will let you have the girl,' Tucker announced to Etna, who stood in Josip Keep's hallway. 'But he wants the boy back. If you don't comply, he will have both children. Under the circumstances, he would almost certainly get them.'

'What circumstances?' Etna asked.

'A mother who has committed an immoral act is seen by the court to be corrupting the morals of a son.'

'Not a daughter?'

'The court does not like to remove a daughter from a mother's protection.'

'This is absurd,' Etna said.

'Nevertheless.'

'What immoral act?' Etna asked.

'A secret residence for possible immoral purposes,' Tucker said, handing Etna the latest of the legalese.

Tucker stood and waited. He would not leave without the boy.

Etna, after consultation with her lawyer, reluctantly complied.

Etna had to return to Thrupp, which, all along, I had known she would do. If I had our son, Etna would have to be near him. She took up residence in the cottage.

I had the boy, and she had Clara, who slept with Etna in the narrow bed in the gabled attic bedroom. Clara resumed her studies at Thrupp Girls' Academy, and Nicky continued his at the local grammar school. On weekends, Abigail, the maid, became a courier, fetching Clara to bring her home even as she was delivering Nicky for a Sunday meal.

I took to watching Etna and Clara through the windows of the cottage – that endless motion picture of humble domesticity. I went at night, when the moon of my face could not be seen at the window. I cultivated stealth and became more proficient at this calling than I had ever been at Rhetoric.

I would leave Nicky in his bed, Nicky whose face I searched daily for clues as to his ancestral identity, Nicky who asked nightly for his mother. I would drive to Drury, where I had found a clearing in which to park the black Ford. I would walk the quarter mile to the cottage and stand in such a way that I could not be seen in the light of the white chandelier, an extravagance so out of keeping with the rude cottage that it was as if a dowager had entered a fishing hut. In its splintery light, I would examine Clara's luminous skin, her pale eyebrows, and the light blue eyes that reminded me of my sisters'. In contrast to her mother, who was taking on a look of transparency, even with her dark features, Clara was a lush bloom of Dutch beauty.

Etna, loving mother, brushed her daughter's hair, unaware of the audience beyond the glass. My wife's face was composed but white, and I could see the strain of skin over the high cheekbones, the nervousness in the topaz eyes, the worry lines at the sides of her mouth.

I could stand for hours in the dark and cold, observing Clara at her studies and Etna at her sewing. I watched Etna at the sink, washing dishes like a common under-cook. She seemed not to mind these chores, some of which were truly odious – the tossing out of slops, the washing and ironing of laundry that froze on the clothes-line at the back of the house, the cleaning of the out-house. Clara, called upon to help, protested like a spoiled girl, and I sometimes longed to step in and upbraid her. At other times, it was all I could do to keep from storming through the door and embracing my child, who was growing tall without me.

Standing in the dark, I considered the matter of Etna's

maternal ancestors, of the unknown parentage. The man who had impregnated the servant girl and then abandoned her could have been anything, I reasoned. Jewish, possibly. More likely a common Yankee with striking features. But then again, he might have been Turkish or Indian or Russian. Each night I would study the cheekbones and eyes of my wife and wonder: Was she Greek? Italian? A Gypsy?

I pondered also the nature of fate and circumstance. Had it not been for the fire, I doubt I should ever have met Etna Bliss. Did I now wish that those few drops of oil in the hotel kitchen had not fallen onto the cooking fire? Might I have eaten my poached sole in solitude and never noticed the young woman in the topaz silk sitting behind me and thus escaped both the joy and anguish of the next fifteen years, only to have met, two months later, say, the daughter of a rare-book dealer from Thrupp whom I then married? Might I never have encountered Etna Bliss at all, but rather have seen a woman emerging from a trolley three days later to whom I gave pursuit and was ultimately betrothed? Or have been introduced at a faculty party at the college to the wife of a colleague (no, never; the sentence does not bear completion, for I should never have stooped so low) . . . or chanced upon, in twenty years' time, after having remained for decades a bachelor, a widow to whom my academic credentials, not to mention my modest fortune, might have been attractive? Or, then again, might I actually have met a *worse* fate than was dealt to me? Might I have wed the daughter of a physician who bore me a child who then died as a result of my wife's carelessness? There are stories more terrible than mine. I do understand this. But the influence of circumstance upon a man's destiny is considerable, is it not?

My nightly visits to that cottage became more and more frequent and then routine. After I had stood at the window for an hour or so, I would walk into the woods and eat a bit of cheese and bread and drink the whiskey that I had brought. Truth to tell, I was drinking rather a lot in those months, and sometimes I had difficulty returning the Ford to its garage in the early hours of the morning. I slept late and was often tardy for or absent altogether from my classes, to which I scarcely paid any attention. My colleagues, concerned and then alarmed and then annoyed, avoided me when an encounter threatened, which was fine with me, who wanted only silence and anonymity, both difficult to come by in that college of mediocre and unruly boys. I would tender my resignation in the summer, I told myself with sweet relief.

Only once in all the times I went to the cottage to spy on my wife did I come near to getting caught. I had gone into the woods to relieve myself, and I must have made an inadvertent sound, because when I was finished and had turned back to the house, I saw that Etna was standing at the window staring straight at me. She tilted her head from side to side, so I didn't think she had actually spotted me. I watched as she left the window and then I heard the door open. She came out, shivering and hugging a shawl around her arms, making delicate footprints in the snow-covered lawn of late March.

'Who's there?' she called out, squinting in the night.

I stood behind a tree and watched her face, longing to reveal myself and wondering how it had come to pass that I, Nicholas Van Tassel, was hiding behind a tree in the woods, the steam from my urine still rising behind me, concealing myself from the only woman I had ever loved.

★   ★   ★

Routine became obsession. (What, precisely, is an obsession? My much used dictionary tells me it is a state of
compulsive preoccupation with a fixed idea or unwanted
feeling or emotion. The word, of course, stems from the
Latin *obsidere* (past participle *obsessus*), which means 'to
sit down before'; *ob*, against, combined with *sedere*, to
sit. Well, I wasn't sitting, but I was certainly standing.)
Sometimes, exhausted beyond sense, I would doze off
and wake only to find that I had been asleep as I leaned
against the white clapboards. This went on for some
time and might have continued indefinitely had I not
seen, one night in early May when I approached the
cottage, a Ford not my own parked in the driveway
beside the Landaulet.

For the first time in weeks, I became painfully alert
and was aware of the workings of my heart, a hard
thumping that made me put my hand to my chest. I
moved silently to my favorite hiding place (a window
behind the Chinese grass chair that was often shrouded
in darkness) and peered in. I pressed hard on my chest
with my fist.

Phillip Asher sat sideways to the small table, one arm
thrown over the ladder-back chair, the other reaching
for a teacup. His legs were casually crossed, and he
seemed relaxed, as if he had been in this house before,
as if he had often been welcomed here. Indeed, Clara
remained unconcerned in a corner with her music stand
and her flute; between the muted bits of conversation
(I seldom ever heard a specific word, so it was mostly
a silent movie I watched those many nights), I could
hear the notes of the practice lesson. Etna was sewing
on the davenport, and it was as if Phillip Asher were a
brother or a cousin who had interrupted a domestic
scene simply to say hello. I looked over to the sink and

saw the remnants of a meal that had not yet been cleaned up. I strained to count the plates and the silverware, for I wished to know if Asher had had his supper with my daughter and my wife.

Had Etna lied to me? Had she and Phillip Asher all along been lovers? (I could hardly be expected to monitor the cottage by day.) Had he been there all afternoon, while Clara was in school, and simply lingered longer than was usual, enjoying the easy company of an arresting woman and her child? But then I had a truly terrible thought: Had I caused Etna and Asher, with my foolish decrees, to come together after my wife and I had separated? Yes, I thought, I had. Asher, under the guise of concern for my well-being and in his position as Dean of the Faculty, would have driven to the cottage to discuss the matter, would he not?

I exercised that night the utmost self-control, for I wanted nothing more than to enter that room and haul the man out and send him sprawling across the driveway. How dare he sit in such close proximity to my daughter! How dare he insinuate himself into my family!

Asher took another sip of tea, which had to have grown cold in the time it had sat on the table; I had been watching this cozy domestic scene for nearly a half hour. Clara put down her flute and asked her mother a question. I could see from the considerate but firm shake of the head that Etna was denying Clara's request to quit her practicing early. Clara, with pained expression, went on, and I could again hear the labored notes of a flute badly played. I watched my daughter stretch her legs in an indecorous manner, a gesture that immediately caught her mother's watchful eye. Asher leaned forward in his chair, as if making a point in his ongoing conversation with my wife. (*My* wife.) He leaned his elbows on his knees and seemed insidiously relaxed. I was afraid that my furious and steamy breaths of air in the frigid night might be noticeable through the window.

To calm myself, I looked away. I shot my gaze up through the tall pines to the stars, wondering why the gods were treating me so badly. I had never before felt such violation. The man had taken my position, and now he was taking my wife?

I turned back to the window, and as I did, Asher and Etna rose simultaneously.

I have played and replayed this scene a thousand times in my head, and I think the paired rising was purely coincidental in its initial moments. Perhaps Etna had been about to go to Clara; possibly Asher was merely stretching. As if in slow motion, and with faint smiles playing upon their lips, they were carried forward by the momentum that had made them stand, first two and then three steps, causing them to meet directly beneath the white chandelier, that extravagant monstrosity. Their hands rose – her right, his left – and quickly, lightly, clasped, as if by the same impulse that makes people who speak the same phrase simultaneously smile at each other in amusement.

That I might have borne. The clasped hands I might have endured and forgotten. After all, the entire incident lasted only a second, perhaps two. But in those moments, I glimpsed something else, something that has stayed with me all these years, that is more vivid to me sometimes than the remembered visages of my children. It was the expression on Etna's face, an expression that was – how can I describe this? *Radiant* is the word I must use. Giddy with delight. An ecstatic expression of happiness that seemingly required the participation of the entire body, as if the body were moving forward at great speed. It was a look I had seen on Etna's face only once before, on the sleigh on that late-winter afternoon so many years ago when the horses, nearly out of control, had sped toward the barn. She had reached for my hand, and I had gone rigid with joy.

Asher and Etna swayed a bit. The moment dissolved in laughter. From the corner, Clara watched, her eyes wary and humorless. My own eyes were dry with anger. I longed to snatch my daughter from that tableau.

The next morning, I sent a note to Etna. I would call that night for Clara, and we would have a meal. She would stay the night with Nicodemus and me, and I would deliver her to school the next morning. Etna was to pack Clara a suitcase with a clean uniform and her nightclothes. I would call for my daughter at five o'clock. I would come up the driveway in the Ford, but I would not enter the cottage. If she would be so kind as to send Clara out to me, I should be very grateful. Yours sincerely, etcetera, etcetera.

Clara was, as she settled herself in the Ford, both timid and angry in equal measure − timid in the face of this rupture of routine, angry because she wanted to blame someone for the dissolution of the family. I did not try to defend myself. She was still a child, too young to know of bargains or of unrequited passion.

I parked on Wheelock Street, and we walked, as in the old days, Clara's arm in mine, toward the college quadrangle. We spoke of her classes and of her music lessons and occasionally, now that she was growing older, of topics outside the immediate circumference of her life, such as a desire to see Yosemite, for example, of which she had heard a great deal from her new friend

Rosemary. We made our way to the hotel, where I had told her we would have a meal, ending with a cup of hot chocolate for each. Gradually she thawed and remembered her love for her father, and at times we were simply a man and his daughter having a meal in the Hotel Thrupp. Who was to say that we might not return to our home on Holyoke Street only to find Etna bathing Nicky, and that life would go on as before?

Lovely thought, but below that happy agenda, I had another.

Three times in conversation, I said Phillip Asher's name. (*Dean Asher*, I actually said, in case that was how he had been introduced to Clara.) After the third mention, when I could no longer bear her silence or her reticence on this subject, I asked, as casually as I was capable of, 'Have you ever met the man?' And Clara, after an initial hesitation, said yes, she had. I, aware now of a sudden heat that had risen to my face, let some seconds pass, and then I asked, as if I had nearly forgotten the topic, 'And where did you meet him?'

Clara answered that Professor Asher was a friend of her mother's and sometimes came to the cottage. The dialogue proved too much for her tender sensibilities, however – this was not a subject she thought she ought to be discussing (she, too, had seen the clasped hands under the chandelier) – and she began to cry.

'Clara dear,' I said. 'I didn't mean to upset you.'

'Why are you and Mother doing this to me?' she asked, weeping like a child now, which is to say messily.

'We are not doing this to *you*,' I said. 'It is simply that for the moment we have chosen to live apart.'

'That's not true!' she said with the wisdom of the keen observer. 'It is Mother who is doing this. You want us back, I know you do.'

'Yes,' I said. 'Very much.'

'Then why did you send for Nicky and not for me?' she cried.

This, I knew, was at the heart of Clara's resentment. 'Nicky is the younger,' I said, groping for an answer.

'You love him more than me!' she accused.

'No, Clara, I do not,' I said truthfully. 'I love you both the same.'

I reached across the table and took her hand in mine, unable, in that public place, easily to embrace her. The touch of my hand consoled her somewhat, so that I was reluctant to let her go. At that moment, a man who was entering the dining room – a man I had never seen before, perhaps a man simply needing a meal – passed by our table and looked at Clara.

It was a subtle glance, in the main inoffensive in its brevity. But as I turned back to Clara, I saw what he had seen. The full lips. The hint of bosom beneath the bodice of her uniform. The slender waist and delicate ankles. It was the first time I saw my daughter as men would for years see her.

'Father,' she said, having blown her nose into my handkerchief, 'why are you staring at me?'

I forced myself to look away. I studied the stranger, who had sat down, oblivious of the plot he had set in motion.

A plan was unfolding. A narrative was spooling itself across the dining room.

'Clara,' I said. 'I think I have a way to bring your mother back.'

My daughter looked up at me, the tears still shiny saucers in her eyes.

In the morning, I delivered three letters. One to my

wife. One to the President of the college. And one to the chief of police of Thrupp.

'My daughter, Clara, has brought something very disturbing to my attention,' I wrote.

The train is lulling me into a kind of stupor. It is the heat. I am told that we have crossed the border into Florida, and I can well believe this true, for it is stifling in my compartment, even with the top half of the window open (which is all that is allowed; to prevent people from jumping out, I should think). We stopped in the morning in Yemassee, where we were all witness to the strange sight of Negro men carrying large bunches of bananas on their shoulders to a freight train parked next to us. They looked both exhausted and resigned in the poisonous heat.

All along the train, men are shedding clothes like boys headed for a swimming hole. First a jacket is laid upon a chair. Then a tie is tugged down, after which the cuffs of the shirt are unbuttoned and rolled. I saw a man with his braces undone. Manners are being cast away with the clothing, it would seem, for tempers are noticeably shorter today than they have been the entire journey. One man snarled at a porter for delivering a drink with no ice (the ice, it would seem, melted in Georgia). I tried to nap but awoke too quickly, my silk sleeping mask wet with both sweat and tears.

Will my daughter come to the funeral if I am there? This is a question that vexes me no end. And if she does come, will she speak to me? I would say ordinarily not, for she has lived with her aunt now for eighteen years and has not spoken or written to me in all that time. But the human heart is a mysterious organ, is it not, and it may be that Clara has forgiven me.

How is it that life goes forward when so many people have been wronged?

There is just one more piece of my story to tell, which is just as well, for soon we shall be approaching West Palm Beach, the end point of my journey. My trip has taken somewhat longer than I thought it would (more than three days due to the derailment near New Haven and the bout of food poisoning in Richmond; it was supposed to have taken thirty hours), and I have realized I will be lucky to make the funeral on time; it has already been delayed, as per my sister's wishes, so that I can be there. Meritable's pronouncement on this matter moved me when I first got the telegram from Berthe, one of our sisters, and indeed motivated me to take the journey, which I might not otherwise have done. It was gratifying to see that Meritable still bore me some affection, despite what can only have been a strong allegiance all these years to Clara. Perhaps Meritable had some design to thrust Clara and me together after her death so that we may repair the rift between us.

I should like to have gone to the library car after breakfast this morning, particularly to the periodicals room, as I feel, in my moving metal cocoon, as though

I have been estranged from the world. I have been writing almost without interruption since I boarded the train at White River Junction three days ago, though I have traveled through sixty-four years of personal history.

What a fraught venture this has been, more perilous than I ever imagined.

As soon as Etna received her letter – the same letter I had written and delivered to Frank Goodspeed, the President of the college, and Merrill Gates, the chief of police – she drove to the house.

Etna and Clara and I gathered in the sitting room. Etna would not sit, however, despite repeated entreaties on my part to do so. She held the letter in her hand as if she had been clutching it all the way from Drury. My heart had lifted when I had seen the green-and-gold Landaulet pull into the driveway, as I had known it would. (I had predicted the time of her arrival to within the quarter hour.)

'Is this true?' she asked of a trembling Clara, who had, as my daughter and I had planned, returned to Holyoke Street after school.

Clara, who wished only that the family be reunited, said yes, it was true, Mr. Asher had touched her.

'Touched you how?' Etna asked, her voice and face as sharp as the point of a thorn.

I watched my daughter carefully. This would be Clara's truest test, her most difficult examination. For a long moment, we all stood in an unhappy triangle, breathing slowly in unison, Nicky safely closeted with Abigail. Clara touched her bosom, a three-fingered brush at the side of her breast that was nearly obscene against the white blouse of her school uniform. It was a breathtaking gesture, not only for its implications, but also for the sight itself – that of a young girl who may never have touched herself in that way before, doing so in such a public manner. It froze Etna's expression. Etna, in unconscious mimicry, brushed her fingers against her own breast, as if wishing (or needing) to feel what Clara had felt.

Clara blushed. She must have longed, as in a child's game, to shout, 'Make-believe!' To call to all the players, 'Allee, allee, in free!' But she was committed to her actor's role, her lines rehearsed, the unthinkable gesture completed. To quit now would be to lose everything.

'Touched you when?' Etna asked in a voice so quiet as to be barely audible. She took off her driving hat and let it fall to the floor.

'After school,' she said, 'when you went to the market.'

'Once?'

'Three times,' Clara said, sealing Asher's fate with a number. A number picked by me both for its damning quality and for its unlikely plausibility.

'Three times,' Etna repeated, struggling, I could see, for comprehension. 'When were the other times?'

Clara, a mirror to a mirror, covered her eyes with her hands. It was one thing to invent dialogue and a playlet, quite another to see the sudden parental incredulity it produced.

But Etna, stern parent, pulled Clara's hands away. 'Look at me,' she demanded of her daughter. 'Look at me. When else?'

'Once when you were late from Baker House,' Clara said in a tremulous voice, speaking her fourth and final line, 'and once when you were in the garden.'

As she so often did when confronted with a disturbing fact, Etna went completely still. Clara and I, witnesses to this maternal immobility, could only wait. Etna was torn between going to the child who had been wronged and withholding judgment – her mother's instinct detecting a covert note (actually, the truth).

Etna placed a hand against the flat of her stomach and turned around, putting her back to us. Clara began to weep, the desperate ploy of an unschooled actress who must resort to tears to convince her audience. Etna, misreading this (as she was meant to do), turned back and folded her daughter into her chest. She put a hand behind Clara's head and pressed her to her own bosom. 'Shhh,' she said. 'There now.'

I watched with a kind of giddy horror.

'Clara, I must ask you,' Etna said. 'Are you very, very sure about this? This is a serious accusation.'

Clara pulled her head away and nodded, and I silently applauded my daughter's lack of hesitation.

'My God,' Etna said.

My wife swayed and briefly closed her eyes. I thought that she might faint and take the child with her. I took a step forward.

'It was so terrible,' Clara wailed. 'Please let us be a family again,' she managed between her sobs, clinging to her mother's delicate body.

(Careful, Clara, I thought.)

But no mother could have resisted that petition. 'Yes,' Etna said, comforting her daughter. 'Shhh. There now.'

My relief was so visceral, I feared it would be visible.

'You must never tell anyone about this,' Etna said to Clara.

I cleared my throat and offered my one and only (and clearly devastating) line. 'The college and the police have already been informed,' I intoned.

Etna looked as though she had been slapped. 'You've

told the school?' she whispered, her voice deserting her.

'Of course,' I said. 'The man cannot be allowed to continue in a position of responsibility. Criminal charges will have to be brought.'

'Oh, dear God,' Etna said.

I didn't dare look at Clara, my accomplice, for fear I would see success upon her face, an expression that would risk the entire venture. I turned away, shaken but elated. I had it all, had I not? My wife and Clara would return home. The family would be intact. Phillip Asher would be removed from his post, his reputation in tatters.

Nicky, who had been waiting in the wings, broke free of Abigail's arms and bolted into the sitting room, where he crushed himself against his mother's skirts. He, too, began to beg.

'Don't go, don't go,' he sang, to which chorus I added my own silent verses.

Etna was not to return to the cottage, I said, taking command of a scene that begged for a leading man. Abigail would go by taxi to fetch anything Etna needed. I would see to it that the building was put up for sale. Etna, too stunned to reply or even to think, did not demur. I guessed that she had no desire now to see that cottage, nor even to show her face in Thrupp. I told myself that with time this shame would go away, that in time we would once again be a normal family.

As for Phillip Asher, he was confronted with the accusation later that afternoon in his office by both Chief Gates and President Goodspeed, an unlikely and awkward pairing. I am told that Asher laughed when he first heard of the informal indictment, thinking it was pure fabrication on the part of a defeated and bitter rival, easily refuted. But when he was informed that it was not me but rather Clara who had made the charge, the color drained from his face, convincing Goodspeed, at least, of Asher's guilt.

Asher wrote to Etna at once, insisting that the imputation wasn't true, that perhaps Clara had misunderstood an entirely innocent gesture, though he could think of no time that he had been in such proximity to her. He would never, he would never. Could he come to see Etna? Could he please speak with her? I intercepted the letter as, of course, any loving husband would have done; though, generously, I allowed Etna to read the missive. She set it aside. Who was a mother to believe: her own child or a would-be lover?

(For I have no doubt now that Asher and Etna would shortly have become lovers. There was no other way to read the look of pure delight on Etna's face beneath the white chandelier. And, in later years, when assaulted with the visions that sometimes plague a guilty man, I would take heart in the fact that I had at least prevented that consummation.)

Asher was told that if he wished, a written accusation would be required of Clara. He could, in fact, take the matter to court. But I had gambled on Asher's being an honorable man who would not put a child on the witness stand nor cause a woman for whom he had tremendous respect — and perhaps even love — to suffer such a second humiliation at the hands of his family. Within the week, after having repeatedly failed to communicate with Etna by telephone and post and even in person (I had Abigail frostily send him away), Asher resigned his position at the college and left the house on Gill Street. Without a trial, there could be no future for the man from Yale in Thrupp, for he would never be able to refute the charge against him.

By the end of June, much to my astonishment and delight, Asher's presence had been so miraculously expunged from the college town – his name never mentioned in public discourse – that it was as though he had never existed. Any hint of scandal is always disastrous for a college badly in need of contributions from alumni.

The matter of a divorce was, of course, dropped. ('I wish to have an amicable and quiet conclusion to the legal deliberations,' I wrote.) I had the cottage in Drury put up for sale. I set a high price on it, thinking to get a little something in return for the near ruination of my family. A week after Asher left for destinations unknown, I was summoned to the college, not by Ferald, whose horse had been disqualified, but by Frank Goodspeed, the very President who had delivered the dismal bulletin to a white-faced Asher. Would I accept the post of Dean of Thrupp? he asked. Left unsaid was the obvious truth that I was second choice, an also-ran, a dean appointed by default. Understood as well was the fact that no one had the heart to initiate another search.

Yes, I said with as much dignity as I thought the scene required. Yes, I would be only too happy to help the college out in this matter.

'Thank you,' Goodspeed said with evident relief. 'I shall make a quiet announcement.'

No fanfare for Nicholas Van Tassel.

'How is your wife?' Goodspeed inquired, almost as an afterthought.

'She's as well as can be expected,' I said.

'We have tried to suppress the incident,' Goodspeed added, 'but I am sure this has been a trial for you.'

'It has,' I said.

'And the young girl? Your daughter?'

'She is trying to put the matter behind her,' I said.

'The young are so resilient,' Goodspeed said.

But, in fact, Clara was not as resilient as I had hoped. In the days that followed Etna's return, my daughter was alternately falsely cheerful and sullen, as if, having been on the brink of finding out who she was, she had discovered, to her dismay, that she was not that person at all. We never spoke, she and I, of the drama we had written and enacted; she seemed as eager to forget the incident as was her father. But I noticed that Clara fretted more than usual and resisted any attempts to jolly her. Whereas before she had lobbied constantly to be allowed to visit one or two close friends, now she never left the house except to finish her classes. She ended the year with a bad report, her grades having plummeted in the last month of the term. I knew this to be a casualty of all the *sturm und drang* of May and hoped for a return to better study habits in the fall.

Throughout the early weeks of that unnaturally hot summer, Etna remained at home, a ghostly presence who performed her duties as if from a great distance. Some days she would not come out of her room at all, and trays of food, largely uneaten, would be sent back to the kitchen. When she did come down, she sewed maniacally, as if having been given a deadline by an overseer at a mill. She would sit in the parlor, in her old chair, her fingers flying, her teeth angrily biting off thread, her hands snapping out the silk or linen on her lap. She sewed bureau scarves and pillow slips and children's dresses and corset covers. She made luncheon sets and then draperies for a nonexistent room. She embroidered monogrammed initials and wreaths with tiny yellow knots. She made a cape coat for Clara and a long-waisted tunic dress, presumably for herself, though she never wore it. I know this inventory by heart, because it has remained in a cedar chest at the foot of Etna's bed all these years, the master of the house not having the heart or the will to send it on to charity, which is where the odd trousseau should go.

No doubt the reader's interest will have been piqued by the phrase *Etna's bed*. In silence and with no fuss, Etna took up residence in the guest room, quickly removing anything of a personal nature from our bedroom. She slept on a high, white, narrow bed, monastic in its spareness, immediately exchanging its colorful quilt for a white chenille bedspread. Sometimes, on the hot nights of that sultry summer, she would leave her door open a crack to catch a breeze. I would pass by on my way to the bathroom and would see her sleeping, her hair tangled upon the pillow, her arms thrown up above her head in an uncharacteristically unfeminine manner. I would stare, mesmerized by this sight, for it was understood that I was as barred from this room as I was from my wife's bed. This was the closest I would get to seeing Etna Bliss Van Tassel at peace. As in the days when I had watched my wife through a glass pane, I would observe the rising and falling of her chest under the thin sheet, the curve of her faintly lined neck as it arched over the pillow, the fluttering of her eyelids as she dreamt. (Of what? Of whom? Of Phillip Asher? Of Samuel?) A knot of desire would sometimes tug at me, and it was all I could do not to step through that cracked door and lower myself onto the bed beside my sleeping wife. But I did not. Such an action was unthinkable under the present circumstances. Even husbandly lust was a subject that could not be admitted into that household. I prayed, insofar as I was capable of praying (our sins are screens between ourselves and God, are they not?), that with time this disgust would pass and we would once again be husband and wife.

This state of affairs went on for upwards of eight weeks.

By August, a poisonous pall had settled over our house and even over the entire village of Thrupp, which always seemed, without its students, eerily, if pleasantly empty in the summer months. Day after day, we woke to dishwater skies that delivered no rain. Our garden at the side of the house was withering from lack of water and of tender cultivation, our gardener unwilling or unable to recreate its whimsical beauty without his mistress's instructions. Only Nicky seemed oblivious to the mood of recrimination and resignation within that household. As a puppy will look for affection even from a listless master, poking its nose against a shin or licking a recalcitrant hand until, almost absent-mindedly, its owner scratches the animal under its chin, Nicky prodded us from time to time into something very like affection. Only Clara, pretending to read, lashed out when Nicky got too close. She was severely reprimanded for these objectionable outbursts, after which she retreated from the family even further. I worked in my study for hours at a time, occasionally distracted by my new duties. In September, I would formally address the faculty, a speech I wrote and rewrote a dozen times.

And Etna. Where was Etna then? Where had my wife of fifteen years gone? In early August, I suggested a trip to the Highland Hotel, a seaside vacation for the sake of the family. Etna would have none of it. (Have I mentioned that we scarcely spoke?) She was growing alarmingly thin, a result of both a diminished appetite and a kind of unattractive and frenzied domesticity. It was as though she had to keep moving in order to ward off the images that her daughter had planted in her mind – Etna, a woman whose stillness had once defined her being.

Did she dream about her cottage? Did she wonder where Phillip Asher had gone? Did she blame herself for having invited the man into her home? I do not know. I took to drinking more and more, beginning earlier in the day, in an effort to anesthetize myself against the pain of Etna's frigid silence, a project at which I was becoming increasingly unsuccessful.

One afternoon in late August, after I had finished nearly half a bottle of sweet wine and had a headache I could not assuage with tonics (the air so still and stifling within that unhappy house that I could not get a decent breath), I came upon Etna sitting in a wicker chair on a side porch. She had no sewing with her, which I took to be a sign of health. Before I went to her (uninvited), I watched her for a moment in repose. Her body and face in profile, she seemed to be staring at something beyond the screen. She had on a sleeveless overblouse and a linen skirt, and her shoulders and long arms were white and bare, a sight I seldom saw those days. She scratched the knob of her collarbone as if she'd been bitten by an insect. Her arms were terribly thin, and without her robust figure, she seemed to have aged considerably since the spring. This was a sight that moved me. I walked out onto the porch and sat on the glider and rocked back and forth, hoping to simulate a breeze. Etna glanced over at me without a greeting. I was aching for the cooler days of autumn which I was certain would bring a swift conclusion to the fever that had infected all of us.

'Perhaps,' I said to Etna, 'we might think of taking the children to the mountains. It would be cooler there. I am sure I could find us rooms in a hotel.'

'What mountains?' she asked plainly. In the weeks since she had returned to the house, she had either lost or forfeited the gift of graceful conversation.

'Well, the White Mountains,' I said, unable to think of any other mountains. The moment I had named them, however, I regretted the reference to the locus of our wedding trip.

'It is not something I should look forward to,' she said.

'Is there anything you would look forward to?' I asked.

'You go,' she said, 'and take the children.'

'I should not like to leave you all alone,' I said, more than slightly irritated with her recalcitrance on every subject. For the sake of the children, shouldn't we get on with life?

Etna stared through the screen at the brown filigree of the seeding Queen Anne's lace that had infiltrated the untended garden. And as will sometimes happen when under the influence of both alcohol and headache at too early an hour in the day, I was seized with a fit of pique.

'Asher is in the Argonne,' I said, naming the most deadly geography on the planet.

Etna turned her head slowly in my direction. Finally something had claimed my wife's attention.

'Phillip in France?' she asked.

Phillip.

'I am reliably informed that Professor Asher has signed on with the British Red Cross,' I announced.

'It's not possible,' she said.

'They'll take men of practically any age,' I said. 'Of course, this is a very brave gesture on his part. I rather think he means to make amends, in some odd way, for his crime. The death rate for medics is near seventy percent. Did you know Asher's a pacifist?'

Etna's eyes were pink-rimmed. Not from crying, I guessed (she seemed too dry for tears), but from malnutrition. She was growing skeletal inside her homemade dresses.

'Phillip in France,' Etna repeated.

'The Argonne.'

'You mean he is gone altogether?'

I flinched and turned to see the speaker. Clara stood in the doorway behind me.

'You mean he is gone altogether?' my daughter asked again.

She crossed the threshold, a silver hairbrush in her hand. Her hair needed a wash, and her white stockings were dirty. She looked from me to her mother and back to me again. 'Professor Asher is gone?' Clara asked again.

I stood, sensing a dangerous turn to the conversation. 'Clara, your mother and I are talking privately,' I said. 'You should learn not to speak unless asked to do so.'

'Very far away?' Clara asked, as if she had not heard my admonition.

'Yes, very far away,' I said. 'We should go and find your brother,' I added, moving toward her.

'Then can I tell now?' Clara asked.

I took in a breath and held it, waiting for the moment to pass without incident. Clara's light blue eyes looked straight into mine. Her question was not an innocent one, I realized then. Was this a malicious act, born of long hours of idleness? A way to draw attention to herself once again? Did she mean to assuage a guilty conscience? Or, worse, was this treachery aimed at me?

'Tell what?' Etna asked.

'Be quiet,' I said under my breath to Clara, putting all the warning I could muster into my barely audible command.

'Tell what?' Etna asked, rising from the green wicker chair. 'Nicholas, what is this all about?'

'It's nothing,' I said, waving dismissively. 'Nothing. Clara, come with me.'

I reached for my daughter's arm and would have dragged her bodily from the porch, but she twisted away from me and went to her mother.

At first Etna's eyes were curious, seeing neither her husband nor her daughter, but rather a scene she had witnessed four months earlier in the sitting room, when Clara had touched her fingers to her breast.

Etna gave a quick shake of her head in disbelief.

Clara embraced her mother, whose long white arms were not yet willing to curl around her daughter's back. Indeed, my wife seemed struck with paralysis.

'I didn't mean it,' Clara said, her nervous voice thinning as it rose to a wail. 'Mother, I thought it would bring you back.'

I watched as Etna replayed that earlier scene in her mind, her eyes alighting on mine. I saw in them the vacant expression of the dazed, and then the sharp focus of the knowing.

'How could you?' she said to me over Clara's head.

'I don't know what you're talking about,' I said.

'You know,' Etna said. 'I can see that you know.'

'I haven't the faintest,' I said.

'Clara, tell me the truth,' Etna said, holding her daughter at arm's length. 'The absolute truth.'

But I turned away before the truth could be confessed. I left the porch and walked through the house to my study.

What did it matter now? I thought as I shut the door behind me. The mother would never leave the family. She would sacrifice herself to the happiness of her children.

I had won, had I not? I had Etna. I had the children. I was Dean of the Faculty of Thrupp College.

Then why was I so frightened?

Etna went to the guest room and slammed the door so hard the walls shook. From time to time, as afternoon wore into evening, we could all hear erratic gusts of disbelief – sharp and breathless, as if she were repeatedly hearing the truth anew. Clara cowered in her room, and Nicky would not leave Abigail's side. Once I saw him walking with his ears covered in case he should inadvertently hear the bursts of weather behind the guest room door. As for me, I stayed in my study, where I had sherry for nourishment and brandy for sustenance. I sat and paced and drank, occasionally as fearful as Nicky of the intermittent cries from overhead.

It was a storm that would blow through, I told myself. No woman, no human being, could physically sustain the intensity of such outbursts. Abigail came to the door, but I turned her away with a peremptory dismissal. I don't know whether her solicitude was for me, by now quite drunk, or for her mistress, whose anguish I could only imagine. Would Etna be thinking about how her family had wronged Phillip Asher (an odd redressing of familial crime, it would appear), of how she had refused even to listen to the man? Of how he had gone away in shame and was now in harm's way in Europe? Might the machinations of her husband and her daughter cause the death of this gentle academic who, at the very least, was her friend? A man she might one day have loved? And on whom did Etna place the burden of guilt? On me, for having devised the plan? On her untrustworthy daughter, who might never recover from having so seriously wronged another at such a tender age (cost a man his job, if nothing else)? Or upon herself, for having goaded me into unnatural behavior with her unnatural bid for freedom?

Or would Etna's guilt go even further back than that, to the day when she stood in an unpainted room in Exeter, New Hampshire, and allowed pity to sway her judgment? Or would my wife, as I had done from time to time, think upon the mysterious conjunction between circumstance and fate? What if she had not accepted the offer of a ride on the night of the fire? What if she and her aunt had stayed home that night and not chosen to dine in the hotel? One could unravel a life in this manner back to the beginning of conscious thought.

Sullen afternoon gave way to stifling evening. The gusts of grief subsided, and Nicky uncovered his ears. Clara came out of her room to find a meal. I discovered my children eating pie at the white enameled table in the kitchen. Clara rose without a word, her mouth stuffed with peaches and crust, and left the room before I had a chance to speak, which, in any event, I had no intention of doing. Abigail, whom I summoned, picked Nicky up and carried the sleepy boy to bed. I lingered in the kitchen, looking for brandy, and when I could find none, I walked out onto the back lawn.

I shed my jacket and stood in shirtsleeves and braces looking up at the sky, too muddy that night to show the stars. All around me was a symphony of insects, whining and scratching, tuning up their nightly instruments. My shirt stuck to my skin, and the evening air offered no relief. We were in the midst of a heat wave of extraordinary dimensions; I could not remember the last time the thermometer had registered a temperature below eighty-nine degrees Fahrenheit. I walked to the edge of the yard and looked back at the building that held the bruised Van Tassel family. I watched as Nicky's light went out and then Clara's. Within moments, I saw a lamp on the third floor go on. (One didn't want to think about the heat in the servants' rooms.) That light went out shortly as well, until the only lamps that remained were the one in my study, which I had inadvertently left burning, and the one in the guest room.

I looked for some sign of Etna, a shadow passing behind the lace curtain, but I could see nothing. I stood on a stone wall for a better view but could make out only the white bureau with its mirror. Perhaps my wife was writing to Phillip Asher, I thought. The notion rankled, and I put it aside. Perhaps Etna had fallen asleep with the light on, I thought instead, in which case I might steal into the room and put it out for her – a husbandly thing to do. I would not wake her, I reasoned; I would merely watch her sleeping for a moment. Possibly I might sit down at that guest room desk and write to her myself – a novel idea! – and seek to explain the events of the past several months. I would convince her of my love. I would ask for her forgiveness.

The more my thoughts went on in this absurd manner (or, rather, the more the alcohol soaked into my organs), I began to conceive the idea – an urgent one – that I should go to Etna at once. I must convince her that with time our little family would heal. I must persuade her that the incident could be forgotten. I would go to her and fold her into my arms and let her cry and tell her, as one would a child, that everything would be all right. In the morning we would wake Clara and help our daughter out of the emotional and moral muddle into which I had put her. We would leave the house and go to the cool of the mountains and exorcize the unhappy memories we had attached to that landscape. And when we returned, it would be autumn, and we could all go on as we had last winter. We had been ill, I would tell my wife, and now we would all recover our health and our wits and once again attend to the routine and the mundane.

Oh, foolish man. Oh, foolish, foolish man.

Sometimes I think that the incident I am about to relate did not happen at all, that in fact I found Etna's door locked and she would not open it to me. That, in fact, this was merely a dream the feverish night produced.

In this dream, I walk without stealth up the stairs, announcing my intentions with a firm step. I make my way down the hallway to the guest room and stand outside. I consider knocking but then decide that such an action might put upon Etna the burden of decision: to open the door or not, to admit me or not. After a few seconds' deliberation, I turn the knob myself.

My wife is sitting on the edge of the bed. Her head snaps up when I reveal myself. Her face is streaked, her overblouse partially unbuttoned. I glance at the desk and see upon it, as I feared, a letter. Lavender ink on a lavender envelope. A name but no address. Address unknown. In the trenches perhaps. Listening to a different symphony entirely.

Etna's face is cold and hard. Her hair is an ugly knotted rope down her back. I see again the unbuttoned blouse, the letter on the desk, the curtains unmoving in the night air.

'You are a monster,' Etna says evenly as I approach the bed.

I walk directly to her, and before she can pull away, I press her face into my formidable stomach. She tries to twist her head but cannot.

'I am not a monster,' I say.

I press her back upon the bed.

'I am your husband,' I say.

'I am not your wife,' Etna says.

I cover her mouth with my hand, and her eyes widen, as they must.

'Don't speak,' I say.

In this dream, or vision, of mine (which may or may not, as I say, be true), I release the hand that is pressed upon her lips and kiss her there instead. Etna becomes quiet, even docile, as though afraid to rouse the children, who might come into the room wondering why their mother is calling out. With gentleness and delicacy, I roll one stocking over her kneecap, feeling the downy hair of her shin. I draw up her skirt and find the opening in the corset covering. She has not, on this hot day, worn the corset itself, which is a boon to my prying fingers. I unfasten the buttons of the overblouse. I touch my wife in every place to which a husband has a natural and God-given right. After a time, I roll Etna in such a way that she is on top of me, both of us looking at the ceiling. Lying in this way, she feels like an extension of myself, as if we are the same person.

Lying in this way, I cannot see her face, which, in any case, might break my heart. Etna makes a sound and tries to stand up, but I cover her mouth once again and clasp her to me. I play her like an instrument, a cello, perhaps, until the violation is complete.

When I am done, I fall into a deep pit, tumbling as in a dream within a dream. I fall until I think I can plummet no more, and then I keep falling.

Just before dawn, I heard a sound that briefly woke me. Had I not drunk so much the night before, I might have roused myself. There was the shutting of a door. Footsteps. Another door shutting. Or do I only imagine this in retrospect? I dozed, half-drugged, sensing that I must try to regain consciousness, that I must try to come awake. When finally I did so, I sat up with a jerk. The sun was already announcing itself in a filigree pattern on the wood floor. I rubbed my eyes and then my temples, for I had the dull, relentless headache of a physical and moral degenerate.

Objects in the room gradually took shape. Where was I? In my own bed, of course, but where was Etna? She was sleeping in the guest room. I remembered then, with sudden and brutal clarity, the events of the night before. I remembered the sounds that had woken me earlier in the morning. I stood and went to the window and looked out over to the carriage house. The door was open, and the Landaulet was gone.

I went out of the house without jacket or hat, still wearing the clothes I had slept in. A sense of urgency propelled me forward. I started the Ford, the sound of the motor shocking me in the silence of the morning. Unable to turn my head without considerable pain, I trusted to luck as I backed down the driveway. I made the turn and steered the motorcar in the direction of town.

I drove too fast up Wheelock Street, past the house of the widow Bliss. I sped by the Hotel Thrupp, which bore no trace of cataclysm, infernal or not. I turned the corner at the college quadrangle, the leaves of its sycamores browning and curling in the August heat. It seemed an early-morning steam rose from the over-cooked grass and that one could almost see, in faint depressions, the ancient paths of students. I urged the Ford past the motley architecture of that undistinguished college, past Moxon's Victorian house, past the driveway to Ferald's limestone manse. I took the turn to Drury. It seemed I traveled in dream-time, unable to move for-ward fast enough. As I drove, I imagined in great detail what I would find.

The body would be lying partially on the Persian carpet and partially on the linoleum, as if, in her last moments, she had been reaching for something near the kitchen sink. There would be an ugly rose, a dis-eased rose, on her throat, quite the boldest splotch of color in that room of white iron and dried hydrangeas. I would give a cry and then turn away, but not before I had seen the unnatural posture of the body, and then the bit of glass from the broken bulb of the chandelier flung against a chair.

I would stagger to the sink and turn on the tap and wet my face in the stream of water. I would stand and shake my head, as a dog will toss the water from its body. Light-headed, I would search for something to support my weight, all the while trying to fend off a distinct sense of nausea.

I would once again look at my wife.

Her face would be grotesque in its contortions,

covered with blood that had spilled from her nose and mouth. (I believe medically one would say that she had drowned.) I would bend my head to her linen overblouse. I would trail my fingers along her thin white arm. I would touch her cheekbone and her acorn-colored hair . . .

No, no, I said to myself, shaking my head violently. This was too melodramatic. This was not how it would be.

I made the left turn into the driveway and brought the motorcar to a stop outside the cottage. The Landaulet was nowhere in sight, but the door to the cottage was open.

I climbed out of the Ford and walked to the threshold, peering tentatively inside. I called out Etna's name and was answered with silence. My eyes scanned the floor, which needed a sweep but otherwise was bare. I glanced up at the chandelier, that white iron monstrosity, all its bulbs intact. I stepped inside the cottage. Apart from the stale air, which even the open door had not been able to dissipate, and a gloom brought on by the curtained windows, the cottage was much as it had been when I had locked it up late in the spring. (That Etna might have kept a second key hadn't occurred to me.) I opened the curtains and the windows and the shutters, letting light and air into the musty room. I looked all around me to make sure that Etna was not there, unwilling to show herself. I climbed the narrow stairs to check the attic bedroom, but I had to climb straight back down again: one could scarcely breathe in the spinous garret.

Etna, I called again.

I took inventory of the contents of the cottage, but apart from Etna's writing case, I noted nothing missing.

My headache reasserting itself, I leaned against the apothecary cabinet. My hand brushed against the front of the white tin cake box. The door banged open, revealing a fan of blue and white and lavender envelopes that spilled across the floor. I picked them up and studied the addresses.

Mrs. Etna Van Tassel, Holyoke Street, Thrupp, New Hampshire

Mr. Phillip Asher, The Hotel Thrupp

Mrs. Etna Van Tassel, Exeter, New Hampshire

Mr. Phillip Asher, 14 Gill Street

I sat hard on the ladder-back chair. After a time, I laid the letters upon the table and put them in order. (Of course, Nicholas Van Tassel must read any series of letters in their proper order.) I read them through once, and then once again. I set them in a neat stack.

Etna and Phillip Asher, my wife and the man from Yale, had married their letters – a marriage, it would appear, more durable than my own.

I threw my head back and howled, a ghostly and guttural cry that might have frightened any sane man or woman.

My wife had come and gone. I understood then that she would not be back. She had tripped the latch of her cage and set herself free.

She had set herself free of me.

What began in fire would end in fire, I decided. Was this an attempt at catharsis on my part or merely the result of a lifelong attention to metaphor? I do not know. What I do know is that it is considerably harder to start a fire than one might imagine. Lacking invention, I stood with a dish towel over the cooking fire, trying to coax a flame into life, only to watch it catch and die, catch and die, disappearing in the humidity-sodden cloth. Finally, after much fluttering of the towel, I had the beginnings of a decent flame. I set it down beneath a curtain.

I took the tin cake box with its contents and, impulsively, the dress form, for which I had no use but which was, after all, the wire ghost of my Etna, having her height and her dimensions. I packed them in the Ford. Hurrying now, I climbed into the motorcar, put the vehicle in reverse, and moved backward down the driveway, hardly daring to watch as first a curtain and then a bit of wall turned orange. At the end of the driveway, just as I was about to make the turn toward Thrupp, I saw a lick of fire poke itself through the open door, and then there was a whoosh of dramatic proportions as the entire cottage went aflame. It was a mesmerizing sight. Fire is truly a beautiful thing.

The blaze raged, its heat impressive even from the end of the drive. It was then, as I was watching the fire, that I had an entirely new thought that intrigued me deeply: If Etna Bliss had set herself free, did it not follow that I was free as well?

The idea was a stunning one. I began to explore it, feeling the tentative relief of someone who discovers that a tragedy has an unexpected bonus. Could it be that I was relieved of the obsession that had been Etna Bliss Van Tassel? The obsession that had dogged me for almost sixteen years?

It could. It could.

I tested my heart and mind as a man will who has been knocked unconscious upon the battleground and wakes and feels for his arms and legs to see if they are still intact – my sense of relief no less exhilarating than that of the soldier who discovers himself to be still alive.

I might have sat at the end of the driveway all morning, trying to absorb this notion, but I began to worry then, for the fire was spreading. I had not intended to burn down the nearby manse as well. I quickly drove away and stopped at the first house I came to. I told the much-surprised man who answered the door that there was a fire just down the road and that he should call the brigade. As it was reported to me later, Etna's cottage was almost entirely destroyed by the time the fire truck arrived, but the larger house, despite the heat and the drought, suffered little damage.

('The cottage belonged to your wife,' said a policeman who came to my house later that day.

'Yes,' I said.

'Lucky she wa'n't in it,' he said.

'Isn't it?' I said.

'Can I speak to the wife?'

'She's sleeping.'

'I see.'

'She's quite distraught.'

'Of course she is. What'd she have it for, anyways?'

'I'm sorry?'

'The cottage. What'd she do there?'

'Sew,' I said with confidence.

'Sew?'

'She gave classes to the indigent,' I said.

'Did she?'

'She did.'

'Unfair then, i'n't it?'

'Unfair?'

'To lose the cottage that way.'

'Yes,' I agreed. 'Most unfair.')

If I had had any intimations of freedom in the moments

when I watched the cottage burn, I had to set them aside when I returned home. For there were my children, Clara and Nicodemus, to whom I had to explain that their mother had gone away for a rest. Nicky cried, and Clara did not believe me. 'You sent her away,' she accused, and, truthfully, it was a charge that was difficult to refute.

In early November, I had to send for Meritable, for I was at a loss as to how to raise a daughter who did not shrink from announcing, at frequent intervals, that she hated me.

'Father killed our mother,' I overheard Clara say to a horrified Nicky as I passed by my son's bedroom not a week after the fire had destroyed the cottage.

'He did not!' Nicky protested, defending the only parent he had left. 'Mother is having a rest.'

'Resting in her grave, more like,' Clara muttered. 'Father is a *murderer*,' she said, drawing out the word with obvious relish.

'Clara, go to your room!' I bellowed from the doorway.

Meritable, whom I'd before thought incapable of being ruffled by the behavior of a young girl, was impressed with Clara's intransigence. Perhaps it would be better, my sister suggested gently, if Clara came to stay with her for a bit, 'just to get her back on her feet.' And so it was that by Christmas, it was just Nicky and myself in that cavernous house, a state of affairs that would remain until he went to Bowdoin College at the age of seventeen.

I believe I was a good father to Nicodemus, more attentive than most, and I do not think he suffered from excessive affection. I was trying to be, as the reader may imagine, two parents and a sibling, and though I could not be all things to my son, we had some good times together, my boy and I.

In the fall, I hired a detective, who informed me (during a perfectly awful interview in my study) that Etna had made her way to London.

'Well, sir,' the short, empurpled man from Boston began, 'I am afraid the news is not good.'

'Of course it's not good,' I said impatiently. 'Get on with it.'

'Etna Van Tassel, your wife, is living in London.'

'London?'

'She has taken up residence at this address.' He handed a piece of paper across the desk. There was only a street name and its number. 'It is the address, sir, of a gentleman,' he added.

'What gentleman?' I asked, bracing for the name of Phillip Asher.

'A gentleman by the name of Samuel Asher,' the detective said.

I started with surprise, which the man from Boston seemed to be expecting. (Detectives are like policemen, are they not, delivering terrible news? Do they steel themselves? Or are they merely prurient witnesses to extremes of human behavior?)

'She is living there?' I asked.

'Most unhappily, she is,' he said.

'My wife is unhappy?' I asked.

'No, I am unhappy to tell you this.'

'Well, you should be,' I said.

(How did the meeting between Samuel and Etna come about? Did Etna go directly to Samuel's town house, her shame abandoned in New Hampshire? Did Samuel, seeing Etna's face, realize the full force of a love he had once known and then given up? Did they revel in this second chance? Did he tell her of his less-than-happy marriage? Did they immediately resume their fully satisfying and somewhat astonishing physical relationship? Did they ever think about the six children they had wronged?)

I actually know nothing of this resumption of their love affair, and the reader will forgive me if I do not linger here in order to try to imagine it. Though I do often wonder if I wasn't a sort of *interregnum* for Etna Bliss. The father of her children, certainly. Her husband, legally. A man whom she never loved, sadly. But mostly, I think, I was a man with whom she lived *in between* the first and second episodes of Samuel Asher. And when I am torturing myself, as I occasionally do, I think of Etna's words in the Bliss bedroom, just before that wondrous revelation of the passion of which she was capable, when she insisted it was a treasure to be able to love so thoroughly, so freely.

(And if I was an interregnum, what was Phillip Asher? An interregnum within the interregnum? A mere echo of a previous love? Did Phillip and Samuel ever speak again? I do not know.)

In June, I will retire from Thrupp College, which is, unhappily, more recognizable than it ought to be from the school it once was in 1899 and 1915. During my tenure as Dean, I hired some thirty faculty members, increased the enrollment of the college from four hundred to seven hundred students, changed the three terms to two, and instituted the teaching of the contemporary American novel, a radical move that surprised everyone.

Three years ago, I was informed, by way of legal

telegram, that Etna had died as a result of influenza. She was fifty-six when she perished. Oddly, her sister Miriam went to great pains to bring Etna's body back from England for burial in the family plot in Exeter; perhaps Miriam felt remorse for her condescending treatment of her sister those many years ago. More oddly still, I was invited to attend the funeral. I went with timid step, fearful that I might encounter either Phillip or Samuel Asher. I needn't have worried, as neither was present, Samuel apparently having decided, for reasons known only to him, not to make the crossing with the body. The funeral itself was a wretched affair, poorly attended, as might have been expected: Etna had, after all, been out of the country for fifteen years. The preacher, who hadn't known her, kept referring to the deceased as *Edna*, a distraction that tended to disrupt the strangely comforting wallow of grief.

For yes, I did grieve then. And I do so still.

I have mostly given up trying to imagine what Etna's life with Samuel in England was like. Though they lived together until her death, they never married. Was this Etna's choice? Or Samuel's? Did she suffer from having lost her children? I believe that she must have. I believe my wife would have lived a life composed in equal parts of shared happiness and private misery.

To date, Nicodemus has been reluctant to investigate the matter of why his mother went away to live in London, abandoning him when he was only seven, and why he was raised without his sister; but now that he is about to become a father himself, I suspect that these are questions he will shortly ask. On re-reading this memoir, however, I see that I have revealed more than I intended, both to the reader and to myself, and that perhaps it is not a suitable thing to pass on to a child.

It seems to me a melodramatic tale as well, the story of a faintly ridiculous man, of little interest to anyone; but then again, so much of life (the joy, the anguish, the words of recrimination, our strange fits of passion) is, sadly, melodramatic in nature, hardly artful.

We are nearing the station, for I can feel the slowing heartbeat of this overheated train, a tired beast wanting to end its day and rest. Soon I shall step onto the platform and search the crowd in vain for my daughter, whom I have not seen in almost two decades. It may be that there will be tears in my eyes as I alight, or perhaps it will be only that I am dazzled from the glare, befuddled by the heat, an old man in the early throes of Florida sunstroke.

But I shall go on. And will, when my head has cleared, summon a taxi to take me to the address of my sister, where I will greet my sisters and brothers and cousins and hope for a word with my daughter. When the funeral is over, I will make the return journey, with perhaps a short stop in Charleston to visit Betty Hazzard. In Thrupp, I shall sit out my remaining days in a study in which I constantly arrange and rearrange my books, as if in ordering a library one could order a life. As to what I shall do with this untidy journal, I think I might slip it next to Dryden's *Palamon and Arcite*, since neither is a volume I am apt to want any time soon.

What was my crime? I taught a child to lie, but my sins were graver far.

I have written quite enough for now, and, as a result, I am feeling rather hollowed out and in need of a cold drink. In this document, its prose chipped and flaking, I have evidence of a life once lived, proof that I once passed this way and thought to have love and understanding, passion and forgiveness, if not finally for my soul then for the condition of all things natural in the body and in the heart, which is always large and hungry and wanting.

Nicholaas Van Tassel
West Palm Beach, Florida
September 23, 1933

Acknowledgments

Thank you Michael, Ginger, Alan, Katherine, and John. (Thanks also to Betsy Uhrig.)

SEA GLASS

Anita Shreve

*'In the wet sand by her foot, a bit of colour catches her eye.
The glass is green, pale and cloudy, the colour of lime juice that
has been squeezed into a glass. She brushes the sand off and
presses the sea glass into her palm, keeping it for luck.'*

New Hampshire, 1929 – when Sexton Beecher proposes to
Honora Willard, she lays aside his flaws as one might
overlook a small stain in a beautifully embroidered
tablecloth. But as the couple begin their new life in the
house at Fortune's Rocks, their love is about to be tested to
the limit. For the Wall Street Crash has as little time for
dreams as it does for the mill workers at nearby Ely Falls,
who are readying for strike whatever the consequences . . .

'Shreve delivers a wealth of historical detail; vivid, often
droll dialogue; sharply drawn characters; and a riveting
story; a gem of a book'
Eve

'Anita Shreve's prose is deceptively simple and her words
are spare and elegant . . . heartbreaking'
Daily Mail

THE LAST TIME THEY MET

Anita Shreve

'She felt for his hand and laced her fingers through his, and there was something in that gesture, in the slow lacing of fingers, the way she lowered their clasped hands to the floor, that told him that she knew.'

When Linda Fallon and Thomas Janes meet at a writers' festival in Toronto, it is the first time they have seen each other for twenty-six years. Theirs is a story bound by the irresistible pull of true passion – a love which begins in Massachusetts in the early 1960s, is rekindled in Kenya in the 1970s, and which is about to play out its astonishing final episode . . .

'A luminous combination of stylistic simplicity and emotional complexity, revealing her to be a supremely elegant anatomist of the human heart'
The Times

'A love story, pure and simple, told with exquisite delicacy . . . beautifully constructed, stylishly written, it is a powerful story, a compulsive read'
Express

Now you can order superb titles directly from Abacus

☐	Eden Close	Anita Shreve	£6.99
☐	Strange Fits of Passion	Anita Shreve	£6.99
☐	Where or When	Anita Shreve	£6.99
☐	Resistance	Anita Shreve	£6.99
☐	The Weight of Water	Anita Shreve	£6.99
☐	The Pilot's Wife	Anita Shreve	£6.99
☐	Fortune's Rocks	Anita Shreve	£6.99
☐	The Last Time They Met	Anita Shreve	£6.99
☐	Sea Glass	Anita Shreve	£6.99

The prices shown above are correct at time of going to press. However, the publishers reserve the right to increase prices on covers from those previously advertised, without further notice.

──────────────────── ⟨ABACUS⟩ ────────────────────

Please allow for postage and packing: **Free UK Delivery**
Europe; add 25% of retail price; Rest of World; 45% of retail price.

To order any of the above or any other Abacus titles, please call our credit card orderline or fill in this coupon and send/fax it to:

Abacus, PO Box 121, Kettering, Northants NN14 4ZQ
Fax: 01832 733076   Tel: 01832 737527
Email: aspenhouse@FSBDial.co.uk

☐ I enclose a UK bank cheque made payable to Abacus for £.......

☐ Please charge £....... to my Visa/Access/Mastercard/Eurocard

☐☐☐☐☐☐☐☐☐☐☐☐☐☐☐☐☐☐

Expiry Date ☐☐☐☐   Switch Issue No. ☐☐

NAME (BLOCK LETTERS please) . . . .

ADDRESS . . . .

. . . .

. . . .

Postcode . . . . Telephone . . . .

Signature . . . .

Please allow 28 days for delivery within the UK. Offer subject to price and availability.
Please do not send any further mailings from companies carefully selected by Abacus ☐